CW01594182

Praise for *How to Train Your Dom in Five Easy Steps*

"A fabulous trip into the minds of a sadist and a masochist who were fortunate enough to find each other."

~ *The Romance Reviews*

"I cannot praise this novel enough. Not only delightfully witty but tender and realistic, *How to Train Your Dom in 5 Easy Steps* is just a marvelous story well worth its five star rating.

~ *The Novel Approach*

"Some of the most delicious filth I've read... Told with wit and style, this is a highly recommended sweet and dirty read."

~ *Boy Meets Boy Reviews*

"To focus just on the delicious filthy sex is to miss the point of this engaging, funny, and ultimately sweet story. Yes, it's BDSM, with pain play and humiliation, but the romance and tenderness more than shine through."

~ *My Fiction Nook*

"This is a fabulous read...I think even if you are someone not into reading BDSM, this book is a journey of enlightenment, not only for our two men, but also readers."

~ *Sinfully Sexy Book Reviews*

"Josephine Myles has written a very good, very funny, sweet and naughty novel with *How to Train Your Dom in Five Easy Steps*. I have never read about a more adorable sadist..."

~ *Prism Book Alliance*

Look for these titles by

Josephine Myles

Now Available:

Barging In
Handle with Care
The Hot Floor
Screwing the System
Merry Gentlemen

The Bristol Collection
Junk
Stuff
Scrap

How to Train Your Dom in Five Easy Steps

Josephine Myles

SAMHAIN
PUBLISHING

Samhain Publishing, Ltd.
11821 Mason Montgomery Road, 4B
Cincinnati, OH 45249
www.samhainpublishing.com

How to Train Your Dom in Five Easy Steps

Print ISBN: 978-1-61922-697-5
Digital ISBN: 978-1-61922-366-0

Editing by Linda Ingmanson
Cover by Lou Harper

First Samhain Publishing, Ltd. electronic publication: September 2014
First Samhain Publishing, Ltd. print publication: September 2015

Dedication

For the original “Sir Bastard”. Your assistance was invaluable!

Thanks also to Prue Tremayne, Kristin, Lou Harper, JL Merrow, Steve Craftman and my editor, Linda. Your feedback has helped shape this novel into something better than I’d ever imagined when I first came up with this porny little idea that just wouldn’t go away…

Chapter One

Eddie gasped as the man he'd been waiting for came into view. Oh yes. Jeff White was everything Eddie looked for in a man—as far as he could tell from this distance, anyway. Broad shouldered, swarthy, built. He ticked all the physical boxes and then some.

"There he is." Maddy tipped her head as if Eddie hadn't yet noticed him. He'd had his nose practically glued to the kitchen window for the last twenty minutes, hoping for a glimpse of the elusive wannabe Dom. He'd made breath marks on the glass, for Christ's sake.

Jeff was out working in the ridiculously oversize garden, doing something with paving slabs, as far as Eddie could make out. Eddie leaned on the breakfast bar, taking in the way Jeff moved, hefting the heavy stone slabs like they were made of polystyrene. As far as Eddie was concerned, that kind of strength could only be an asset in a top. He could just imagine those bulging arms pushing him down to his knees and grabbing hold of his hair. Yummy. Eddie made an appreciative noise. "So far, I like what I'm seeing. Niall's wrong. He's not too low rent for me." They were sitting in Niall's kitchen, but the man himself was nowhere to be seen. Maybe Maddy had worn him out already. She had a well-sated gleam in her eyes.

But right now she was eyeing up Jeff White. "He definitely looks better in the overalls than he did at the last Fetish Club social. He turned up in double denim, and I'm not talking indigo, which he might just have managed to get away with. I'm talking grungy old stonewashed jeans and a black denim bomber jacket."

Eddie pondered this crime against fashion and its stocky perpetrator. “The overalls are kind of sexy, though. Especially all muddy like that.”

“Maybe he should turn up in those next time. Can’t imagine it will make much difference to his chances, though. No one’s going to give him the time of day, after what Gwen told us.”

“He didn’t do anything that awful.”

Maddy made a face. “Maybe not, but he’s also a bit of a short-arse, hairy as a gorilla, and he’s absolutely crap at small talk. And let’s face it, there’s more than enough straight Doms to go around. Some days I can’t seem to move without tripping over some arsehole who wants to tie girls up and beat them. We can afford to be choosy.”

Eddie sighed. “Wish it was as easy for me.” He didn’t have any direct experience of the straight BDSM scene, but according to Maddy, it was brimming with men—dominants, submissives and switches—with precious few women to go around.

“Oh come on, darling. You never seem to have a problem finding a Dom.”

“I’m not saying it’s not easy enough to get a good seeing to, but I still haven’t found anyone I’d actually want to have a relationship with.”

“Who needs a relationship? Totally overrated. I like being a free agent.” Maddy grinned and went for Eddie’s half-eaten croissant. “Are you planning on finishing that?”

“You’re a bloody dustbin, you are.” Eddie shoved the plate in his friend’s direction and watched her set to work on the croissant. “Anyway, you can talk. You’ve been seeing Niall for ages now.”

Maddy shrugged. “Yeah, but it’s not like we’re exclusive or anything. And I’ve still got my own place. I can come and go as I please. Suits us both fine.”

“Sounds like you’ve got him well trained.”

Maddy just grinned and winked.

Eddie turned back to watch Jeff. He was doing something with a bucket of cement, and he'd stripped the overalls down to his waist. Shame there was a T-shirt underneath, but it was only half nine in the morning. Perhaps he'd strip properly as the day warmed up. Or perhaps Eddie had him confused with a model.

"I always had a thing for working men," he said, admiring the obvious strength in Jeff's legs. "Builders, mechanics, whatever. My sister had this poster up of this gorgeous bloke—"

"I know the one. Black-and-white with the guy stripped down to the waist?"

"You had it too?"

Maddy rolled her eyes. "Didn't bloody everyone for a while?"

"I never did. Stuck to footballers and rugby players until I was sixteen." It had taken him that long to come out to his family, but in the end he'd wished he'd done it sooner. There was a total lack of surprise or concern about his big, terrifying revelation. "After that, I went mental with the porn star pinups, but Belinda made me put stickers over any naked dicks and arseholes. She said she didn't want the girls seeing any of that sort of thing until they were a bit older. I told her they shouldn't have been in my room in the first place." He loved his step-mum and half sisters dearly, but he hadn't exactly wanted them snooping around in his bedroom once he'd hit puberty.

There was something about Jeff that was vaguely reminiscent of one of those blokes he'd stuck up on his wall all those years ago. He had the closely cropped hair, thick neck and broad shoulders of Eddie's favourite porn stars. From across the lawn, it was hard to get a really good look at Jeff's face, but as far as Eddie was concerned, a few laughter lines would be a bonus. Made him feel younger in comparison, which had to be a good thing now he was approaching his mid-thirties. "Thirty-four still counts as early thirties, doesn't it?"

Maddy shook her head. "Face it, babe. You're getting on a bit."

"So are you, then." They'd been in the same year at school.

"Yeah, but I don't give a shit. And I'm still looking hot."

Eddie had to give it to her. She was. Maddy had always been a tall, awkward teenager who carried a fair bit of extra weight, but at some point in the last ten years, she'd slimmed right down. Now she worked as a personal shopper for women with way too much money to throw away on clothes, and looked like some kind of celebrity, in her designer shades and fancy tracksuit.

"Thought you were supposed to be exercising, anyway. Not troughing pastries."

"It's fine. I'll run it all off." But Maddy did put the croissant down with a sigh, and Eddie picked it right back up again.

"Mmm, delicious. Your boyfriend has good taste. You sure he doesn't want to take me on as a second sub? I'd totally respect your place in the hierarchy."

Maddy snorted. "As if. You're the least respectful sub I've ever met. And you're not getting your hands back on him, anyway. You had your chance, and you blew it."

"I blew *him*, you mean."

Maddy flipped him one very well-manicured finger.

"Who blew who?" Niall asked, wandering into the kitchen wearing the most eye-bending shirt Eddie had seen in a long time.

"No one," Maddy said, while Eddie drawled, "Me blowing you."

Niall just smiled and walked up to Maddy, giving her a kiss on the cheek. "Hey, gorgeous, good to see you still around. And you, Eddie."

"I had to hang on for Eddie's sake," Maddy said. "He wanted to check out Jeff and see if he could help him out with his little problem."

"What problem?"

Was Niall being deliberately obtuse? "The whole Dom-training thing. I reckon I'd be the perfect sub for him to practice on."

Niall stared at him with those unsettling pale blue eyes. "You do know he's straight?"

"Wouldn't be the first otherwise straight bloke to fall for my charms." Eddie winked, and Niall got a faraway look, like he was remembering something from their very brief time together. Eddie hoped it was that time he had Eddie in a sling in a club and fucked him stupid while everyone watched.

Niall blinked and came to. "Look, I've known Jeff since he was still wet behind the ears. He's never shown even the slightest hint of being that way inclined."

"So you're saying I should go and flirt with him first? Test the waters?"

"You might get a punch in the face for your trouble. No. Let me go and ask him first. But be warned, he's going to say no."

"And then I'll persuade him otherwise."

Niall and Maddy were both giving him the full benefit of their raised eyebrows. "What? I'll have you both know I could sell sand to the Bedouin. But you do your introductions first, and then I'll mosey on out. Can't hurt, can it?"

"Famous last words," Niall muttered before heading out of the back door.

Chapter Two

Jeff moved the last paving stone into place and stood up carefully. He couldn't afford to put his back out again—he'd lost a whole two weeks of work the last time, as well as pissing off one client so much they went to one of his rivals instead. Being self-employed was great in many ways, but the lack of any sick pay was a real bugger. You had to look after yourself when you were your own boss.

Thinking of which, Jeff rolled his shoulders and stretched before going through a couple of the exercises the physio had shown him. Always made him feel like a bit of a prat, but at least no one could see him down here at the end of Niall's garden.

He glanced up at the house and froze. Two faces stared out at him from the kitchen window. He couldn't focus on them with the sun in his eyes, but it must have been Niall and his missus. You'd have thought the lazy bastard would have at least come out to offer Jeff a cuppa. Or sent Maddy out. Although, despite being Niall's sub, she didn't seem to do any of that domestic-service type thing. Pity. Jeff rather liked the idea of having a slave to see to his every creature comfort.

Jeff eased out of the stretch, trying to make it look like he'd been doing something gardening related. Inspecting the rose bushes. Actually, that was something Niall really did need seeing to. It was all very well sorting out the hard landscaping, but if the plants were a mess, who'd actually want to stroll around the garden on the brand-new path?

"Jeff, mate!" Niall's hearty tones rang out across the lawn. He was standing at the open conservatory doors, but the two faces were still peering out of the kitchen window. "Fancy a coffee?"

"Nah, but a cuppa would be good." Jeff sat on the low brick wall of the raised flowerbed, basking in the sunshine and peeking through his lowered eyelids at his mystery audience. Did Maddy have a friend round? Niall had promised he'd find Jeff someone who was up for a bit of erotic punishment and humiliation. After all, there must be a kinky bird somewhere who hadn't heard about the incident. Or even if they had, who wouldn't be put off by it.

Could have happened to anyone. And how was he meant to improve if no one would let him practice on them?

Jeff shaded his eyes and peered up at the house. Yes, there was Maddy with her sleek black bob, and there was her friend.

Oh, it was just some bloke. Jeff peered at him for a moment, trying to figure out if it was anyone he knew. Niall moved in different social circles to him—the only reason they even knew each other was Niall had sold Jeff his house all those years ago, and for some reason, they'd hit it off—but Jeff had met one or two of Niall's other friends over the years.

This bloke didn't look like one of Niall's estate agent buddies, though. He had a boyish look about him, what with his fair hair and big smile. Tall, though. He stood about a head taller than Maddy. Seemed to be a good friend of Maddy's, as the two of them were now laughing. The sound carried from out of the open window and down to the end of the garden. Maddy's dirty chuckle combined with a deeper, infectious kind of laugh.

Bloody hell, if Jeff were Niall, he wouldn't let his girlfriend hang around laughing like that with such a good-looking bloke. Still, Jeff didn't pretend to understand the so-called open relationship those two had. Was Maddy sleeping with this new bloke? Jeff looked at him with fresh interest. He didn't look like any of the Doms at the local group—didn't have long black hair and piercings, for a start—but you never knew. Niall didn't look all that typical either.

Niall proved Jeff's point by heading out into the garden in the most god-awful Hawaiian shirt Jeff had ever seen. It was a mishmash of greens, reds and golds, and featured pineapples, hula dancers and palm trees.

"Bloody hell, you trying to blind me or something?" Jeff took the cup he was offered.

"Got it on holiday," Niall said. He'd brought back a nice case of sunburn from the Seychelles too.

"You should have left it there. I'm surprised Customs let you bring it through."

Niall chuckled. "Next time, I won't bother bringing you a present."

"You shouldn't. That stuff was rank." Niall went on holiday every other month, it seemed, and he always brought back Jeff some of the local booze. When it was beer or wine, that was fine, but this time it had been some awful sweet liqueur. Jeff had added it to the cupboard where he stashed all of Niall's more dubious gifts. "I'm going to have to hold a cocktail party or something to use all the nasty stuff up. Hey, maybe we could make it a kinky cocktail party. You know any girls who might come?"

Niall snorted. "You, having a cocktail party? You know you have to provide sophisticated nibbles and actually follow drinks recipes? If you're going to have a party, you'd best stick to what you're good at. Beer and peanuts."

"You're saying peanuts and pork scratchings aren't sophisticated nibbles?"

"And you wonder why you can't get a girlfriend," Niall deadpanned.

"It's not that I can't get a girlfriend. It's that I can't get the right kind of girlfriend." For some reason, the kind of women who went for Jeff were the overconfident ones. The ones who intimidated him. "Besides, she needs to be kinky."

"Sandi's into you. You should give her a go."

"Sandi's a bit...extreme." Why couldn't the women who were into BDSM look more normal? Jeff had never been attracted to alternative types, and every time he went to one of the local fetish club meetings, all the women seemed to have weird-coloured hair, be covered in tattoos and had their skin punctured all over the place. They looked like patterned pincushions, and try as he might, someone who looked like they'd fallen out of a sewing basket just didn't turn him on. "I don't mind the tight leather miniskirts and the big boots, but Sandi's kind of scary too. And she's definitely more of a Domme, even though she says she switches. Why? Would you do her?"

Niall pulled a face. "I don't think she'd let me even if I wanted to."

"Exactly. And you don't want to. So, did you find me anyone else yet?"

Niall grinned in a sharklike way that wasn't entirely reassuring. "Actually, now you come to mention it, I have found someone who's interested in meeting you. And amazingly enough, that's even after hearing about what happened with Gwen."

"What the hell did you have to go and tell her that for?"

"Jeff, chill. It's fine. I wanted to find you someone really experienced who'd know how to deal with your, uh, *issues*."

Issues-schmissues. "There's nothing wrong with me. I just haven't been able to find the right girl yet." And when he did, his little soldier would leap to attention again, he was sure. And this time he wouldn't fire his load prematurely either.

Niall held his hands up. "Whatever you say, mate. I just thought you'd be better off with someone who knew the score. BDSM works much better when you're honest with your partner."

"I'm always honest."

"I know you always say exactly what you're thinking, but that's not necessarily the same thing."

Fuck knew what Niall was on about now. Jeff decided to concentrate on the more pressing questions. "What's she like? Is she pretty? No, that's not all that important. She's got to like pain, though. I mean *really* like it. It's no fun hurting girls who don't get a kick out of it. In fact, it's kind of painful." Jeff rubbed his jaw, remembering the well-aimed punch he'd received from one girl who most definitely didn't get a kick out of it.

"Don't worry. I've only been looking at total painsluts."

Jeff nodded approvingly. He'd come to this BDSM thing relatively late in life, after suppressing all those urges for his twenties while he was with Sarah. But after Sarah moved out last summer, all bets were off. Luckily, Niall had been around to help him through that whole readjustment period, and when Jeff admitted he was interested in the lifestyle, Niall had taken him along to the local fetish social club to meet others. Well, he'd called it a club. Really it was just a bunch of weirdos who met up in a pub in Frome once a month. Nothing exciting going on, unless you had a fetish for overpriced beer.

Unfortunately for Jeff, he just didn't fancy any of the women Niall had introduced him to so far, and to be honest, it seemed like the feeling was mutual. Why couldn't they just leave their bodies alone, rather than marking them with all those tattoos? Jeff wanted to be the one to leave marks on their skin and stick needles into them. If someone else had been there first, it was off-putting. And kind of intimidating too, not that he'd ever admit that to anyone.

After a couple of spectacularly unsuccessful dates with women he'd met through Niall, Jeff tried a different tactic. But introducing kink into dates with the vanilla women he met through a local dating agency had proved disastrous. He'd tried suggesting it in conversation over dinner several times, but quickly learnt that most birds looked at you like you were one sick puppy if you admitted that what really turned you on was the idea of hurting them. Yep, he'd had a fair few dates that ended in women running away and telling him to lose their phone numbers. One had even done that before he got to the kinky bit of the conversation, saying he was a rude arsehole. All he'd done was tell her that the frilly dress she was wearing made her look like an old-fashioned doll, and that she'd be sexier in something sleek and tight. Honestly, women could be so bloody sensitive sometimes.

He'd tried waiting until he got them in bed too—after all, people went on these dates for a shag, didn't they? Even the women did, despite pretending they were after friendship rather than sex. Unfortunately, Jeff had discovered that most normal-looking women ran a mile when you started calling them a dirty bitch and pinching their tits. Probably Jeff should have waited till the second date before starting on all that, but then again, he hadn't wanted to waste time and effort on dating someone who wasn't going to share his special interests.

But if Niall had found someone perfect for him...

"Come on, spill the beans. You got a picture of her? I don't want some goth girl. You promised me natural hair colour and no tattoos. Or at least just a small butterfly or something."

"Eddie has completely natural hair and just one very small tattoo. No piercings either, so you're safe there. Pretty fit too. Works out regularly." Niall's smile was still odd.

"What's the catch? There has to be one. She's not a real doormat is she?" Wet and clingy just wasn't his thing. Jeff might find some women way too intimidating, but the opposite was no more appealing. "Come on, what's she like?"

"Other than being a very experienced and kinky painslut? Eddie's a graphic designer. Pretty successful. Own business, own place. Good sense of humour. Fun."

"Sounds perfect. Where's she been hiding all my life? You got a picture of her? And what's Eddie short for? Edwina?"

"Edmund."

"Edmund? Jesus, some parents are so fucking cruel. Edmund isn't a unisex name, is it?"

"No, but then again, Edmund isn't a girl."

What the fuck? "Niall, what are you saying?"

"I'm saying Edmund is a very nice young masochist with years of experience, and he's willing to let you hone your Dom skills on him. You can practice all kinds of pain and sensation play, humiliate him, tie him up, stick things up his arse, whatever. He'll do just about anything. I'm not saying he's got no limits, but I don't know that anyone's ever managed to get close to them."

"I am not having sex with a man."

"Who said anything about sex? BDSM is more about the power play than getting your rocks off."

"For you, maybe. For me, it's about sex."

Niall shook his head. "You're missing the whole point of it, but you'll learn over time."

"You know you can be a right patronising git sometimes, don't you?"

"Takes one to know one."

Jeff smiled reluctantly. It was hard to be mad at someone who'd just bought you a bottle of booze, even if it was something sickly sweet.

But that still didn't change the way he felt about this Eddie fella. "Look, I appreciate the offer and all, but I need a female sub. End of story. There's no way I'm whipping some bloke's arse. It just wouldn't feel right."

"You sure? I'd have thought you'd be better able to concentrate on learning how to do things properly if you weren't ridiculously turned on. You know, your little brain has a way of overpowering your big one. Not that it puts up much of a fight."

"You saying I'm thick?"

Niall punched him in the arm. "You said it. Not me."

Jeff glared at his former friend.

"Oh, all right," Niall relented. "You're not thick. Maybe it's just because you've been out of the game for so long, but you act like an oversexed predator when you're chatting women up. Way too sexually aggressive too fast. You've got to learn to tone it down. Act more like you're in control. No sub's going to feel safe with an out-of-control Dom."

"I am in control!"

"That's not what Gwen's been saying. Believe me, your name is mud right now."

"Cheeky mare." Jeff could have a few choice words to say about her gossiping, but since he really didn't want to rehash the whole embarrassing incident, he kept his mouth shut.

"So, you want to meet Eddie? Just to talk. See how you feel after that."

"Not particularly. I'm not gay, so chatting with the bloke isn't going to make any difference, is it?"

"What am I going to do with you, eh?" Niall sighed and took hold of Jeff's empty cup. "All right, then. Have it your way. But I'm warning you, I don't think any of the girls round here are going to want to have anything to do with you. They've been chatting about you on Fetlife. You know how fast gossip spreads there. You're going to need to set up a new profile and start over."

Fuck. Ah well. What did Jeff need that stupid bloody site for anyway? It wasn't like he'd had any luck approaching women there either. This whole bloody thing was getting too complicated. All he wanted to do was submit a normal-looking woman to erotic torture and then shag the living daylights out of her. Was that really too much to ask? Jeff glowered at the paving slabs he'd been laying.

"Well, if some bloke is the best you can do, I think I'd better get back to work. Hey, you want me to tidy up any of the plants after I've finished? That shrubbery's got well out of hand. Gardens don't just look after themselves, you know. Really, one this size needs a day a week putting into just maintaining it."

Niall waved distractedly. "Yeah, fine. If you want the job, it's yours." He turned to the house. "Better go. I've got a visitor to entertain. Just give us a knock when you're leaving."

Chapter Three

Eddie had watched the conversation between Niall and Jeff with interest, wishing all the while he could lip-read. Jeff was doing the whole macho posturing thing, folding his arms so his biceps bulged, and while he wasn't as tall as Niall, you could see how easily he could intimidate him. However, Niall acted totally unimpressed by it all. You could tell they'd been friends for years.

"He's not interested," Niall said when he entered the kitchen. "Sorry, mate."

Damn. "Are you sure he couldn't be persuaded? So far I'm liking what I see."

Niall shook his head, grinning. "I doubt you'll still be feeling that way once you've met him. The man's as stubborn as a mule and just as likely to kick. Honestly, you won't be able to teach him anything. Thinks he knows it all already. He just told me there was no point in BDSM without sex."

Eddie rubbed his hands together. "Sounds like my kind of man. I can't see the point in it if I don't get off. It's so bloody irritating when you meet a hot Top who won't even let you get hard, let alone come. If I wanted to spend my time acting like a servant with no sexual reward in sight, I'd have got a job as a flight attendant. Actually, that's not a very good analogy. They probably get loads of cock."

"There's nothing wrong with a bit of delayed orgasm," Maddy chipped in.

"There's nothing right with it either."

"Well, yes, but so long as you do finally get to come, it can make it all the sweeter. Mind you, I'm not into all pain and no gain. I've got to come eventually. I'm with you there, darling."

Niall threw his hands up in the air. “Oh God, not you too! There used to be a code, you know. Protocols and so on. Now it seems like everyone’s just in it for the pervy thrills.” Maddy rolled her eyes while her boyfriend gave his little speech, and Eddie had to fight not to laugh.

“Well, yeah. I am a pervert after all,” Eddie said. “And I don’t see what the problem is, anyway. He wants kinky sex; I want kinky sex. He’s a sadist; I’m a masochist. It’s like we’re meant to be together. A match made in heaven and all that bollocks.”

“Don’t forget he’s straight, and you’re a man,” Maddy added.

Eddie shrugged. “I’ve had straight blokes before. Get ’em in the right head-space and they stop caring about where they’re sticking their dicks. It’s all just warmth and friction, and one hole feels much the same as another. So I’m told, anyway.”

“I can get that it might feel the same,” Maddy said, “But it’s not going to look the same, is it?”

“He can always close his eyes.”

“Why don’t you go and tell him that, then?” Maddy grinned like there was something amusing about the idea, but really, it was the logical next step. Eddie would be able to do a much better job of convincing this grumpy gardener than Niall could. In fact, he’d be doing Jeff a favour. Giving him a different perspective on BDSM. Niall was probably filling his head with all kinds of rubbish. For God’s sake, Niall had a ponytail. What kind of role model was that for a Top?

“Okay, I’m going.” He rubbed his hands together and walked to the doors. “Wish me luck.”

“Break a leg,” Maddy called out cheerfully. “Oh, and pick some rosemary while you’re out there, would you? I could use some for lunch. There’s a few bushes growing down near where Jeff’s working.”

“Rosemary, rosemary, rosemary,” Eddie muttered to himself, walking along by the flowerbed. He thought it would be easy enough to spot, as his stepmum’s farmhouse kitchen had tiles with a botanical illustration of a sprig of it scattered between the plain ones, but nothing out in Niall's overgrown flowerbeds resembled the piney-looking twigs with the blue flowers he had etched into his memory.

He was drawing closer and closer to Jeff. Maybe he could just forget about the herbs and start chatting to his future Top instead. Although it could make a good icebreaker... "Hi," he called out cheerfully. Jeff straightened up from whatever it was he was doing with a stone slab and peered at him with a suspicious expression.

Okay, so not the most promising start, but Eddie wasn't about to let it break his stride. "Maddy sent me out for some rosemary. I don't suppose you've seen any, have you? She said there was some down here somewhere."

Jeff squinted at him. "Look down."

Eddie's nerves thrilled at the gruff order. "I beg your pardon?"

"You're bloody well trampling the stuff right now. Surprised you can't smell it."

Eddie looked down to discover he was indeed standing next to a low bush covered in dark green, needlelike leaves. No little blue flowers, though. "Huh, is this it?" He leaned down and plucked a sprig, then lifted it to his nose. "Can't smell much. Are you sure this is the right plant?"

"Rub it between your fingers."

Eddie did as he was ordered, and the most delightful scent drifted into his nostrils. "Oh my God, I'm getting flashbacks to Sunday lunch at my dad's place. It's gorgeous. My stepmum cooked a mean roast lamb."

Jeff grunted and turned back to his stone slabs.

Okay, so not the most adept at small talk. Good thing Eddie could talk enough for the both of them. "You any good at cooking?"

Jeff gave him a "what's it to you?" kind of glare.

"Okay, so I'll admit it, I'm a total disaster when it comes to the kitchen. How much do you think I need?"

"Didn't Maddy tell you?"

"I wouldn't be asking if she had."

Jeff sighed and let the slab fall—*thud*—onto the lawn. "What's she making?"

"Just some roast spuds I think. Something veggie, anyway."

Jeff pulled a face like he didn't consider veggie food to be worth his time, but he took a step closer and bent down to the rosemary bush. He brushed through the branches, tutting disapprovingly. "This needs a bloody good pruning, and I don't expect Niall's going to bother. A place like this is wasted on a bloke like him."

"He's not the gardening type, then?"

"Hardly. Never understood why rich folk want these massive gardens if they don't actually enjoy working in them. Now if this were mine, I'd be out here every day, rain, sleet or snow."

Jeff straightened and looked around, his eyes glowing with something like artistic appreciation. It was the look clients got when Eddie had wowed them with one of his designs. The moment when they realised the potential it had.

"I bet you have a great garden yourself, then," Eddie said.

Jeff smiled wistfully. "It's nice enough. Nowhere near as big as this one, though. If I ever win the lottery…" His voice drifted off, and Eddie had to wonder what dreams were filling his head. Jeff dressed and sounded like your perfectly average local straight bloke. But he didn't look like Eddie had expected. He was far more striking, what with his strong features and the dark stubble just starting to shade his jaw. And better yet, a pair of remarkable deep brown eyes, along with lips that veered on the side of plump rather than thin. If Jeff was a kisser, that could only be a good thing. Oh God, and his nose was just that little bit out of kilter. Broken? It certainly made him look tough. Eddie shivered. Why did the rough-looking ones always do it for him?

But aside from Jeff's good looks, he really didn't seem in any way out of the ordinary. There was a west-country twang to his vowels, and he wouldn't stand out if you saw him down the pub during a football game. Well, he might in the overalls with all that dirt on his hands, but in jeans and a T-shirt he'd be totally unremarkable. Jeff was even a good few inches shorter than Eddie, although at six two, he was kind of used to that. Besides, being tall didn't make any difference to how well you could dole out pleasure and pain. Eddie let his gaze drift over Jeff's body, checking out the broad shoulders and hairy, thickly muscled arms and legs. Yeah, the man looked like he could dole out a good beating in terms of strength, and the way he'd handled the rosemary promised dexterity and finesse. All Jeff needed was the right training, and Eddie was just the man to do it.

He lifted his gaze to meet Jeff's, only to find his eyes now narrowed. Uh-oh. Had he been a bit too obvious in his appraisal? He had to remember he wasn't at a club. He was in a back garden, with a straight bloke who didn't even know who Eddie was yet.

Jeff handed over a sprig of rosemary. "Reckon you'll need another couple of these. I should be getting back to work."

"Cheers. Much appreciated." Eddie smiled his best charming-the-clients smile and stuck out his hand. "I'm Eddie, by the way. Eddie Powell. Good to meet you."

"Jeff White." Jeff stuck out his hand, which Eddie grabbed hold of quickly, and Eddie watched as delayed recognition of Eddie's name dawned on his face. Jeff's eyes widened in alarm, then narrowed down, and his expression set into hard, forbidding lines. But in between the alarm and the hostility, Eddie could have sworn he saw a flicker of interest. Perhaps not sexual interest—not yet—but Jeff was intrigued by Eddie. Or by what he represented. Whatever it was based on, Eddie could work with it. He always rejoiced when he saw that fleeting expression on a client's face, knowing it might be a slog, but he'd be able to sell his work to them.

And what was this if it wasn't selling his work as a trainer? Yeah, a Top-trainer. Eddie liked the sound of that.

"I think Niall's already mentioned my offer to you."

Jeff folded his arms. "He has. And I told him where you could shove it."

"Excellent. I can see you're thinking about anal play already. And if you decide to let me be your trainer, I'll happily let you shove whatever you like up there, within reason. Nothing that could break apart and require a trip to the hospital to extract, and definitely no gerbils. Although to be honest, I'm not sure anyone's actually ever done that. No one I know has ever admitted to it, anyway. And I've known some right perverts."

Jeff glared, like he was trying to vaporise Eddie through the power of his eyes. "I'm not gay," he grunted.

"Never said you were. Of course, if all you want to do is talk, I'm happy to do that too. Give you a painslut's perspective on things. Or be a handy body for you to practice whipping and what have you. Doesn't have to be anything sexual, if that's what's bothering you."

"Still not going to happen. I've got no interest in men."

"Yeah, I hear you. But sometimes that makes it easier to learn, doesn't it? If you're not distracted by lust. Much easier to concentrate on the technical aspects of a good flogging if you're not getting excited by it. You know what I mean?"

Indecision wavered across Jeff's face, but only for a moment before his expression shut down again. "I don't need teaching."

"No one's saying you need teaching." Which was a blatant lie, but Eddie would allow the man his pride. "Just a bit of practice. Come on, no shame in that. Everyone can use a bit of practice, no matter how experienced they are. And look, there's no need to make a decision now. My offer's open, and if you decide you want to meet up—just to talk, if that's what you need—then just call me. Or text. Or e-mail, whatever. I'll send you all my contact details."

"No point. I'm not going to change my mind."

Ooh, he really was pigheaded! You had to love a man who stuck to his guns. Or Eddie did, at any rate. So sexy. Made him want to drop to his knees and start sucking cock.

But he wasn't about to let Jeff know just how horny that forbidding glare made him. "Okay, I hear you, but I'm still going to send you my details. Then if you do reconsider, you'll know how to get hold of me. Anyway, I'll let you get back to work." While he was tempted to stay there and bask in Jeff's surly attitude, he knew he'd probably end up doing his cause more harm than good if he outstayed his welcome any further.

Or was it just Eddie's cause? Now he'd actually met Jeff, Eddie kind of wanted to help him for his own sake. Jeff might put on a macho front, but there was definitely more going on beneath the surface. The way he'd looked when he was contemplating the garden revealed a man who had some artistry in his soul.

Jeff grunted something that sounded a bit like "bye," and Eddie took it as his cue to leave, but not without throwing a "See you soon," over his shoulder.

And so what if Jeff did mutter "not bloody likely" loud enough for Eddie to hear? The man was definitely protesting too loudly.

Chapter Four

When the text with Eddie's contact details came through to his phone, Jeff was all set to delete it. But as his finger hovered over the screen, something stopped him.

Eddie hadn't been anything like Jeff had expected. He wasn't coy and mincing or in any way camp. There was no way Jeff would have known he was a bummer if it hadn't been for Niall telling him. Made him wonder how many other gay blokes he'd met without being any the wiser. And Eddie wasn't someone Jeff would have expected to be submissive either. He'd been confident and laid-back. Although going along to the local fetish club meetings with Niall had made him realise that subs came in all different shapes, sizes and personalities.

All that flitted through his head as his finger paused over the Delete button, and so he saved the message instead. It wasn't like he was about to reply to it, but Eddie had seemed like a nice bloke, despite being posh as you like with his brown loafers and voice like someone off the BBC.

Maybe there'd come a point when Jeff might want to meet up with him again—just to talk, of course. No funny business. It wasn't like there were many people Jeff could talk about all this sort of thing with. Well, there was Niall, but Niall was a busy man these days, and besides, Jeff didn't particularly enjoy admitting the extent of his ignorance and inexperience to his friend. In some ways, it might be easier to ask a near stranger all those stupid questions.

Jeff shoved his phone back in his pocket and picked up his spirit level. He didn't have to make a decision right now. He had all the time in the world. And who's to say there wouldn't be someone new at the next fet club? One of these days, that perfect woman was bound to turn up, wasn't she?

Yeah, no hurry. He could afford to wait.

Two weeks later, and Jeff headed into the Lamb and Flag in Frome, with what he hoped was an upbeat, commanding attitude. He got a pint of Guinness in and attempted to check out the fet club lot from behind the pillar without actually looking like he was doing something as lame as spying on them. They were impossible to miss. Although their Fetlife profile insisted they should dress normally and not draw attention to themselves as kinksters, you couldn't miss them, what with all those blokes wearing long black duster coats in the middle of summer, the birds with purple hair, and that bloody teddy bear on the table. It had a studded collar on, for Christ sakes. What possessed a bunch of adults to put a teddy on their table?

More to the point, why did Jeff keep coming along to these things? He really didn't fit in.

Then Sandi bent over the table, revealing a teasing strip of lacy stocking-top under her short leather skirt, and Jeff remembered exactly why he kept coming along. Not that he was interested in Sandi or anything she had to offer.

Sandi caught his eye. Uh-oh. He let his gaze veer off and noticed a new girl. She was pretty. Dark hair in ringlets, not too much makeup, and a fit body showcased in tight jeans and an even tighter T-shirt. She was sitting next to Maddy and looked kind of nervous, but not like a wallflower or anything. She was talking and smiling lots. Nice smile. Hmmm. Why hadn't Niall let him know he'd found him a sub? Shame there was no space next to her.

Still, never one to let the lack of a seat thwart his intentions, Jeff set off to chat up the girl of his dreams.

Half an hour later, and Jeff still hadn't managed to exchange more than a brief introduction with the new girl. Her name was Francine, and she was just curious, apparently, but the way she kept sending flirty glances in the direction of every other woman there had warned Jeff he was barking up the wrong tree. Maddy had confirmed it in a hushed conversation over by the bar.

"She's a lesbian. Always has been, always will be. No point thinking you can convert her."

"I wasn't thinking that." Jeff attempted to sound outraged, but Maddy just raised her eyebrows.

"Come on, every straight man thinks that, don't they? Just like gay guys have fantasies about converting straight men. It's human nature. The boost to your sexual prowess in turning someone's sexuality would be off the scale."

"What about you?" Jeff countered. "If it's human nature, does that mean you fantasise about turning gay blokes straight? What about that friend of yours, Eddie?" He realised he'd made a mistake in mentioning Eddie when Maddy broke out in a sly smile.

"Oh, you still thinking about him, are you? You really should take him up on his offer. He's a good bloke, and there's nothing he doesn't know about bondage, pain and humiliation."

"You didn't answer my question."

Maddy took a sip of her drink and appeared to be thinking about it. "I did fancy him when I first met him, so I suppose I might have daydreamed about it then. But you know, what would be the point in me turning another submissive straight? Or bi, or whatever. Sub energy isn't what turns me on. I've got enough of that myself. I need the yang to my yin. And likewise, I wouldn't have what Eddie needs." Her smile turned mischievous. "Whereas you have it, in spades. I'm not surprised he's interested in training you."

"Couldn't you train me instead?"

Maddy shook her head. "Not going to happen. Letting someone who doesn't know what they're doing experiment on my body? Uh-uh. You'll just have to find someone yourself. Maybe another dominant would do a better job." Maddy's eyes widened as she looked over his shoulder. "Speaking of which, hi, Sandi."

"Well, if it isn't my favourite switch-in-denial," Sandi purred, sidling right up to Jeff and pinching his bum. "I'm still planning to get you into my dungeon one day. You'd look great all tied up in red rope."

"I'll leave you in Sandi's capable hands, then," Maddy said, smiling wickedly.

Bitch!

Jeff turned to face his tormentor, who was now attempting to sneak another pinch in.

He swatted her hand away. "Oi, hands off."

"Oh come on, sweetheart. You'd make a lovely little slut. You just don't know it yet, but once you've felt my heels digging into your balls you'll know you made the right decision."

The balls in question attempted to climb back up inside Jeff at the very suggestion. "Is that really what you do?" he asked, curious despite himself. "Blokes want that kind of thing?"

"Absolutely."

Jeff's insides did something peculiar. Was that the kind of thing Eddie would be into? No, of course not. There couldn't be many male Doms who'd wear high heels. But maybe they crushed balls in other ways. He could google it when he got home...or not.

He shouldn't have let himself be distracted, because now he'd been trapped in the corner by Sandi, who towered over him in her ridiculously high stiletto boots. He was trying very hard to keep eye contact and not let his gaze slip down to her tempting cleavage. Wouldn't want to give her the wrong idea.

"You really should let me tie you up sometime, sweetie. I know you don't think you're a sub, but trust me, I can always tell when a man wants me to dominate his arse."

"Piss off, Sandi. Why don't you go and chat up that new girl instead?"

"What, Francine? Nah, I've met her sort before. She's not really into it. She likes the idea more than the reality. But you, on the other hand—I can tell you're a very *physical* man, Jeff

White. I don't care what they say about you, you've got the makings of a wonderfully smart-arsed masochist."

Jeff really hoped the barman wasn't listening in. "I don't enjoy pain."

Sandi burst out laughing. She had a raucous laugh that always made people turn and look. "Sweetie, that's what they all say, but trust me, you just need to be trained. Once you've had a few orgasms while in pain, you'll start to reprogramme your body. Then you'll start getting hard at the mere thought of being hurt."

"What, like getting a paper cut? Never found that particularly sexy."

Sandi cocked her head to one side. "Well, I once knew a man who wanted paper cuts to his nob, and so I said—"

"Shutupshutupshutup!" Jeff clamped his hands over his ears. "You're one sick fucker, you know that?"

"Well, duh. Takes one to know one." Sandi stuck her tongue out at him, and all of a sudden Jeff found himself laughing too. "That's it. Lighten up, mate. You know I'm not seriously going to carry you off to my dungeon."

"You really have a dungeon?"

"Yeah, well, I call it that." Sandi grinned sheepishly, and Jeff felt himself relax further. "Actually, it's more of a box room. The estate agent called it a second bedroom but I've got to take issue with that. Couldn't get a full-sized bed in there, although a spanking bench fits just fine. And you know what, it literally is a box room most of the time. I have to keep a bunch of empty boxes stacked up in there when I'm not using it, so my mum doesn't see all the cuffs and shit when she comes round. Always poking her nose in places she's not wanted, that woman. She's a bloody nightmare."

"Why don't you just put a lock on the door?"

"Oh, that'd be like a red rag to a bull. She'd have to know what was in there then. I'd never hear the end of it. As it is, she wants to know why I haven't finished unpacking yet when I moved two years ago. I think she wants me to set up a nice little craft room."

"Maybe you should. You could make it a leather-working room."

"Hey, I like your thinking!" Sandi leaned back against the bar, and Jeff decided to perch up on the barstool. It made him a bit taller than her for a start, which was always good for the ego. "So, where do you keep all your kit?" she asked.

"In a suitcase," he said, without thinking first how pitiful that sounded. Still, she wasn't to know it was one of the little carry-on ones you could fit in the overhead locker of a plane. For all she knew, it was a family-size one bursting at the seams.

Sandi patted him on the back. "Hey, don't worry about it. We've all got to start somewhere, haven't we?"

Busted.

In the end, Jeff managed to have an enjoyable conversation with Sandi about her garden of all things, but as far as finding that elusive sub went, the night was a washout. But as he drove the twenty miles back to Hook St. Norton, he got to thinking about Eddie again. Maybe it wouldn't be so weird to meet him for a chat. After all, the one with Sandi had gone all right. Perhaps he and Eddie could meet up for a drink or two and talk a bit more about pain and pleasure. After the Gwen disaster, he could do with a better understanding of what went through a submissive's brain.

Yeah, just a drink. They could do it somewhere far enough away from Jeff's home that there was no way he'd be tempted to invite Eddie back for a more practical demonstration. Because that wasn't going to happen, ever. No matter how much the idea made him hot and cold all over. It wasn't like he was uncomfortable being around naked blokes. He'd always enjoyed the whole towel-flicking locker room atmosphere after sports at school. And he had no problem checking out the erect cocks in pornos, just for comparison's sake. But yeah, having a naked, turned-on bloke in his house just wasn't going to happen. Not unless the bloke in question was him.

But they could talk. No harm in that.

Buoyed up by his decision, Jeff fired off a quick text asking if they could meet the following evening. His phone buzzed ten minutes later while he was making himself a cup of Ovaltine.

Sure thing, Eddie said. *How about the Globetrotter in Bramble Bottom? That's about halfway between us. I could get there at seven but would need to eat. Fancy joining me for a meal?*

It was a little closer to home than Jeff might have liked, but at least he was unlikely to run into anyone he knew there, as it was a bit too swanky for most folks in Hook St. Norton. He sent back an okay and took his drink out to the garden. It wasn't a very wide garden, as his house was a terraced two-up, two-down miner's cottage, but he'd landscaped the downhill slope and created a different sort of area on each level. His back door led directly out onto a patio surrounded by herbs and scented plants, with a pergola and grapevine over the small table and chairs. He sat down and looked out over the moonlit valley.

Bats swooped overhead, and an owl called from somewhere in the woods down by the river. He loved this view. He'd really lucked out managing to buy this place before the property prices went mental with rich Londoners buying their second homes out here. And he'd been lucky it had just been his name on the mortgage because Sarah had still been in college when he bought the place. It had made the whole splitting-up-the-assets thing go that much smoother than it might have done, although it did now mean he had little spare income managing the repayments all by himself.

And he felt kind of lonely these days, he had to admit. Nowadays, most of the lads he'd grown up with couldn't afford a place in the village and were moving out to cheaper towns. His own brother was moving to Trowbridge at the weekend, poor fucker. Jeff and his folks would be the only ones left in Hook St. Norton.

He looked down at their rooftop, checking that the usual lights were on. They probably didn't need him looking out for them just yet—they were both still relatively hale and hearty, and his mum had even started doing his cleaning for him every week. He'd tried to pay her, but she insisted he couldn't manage without a woman in his life, and if it made her feel important, he didn't want to take that away from her.

Plus he was still confused by the washing machine.

Jeff drained the last of his drink and headed inside.

Chapter Five

It was only when he was showering after his day of sinking a pond—hard, messy work at any time of year—that Jeff realised he was going out to dinner with a man. A gay man. Shit.

Was this a date?

No, it couldn't be. A date implied both parties were expecting sex, didn't it? And Jeff certainly wasn't. He stood in front of his wardrobe, wondering what would be the most off-puttingly heterosexual outfit he could wear.

A football shirt. Perfect. That definitely wasn't date wear. Jeff teamed up his favourite Chelsea shirt with his oldest, tattiest jeans and a pair of scuffed trainers. He definitely didn't look like he'd made an effort.

But even he couldn't explain just why he ran back to the bathroom to brush his teeth before he left.

He pulled up outside the Globetrotter at ten to seven. The evening was mild and still light enough to only need your sidelights on. He scanned the other cars there, wondering which was Eddie's. Could it be the fancy little yellow Porsche? Or was he more of a Mini Cooper sort of man? Jeff's battered old work truck stood out like a sore thumb among all the shiny new cars, but it wasn't like he could afford to run two vehicles.

He got down from the truck and stood there, not wanting to look too keen by getting there early.

A vintage E-type Jaguar pulled in and eased into one of the last parking spaces, its shape marking it out as a different breed to the rest of the cars. Jeff was admiring the dark green paintwork when a voice rang out.

"Jeff, what are you doing loitering around in the dark?" Eddie got out of the Jag, grinning. Of course, it had to be his car, didn't it?

"Just admiring your wheels," Jeff said. "Must have set you back a fair bit."

"Actually, she was a bargain. Bit of a fixer-upper, but I've got a friend who's a mechanic, so she took her on as a project. Mates' rates."

"You're friends with a mechanic?" You could have knocked Jeff down with a feather. Men like Eddie weren't friends with mechanics. They hung out with other trendy city types. You only had to look at Eddie's outfit to see that. Okay, so he was in jeans and a T-shirt too, but the royal blue T-shirt was a close fit and bore the logo of something or other—a computer game perhaps?—and the jeans had all kinds of weird shit going on that marked them out as designer. Even his neon-orange trainers were squeaky clean.

Men like Eddie didn't hang around with grease monkeys.

"Yeah, she's my cousin's ex. You needn't look so surprised. Never know when it's going to be handy to have friends in different places, do you? I've been collecting them from all walks of life. It's a bit of a hobby of mine. And now I've added a gardener to my collection. All I need now is a rat-catcher, and I'll have completed the set."

Jeff knew he was being teased, but he didn't really mind when Eddie did it with such an open smile. Still. "I'm not really a gardener," he said. "Hard landscaping is a whole different thing to horticulture, and I don't have the qualifications for that."

"But you'd like them?"

"Yeah. I love flowers." It wasn't something Jeff had ever admitted before, but this man had no connection to the rest of Jeff's life. It wasn't like word would get back to Jeff's family, was it? Well, unless Eddie told Maddy, and she told Niall, and Niall ran into Tony in the village... Shit, that was a connection, wasn't it? "Don't tell anyone that, though," he ordered.

"Don't worry, your secrets are safe with me." Eddie's eyes crinkled at the edges, and Jeff had to wonder how old he was. He dressed and talked young enough, but Jeff's skin hadn't started creasing up like that yet. Shit, was Eddie older than him?

"Come on," Eddie said. "I'm dying for a beer."

He drank beer too? Posh blokes didn't drink beer, did they? They were meant to like wine and single malt whiskies or something. And Jeff was fairly certain gay men drank cocktails, not pints.

However, it turned out Eddie drank real ale by the pint, which actually shamed Jeff from buying his usual fizzy lager. The pub had six different ales to choose from, and he went for one called Skullcrusher. That was a suitably macho name, wasn't it? Yeah. And no one was going to think him and Eddie were a couple. Not with Eddie dressed in fairly normal clothes.

Jeff began to relax as they found a corner table and sat down. He ordered steak and chips, and Eddie lived up to expectations and ordered the mussels with the fancy French name. Seafood. Ugh.

"So," Eddie said after the waiter had taken their order, "what's all this I hear about you being a switch?"

Jeff choked on his mouthful of beer.

Eddie watched Jeff struggle to clear his throat. He wasn't blushing, but he was definitely floundering.

"Where did you hear that? It's a lie."

"Oh, I have my sources. Like I said, friends all over. Never know when they're going to come in handy."

Jeff was looking really worried now, playing with the foam on the top of his beer with one fingertip as an excuse not to have to look at Eddie. Eddie took pity on him. "Don't worry, it was only Maddy. She said some Domme wants to take you on as her sub."

"She's nuts. Sandi, I mean, not Maddy. There's no way I'd ever let anyone hurt me or order me around."

"Why not?" *Please don't let it be because you think subs are weak.* Eddie refused to be thought of in that way.

"Just because." Jeff glowered into his pint. "I don't like pain, and I don't like being told what to do."

"What happens when you feel pain?"

"What do you think? It bloody well hurts!"

"And that's unpleasant?"

"Of course. Isn't it for you?"

Oh, and there it was. A question from Jeff about how Eddie experienced things. Marvellous. They were getting somewhere at last. Eddie considered carefully before answering. "Some kinds of pain are just as bad for me as they are for you. I'm a complete wuss when it comes to a headache or toothache or any pains from the inside of my body. You know. Stomach cramps or torn ligaments or what have you. But for some reason, I've never been all that bothered by pain coming from the outside."

"So you just don't feel pain all that much, then?"

"I feel it the same as anyone else, I think. I reckon I just process it differently. It feels sparkly or warm or just plain interesting. Used to always be getting the other kids to give me Chinese burns because they felt so tingly afterwards. And grazed knees were really intense, but not altogether bad. Used to love pressing on scabs just to feel that crackly sort of pain. It gave me a kind of high. The endorphins, I suppose." Eddie realised Jeff was now staring at him like he was some kind of bizarre museum exhibit. "What? You're telling me you never worried your scabs?"

"You end up getting scars if you do that."

Wasn't that the truth? "You sound just like my mum. And yeah, you're right, but I just can't bring myself to be bothered about them. Every scar tells a story, you know? Even if it was just about the time I totalled my bike because I was showing off in front of Ralph Tidyman. He was seriously fit for a fifteen-year-old." Eddie smiled to himself, thinking about that one time he had persuaded Ralph to drop his trousers so Eddie could blow him. It was over way too fast, and Ralph completely ignored him after that, but he'd recently seen Ralph's Facebook status updated to him being engaged to some guy named Marcus, so he liked to think he'd been instrumental in giving the teenage Ralph his first taste of gay sex.

Belatedly, Eddie realised he'd gone off in a bit of a daydream there, but when he drew his attention back to Jeff, it was to find him worrying his beer mat, obviously deep in thought.

"Do all submissives feel that way?" Jeff eventually asked, in a tentative kind of voice that was different to his usual swaggering growl.

Now this was something Eddie could definitely answer. "No, not all of them. For some subs, it's all about following orders, having choices taken away from them or being humiliated. Painsluts are a distinct group on their own, and not everyone who's a painslut is all that submissive either. I can be submissive with the right Top, but too many orders without enough sensory gratification make me feel rebellious. And I'm not remotely submissive outside of scenes. You tried ordering me about right now, I'd tell you where to go."

"Is that so?" Jeff quirked a challenging smile. If Eddie didn't know the man was straight—or thought himself straight at any rate—he'd definitely call that a flirtatious smile. And oh my God, Jeff looked sexy like that. Kind of devilish with his lifted eyebrow and sharp canines.

Eddie fluttered his eyelashes. "You could always try it and see what happens."

Jeff took a deep draught of his ale and then leaned back in his seat. For a moment, Eddie thought he was about to take him up on his challenge. What would it be? Something humiliating in front of a pub full of people?

"So you get high off pain? It's never too much for you?"

Yeah, that was more like it. "If the Top knows what he's doing, I get high. All swimmy-headed. It's like being drunk or something. But that doesn't mean I love every last crack of the whip. In fact, I'm not all that fond of canings and whippings when they're being done. Fucking smarts, but then afterwards I soar."

"And it turns you on too? You know, sexually?"

Would knowing it did put Jeff off? Fuck it. Eddie would take his chances. "Yep. Like I said, endorphins. Of course, I'm happiest if they're helped along by the occasional tug. I really hate it when a Top ties me up and tortures me but never once touches my cock. It's bloody hard to come without any contact."

Jeff pulled a face. Bugger. He'd gone too far then. But all Jeff said was "You're right there."

Intriguing. "So you have tried subbing for someone, then?"

"Not exactly." Jeff's pint was being all fascinating again. Eddie could see the moment when he reached a decision to confess. "It was my ex. We were together thirteen years. Thirteen years! You think you know a person after that long." Jeff trailed off, but Eddie kept quiet, waiting for him to continue. "Anyway, things had gone stale, and we decided to spice it up a bit. She didn't want to be tied up, though, so I said I'd let her do it to me. Fucking stupid decision, that was. She did a strip tease, then something I said pissed her off for some reason, and she stormed out of the house in her dressing gown. She left me tied to the bedposts. Took me ages to work free."

"Ah. So I'm not going to need to tell you about the cardinal rule of not leaving a bound sub on their own, then."

"No, you're all right there. I'd never wish that on anyone. Almost dislocated my arm getting out of that one. And she'd only used a couple of her silk scarves. I dread to think what it would have been like with rope."

"Actually, silk's an extremely strong fibre."

Jeff smiled ruefully. "Well, I say silk coz she used to call them that, but I don't reckon they were that fancy. She bought most of her clothes down the market."

"A style icon by the sounds of it."

Jeff gave a sad smile, and Eddie told himself off for being catty. "So when did the two of you call it a day?"

"Only six months ago. I'm still getting used to this whole dating thing."

Eddie looked at the tea light burning at the centre of the table, then up at Jeff. He couldn't keep the wicked smile from his face. "Bet you never thought you'd end up having a dinner date with a man."

"Fuck off, this isn't a date." Jeff folded his arms, which just made him ten times hotter. Why did Eddie have such a thing for riling a Top's temper?

But just then their meal arrived, and the young woman serving it gave them a knowing look. Jeff glared at her, and Eddie smiled sweetly. "Thanks, love," he said. "And can we see the dessert menu later please? Do you have any sharing desserts?" He turned to Jeff and said casually, "They're so much more romantic, don't you think, darling?"

"Fuck off." For a moment, Eddie was sure he'd pushed him too far, but then Jeff shook his head and smiled. "You're a right pain in the arse, you are. You deserve a good punishment for that."

Eddie waited for the waitress to move out of earshot before leaning forward. "I'll happily accept a spanking. You look like you've got great hands for it. Big and wide. And those arm muscles look like you could pack a good wallop. There'd be no need to hold back with me, you know. I can take as much as you can give."

Jeff's pupils flared, and though he shook his head, he kept eye contact with Eddie. Yep, he was thinking about it all right. Now all Eddie had to do was keep him happy for the rest of the meal, and see where things led from there.

Jeff didn't know what the fuck was happening to him, but at some point in the last hour, he'd gone from being determined nothing was going to happen with Eddie to being equally determined to give the man a royal spanking for his cheek. It wasn't like either of them would have to take any clothes off. There'd be nothing sexual about Jeff putting a fully clothed man across his lap and giving his arse a bloody good wallop.

Teachers used to do it, didn't they? And his dad had done it to him once or twice.

Yeah, it would be more like Jeff asserting his authority and showing the cheeky bastard just who was boss.

They didn't end up getting dessert after all, because when the waitress arrived to clear their plates, Jeff told her not to bother with the menu.

Eddie gave him a quizzical look.

"We're leaving," Jeff announced. "For my place."

"Really?" Eddie leaned back in his seat and gave Jeff a lazy smile. "And what makes you think I'd be willing to go back to some isolated cottage with a man I barely know?"

"Because you're gagging for it."

"Am I now?"

"You've been making eyes at me all evening."

Eddie raised one eyebrow. "I'm surprised you noticed. Most aggressively heterosexual men choose to ignore it when I flirt."

Jeff had had enough of the banter. He stood up. "So, are you coming or not?"

"Well, that depends. We haven't talked through what we're going to be doing yet. I haven't let you know my limits either."

"Niall said you don't really have any."

Now Eddie leaned back in the booth, crossing one leg up on the other knee. "Well, that's blatantly untrue. I have some limits. There's really gross and dangerous stuff I won't do, but yeah, he's right. I've tried most things."

"So what's the point in discussing it? I'm not going to do anything gross or dangerous."

"The point is, I do have limits for a first hookup with someone I don't know well, especially when it's on their territory. For instance, you'd have to use a condom for oral. I'm not into taking stupid risks."

"Who uses a condom for a blowjob?"

"Anyone who doesn't want to risk sexually transmitted diseases."

"I don't have any sexually transmitted diseases!" Jeff realised he might have said that loud enough for the neighbouring diners to hear, but he had nothing to be ashamed of.

"I'm not saying you do, but how would I know? It's a lot to take on trust. After all, you've been dating recently, haven't you?"

"Yeah, but I nev—" Jeff clammed up, realising what he'd been about to admit. Not cool. Not remotely cool. "It hasn't always got to that stage."

"Oh yeah. I heard about what happened with that girl. What was her name, Gwyneth?"

"Gwen," Jeff corrected, and he bloody well didn't have anything to be ashamed of there, he told his burning cheeks. Premature ejaculation could happen to anyone. Even really premature, before-the-first-spank ejaculation.

Even premature ejaculation that ended up all over a pussy. And not the right kind of pussy either. He knew he should have insisted Gwen locked her stupid bloody cat out of the room. To his credit, Eddie wasn't smirking, but that didn't stop Jeff giving him a forbidding glare. "It's none of your business, anyway."

"Hey, chill. It's no big deal. Everyone gets a bit overexcited their first few times. I blew my load within minutes of starting my first scene. The top really wasn't impressed with me. Earned me a right walloping." Eddie looked positively proud of himself.

But who disciplined the Dom when they fucked up? Gwen had given him a withering look and started fussing over her cat. She'd named him Mr. Tiddles, for fuck's sake. Wasn't Jeff's fault he couldn't get it up again after that. It was just... Well, he'd been embarrassed. And humiliation really wasn't a kink of his. Humiliating someone else was fine, though. So long as they enjoyed it. Would Eddie enjoy it? He was about to ask, but then he remembered what they'd started out discussing. Definitely a safer topic of conversation than the whole Gwen thing.

"Anyway, we're not going to need rubbers, because a blowjob isn't going to happen. No way."

"Okay, well, we'll see. And no bondage and no gags. No blindfolds either. And my safeword is pancetta."

"Pancetta?" Now Jeff had heard it all.

"What's wrong with pancetta? I love the stuff."

"That's such a middle-class safeword. I bet it's Waitrose pancetta too, isn't it?"

"Actually, I do all my grocery shopping in Marks and Spencer."

"No one does all their shopping in M&S. It would cost a bloody fortune. What's wrong with Tesco?" Jeff shopped in Tesco, and they had everything he needed, including a few luxuries he didn't.

"I've never even been into a Tesco. Or an Asda. Or a Morrisons, come to think of it."

Jeff couldn't believe his ears. Were there really people out there who didn't care about saving money on food? "You're so bloody posh," he said.

Eddie grinned. "Well, I am at the upper end of middle class. Can't really help that. What? You don't have a problem with that, do you? I'd have thought it would add a bit of extra spice for a working-class man like yourself, being able to dominate someone of a higher social status."

Jeff felt a bit miffed at being called working class and lower status, but there was nothing to be ashamed of in honest toil. "You're no better than me just coz you talk all fancy."

"Right you are." Eddie stood, which disconcerted Jeff for a moment because he'd forgotten how tall Eddie was while he was seated. Fortunately, Eddie then sat back on the edge of the table, which evened things up a bit. "Then part of the fun for you will be in making sure I know you're superior to me. Go on. Have a go. Insult me and put me in my place."

Jeff gulped. The last time he'd tried to insult a woman, it had gone spectacularly badly and ended up with him doubled over, holding back the tears after a knee right in the happy sac. But Eddie was inviting Jeff to put him down, so he was hardly likely to get violent, was he? Besides, despite Eddie's height advantage, Jeff had the feeling he could take him in a fight. He didn't have the same qualms about hitting blokes as he did about hitting women.

Trouble was, he didn't really know any good insults for men. Fuck it. He'd try what he'd called that bird from the dating agency. He pulled himself up as tall as he could and glared. "You're just a dirty bitch, and you need a man to show you what's what. Now get in your poncy little car and follow my truck back to my place. I'm not going to let a tramp like you soil my seats."

"Ooh, that's the stuff." Eddie's smile turned downright dirty. "Tell me, Sir, have you got any instructions for when we get to your place? Want me to stay in the car until I'm fetched? Or should I get out and stand with my hands on my head?"

Christ. That idea was strangely appealing, but Jeff couldn't risk his neighbours seeing anything so odd going on. There was nothing weird about a mate coming back to his house in the evening for a bit, though, was there? Okay, so they might remark on Eddie's wheels, but it wasn't like the man was driving something naff like a Fiat Panda.

"You just get out and act normal. I'll let you know what I want when we get inside."

Eddie's eyes flicked down, and Jeff knew he was being checked out. He adjusted his bits, surprised to feel just how much blood had pumped down there. Huh. He wasn't hard by any means, but he wasn't exactly soft either. Must be all the testosterone from ordering Eddie about and calling him a bitch.

"Come on, then, slut. You've had your orders."

Jeff turned and strode for the door. After a moment's pause, he heard Eddie's footsteps rushing to catch him up.

Jeff smiled to himself. He could get used to this feeling of power.

The heady feeling didn't last the whole way home. Alone in his truck, Jeff began to wonder what he was doing. Was it totally gay to feel even a little bit turned on by dominating a man? Last thing he wanted was to start mincing around and acting like one of the queens off the telly. But then again, Eddie didn't act like that, and Eddie was gay. It was confusing, that was what it was.

Nah, it'd be okay if Jeff got turned on. It would just make the whole thing more authentic as a practice session, wouldn't it? Like Niall said—not that he'd admit it to the arrogant bastard—he had to learn how to do this without letting his little brain take over. No point figuring out the perfect way to do stuff if he screwed it all up again the next time he got with a woman.

Jeff idly stroked his dick through his jeans whenever he wasn't changing gear. Only took a couple of miles to get it excited again. Not excited about Eddie, but excited about learning how to do this whole dominating thing properly. And the sadism thing. He was really, really looking forward to hurting Eddie.

Now he was properly hard.

Good thing they were nearly home. Jeff turned onto Featherbed Lane and checked in his rearview mirror to see if Eddie's Jag was still behind him. Still there. Nice one.

Jeff pulled into his usual spot right outside the house and watched in amusement as Eddie crawled down the street, trying to find a parking spot. Featherbed Lane was a narrow dirt track right on the hilltop, and the ground sloped away steeply on one side, with the houses huddled on the other. There was a designated parking space opposite each house along the open side of the road, but since most households owned more than one car, they'd turned their front gardens into parking spaces. Jeff refused to do that to his. Besides, he didn't need to. For some reason, none of his neighbours ever took the space opposite his house. He probably should have warned Eddie to park around the corner, but hey, where was the fun in that? Featherbed Lane was a dead end, with only a very tight turning spot at the end of the road, and so he wasn't surprised to see Eddie reverse back along the street a minute later.

Eventually, Eddie pulled up alongside where Jeff was standing and rolled down his window. "Okay, I give up. Where do I park?"

Jeff cocked his thumb to indicate the way to turn at the end of the road. "Just up there and round the corner. I saw a few spaces as we drove in."

"I hate reversing that far," Eddie grumbled. "You could have bloody warned me."

"Where's the fun in that?"

"Fucking sadist."

"Exactly."

Eddie's eyes sparkled, and somehow that made this even more fun, knowing he was playing at being pissed off. Jeff decided to try some orders now they were here.

"Park up and walk back to the house. I'll be inside, but I'll leave the door unlocked. Let yourself in and head over to the coffee table. I want you leaning over it, arse in the air."

"Yes, Sir." Eddie grinned, blatantly checking out Jeff's crotch, and fuck it, Jeff was going to do the same. It wasn't gay. It was just him making sure his sub was turned on. That was responsible Dom stuff, right?

In the glow of the streetlight, Jeff could just make out the bulge in Eddie's jeans, proving he was as hard as Jeff was. That was good, wasn't it? He thought it must be. After all, he'd be wanting his future female sub to feel turned on when he was doing his shit, so it made sense for Eddie to be horny when they were practising.

"Be quick about it," Jeff growled and slapped his hand down on the roof of the Jag. "Don't keep me waiting, bitch."

Eddie revved the engine and reversed back with a squeal of wheels, like he was so keyed up he couldn't manage to slip the clutch properly. Yeah. Jeff was having the right effect on him.

So far, so good. It just remained to be seen how it all went when a bit of pain was added into the mix.

Jeff let himself into the house and ran up the stairs, retrieving his suitcase of kink from the top of his wardrobe. Now he just had to quickly unpack the stuff and lay it out on the sofa, then hide the case so Eddie wouldn't realise that was the full extent of his collection. Ever since speaking to bloody

Sandi, he'd been increasingly self-conscious about how few tools of the trade he had. But the proper kit was bloody expensive, and he'd learnt the pitfalls of buying cheap tools the hard way. Nothing like having a trowel handle break on you when you were in the middle of building a wall to realise that you should have forked out the extra twenty quid and got yourself a professional-quality one.

But when he got downstairs, he spotted Eddie striding down the garden path through the front room window. "Fuck." Jeff legged it through to the kitchen and plonked the case on the table. Hopefully, Eddie hadn't seen him. It was always harder to spot people inside a house than it was to look out of the windows. Well, unless you had the lights on, in which case everything in your house was on display for any old potential burglar to check out.

Jeff unzipped the case and pulled out a paddle, a flogger, a tawse and a riding crop. He contemplated the dressage whip. It had stung like bloody buggery when Jeff had tried it out on his thigh. And Eddie had said he didn't much like those kind of stinging implements.

Jeff added it to the bunch in his hand, along with the cane. Fuck it. Why not? Eddie said he could take all this stuff and enjoy it, hadn't he? And something about getting a high even off the kind of pain he didn't much enjoy at the time. Jeff had to stop feeling guilty about the prospect of hurting someone. Painsluts wanted to be hurt. That was part of the whole job description. And sadists enjoyed hurting them.

Right. He could do this.

"I hope you're ready and in position, bitch," Jeff called.

"Yes, Sir, right where you asked me to be."

Jeff opened the kitchen door and got a prime view of naked backside bent over his table.

Fuck. He really wasn't meant to find that sexy.

Jeff closed his eyes, trying to erase the memory of Eddie's bare bum. Actually, as bums went, it hadn't been a bad one—lots of smooth white skin and perky cheeks—but it hadn't had the right shape. Women's arses were rounder. Softer. They wobbled. Eddie's had been kind of...

Jeff opened his eyes briefly. Firm, that was the word he was looking for. Muscular, even. He couldn't bloody well erase the image from his head. Felt like it had been burned onto the back of his eyelids. At least Eddie had kept his legs together. Jeff didn't think he'd have been able to cope with seeing his meat and two veg as well.

"Did I ask you to get undressed?" Jeff demanded. He wasn't going to let his voice crack either.

"No, Sir. You didn't."

"Then explain yourself, bitch."

Eddie's head twisted round. His expression was all wide-eyed and innocent. *Yeah, innocent my foot.*

"If you're going to punish me, you'll need naked skin so you get visual feedback on your strokes. That's half the fun of it for you, so I'm told. Going through clothing doesn't hurt as much either, so this is more fun for me. It's a win-win situation."

Jeff could see the logic, but still... "I don't remember saying I was going to punish you."

"But you're holding a flogger and a paddle, Sir. And is that a tawse? Ooh, I haven't felt one of those in a while."

"I've got a whip and a cane too, so you'd better watch your mouth, bitch." Jeff walked over and put the implements down on the coffee table in front of Eddie before heading over to pull the curtains shut before he turned the lights on. You didn't tend to get many walkers down Featherbed Lane, but he really didn't want to give anyone a free show.

Eddie grinned. "Much as I'm enjoying this, Sir, can I suggest something?"

"All right, go on, then."

"You'll want to start with a bare-hand spanking to warm me up. That's most pleasurable for me, and it'll give you a good feeling for how hard you're hitting as it'll make your palm smart too."

"No way." Jeff looked down at the arse in question. It was hairy. Just a light blondish fuzz, but still, women didn't have hairy arses. "I'm not touching your bum. That's too gay."

"Are you implying that there's something wrong with being gay?"

Was he? "I haven't got a problem with other blokes being gay, but since I'm not, then yeah, there's something wrong with me doing gay stuff."

Eddie huffed. "Fine, well, if you won't use a bare hand, then a flogger would be the next best thing. I'm not saying you can't give a good caning without warming up first, but it's a different kind of pain and not one that most people will enjoy. If you want to learn how to give the pleasurable sort of pain, then you need to master the warm-up first. Do you know how to wield a flogger? It's all in the wrist."

"Yes, of course I bloody well know." Jeff had practised on a cushion.

"Fine, just checking. Well, I'm ready when you are."

Jeff picked up the flogger and tested its weight. He'd gone for one with lots of long, thin suede tails. In black, of course, as there had only been a choice of black or purple. These fetish people were certainly predictable with their gothy ways. He flicked the flogger against his sofa, pleased at the whumping sound it made. Was it going to sound like that on Eddie? He eyed his sub, considering it, and Eddie grinned at him.

"You know, I've never done a scene with a Top in a football shirt before."

"Did I give you permission to speak, slut?" Jeff flicked out the flogger, and the tails just caught Eddie's flank.

"Ow. No, Sir. You didn't, but since you hadn't forbidden it, I went ahead. And you know, this is supposed to be a learning session. I can't instruct if I can't speak."

If the cheeky bugger thought he was going to get a chance to lecture Jeff, he had another thing coming. "I learn best through teaching myself, so I don't want you speaking unless I'm doing something wrong or dangerous. You got that?"

"I hear you, Sir, but you should probably know I'm fairly disobedi-*ow*!"

Jeff had flicked the flogger harder this time, the tails whacking down right across both cheeks of Eddie's arse. Yeah, that was satisfying. The skin didn't look any different yet, but he'd only just got started. Jeff gave another few fierce whacks, then walked around to the other side so both cheeks would get a good toasting.

Eddie stuck his arse out farther and groaned. A deep exhalation of pleasure that tingled up and down Jeff's spine and ended up zipping down his legs and making his toes curl up. And on the way there, it took a detour to Jeff's balls, making them churn. Yeah, those were the sorts of sounds he wanted to hear from his sub. Of course, he wanted it in a higher-pitched voice, but a groan was a groan. Jeff adjusted his package, trying to get more comfortable in his jeans. The temptation to loosen the zip was there, but if he did that, then who knew what would happen. And letting another man blow him would definitely be gay.

Jeff's dick ached at the thought of plunging into wet, sucking heat. God, he did love getting blowjobs.

What about if Jeff ordered Eddie to blow him? Would that be more or less gay than just opening his fly and letting Eddie do what he wanted?

The question refused to resolve itself, but the swings of his flogger were somehow both calming and exciting. Jeff got a bit more adventurous, working up Eddie's back and then concentrating on his shoulders. Eddie made even more noise. Fuck. What if the neighbours could hear? But no, these walls were solid stone, and you could only hear their telly when they had it on really fucking loud, and even then only because it was right by the chimney breast, which acted like a sound box.

He had Eddie right by the chimney breast. Shit. What if Mrs. Davis thought that was Jeff making all that racket? He chucked the flogger over onto the sofa. His work with it was done, anyway. Eddie's skin had gone a nice shade of pink, like that clematis he had growing over the pergola.

Fuck. He really wanted to see his handprint there in pink.

No, touching another man's arse was definitely gay. No two ways about it.

Unless he was just experimenting.

Yeah. Experimenting was okay. That didn't mean anything, did it? Lots of people experimented with stuff. Jeff had once had a guitar lesson, but that didn't make him a musician, did it? It was fine to just try new things out. Thinking of which...

"Get up." Jeff grabbed hold of Eddie's hair, which wasn't like touching bare skin, so that was okay. He pulled Eddie's head up and got him onto his knees.

"Arrrgh, that hurts. Bastard."

"I think you'll find that's Sir Bastard to you."

"Yes, Sir Bastard." Eddie's expression was a little dazed, like he'd had a toke on a joint or something, but he wasn't completely out of it yet. He was with it enough to give Jeff a wink and a cheeky smile. Jeff wanted to see Eddie flying on an endorphin high, like he'd talked about back at the pub.

So Jeff stepped over to the sofa, pulling Eddie with him by the hair, and sat slap bang in the middle. He grabbed hold of Eddie's waist—because if he was going to spank him, fuck it, he'd be touching bare skin in a moment anyway—and shoved him down over his lap.

Eddie squirmed a bit, so Jeff slapped his hip. "Keep still."

"Just trying to get comfy."

"You don't get to be comfy, bitch."

"You know, you're really very good at this whole domination thing."

"Shut up," Jeff barked, but the compliment left him glowing. Yeah, this was going well. It was odd, really, because he wasn't doing anything particularly different than he had with the last woman he'd tried this with—not that he'd ever got this far. She'd had a right go at him about ripping one of her hair extensions out, then flounced out of the door and told him not to bother calling back. Honestly, how was he supposed to have known it wasn't all real? If she'd only gone and told him to begin with, he'd never have tried grabbing her hair.

But Eddie seemed to be made of sterner stuff. And he definitely wasn't wearing hair extensions. Jeff tugged on Eddie's hair again. "Look at me. I want to see your face when I'm doing this." He hadn't thought he would, but he really wanted to find out what expressions went with those sexy noises Eddie made.

Uh, not sexy noises. Sexual noises. There was an important difference. Yeah. Of course there was.

Eddie turned his head so Jeff could see most of his face, all squashed up against the sofa cushion. "Go on, then. Show me what you've got," he taunted.

"That's show me what you've got, Sir." Jeff punctuated the sentence with a good wallop to Eddie's left arse cheek.

"Fuck! That was hard."

Jeff went for the other cheek and gave it the full benefit of his arm muscles.

"Arrrgh!" Eddie seemed to be having problems catching his breath. His eyes were scrunched shut and his brow all crinkled.

Jeff hit him again and again, as hard as he could. The skin was coming up bright red now. Eddie's hands scrabbled on the sofa and his body bucked and twisted. He was making a sobbing sound. Jeff's dick was fucking well throbbing now. He wanted to press Eddie down against it and feel his body writhing as Jeff walloped him. What a way to get off.

Eddie looked like he was trying to say something. His mouth was working, and his eyes stared wildly. Jeff slowed down his smacks a bit, letting Eddie catch his breath enough to speak.

"Stop! Fuck, too much."

Shit. Jeff thumped the sofa cushion instead of landing another blow to Eddie's backside. The skin there was so dark it was almost purple. He'd bloody well done it again, hadn't he? Gotten way too carried away. Eddie wouldn't want anything to do with him now.

"Sorry," he choked out.

Chapter Six

The blows raining down on his backside had stopped at last, and Eddie fought for breath.

Wow. He hadn't had a spanking like that since... To be honest, he wasn't sure he'd ever had a spanking like that. What Jeff lacked in finesse, he made up for in brute force. He'd whacked Eddie so hard his blood was roaring in his ears, muffling everything.

Jeff was talking. Eddie forced himself to concentrate.

"Didn't mean to lose control," Jeff was saying gruffly, a humble expression on his face. He wasn't meeting Eddie's gaze but instead staring at Eddie's arse. Okay, it probably did look pretty impressive after all that. Bruises, hopefully. Eddie didn't seem to bruise as readily these days, for some reason. He figured his blood vessels had gone into hiding after all the voluntary trauma he'd put them through.

But he needed to stop thinking about his arse and reassure Jeff, didn't he?

"S'okay. I was enjoying it."

Jeff looked at him then, all confused. "But you told me to stop."

"Yeah, but I didn't safeword, did I?"

Jeff's brow crumpled. He was cute when he was puzzled. "No, but you said stop. I thought maybe you'd forgotten your safeword."

"Trust me, I'm not going to forget pancetta in a hurry. And even if I had, I'd have used red. That's kind of the industry-standard safeword."

"So why did you tell me to stop?"

Okay, this would demand some concentration to explain. And being in this awkward position with his head lower than his body really wasn't helping matters. Eddie eased himself up off Jeff's lap, bracing himself against the arm of the sofa when he felt dizzy. He went to sit, then thought better of it and sank to his knees in front of Jeff instead. At least Jeff had a nice soft rug on his living room floor. "It's all part of letting myself go. Having the freedom to protest and say *no* and *stop*, even if I really want it to carry on. And knowing that you'll carry on pushing me past what I think I can take." Eddie paused, gathering his thoughts. "Actually, that's the first time anyone's got me to that stage with just a bare-hand spanking. Your hand must be killing you."

Jeff flexed his fingers and winced. "Yeah. It is."

"Right, and we don't want either of us to sustain any permanent injury, so you need to learn to listen to your body too. I'm guessing you didn't feel it while you were spanking me because of all the endorphins coursing through you."

"I thought it was just you who got high off them."

"Trust me, you're getting them too. Didn't you feel euphoric? I could feel how turned on you were."

Jeff's hands went to his crotch again, and Eddie was pleased to see there was still a distinct bulge in the denim. The man looked hung. Fuck it, Eddie couldn't resist licking his lips.

"You got off on it too." Jeff gave a very deliberate look at Eddie's erection—now drooping slightly, but it wouldn't take much to make it perk up again. Just Jeff's gaze might be enough, in fact. Eddie's cock stirred with an infusion of fresh blood.

Eddie grinned at Jeff's wide-eyed appreciation. At least, he thought it was appreciation. Eddie liked to think he had a nice cock. Might not be the largest around, but it had a good curve to it and a nicely flared head. If there were penis beauty contests, he thought he'd be in for a chance of winning the sash. And then he'd tie it around his balls. Mmm...

Eddie wiggled his arse, feeling the soreness as he moved his muscles. Lovely. "How about you try out something else next. The crop, perhaps? Just don't put quite as much welly into it as you just did, or you'll probably break it."

Jeff's eyes narrowed. Was Eddie being too bossy? "Bring me the tawse," he said. "And the cane."

"You're not seriously going to cane me after that, are you? It'll fucking kill."

"Are you a painslut or not?"

Eddie folded his arms.

"Well? Answer me, bitch!"

Oh, that tone of voice had done the trick, making Eddie's little beauty queen stand to attention. "Yes, Sir. I'm a painslut."

"Then bring me the cane. Now. Come on. Faster. No, stay on your knees."

Eddie dropped back down again and shuffled over to the table. Jeff could dole out humiliation too. This boded well. He grabbed the cane and tawse, then paused. What the hell, he might as well bring the whole lot.

Jeff was still sitting there, looking insanely hot in his football shirt. It added to the whole thuggish, working-class vibe. Eddie did love a bit of rough. The glare worked with it too, especially under those dark, lowered eyebrows.

"I said the cane and the tawse, slut," Jeff snarled.

Eddie's toes curled with anticipation. "I've been a bad boy." He tried to keep his face straight, but it was impossible not to smirk just a little. "You'll have to punish me for my disobedience."

"You're bloody right I will. Over my knee. Now!"

Eddie flopped down over Jeff's lap eagerly, making sure he rubbed up against Jeff's cock while he did so. Jeff grunted and turned it into a cough, but he wasn't fooling Eddie. Oh no. The man wanted to come, and there was a very good chance he'd come inside Eddie. Or perhaps over Eddie. God, that would be good. He loved being covered in spunk.

The first crack of the paddle took him by surprise, shocking him out of a fantasy of Jeff's monster cock splurting all over his face. It was followed by another in quick succession, and Eddie had to wonder if that was the paddle after all. Not the crop or the cane, definitely, but there was something of a sharp edge to it. Oh yeah, the tawse. He'd only had them used on him a few times, and not for ages, but now he remembered the sting you got from that gap down the middle. Made it faster than a paddle too, raining down on Eddie's arse like a hailstorm. Eddie groaned out all the pain and pleasure, humping against Jeff's meaty thigh as the blows continued. If he could only get a bit more friction...

"Stop that." A hand crashed down on the small of Eddie's back, pinning him down, and then he couldn't move anywhere. He just had to endure.

"Enough!" he gasped at one point, and "Stop, you bastard!" but Jeff just laughed and carried on giving him what he wanted. The bastard learnt quickly, that was for sure.

By the time Jeff stopped, Eddie was soaring. It didn't feel like pain anymore. Each blow was a burst of electricity, sparking off a chain reaction all through his body. All thoughts were gone from his brain. He couldn't move. Couldn't protest. He was like a rag doll.

"Eddie, Eddie? Are you okay?"

Eddie grinned. He was drooling a bit, but he didn't care. Couldn't Jeff see Eddie was still rock hard? He'd have pointed at his cock, but his arms were stuffed with cotton wool.

Jeff didn't look reassured. And he was cradling Eddie's jaw in a way that was more sweet than commanding. Shit. Eddie had to try for an explanation, but words were near impossible like this. Bugger. He pulled his brain cells together, that wonderful feeling slipping away as he did so.

"Subspace," he eventually managed to say, although it came out kind of slurry. "S'good."

Jeff obviously understood enough to get what was going on, as his frown cleared and lust took over. Mmm, his face was more beautiful than Eddie had thought. When he looked like that, he was possibly the best-looking man in the universe. Even with the broken nose.

"On your knees, bitch," Jeff said

Eddie tried to move, but his arms and legs didn't want to listen to his brain. "Can't move," he explained and was grateful for the rough hands that shoved him down to the floor. Oh yeah, that made him feel like a proper slut.

Eddie sat back on his ankles and smiled up at Jeff. What would come next? Jeff let go of Eddie's hair. Fuck. Without that to anchor him he was going to fall backwards and probably bugger up his knees in the process, but he didn't have the vocabulary to explain all that right now.

Jeff's eyes turned black, and his hands went to exactly the right place. His crotch. Oh yeah. Eddie willed them to undo the zip. He somehow managed to raise his own to help, but Jeff batted them away. "Hands behind your back. Now."

Mmm, his favourite position to give a blowjob from. How had Jeff known? It was like he'd reached into Eddie's brain and ransacked his store of fantasies.

When Jeff's cock finally sprang out, Eddie gasped. "Fuck!" It was the thickest, reddest, meanest and veiniest dick he'd ever seen. Oh yeah, that was another page torn out from his fantasy book. It looked almost evil, especially with that bush of black hair at the base. And those large, pendulous balls hanging behind.

Eddie was drooling again.

"Please, Sir," he whispered, but he couldn't force the rest of the words out. Little bastards were still not cooperating. "Please." He could manage that one at least.

"What do you want, slut? Answer me."

Eddie struggled, and eventually the words came unstuck. "You. In my mouth. Please." Balls or cock, he wasn't fussed which. Hey, he'd even settle for a finger or a tongue. Or a toe. Toe-sucking was degrading in a particularly hot way.

But Jeff's cock would be best of all.

Jeff wasn't smiling, but he had an intense look on his face that Eddie wanted to see so much more of. *I did that. I did it to a straight man. Or one who at least thinks he's straight, even if his cock doesn't.*

The cock in question battered against Eddie's lips, and he opened eagerly and sucked on that head. Ooh, tasty. Bitter and ripe, like Kalamata olives. Eddie hoped Jeff liked drool, because he was going to be salivating like crazy with that flavour in his mouth.

Oh, but Jeff had to use a condom. Bugger. But those were Eddie's rules, and no matter how tasty Jeff was, he had to wear one. "Condom," he said, staring up at Jeff.

Jeff frowned. "I honestly don't have anything you need to worry about."

"But I don't know that for sure." Eddie slumped sideways and found his jeans. There were rubbers in the pocket. And damn it, he didn't want Jeff to have second thoughts, but he didn't want to give in too easily. It was so fucking tempting just to take Jeff's word for it.

He eventually found one of the packets and rolled a cola-flavoured condom onto Jeff, who wrinkled his nose. "Can I still come on your face?"

"Yes, please."

Jeff smiled then, briefly, before pulling a stern expression. "Hands behind your back and stick your tongue out. Right out."

Yeah, like Eddie needed someone to coach him in how to give head. But he did what Jeff asked anyway, because deep throating this baby was all he wanted to do right now. He shoved his head as far forward as he could manage, but it wasn't deep enough without anything to grab hold of. Fuck it. It was time to break some more of Jeff's rules.

He grabbed hold of Jeff's buttocks. Oh yeah. Firm and strong. Jeff had a great body. He dug his fingers in and took down that last inch. Couldn't breathe. *Yeah, so good.*

"What did I tell you?" Jeff growled. "Hands behind your back, bitch."

Eddie looked up into Jeff's eyes, and he liked what he saw there. Lust and wildness, with just enough determination to stay in control. He dropped his hands and tried to get that deep again without them, but it just wasn't happening. He moaned in frustration.

"You want my cock deep in your throat, do you? Yeah, you do, dirty slut like you. Bet you love choking on cock."

Eddie did his best to nod and say *hell yes*, but it came out as a needy-sounding whine. He tried again, but he still couldn't quite bury his nose in Jeff's pubes.

His scalp pulled as Jeff took two handfuls of his hair, and then it was all about trying not to gag as Jeff pushed in deeper than Eddie thought he could take. So good!

"Yeah, that's it. Take it all, you dirty slut. That's what you came here for, wasn't it? You were hungry for my cock. And now I'm going to fuck your face with it, bitch."

Eddie moaned with pleasure as Jeff made good on his promise. There was almost no time to breathe, Jeff fucked him so hard and fast, keeping up a string of dirty talk, but Eddie managed to snatch the occasional breath when he had to. Bloody hell. His lips were going to be bruised and swollen with the way Jeff was battering in. Saliva ran down his chin. Tears ran down his face. It was heaven. Or at least, it would be if he could taste Jeff rather than the sickly cola-latex combination.

"Yeah, that's it. Oh yeah, I'm gonna come. Come all over your face, coz you're such a slut. You don't deserve me coming in your mouth."

Eddie could come like this, he was sure. If Jeff just kept up a bit longer.

Jeff pulled out and whipped the rubber off.

Eddie whined.

Jeff's cock hit him in the cheek. One side, then the other. Oh, he loved a good cock battering.

Jeff pumped his hand while Eddie looked up into his face. He was concentrating hard, deep lines between his brow. So fucking sexy.

Jeff's face went slack, and wetness hit Eddie's cheek. Fuck his rules. Eddie wanted a taste. He stuck out his tongue, eagerly chasing the tip of Jeff's cock. But Jeff kept hold of

Eddie's hair and wouldn't let him suck him down again. Instead, he painted it over Eddie's face. It was joining the spittle and tears and dribbling down Eddie's chin and onto his chest.

Fuck. Jeff came like a bloody war horse.

Another spurt hit him square in the mouth, and Jeff grunted. This time he didn't resist as Eddie found the head of his cock and licked it clean. Jeff's body was heaving, and it felt like he was using Eddie's head as support to stop him from falling over, but that didn't matter. Eddie's lust was keeping him upright.

"Enough," Jeff finally said, his voice all hoarse.

Yeah, Eddie had done that to him.

He looked up into Jeff's face. He had this look of utter bliss there. Eddie should take advantage of it. Who knew when the weirdness would hit? Because it was bound to, wasn't it, with a straight bloke like Jeff.

"Do I get to come too, Sir?" he asked.

Jeff stared at him, and for a moment Eddie thought he might have pushed him too far. But then Jeff gave a kind of what-the-hell grimace. "Touch yourself," he croaked. "Come at my feet."

Oh yeah, Eddie didn't need asking twice. The moment he took hold of his erection, his balls responded, pumping jizz out. Eddie tried to keep his eyes open to watch it spurt over Jeff's tan-coloured Caterpillar work boots and his rug. Oh yeah. That was the stuff.

His body finally gave up holding itself upright, and Eddie flopped forward, catching hold of Jeff's legs for support. It was like hugging a tree trunk or two. If they were rather short trees. Not that Eddie was exactly the tree-hugging type, despite a brief flirtation with vegetarianism in his teens.

But these trees shifted uncomfortably, and as Eddie pulled himself together, he remembered that he really didn't want to spook the straight bloke. Not if he wanted another chance at that.

Which he did. Oh yeah.

Which was why he pushed himself back so he was sitting on his ankles, wobbling dangerously. "Now, this is the part where I should probably go through aftercare of your sub after an intense scene."

Jeff looked down and frowned. "Never mind that. What about the aftercare of my rug and boots?"

Eddie blinked as he gathered his thoughts. He'd never have taken Jeff for being particularly house or clothing proud, but now he looked around, he could see that the place was well looked after. There wasn't a great deal of furniture or ornamentation, but the pieces Jeff had were sturdy and comfortable, and everything looked clean enough to eat your dinner off.

Except the rug. "Don't worry. Spunk cleans off easily enough. You must know that from washing your sheets, surely."

Jeff shrugged. "Mum does my laundry. And she comes round to clean too. I can sort out the boots easily enough myself, but I don't want her finding that on the rug. What's she going to think?"

"I imagine she'll think it's yours, and that you've seduced some woman down in front of the fire." Eddie pushed himself to his feet. Last thing he felt like doing right now, but since he didn't want Jeff weirded out, he'd make a sacrifice. "If you're not up to cleaning a small spot on your own rug"—and how pathetic was that?— "then you could always order me to clean it up for you."

Jeff crossed his arms. The tough-guy look was kind of ridiculous with his spent dick hanging out of his jeans. "And would you?"

"Only one way to find out. But it'd be a pretty hard-line approach, and I wouldn't recommend you try it with anyone else. Especially not a woman. They don't usually take kindly to that kind of thing. Especially if they're coming down off the high of a scene."

Jeff scratched his neck. "Shit. Like you are. I'm not doing too good here, am I?"

Ooh, vulnerability. That was nice. Maybe Eddie could utilise it for a teaching moment. "After a scene, you generally want to spend some time with your sub, bringing them down gently. Cuddling and kissing is good, although obviously that's out of the question here. But something like offering me a shower or a flannel to clean up with would be good. And then a warm blanket to wrap up in. And a cup of tea with two sugars. Builder's strength."

Jeff looked at him with something like respect. "Wouldn't have had you down for drinking proper tea. Thought you'd have gone for that herbal muck."

"Nope. I like my tea strong and sweet." He bit back the urge to add that was just like Jeff, because he had a feeling the bloke wouldn't be flattered by being called sweet. And Jeff probably wasn't, by most people's definitions, but there was a sweeter side buried under the gruffness, Eddie could see. It was intriguing. It would definitely make Jeff easier to get along with between scenes, because full-on testosterone-fuelled machismo could be tiring. Eddie had figured that out the last time he'd tried to have a romantic relationship with a Top.

Not that romance was ever going to be in the air for him and Jeff, but still. Friendship and occasional sex would be good. More than good, if he got more of that.

Jeff grunted as he tucked himself back into his trousers. "I'll find you a cloth to clean up with." He disappeared into the kitchen.

Great. So much for the sweetness. Jeff wanted a domestic slave after all.

When the wet dishcloth was handed to him, Eddie sighed and bent forward, scrubbing at the rug.

"What are you doing? That was for you. To clean up your face and...you know. Whatever else needs cleaning."

"Oh." Eddie's heart warmed. "Thanks."

Jeff shrugged awkwardly. "S'all right. I've got the kettle on. You want normal tea or decaf?"

"Normal, please. I'm going to need it to be able to concentrate on the drive home." Then it struck Eddie. "Now I wouldn't have had you down for a decaf man."

"I'm not, but my dad is, so I keep it in for him."

And there it was, another sign of Jeff's innate sweetness.

Eddie cleaned up and got dressed again, all the while playing through his evening. Sometimes it could be hard to remember the details of a scene afterwards. Something about the endorphin haze made it tough to put together a narrative, but moments would leap out. Eddie found if he reviewed it soon enough and made some notes in his diary when he got home, it was easier to fix the good times in his memory. He sat on the sofa, strangely reluctant to follow Jeff into his kitchen. He didn't want him to feel crowded.

But eventually Jeff came through with the tea.

"Cheers," Eddie said. "Appreciate it."

Jeff did that awkward shrug again. "Least I could do for you. After all that...you know."

Eddie made an effort to shift back into trainer mode. "That's great. You've helped me to clean up and given some refreshments. The only other thing that's really important after a scene with a new playmate is to have a little chat about how things went."

"Playmate." Jeff frowned. "That sounds so childish."

"There was nothing childish about what we just did."

"No." Jeff hesitated, something clearly on his mind. "But it was a bit like I was playing teacher or parent. You know, having you, erm, over my knee."

"Did you feel like that was something you wanted to role-play? I'm not into doing incestuous scenes, but I don't mind being a naughty schoolboy."

"No! I don't know. Maybe. It kind of... It stopped it feeling so gay."

Eddie sipped his tea as Jeff paced back and forth. He had to handle this carefully. Casually. Not make a big deal out of it so Jeff could put it in perspective and not let it ruin his peace of mind.

"There wasn't really anything gay about what you were doing."

"I was touching your arse!"

"No, you were spanking my arse. Not that a bit of touching wouldn't go amiss. When you do that with a girl, I'd suggest sometimes switching to stroking, rubbing, and even kissing the skin. The changing sensations make it all even more overwhelming."

"But still. I got hard."

"Yeah, but that's not because you're gay. That's because you're a sadist."

Jeff looked glum. "I really am, aren't I?"

"You're making it sound like a bad thing."

"It's not exactly the done thing, though, is it? Admitting you get turned on by hurting people. My parents would think I'm a monster."

"Yeah, but it's not like you're hurting anyone against their will. Would you have enjoyed it if I hadn't been enjoying myself?"

"I don't know. I don't think so. I think it's more about having the control. About knowing you were putting up with it all for me. Because I wanted you to."

"Well, there we go, then." Eddie slurped the rest of his tea down in one. Although there was plenty more about the scene they could discuss—the whole condom issue, for a start—with Jeff's brain fixated on the whole gay issue, he didn't think the man would be taking any of it in. "Look, don't overthink it. There's nothing to be ashamed of in being a pervert, and there's no reason to go worrying about your sexuality just because you let me suck you off. Different rules apply in a scene. It's like you take a step outside of your everyday reality. Your personality changes. It's all fine. It doesn't have to affect the rest of your life. You're still exactly the same Jeff White you were earlier today."

"You think?" The uncertainty dropped from Jeff's expression, and his usual mulishness returned. "Yeah. You're right. Of course I am. This was just an experiment. That's all."

"Exactly." Eddie stood. "Now, I should be going. I'll see myself out. And I'll call you in a few days in case you have any questions about anything. And if you feel like it, maybe we can set up another session."

"That's not going to happen."

"No need to decide now. Just see how you feel." Eddie darted out of the door before Jeff could say anything else to burst his bubble.

Chapter Seven

He wasn't gay. Jeff had to keep telling himself that. He told himself first thing in the morning when he woke up with a stiffy, and he told himself last thing at night when he had his usual bedtime wank. He told himself all through the day too, constantly on guard against any behaviour that might mark him out as being anything other than a heterosexual man.

It was five o'clock—nearly teatime—so Jeff packed up his tools and headed back to the truck. It was like an oven inside, as there'd been no shade to park in at this client's place. A particularly stinky oven. But it was a proper manly smell, Jeff told himself. Sweat and dirt. And something else. Something that turned his stomach. Jeff rooted around in the mess littering the passenger side foot well, trying to find the source of the stench. Eventually he found a plastic container with something vile-looking at the bottom. Rotting cabbage. Bloody hell, that had been his mum's chicken pot pie. She'd shoved some greens in there too, even though she knew he hated cabbage. Jeff sighed and eyed the space under the rearview mirror where the cardboard pine air freshener had hung up until two days ago. He'd liked the smell of that thing, but then he'd decided that maybe it was just a touch too precious. Straight working-class men had no need for such fripperies. They didn't even need to shower every day. Or wash their clothes all that often.

However, after a single day's experiment with not washing, Jeff decided he wasn't going to let his personal hygiene slip too. A smelly truck was one thing—it wasn't like he had to be in there all day—but he had to live with his body odour all the time. And besides, he reckoned most straight working-class men didn't sweat like pigs all day, rebuilding stone walls in the sweltering heat. Yeah, manual labourers were allowed to shower twice daily. It wasn't like he used moisturiser afterwards or anything.

He wasn't going to feel weird about showering when he got home. Showers were great after any kind of physical activity. Shit. Maybe he should have suggested Eddie had one instead of just throwing him a dishcloth. It had been a clean one out of the drawer, but Eddie probably didn't know that. Or he could at least have gone upstairs for a proper flannel. Niall had been right. He really was a crap host.

Maybe that was why Eddie hadn't called him back yet.

Not that he cared. Women always irritated him when they got clingy after sex, so he should be glad Eddie was just keeping it real. He was glad, wasn't he? Jeff peered into the rearview mirror and faked a smile. Yeah, look at him being glad. For fuck's sake.

Why hadn't Eddie phoned? Jeff would do things better next time. He didn't think he should be judged too harshly on his first time. Everyone had to start somewhere, right? And anyway, that wasn't a proper first scene. It was just a practice experiment. A training session. Yeah. And nothing that happened in it counted. Eddie had made that really clear.

Jeff should probably check that. He should call Eddie. Make sure he was okay. That was the responsible Dom thing to do, wasn't it? Eddie might have got himself in a stew over something. Were gay blokes like women, constantly overanalysing every last little thing Jeff said and did? He should explain himself, just in case Eddie had got the wrong end of the stick about something like Sarah always used to.

He pulled out his mobile before he could second-guess himself, and pressed Call.

"Hey, Jeff. Good to hear from you. How's things?"

Jeff had been expecting standoffishness, so Eddie's warm friendliness caught him off balance for a moment. "Me? Oh, you know. Working hard. Got food in the fridge and money in the bank. Can't complain."

Eddie chuckled. "I can see you're a man of simple tastes."

"Are you calling me common?"

"Simple pleasures, I meant. That was meant to be a compliment. I think people with simple tastes are generally the happiest. I've got pretty simple tastes myself, believe it or not."

"Like M&S ready meals?"

"Okay, you've got me there." Eddie chuckled again. It was a good sound. "But on the whole, I know you think I'm some posh wanker, but really, I'm pretty ordinary."

"I don't think you're a wanker." Jeff reconsidered that. He had ordered Eddie to toss himself off, after all. "I mean, no more than any other bloke is. You are a bit posh, though."

"Ah, not that posh. There's plenty posher than me. Anyway, to what do I owe the pleasure of this call? Fancy meeting up for a drink or something? We could talk through what happened. Make plans for next time."

Next time? Jeff's stomach gave a flip, and he sent Eddie a silent thank-you for not making him be the one to broach it. "Yeah. I s'pose we could." He didn't want to sound too keen.

"Your enthusiasm is overwhelming." Yeah, Eddie could do sarcastic. Jeff had figured he probably would. Clever clogs types always did.

Jeff went for firm and challenging. Best way to meet sarcasm. "I just said we could, didn't I?"

There was a huffing sound down the phone line. "Yes, you did. God, I hope you don't treat women like this, that's all I can say."

"I don't. I'm not trying to impress you, am I?"

"So I'm getting the real, uninhibited you, am I? I suppose I should be grateful for that."

"You're bloody right you should."

For some reason, that seemed to cheer Eddie up, as he chuckled again. "Okay, then. No time like the present, so how about we meet after work? I'll be finished up in half an hour or so, and I could swing by your neck of the woods on my way home."

"Can't do it today." He wasn't going to stand up his folks. And besides, he needed to get his head straight about a few things first. "How about tomorrow?"

They made arrangements to meet up at the Globetrotter again—Jeff didn't want to do it anywhere too local in case people saw him with Eddie and wondered what he was doing. Or worse yet, came over for introductions. But Eddie didn't seem to realise that was Jeff's ulterior motive, and his "See you tomorrow, mate," was perfectly cheerful.

There. That was a pretty successful phone call. Jeff hadn't put his foot in it once. Not in a way that he hadn't been able to get out of again, anyway. And that was pretty much the same thing.

Jeff started the engine in a better mood than he'd been in all day. He wasn't going to be inviting Eddie back again tomorrow—that'd look way too keen—but he'd make sure he was ready for next time and get tips on being a good host from his mum, right after he'd been back for a shower and a set of fresh clothes.

"There you are, love. We were wondering if you'd been held up with work. Doing the Allinson's stone wall, aren't you?"

"That's right. It's been hard work in this heat." Jeff accepted his mum's hug and kiss on the cheek before doing the mutual back-slapping thing with his dad. "I could murder a beer."

His mum bustled off to fetch him one, and his dad limped his way back to the sofa. "Any news from the village, son?" he said after easing himself back into his chair with a groan.

"Reckon you probably know more than I do. I've been busy with work." The village grapevine was clearly still thriving, as Jeff didn't recall having told his parents anything about the job at the Allinson's the last time he'd seen them. That was the trouble with living in a small place. Everyone knew everyone else's business all the time. Thank fuck they hadn't heard about Eddie calling round.

His mum came in with a can of Stella for him and a Diet Coke for his dad.

His dad scowled at the can. "Oh, come on, Mags. Let me have a beer too."

"Not at this hour," Jeff's mum scolded. "You haven't been busy toiling away all day and burning off the calories. You heard your GP as well as I did. You've got to watch what you eat. Can't have you getting all lardy now just coz you can't get about like you used to."

Jeff's dad waited until she was back in the kitchen before muttering that being fat and happy was better than skinny and miserable.

Jeff eyed his dad's pot belly. He and his dad had always had similar builds—stocky and muscular—and seeing what had happened to the man since his accident was a warning to Jeff about keeping fit and eating well. "Dad, I hate to break it to you, but you're not skinny."

"What are you saying, boy?" His dad grumbled. "I ought to have you over my lap for that cheek."

Oh God. What had they heard? Has his mum known from the smell in the room or something? Had Eddie left hairs in the carpet? Or a lipstick mark on his mug? Not that Eddie wore lipstick, but maybe there was some way Mags could tell that someone other than Jeff had drunk out of that one. Jeff pictured her as some kind of forensic specialist like on CSI, combing the room for evidence of her son's sex life. She was certainly nosy enough to do that. That was why he kept his suitcase of kink on top of the wardrobe.

But no, that couldn't be it. She came to clean on a Friday, and the place had been freshly done on the day Eddie came round.

Jeff took a swig of Stella, feeling liquid relaxation pouring down his gullet.

"So, how's the Gherkin coming along?" His dad was building a scale model of the London skyscraper out of matchsticks. It was the kind of hobby he'd have scorned had Jeff ever taken it up as a teenager, but it seemed that early retirement and a gammy back had changed Bert White's views on dainty handicrafts.

"Go take a look," Bert said, looking rather smug. "On the home stretch now, my lad. I'm trying to decide whether I want to go for the Eiffel Tower or the Taj Mahal next."

Jeff stepped over to the table in the chimney alcove and carefully removed the box his dad used to cover his creation. He hated doing that, always worried he'd do something stupidly clumsy and send the whole thing flying into pieces. Bert insisted the glue he used made it stronger than it looked, but still, Jeff didn't like to take the chance. He'd been on the wrong end of his dad's temper way too often as a child.

The model was incredibly intricate, and while it wasn't exactly something he'd want to decorate his own house, Jeff had to admire the level of detail that had gone into it. He grunted his approval. "Don't know how you do it," he said, before carefully putting the box down over the top again. "Think I'd go nuts trying to do something like that."

"You should give it a go. Reckon you'd do well, what with you being a builder too."

"Nah, you're all right."

"Come on, lad. Everyone needs a hobby. You can't just spend all your free time down the pub or watching telly."

"Suited you well enough for most of your life."

"Oi! You really aren't too old for a clip round the ear."

Jeff grinned because it sounded like the old man was joking, but he took a step back anyway. "Anyway, I don't spend all my time down the pub and watching telly. I've been working in the garden most evenings."

"Huh. You'd have thought you get enough of that during the day." Bert White sniffed, reminding Jeff of the way he'd sneered when Jeff had first announced his plans to quit the building site and work on people's gardens instead. What would the old man have to say if Jeff told him he was now starting to do proper gardening work too? Mowing lawns was one thing, but he had a feeling he knew what his father would say about men who spent their days sniffing roses.

"I'm building another shed," he said. That much was true, although it was the vegetable garden that was taking up most of his time this year. "It's not a prefab. I'm doing it all from scratch and laying on electricity and running water and all. It's keeping me pretty busy."

"Not that busy. You had some new friend round the other day, I heard."

"Oh?" Jeff took another chug from his can, just to avoid answering that. But by the time he'd wiped his mouth with the back of his hand, his old man was still staring at him. Fuck, his eyes were sharp. Like a bloody jackdaw's, they were. You never could get one past him. "Yeah. Not a friend, though. A new client." Jeff really didn't feel like explaining his friendship with a man like Eddie, who his dad would no doubt hate on sight.

"They're making house calls now? You should be the one going to them, you know."

"He wanted to have a look at what I'd done in my garden. With the pond. Could be a big job if I land it."

"One of them fish collectors, is he? Bunch of weirdoes. Heard he had a Jag. Some of those posh cunts have more money than sense. What's the point in collecting a load of fish? You can't stroke 'em or anything."

"What's the point in building a tower out of matchsticks?"

"Keeps my fingers working properly. The physio recommended I do something using fine motor skills, and I didn't much fancy knitting."

"Oh yeah. I remember." But still, it was the principle of the thing. Jeff didn't like hearing Eddie's hobby criticised. Even if it was an imaginary hobby. Unless Eddie really did collect fish? But he didn't have a garden, did he? Just a sad little balcony, by the sounds of it.

Jeff felt sorry for the bloke. Maybe he really should invite him round to see the garden. He could sunbathe. Get a bit of colour to his skin. He was way too pale. The way Jeff's hand had looked against Eddie's pale arse... It was like they were different races or something.

Fuck. He wasn't meant to find that memory a turn-on.

Jeff squirmed in his seat, willing his cock to calm the fuck down. Fortunately, just then his mum brought the tea things through, and the distraction of the teapot and slices of Battenberg was enough to lull his dick back to sleep.

"Here you go, love." Mags handed out the plates of cakes, reminding Jeff about his plans to observe what a good host did.

He watched his mother closely, but it was no use. As far as he could tell, it was all about lining the plates with paper doilies and pouring tea for people. Somehow he couldn't see that working for him and Eddie. He'd have to think of something else. Or ask someone else. Maybe Niall...

Or what about Eddie himself? Yeah, he could ask that tomorrow. Just come right out with it and ask him how to set up a scene and treat him right and all that.

It occurred to Jeff that that would be a bit like admitting he didn't know what he was doing, but he smothered the doubts in another chunk of Batternberg washed down with a milky cuppa.

Chapter Eight

Eddie strolled into the Globetrotter garden, on the lookout for Jeff's dark head. Ah, there he was, halfway through a pint and scowling at the sunset. Or at least, it might have been a scowl. He could have just been squinting against the light. What Eddie had first mistaken for general all-round surliness, he was now inclined to think was just a quirk of genetics. Jeff was simply cursed with one of those serious faces, and unless he was actively smiling, he tended to look like he was in a bad mood. Combined with his muscular breadth and shorn head, he probably scared most people away.

Maybe that was why Jeff had such a hard time finding a sub. Lucky for him Eddie found the whole mean-and-thuggish look a right turn-on. Even better if he knew it was just a veneer. After all, it wasn't easy to trust someone who genuinely was a violent psychopath.

Eddie put his latte down on the table. "You know if the wind changes, you'll be stuck with that frown forever."

Jeff stared at him. "It's not windy."

"Never mind. Just something my stepmum used to say whenever I pulled a silly face at her." Eddie straddled the bench of the picnic table so he was facing the sunset too. The Mendip hills rolled away before them, crisscrossed by hedgerows and dotted with church spires and farmhouses. "It's no wonder this place is popular with a view like this."

Jeff just grunted in response.

"What, you don't think it's beautiful?"

"I like the view from my garden better. Too many quarries in this view."

"Where?" Eddie followed Jeff's finger as he pointed out the quarries. Now he was aware of them, he could see the scars to the landscape like limestone cliffs. "I always thought those were natural cliffs."

"Nope. All blasted out of the hillsides."

"So you object to them? Funny, I didn't have you down as an environmentalist."

Jeff rubbed the back of his neck and looked down at the tabletop. "Yeah, well, I just don't think they need to have so many of them around here. All those lorries are well noisy. And you get rock dust coating all the trees in the woods nearby. And, you know, it's bad for the wildlife and shit. Destroying their habitats."

Eddie gazed on Jeff with a newfound respect. "I had no idea you'd care about all that."

"Yeah, well, you haven't grown up round these parts."

"What makes you say that?"

"You don't talk like a local."

"That's because my family don't talk like locals. I grew up in Bradford on Avon."

"Right. So you're not local. That's in bloody Wiltshire."

"You got a problem with people from Wiltshire now, have you?" Eddie teased. "You know it's right on the border with Somerset. I drank scrumpy as a teenager too."

"So, what, are you drinking posh coffee for now, then?"

Eddie took a sip of the beverage in question and smacked his lips ecstatically. "Mmm, well, not only does it taste heavenly, but since I'm driving and really want to keep a clear head for our little chat, I thought it was for the best."

"No one drinks coffee in a pub," Jeff insisted.

"And yet here I am, doing just that." Eddie took another slow and sensual sip just to annoy Jeff.

"Makes you look soft."

"And that should bother me why, exactly?"

Jeff didn't seem to have an answer to that, and while he could think of a thousand and one things to chat about, Eddie let the silence stretch out. He wasn't going to drag Jeff into this conversation kicking and screaming. Let him decide for himself when he was ready to talk. Grumpy-bear types preferred to feel they were in charge of things, and Eddie was a patient man.

Most of the time, anyway. He did have an almost irresistible urge to wind his legs around Jeff's under the table, but since he wanted to keep his original set of teeth, he decided he'd best not. It was a shame, though, as he'd bet anything that deep down, Jeff was a snuggler, even if he didn't like to admit it.

Eventually, Eddie's patience paid off, and Jeff cleared his throat. "Listen, I've been thinking..." Jeff looked at Eddie as if for a prompt, but Eddie just nodded encouragingly. Jeff didn't seem to blush when he was embarrassed, but he was scratching his neck like he had fleas or something. When he did speak, it was directly into his empty pint glass. "It went all right last week, and I was thinking maybe we should set something like that up regularly. Let me practice something different each time. You seem to know what you're talking about, and I reckon I could probably learn something off you. I just don't want to cock this all up again next time I'm with a woman."

"So what exactly do you want to learn from me?"

Jeff shrugged awkwardly. "You know, the usual. Bondage and all that. Nothing gay, though. Just whatever kind of stuff you think women are into."

"What if I said a lot of female submissives are into anal play?"

Jeff's eyes widened. "They are?"

"Yep."

"Why?"

"Probably the same reason a lot of vanilla women enjoy it. It feels good. And then there's that added frisson of wrongness for the pervs."

"How come you know so much about what women like?"

"I could ask how come you know so little." Jeff frowned, and Eddie relented. "I've always had close female friends. And then Maddy and I have been friends since college, so I know plenty about what female subs are into."

"You really talk about that kind of thing?"

"Yep. Not all the time, because that would be boring, but sometimes I go round for the evening, and we drink wine and stay up scoffing chocolate and chatting about all kinds of rubbish. I kip on her sofa quite often."

"That sounds suspiciously like a girly sleepover."

"Are you seriously telling me you and your ex never used to sit up with a bottle of wine and chat?"

Now Jeff looked so awkward Eddie wanted to take his words back. "Sarah didn't drink. And she was always out doing things. Sports and aerobics and shit like that. Nights we were in together, we'd just crash in front of the telly."

"Oh." She sounded like a riot, but Eddie bit back the sarcastic comment. Who knew what sort of feelings Jeff was still harbouring for his ex? "And what did you do on the nights when she was out?"

"Sometimes telly. Sometimes watching a game of footie down the pub. Sometimes pottering about in the garden." Something about the way Jeff's voice softened at the end made Eddie suspect that the gardening had been his preferred occupation.

"I'm going to have to see this famous garden of yours next time. It must be amazing."

Jeff shot him a wary glance. "It's not finished yet."

"I'm not bothered about that."

"Maybe If it's a nice evening."

"It's a nice evening tonight."

That got Jeff's attention. "You want to come back tonight?"

"Why not? Like you said, there's plenty to be practising. I thought of a five-step plan. You worked on corporal punishment last week, so what about some sensory play this time?" Jeff looked confused, so he clarified. "Stuff like wax and ice, electricity and so on."

"I don't think I've got any of that sort of thing."

"Doesn't matter. Lucky for you, I came prepared. I've got a suitcase of kink in the back of my car."

Jeff's head snapped up. "You have a suitcase of kink too?"

"Yeah. It's not so strange. Lots of subs collect their own toys too."

"Oh." Jeff was staring at Eddie with something like wonder, which was kind of weird, but who knew what was going through that head of his? Still, wonder was something Eddie could work with. "Once we've tackled sensory play, if I feel like I can trust you enough, then we'll do restraint the week after."

Jeff's pupils flared with interest. "You'll let me tie you up? With rope?"

"No promises, but yeah, that'd be fun. Maybe just some cuffs first, though."

Jeff looked crestfallen. "Oh. Okay."

"Are you really into trying out shibari, then?"

"Shi-what, now?"

"Shibari. Decorative rope bondage. It's an ancient Japanese art."

Jeff pulled a face. "Dunno nothing about that. I just want to tie you to my bedposts."

Now that was something Eddie could get behind. "Ooh, face up or down?"

"Down." Jeff sounded pretty damn certain about that.

"And when you've got me facedown in four-point restraints, what will you do to me?" Yeah, Eddie was flirting, but hey, this was a conversation about sex, so it was allowed, wasn't it? "Come on, Sir. Let me know what fantasies you've got going through that shaven head of yours."

Jeff was scratching the back of his neck so fiercely it was a marvel he didn't draw blood. "Just wanted to beat you some more. Didn't get a chance to use the cane yet."

"And when you've covered my arse in red welts, what then?" Could Eddie get him to admit to it? He continued in a low voice. "I'd be completely at your mercy. I wouldn't be able to stop you if you wanted to ream my arse. You could fuck me like that, facedown and helpless. You could do it hard and deep, and while you're doing it, you could look down at the welts you made all over my arse. And then you could pull out and come all over them. Yeah, you'd like that, wouldn't you? I thought as much."

Jeff shifted uncomfortably on his seat and cast a nervous look around the garden. "So what if I do?"

"Then great. I'd love that too." Of course, Eddie would enjoy it even more if the shagging was interspersed with kisses, and if he'd been fitted with a cock ring first, but he wasn't going to add those little details of his fantasy in because he was fairly sure they didn't feature in the "I'm not gay, honest" version that Jeff had playing out in his head. But he did now risk a minor footsie manoeuvre, running the tip of his shoe up the inside of Jeff's left shin.

Jeff jerked and looked around wildly. "Watch it. We're in public," he hissed.

Eddie deliberately did not look around. "The garden's nearly empty and you know it." It was a lovely evening but too chilly for sitting out for long. The tables nearest the back door were filled with the terminal nicotine addicts and their hangers-on, but the rest of the garden was all theirs. But it was getting chilly…

Eddie drank down the last of his coffee. "So how about we head back to yours, then?"

"Yeah. Okay. Good idea."

But when Eddie stood, Jeff remained sitting, scratching his neck again. He was going to rub it raw if he wasn't careful. "Not having second thoughts, are you?" Eddie said lightly. "I meant what I said before. This is like taking a step outside your normal life, and no one ever has to know anything about it. It doesn't make you any less heterosexual, and you don't even have to think about me outside of the time we're together."

"That's easy for you to say," Jeff muttered. "You've bloody well wormed yourself into my head, though, haven't you? What if you start wanting a relationship with me and go getting all obsessed?"

"Trust me, darling, I don't do relationships. Nothing serious, ever." It was a lie, but Eddie did his best to channel Maddy so he could put Jeff at ease. "I'm too happy being a free agent. Come on. No need to worry about me."

"Yeah, okay. Just, erm,"—scratch, scratch, scratch—"could it wait a minute or two. I can't really stand up right now." Jeff finally met Eddie's eyes. "That fantasy of yours got me a bit overexcited."

"Ohhh." Eddie couldn't suppress the grin as he leaned forward to peer down into Jeff's lap. His shorts were tented proudly. "I see your predicament."

"How come you're not hard?" Jeff complained. "You're the one who's actually gay, after all. Doesn't seem fair."

"Maybe I've just got excellent self-control."

Jeff glared at him.

Time for honesty, perhaps. "Oh, okay. I did get a semi-on while I was outlining that little fantasy, but since I know you're not going to be kissing me and subjecting me to genital torture, it's not as much of a turn-on as it could be."

"Do gay Doms do that, then?"

"Genital torture is usually pretty high on their list of favourite pastimes."

Jeff went pale under his tan. "I meant the kissing."

Interesting. "Not all of them do, but I've always liked it best when there's snogging. Even your most degraded piss pig enjoys a kiss now and again. Submissives do want to feel cherished, even while they're being hurt and insulted. It's kind of what makes it fun rather than being an ordeal. Otherwise, it's only a step away from sexual assault."

"Huh." Jeff appeared to be mulling that one over. "What's a piss pig?" he eventually asked.

"Subs who are into extreme humiliation, usually involving watersports and drinking piss. It's a gay thing. I mean, I know women can enjoy that too, but the whole gay scene tends to be more extreme. Straight fetish clubs are incredibly tame in comparison."

Jeff had gone almost green now. "That's taken care of it," he said, rising from the bench.

Eddie checked him out. While Jeff's dick was still prominent, he had a feeling that was just the natural state of affairs for a man as large as him. Yet again, he had to wonder why the female subs weren't going for him. Okay, his manners were pretty shocking at times, but once he'd got the hang of when to finesse and when to go for brute insults, he should be able to carry home any sub he wanted. The man had a fine body, so long as you liked them hairy.

Shame about the awful clothes. A faded old promotional John Deere T-shirt, baseball cap and badly hacked-off stonewashed jeans really wasn't Eddie's fantasy-Top outfit.

"You got any leather jeans?" he asked. "You'd look super hot in them."

Jeff rolled his eyes. "I don't go for all that goth stuff."

"Leather isn't goth. It's sexy. Tactile. Smells good. Trust me, nearly all subs love a man in leather. And if the goth thing's worrying you, you don't even have to get them in black. You could go for brown, if you wanted. Or maybe a nice pair of suede chaps over jeans..." Eddie trailed off, imagining just how hot a shirtless Jeff in chaps could be. Forget about the bloody jeans.

"I don't want to look like one of them gay cowboys."

"But you've got the tan and the body to carry it off. Just a thought, anyway."

"You should be thinking less about that and more about what I'm going to be doing to you when I get you back home."

Ooh, that was more like it. Confident Jeff back again. "I can't think about that too hard, or I won't be able to drive. And you don't even know exactly what I've got in my suitcase, do you, Sir?" Eddie winked and turned to leave.

Jeff growled, and Eddie smiled to himself. Teasing Tops was way too much fun to ever stop.

Jeff climbed up into his truck and took a moment to sort his head out before starting the engine. Fucking hell! Eddie was a bloody tease, there was no two ways about it. Jeff was out of his depth with this one. He could admit it to himself, but he was buggered if he was about to let on in front of the bloke. Eddie would probably just wink and wiggle his arse and do something annoyingly sexy, like that way he made his voice all purry and low. Or the way he batted his eyelashes. Sodding hell, why had Jeff ever taken him for a just a normal bloke? Normal straight blokes didn't flirt like that, did they? No, they went for the caveman approach and just told birds what they wanted to do to them.

Eddie was flirting like a girl.

Except he wasn't. Not really. There was none of that crazy hidden agenda Jeff kept tripping over when women were involved. And Eddie didn't get all emotional and burst into tears for no reason when Jeff spoke his mind.

Eddie was much easier to understand than any woman Jeff had ever met. What did that say about him, that he understood gay blokes better than he understood chicks? He'd lived with Sarah for almost fourteen years, and she'd still been a bloody mystery to him at the end.

Maybe straight blokes and gay blokes had more in common than Jeff had realised. And Eddie did have an amazing car. Which, right now, was waiting for him at the exit to the car park. Shit. He should get his arse in gear.

Jeff started up the engine, not sure whether to curse the day Eddie entered his life or to celebrate it. He'd never been this bloody confused and turned on all at once. Things in Jeff's world were meant to be simple. Straightforward. No messing.

And yet here he was, leaping dick-first into a situation that bloody well terrified him.

Fuck it. Sitting around chewing on it wasn't going to make things any easier to understand. Jeff needed to work Eddie out of his system with a few more sessions together. It was the only way to do it. Familiarity breeding contempt and all that.

His mind made up, Jeff flicked his headlights on, revved the engine and peeled out of his parking space. Let the good times roll.

Chapter Nine

This time Jeff followed Eddie back to Hook St. Norton, growing increasingly envious of the power behind the Jag's engine. Eddie was sprinting ahead while Old Maud was huffing and puffing behind her, like the unfit kid who came in last on school sports day. If only Jeff could afford to run two vehicles, but he didn't have the funds, and there was no way he could manage with just a car when he had to lug tools and materials around. It was a pain in the backside, though.

Would Eddie let him have a go driving her? Maybe if Jeff treated him nicely enough. Eddie had liked the rough stuff, but he'd also said something about liking kissing, hadn't he? Could Jeff bring himself to kiss another bloke? Like full-on snogging, with tongues?

Nah, that'd be well gay. He'd have to think of something else that didn't involve exchanging bodily fluids.

Maybe just a kiss on Eddie's back. He'd had a nice back. Good definition, even if he wasn't built. Jeff could appreciate the effort that went into developing muscles like that, especially when you had a desk job. Watching his dad's muscles waste away had been a real eye-opener. There was no way Jeff'd ever let that happen to him. He'd be straight down the gym if for any reason he couldn't work the way he was anymore.

Planning future workouts managed to keep Jeff distracted for much of the way back, which was definitely better than thinking too hard about getting Eddie naked. Especially with the way that made his dick perk up. Although, to be honest, thinking about pumping iron at the gym was having a similar effect. What the fuck was wrong with him these days?

Eddie parked around the corner on the main road, and by the time Jeff had manoeuvred into his parking space, Eddie was outside his front door with his little suitcase, inspecting Jeff's climbing roses.

"These have the most amazing fragrance," he said. "I didn't know roses could actually smell this strong. My stepmum's never did."

"It's a nineteenth-century variety. The older varieties always seem to have the best fragrance. Nowadays most people breed for colour and size of the blooms, but if you don't mind smaller, simpler flowers, you can get a lot more fragrance. It's the same with sweet peas."

"You grow sweet peas too? You're a regular Alan Titchmarsh, aren't you?"

Coming from Jeff's dad or one of his mates, that would have been an insult, but Eddie had sounded admiring, so Jeff volunteered a bit more information. "I've planted the parts of the garden nearest the house for fragrance. It was for Sarah, really. Girls like stuff like that," he added, just in case the whole thing made him sound like a nancy boy.

"I like stuff like that too. Flowers aren't just for girls. I always buy a bunch when I'm at the supermarket."

"What, M&S? That must cost you a bloody fortune. You know you could grow your own."

"But I've only got a flat. My balcony's hardly big enough for a flower garden. And besides, I don't have green fingers. Not like some people I could mention."

Jeff grunted, not wanting to show just how much the compliment warmed him inside. He opened the door and was about to head on through when he remembered his manners. Instead he stepped back down the path and waved Eddie in. "After you, mate. Oh, and let me take that."

Eddie raised his eyebrows and handed over the case but didn't say anything. But his body brushed dangerously close to Jeff's on the way past, allowing Jeff to get a whiff of Eddie's scent too. After the sweetness of the flowers, it smelled sharp, but there was a whiff of herbs that reminded Jeff of woodland in the spring after a rain shower.

He wondered if he smelled anything like as good, considering he'd run out of shower gel and had had to wash with Tesco medicated hand soap. Shit, he needed to stock up on some decent grooming shit. He just had to hope no one saw him when he did. His mum'd rip the piss out of him when she saw it in his bathroom too.

"You coming in then, Sir?" Eddie called from inside. "I want to show you all the toys I brought."

Bugger. Jeff looked up and down the road. His neighbours' windows were closed, so hopefully they hadn't heard any of that. He scurried in and slammed the door behind him.

"Now, I'm hoping you've got an old sheet or towel or something so we can play with wax, as that's great fun. But it's messy."

"I've got something." There was that old tablecloth Sarah had left behind. It wasn't like Jeff had any use for tablecloths now, was it? He went to pull it out of the cupboard under the stairs. "Where do you want to do this?"

"In the bedroom's probably best, if there's room for you to move around the bed. Otherwise, on the floor is okay. Could do with a touch more heat in here, though."

Jeff pictured the bed he'd shared with Sarah for so many years. He had a feeling if he got Eddie into bed, then sex would be inevitable—that was what beds were for, anyway. Besides sleeping, that was. And Jeff wasn't sure he was ready for taking that kind of step. A blowjob was one thing. Anal was a whole different hole.

"I'll get a fire going," he said, glad of the excuse to crouch down and turn his back to Eddie, hiding his confusion. "You start telling me about what you've got with you."

"First of all, have you got any ice?"

Shit. Already he was being a bad host. Jeff sprang up and walked to the kitchen. "What do you want to drink? I've got Coke and beer. Oh, and milk." Not that he'd heard of people putting ice in beer or milk, but who knew what the posh folk got up to behind closed doors?

“Actually, the ice was for playing with. Just a few cubes would be great, but if you’re offering drinks, do you have any mineral water, please?”

Jeff gave him a look. “I don’t see the point in paying for bottles of water. Not when there’s plenty of decent water flowing freely out of the tap.”

“Why am I not surprised? Okay, tap water would be lovely, thank you. And ice in that too, if you have some.”

“Yeah, don’t worry, I’ve got ice.” Although, when he got to the freezer, Jeff remembered that Sarah had taken the normal ice cube tray with her, and all he’d been left with was the novelty one his brother had given him for his birthday a few years back. The one that made ice cubes in the shapes of cock and balls. Jeff groaned. Bloody perfect. *Thank you, Tony. Not.*

“You can put ’em in your own drink,” Jeff said, plonking the pint glass of tap water and the bowl of ice cubes down on the coffee table. There was a mysterious old leather-bound case on there now, which intrigued him no end, but he wasn’t going to ask about it. Always best to act like you’d seen it all before.

“Nice.” Eddie held an ice cube up, grinning. “I can see you’re a man after my own heart.”

“Not bloody likely,” Jeff muttered, settling down to finish building the fire. Once he’d got the kindling ablaze and was reasonably sure the logs would catch, he turned to head back to the sofa. He’d been worried Eddie might have taken the opportunity to get naked again, but he’d managed to resist. And Jeff definitely wasn’t disappointed about not having all that skin on show.

“Did I leave any bruises?” he asked once he’d dropped down to the seat at the other end of the sofa. Fuck. Now Eddie would know he’d been thinking about his arse.

“Oh yeah, it was pretty impressive. Faded now, but you can still see something.”

“Show me.” It was out of Jeff’s mouth before he could stop it, but he sat firm and refused to act like there was anything remotely gay about the request. It wasn’t that he wanted to see Eddie’s arse because he found it sexy. It was because he needed to know what the bruising was like. Responsible Dom stuff again.

But when Eddie pulled his trousers down, Jeff gasped. "Shit. That really did bruise. Bloody hell, that must have been sore the day after."

"Eh, not that bad. I'm kind of used to it now."

"Oh." Bugger. He'd wanted Eddie to be feeling the aftereffects for days. But still, the bruising was impressive. Both of Eddie's cheeks were a mottled greeny-yellow, with smaller purple spots speckled across them, along with a few stripes. It definitely wasn't like any other kind of bruising Jeff had seen.

He frowned at the stripes and reached out to prod one.

"Ow!"

"Thought you said it didn't hurt."

"It does if you do that."

Something about those stripes was bothering Jeff. Then it hit him. He'd never used the cane or the crop in the end, had he? Had Eddie been to see someone else after their session?

"How did you get these?" He demanded.

"I'd have thought you of all people should know that."

"What the fuck's that supposed to mean? These stripes. I didn't do them."

"Yes, you did."

The bloody liar. If there was one thing Jeff couldn't stand, it was being lied to. That and the thought of Eddie sneaking out to see some other Dom. One who was better at all the gay kink than Jeff was. Fuck. Jeff was going to need to learn how to do all that kind of stuff if he wanted to keep Eddie satisfied. It was a tough job, but someone had to do it.

"Jeff, you did these. I promise." Eddie was stroking Jeff's cheek, which was a bit much, but somehow he couldn't bring himself to push Eddie's hand away. It felt...nice. "It was the tawse," Eddie was saying. "That slit in the middle has edges which sometimes leave a mark like that if you hit hard enough."

"I didn't see any stripes when I was doing it."

"No, but then again, you had got me bright red already. I'm not surprised they didn't show up till the next day."

"Huh."

"Where did you think I'd got them? I'm not seeing anyone else. One Top at a time is plenty for me. Especially when that Top packs a wallop like you do."

Did Jeff trust him? He must have looked doubtful, because Eddie grasped his other cheek. "How about tomorrow I text you a picture of my arse so you can see any new bruises while they're fresh. Will that reassure you?"

"I s'pose." And really, he probably should take Eddie's word for it, in the same way Eddie had taken his about not having an STD. Jeff took hold of Eddie's wrists and pulled his hands down off his face. They had felt good there, but he was feeling a bit weirded out by a bloke holding him like that. Especially when the bloke in question was standing in front of him with his trousers round his ankles. It all looked a bit too much like Jeff was about to give him a blowjob.

Which absolutely wasn't ever going to happen. Ever. Not in a million years. And Eddie wasn't even hard yet. Unlike Jeff.

Jeff cleared his throat. "Sit down," he ordered, trying to make his voice as gruff as he could. "And keep your trousers down."

"Kinky. I do love a bit of humiliation."

Jeff eyed the kit on the table properly for the first time. "Okay, why don't you talk me through what you've got here?" He picked up one of the candles. Just an ordinary thin straight one like you'd find in a packet of six at the hardware shop in case of power cuts. "I'm surprised these aren't black or purple."

Eddie chuckled. "I know what you mean. Sometimes I think I'm one of the few pervs who actually likes a range of different colours. But yeah, you can get black candles if you want to, but these were just from the supermarket. No need to buy pricey kit if you can find something that works just as well for next to nothing."

"So the candles don't have to be a special kind?"

"So long as they're not beeswax, they're fine. That stuff gets way too hot, but any cheap paraffin ones should be perfect. Now, before you use wax, some subs like to be rubbed in baby oil so the wax comes off easier. Personally, I'm fine with it on unprepped skin. The trick with this stuff is to start with the candle high, and then get closer and closer to increase the heat of the wax. You'll probably want to start somewhere fairly neutral to begin with. The stomach or clavicle. Work your way to the nipples and genitals once you've judged how your sub reacts to it. Ideally, you want to use four-point restraints, as it can really make some people writhe"

"What about doing it to someone's back?"

Eddie pulled a face. "Yeah, you could, I suppose. Not nearly as much fun, though, as you don't have many pain receptors in your back. And none of the pleasure zones are there."

Jeff wasn't sure he was up to having Eddie lying faceup and naked, but he kept that to himself for now. Maybe he could try it and see.

"So what's the ice for? Cooling you down afterwards?"

"Kind of. You could, but really I prefer them to be alternated. Bit of hot, then a bit of cold. The contrast makes them all the more intense."

Okay, Jeff could see that.

"And this thingie?" He picked up a bit of what looked like either medical equipment or perhaps a crafting tool. There was a steel handle with a steel wheel attached at one end, with spikes sticking out of the wheel. He tried rolling it across the palm of his left hand and winced. "Ow!"

"Yep, that's exactly what you do with it. The pinwheel is one of my favourite toys. It gives an almost ticklish sensation."

"That wasn't ticklish. It bloody well hurt."

"Yeah, but that's because you're not a masochist. Trust me, for me it's great."

"Looks kind of medical."

"That's because it is. They used to be used to check nerve sensitivity. And you can still role-play with them. You know, there's a whole subculture of kinksters who get off on being medically examined? Once had a guy use a speculum in my arse. He cranked it really wide. Incredibly humiliating, that was. And painful." Eddie smiled fondly. "Fun times."

Jeff felt kind of hot and sick, which had to be down to the idea of someone getting off on having a speculum up his arse. Yeah, Eddie certainly was a pervert. Possibly even more of one than Jeff was. Jeff wished he'd been there to witness his humiliation.

No, Jeff wished he'd been there to shove that other Dom out of the picture and take over himself.

Uh-oh. Where had that come from?

Jeff's fingers trembled a bit as he went for the leather-covered case on the table. What the fuck was wrong with him? Getting possessive over a girlfriend was one thing, but getting possessive over a bloke you were just fuc—uh, practising BDSM with was just ridiculous. He needed to get a grip. He fumbled with the case and nearly knocked it off the table.

"Whoa! That's some pricey kit in there. Careful. Here, allow me." Eddie took the case from Jeff and stroked it like it was a bloody dog or something.

"What is it?"

"This, my friend, is a genuine antique electrotherapy device, better known these days as a violet wand." As he spoke, Eddie lifted the lid. The case was velvet lined inside like something out of a jewellers, and a collection of differently shaped hollow glass rods nestled into custom-shaped cutouts in the lining.

Jeff had to admire the workmanship. "This is amazing. I've seen these things on the Internet, but they didn't look anything like this."

"Modern ones aren't nearly as stylish. I found this one on eBay, amazingly enough, but got in a bidding war, so it set me back a fair bit. It's from the 1920s. Back then it was a huge medical craze. People thought it was a cure-all, so all these bits are shaped to stimulate different parts of the body. This one here...” Eddie lifted out something that looked like a large test tube. “Can you guess what it was used for?”

Jeff squinted. He didn’t want to go for the obvious. “A back massager?”

“Nice try, but this was to be used vaginally to supposedly cure all kinds of things, including general malaise. I bet it worked too, lucky ladies.”

“So how do I use all this on you?” The fact it was an antique was kind of intimidating. Jeff didn’t want to drop one of those glass thingamabobs. Maybe Eddie had brought it along just to show off, though.

But Eddie gave him a hungry kind of look, then pointed at a mushroom-shaped attachment. “Well, this one is meant for nipple stimulation, so you could always try that one first. But you know, I always think you should try out stuff on yourself first. A good Top knows what he’s dishing out from firsthand experience.”

“You saying I should be a sub for a while?” Jeff bristled at hearing Sandi’s advice coming from Eddie too.

“Nah, don’t worry. That’s not necessary. I’m just saying you should try it on yourself, that’s all.”

“Oh. Okay.”

“I’ll plug this in. You get your shirt off. Sir.” Eddie stood and looked down at Jeff, somehow managing to make it seem like he was looking up through fluttering eyelashes.

Fuck. Jeff’s dick was hard enough to smash through concrete. Next time he was breaking up old foundations, there’d be no need to get out the pneumatic drill. He’d just need to think about Eddie and whack his dick down on the ground.

He stripped his shirt off, trying not to show how hot and bothered he was getting. Think about something to calm down his arousal. Nipple torture. His dick went to titanium strength. No, *his* nipples being tortured. That was better... Wasn’t it? Fuck. It wasn’t much better. Not if Eddie was still in the room.

“Oh my. I had a feeling there’d be the body of my wet dreams hiding under your awful T-shirts.” Eddie was leering at him openly, his dick now sticking out and waving around between them like it was happy to see him too.

"Fuck off." But Jeff flexed his pecs a bit, kind of pleased at the attention. No one had looked at him with that level of admiration since...well, since he first got together with Sarah. Which was almost fourteen bloody years ago. But here Eddie was, looking at him like he was the sexiest man alive. He could get used to that kind of thing.

"Mmm, you know if you were gay, you'd definitely be a bear. Love all the hair."

Jeff snorted. "There's more of it on my body than there is on my head. Sarah used to say I didn't need to wear clothes because I was already covered in a fur coat."

"I like Sarah's thinking. If you were mine, I wouldn't allow you to wear any clothes at home. Uh-uh. No way."

"Maybe I'm the one who wouldn't let you wear any." Oh fuck. Now he was flirting back. *Stop it, stop it, stop it.*

"Now that's my big, bad Top." Eddie seemed to take that as a cue to strip off the rest of his clothes, and Jeff wasn't about to stop him. Subs were meant to be naked. It had nothing to do with Jeff wanting to check out those lean muscles again.

Eddie knelt down between Jeff's knees and squinted at his chest. "Hmmm, think we can locate a nipple somewhere there in all that fur?"

Jeff rolled his eyes and pointed them out. "They're not that hard to spot."

"No, but I just wanted to see you touch your own nipples."

"Pervy bastard."

"Yup. Now, this is all ready to go. I've got it on the lowest setting, so it shouldn't really be more than a tingle, but maybe we should try it on a less sensitive part of your body first. Like your arm."

Good idea. Now that he could see the violet wand all plugged in and ready to go, Jeff was starting to get the fear. The glass part was glowing with a soft purplish light, and it was attached to the box with a curly wire just like they used to use for telephones. The thought made him laugh out loud, but it came out sounding a bit hysterical.

Eddie smiled calmly. "Here, take hold of this."

Jeff's hand shook as he tried to reach out for the wand.

"Want me to assist you, Sir?" Eddie lowered his eyes submissively, and that humble look kicked something off inside Jeff. Something that didn't just want to abuse Eddie but that wanted to protect him. What had Eddie said he wanted? To feel cherished. That was it.

Before he could talk himself out of it, Jeff pressed a quick kiss to Eddie's forehead.

"What was that for?" Eddie stared at him, eyes wide with surprise.

"Just letting you know I trust you. Not to hurt me. You won't, will you?"

"It's just a little tingle. No worse than getting a shock from static electricity."

Jeff hated those, but he kept his trap shut.

"Here, I'll just touch it to your upper arm so you can feel what it's like," Eddie said, doing just that.

Bloody hell. Jeff's arm trembled, but he forced himself to hold still. It was painful. Okay, not as bad as having his tetanus shot had been, but still, if it felt like that on the lowest setting on a not very sensitive part of his body… "There's no way you're using that on my nipple," he said.

Eddie pouted. "Are you really finding it that bad?"

"It's horrible. How can you enjoy this?"

"I don't know. Just the way I'm wired up, I suppose. Oh no, please don't cover up again. Even if I can't touch your nips, can I at least look at them?"

"I suppose. But I'll need to put another log on the fire." Jeff gladly took the excuse to turn away from Eddie for a minute. He'd been this close to ordering Eddie to suck his nipples. And if he did that, it would be his cock next, and then Jeff wouldn't get a chance to pour all that lovely hot wax all over his lily-white skin. And he'd die if he didn't get a chance to do that.

Chapter Ten

Eddie watched Jeff stoop down to mess about with the fire—classic displacement activity if ever he'd seen it—and pondered his next move. He'd never had to deal with a Top this twitchy before, and it definitely wasn't just the gay thing. Jeff's lust had carried him through that last session, but in the calmer, more intellectual atmosphere of a teaching session, his nerves were really starting to show. The way his arm had trembled!

While Eddie knew he shouldn't trust a Top this nervous and inexperienced, he really, really wanted to help Jeff find his groove. If he could get over the wibbles and find his confidence, he'd be amazing. Last week had shown what he was capable of when inspired.

Maybe Eddie just needed to put himself into an even more submissive position and let Jeff take over. He grabbed the tablecloth and shook it out over the rug, then lay down on it, faceup. There were a couple of handy armchair legs he could grip on to which would simulate being cuffed. Again, that might help Jeff feel he was in control.

"What are you doing?" Jeff stopped with his unnecessary fire tending and was scowling at him, although his eyes still gave away his terror.

"I think I've spent enough time boring you with explanations. It's time you did a bit of kinaesthetic learning."

"Kinna-what, now?"

"Kinaesthetic. It means learning through hands-on experience. I have a feeling you're the kind of person who learns better that way than through lectures or books."

"I'm not stupid."

"I didn't say you were." Eddie sighed and propped himself up on his elbows. "It's just a different learning style. Unfortunately we live in a society that tends to favour those with aural learning styles who can sit and concentrate through lessons and lectures. Those are the people who do best at school. But when it comes to learning practical, useful stuff, the kinaesthetic and visual learners come into their own."

"Oh. Yeah. I guess I am a kinna-whatsit, then."

"Right. So rather than listening to me wittering on about violet wands, wax play and so on, you need to try these things out and learn for yourself. And if you really don't want to try them on yourself, then I'll be your willing stunt double."

That made Jeff smile. "You'd be a crap stunt double. You look nothing like me."

"Yeah, I'll just have to be a stunt double for your future girlfriend."

"You don't look anything like a bird either."

"Sorry. Not a lot I can do about that. I would offer to shave my body hair off, but it always gives me a rash. And I might be a masochist, but I hate having an itchy crotch."

Well, what about that—Jeff was actually checking out Eddie's body and staring at his groin. He didn't even look revolted like Eddie expected, but instead was intense, considering. Eddie forced himself to relax back down again and hold on to the chair legs. He wasn't about to jinx this by coming on too strong.

Eventually, Jeff spoke in a low, halting voice. "I don't want you to shave. It's kind of nice. Being with someone a bit hairy. Means I don't feel like such an ogre."

"You don't look like an ogre to me."

Jeff found something fascinating to look at in the corner of the room and scratched his neck again, and for a moment, Eddie thought it had been too much. But then the scowl melted away, and Jeff met his gaze again. "Do you want the wax first?"

"I want whatever you want to try out first. Use me however you like."

Jeff's eyes darkened, and he adjusted his shorts, which were starting to tent again. "Okay." He went over to the coat pegs by the front door and took down a scarf. Not a woolly one, but a dark, fine-looking one. What exactly was he planning?

"You remember I don't do bondage until I say so?"

Jeff wound the scarf around his hands and walked over. "I remember. I'm not going to tie you up. I just want to blindfold you."

"Oh." Eddie should probably object to that too, but if he wasn't bound, it would be a piece of cake to remove the blindfold if he needed to. Provided Jeff wasn't trapping his wrists. But he trusted Jeff not to do that, didn't he? Yes, he did. "Okay. That's not a bad idea, actually. Makes the sensations more intense."

"You need to stop the lecturing now. Just lie back and feel." Jeff knelt by him, and Eddie lifted his head to give better access. Jeff continued in a low, gruff voice, "Can you do that for me? Just give in to the sensations."

"Sounds good." Eddie's heart was thumping away like crazy, and his cock strained up, desperate for a touch from Jeff. Wasn't going to happen, but he could dream. He gripped on to the chair legs as the world went dark and the soft fabric pulled tight around his head. Normally he could see out from under improvised blindfolds—not that he'd ever admit as much to the Top he was with—but Jeff had somehow folded the scarf so it was padded out enough to make him completely blind.

Eddie had to force himself to relax. Shit. Was he nervous? Or just turned on? The anticipation was killing him.

"Hmmm."

Eddie strained his ears for sounds of Jeff, hoping to prepare himself for what came next. There was some clattering over in the direction of the fireplace, and a momentary loss of heat against his side. Still tending the fire? Maybe it wasn't a displacement activity after all. Unless Jeff really was more anxious than he was letting on right now.

There was a hiss of a match flaring into life and a tang of sulphur on the air. Aha. Wax play first. Eddie breathed deeply, forcing his muscles to unclench. Hot wax was always a shock when you didn't expect it, but at least now he knew what was coming.

He felt the stirring of air as Jeff settled down beside him.

Here it comes. Probably the centre of the chest first. That was where most people started.

Electricity sizzled under his arm.

"Arrrgh! Fucking hell."

Jeff laughed, rich and deep. The sound was almost textured, pouring over Eddie like honey.

"I was expecting wax, you bastard."

"Sir Bastard to you."

"Sir Bastard." He couldn't help smiling himself. Then prickling pain shot up his chest from his navel to his collarbone. "Shit! Wasn't expecting that either." The pinwheel felt unusually intense. Jeff slowed its movement so it crawled across Eddie's pecs, just above his nipples. He whimpered, shifting slightly to try to encourage Jeff to venture just that little bit lower.

"You want this on your nipples, don't you?"

"Yes."

"Why?"

"Hurts so good."

"Where else do you want it? Tell me."

Well, if Jeff really wanted to know... "On my balls. And my cock. Not under the foreskin, though. That's too much." He wouldn't normally admit to that—telling a sadist you didn't want something was generally a sure-fire way to make sure you got it. But there was no way Jeff would venture that far south, so he was probably safe.

The pinwheel circled round his nipples in a wide figure eight. Was it Eddie's imagination, or were the loops closing in? He realised he'd pushed himself up onto his curled toes, and consciously relaxed back down again.

The pinwheel ceased, and his nipple caught fire.

"ARRRGH!" Wax. It was just wax. "Fuck, you could have warned me, you bast—Fuck!" There went the other one.

"Where's the fun in warning you? Anyway, I think you're being a baby. I'm holding it really high. Could go much lower than that."

Drops rained down on Eddie's nipples and between them, from one to the other, hotter and hotter. God, he was out of control now, writhing and wailing.

"Keep still." Jeff's hand pinned down Eddie's chest, keeping him from moving. "Anyone would think you didn't like this."

"I do, I do. Just too much. So hot! No, don't stop!" The candle had stopped dripping, and then Jeff's rough hand scraped the wax away from his nipples.

Oh my God, Jeff was touching his nipples.

Eddie held his breath, not wanting to spoil the moment. Jeff's hand slowed. Came to rest. Then took hold of his nipple and pinched hard.

"Oww, fuck!"

"You like that, bitch?"

"Yes! Yes, Sir Bastard, thank you very much, Sir." Eddie kept babbling because it was either that or sob with the intensity of the pain. So fucking good. It shot down to his balls and set his whole body humming with arousal.

"Your nipples are huge," Jeff said, sounding intrigued. He let go of Eddie's nipple and then flicked it. "Not wide or anything, but you know, they really stick out."

Eddie was rather proud of his nips, but he could see why they might seem a bit odd if you hadn't had much experience with painsluts. "That's what years of nipple torture will do to you. They used to look fairly normal."

"I like them. Gives me more to grab hold of."

Suddenly, Jeff wasn't pinning Eddie down anymore, but then both nipples exploded in pain. Eddie cursed and writhed, trying to hold on to the memory that Jeff had just said he liked his nipples.

He *liked* them.

"Why are you smiling?" Jeff asked.

"S'good," was all Eddie could manage in response while Jeff was pinching and twisting his nipples. He didn't have to admit exactly what was good, did he?

"You masochists are a weird lot."

"So are you s-s-sadists. Ow!" Sometimes the moment of release was more painful than the torture that had gone before.

"Your cock's dripping. You really did like that, didn't you?" Jeff sounded dazed with wonder.

"Abso-fucking-lutely. Yes, Sir. Please feel free to torture my nipples as much as you— Ow, fuck!" That was the violet wand on one of them now, he was sure of it. The crackling electricity was less of a tingle, more of a sharp buzzing on his abused skin.

"Yes, I think I will torture them. It's fun watching you getting all carried away with it. Can't say as I get why you enjoy it, but I'm glad you do."

"Why?" Oh, why did Eddie have to say that? He didn't want to push Jeff so far he got defensive again.

But Jeff only paused a moment before answering. "I don't know exactly, but I guess it's just the way I'm wired up."

"Bloody good thing too, Sir. I do love a man who enjoys hurting me."

"Yeah, I really do." Jeff's voice had gone all deep and husky, and Eddie turned his head towards him, taking a deep breath. He swore he could taste Jeff's arousal on the air, mingling with the sharp ozone from the violet wand. If only Jeff was one of those Doms who'd get off on sucking Eddie a little, then torturing his cock and balls, then sucking him some more. Those mingled bursts of pleasure and pain were the best.

But Eddie was hoping for too much there from a straight man.

Hot wax splattered on his chest again, distracting him from thoughts of oral sex. The dribbles of molten heat moved down towards his navel. "Fuck, oh fuck. No, no, no, no, no. No! Don't stop!"

"Hard not to when someone's yelling no," Jeff muttered, but the wax splashing resumed. The heat moved down, agonisingly slowly. Felt like Jeff was trying to mummify him in wax. The hot spots skated round his groin and splashed onto the tender skin of his inner thigh. Oh God, was he really going to go there, or was this just a monumental tease?

Eddie was almost hyperventilating. He gripped on to the chair legs, arching his back and opening his legs in a giant *yes, please.*

The wax stopped for a moment, and Jeff moved. Where was he off to now? "Please," Eddie rasped. "Please don't stop there."

"Shut up, bitch. You don't get to say what goes on here."

Eddie moaned his protest and arched his back further.

Jeff moved between his legs. Oh fuck. Eddie could feel the fabric of Jeff's shorts rubbing against his ankles. What was he planning?

The temptation to rip the blindfold off was unbelievable, but he had a feeling this would all be over if he challenged Jeff like that.

Eddie held still, tensed in anticipation.

"That's it. Nice and still. Good boy." Jeff's breath gusted over Eddie's groin with his words. He must be leaning down. Did that really mean what Eddie thought it meant?

Chapter Eleven

Jeff knelt on Sarah's old tablecloth, staring at another man's erection. This wasn't somewhere he'd ever thought he'd be, but so long as he didn't touch it, that was okay, wasn't it? Torturing another man's genitals wouldn't make him gay. This was just...rewarding Eddie for being such a good boy. Erm, good slut. Boy sounded a bit weird, actually. Bit too much like they were in a relationship or something.

Jeff eyed the instruments of torture he'd been using. The tip of the violet wand gave off that eerie light, and the candlelight was glittering in both the glass of that and the steel of the pinwheel. They were all fun in their own special way, but which should he start with? And where?

Jeff squinted at Eddie's bollocks. They huddled up next to his body, all neat and tidy and covered in just a light blond fuzz. Nothing like Jeff's swinging, hairy sac. They were much more attractive.

Had he just thought another man's balls attractive? Fuck. He bloody had as well.

Jeff determinedly swept that thought into the dustbin of his brain, never to be mentioned again.

Would Eddie really enjoy having his bollocks tortured? Jeff found it hard to believe, but then again, he was willing to admit he was a bit of wuss about any kind of pain, so maybe he was no judge. Still, a man's nuts were bloody sensitive...

He should go for Eddie's cock instead. Erm.... He snuck a glance at it, kind of nervous now he was up close and personal. And about to get a whole lot more personal. Eddie's dick was a bit of a weird shape what with being all bendy and a bit wider in the middle than at either end. It sort of reminded him of a banana, which would explain why he felt hungry. He definitely didn't want a taste of cock banana, though. No, gross. It would be, wouldn't it? All sweaty and spunky and nasty.

Jeff took a sniff. Actually, Eddie's bits smelt all right. More like soap and sex. Jeff's cock jerked as if it wanted a sniff too. Jeff growled at it, hoping that might calm him down.

Eddie made this weird sound then, kind of helpless and like he was about to come. Yeah, a sex sound. Not a sexy sound. Just like the smell of him was sex, not sexy.

Good thing Jeff had that all sorted.

He picked up the violet wand and held it over the base of Eddie's cock. Okay, here went nothing.

He pressed it down.

Eddie yelped and jerked his legs wildly.

The candle fell over. A burning-hair smell filled the room.

"Shit!" Jeff whacked the candle flame out. There was a singed patch on the rug and a splatter of wax. If only the fucking tablecloth had been bigger.

"God, are you all right? What happened?" Eddie had pushed the blindfold up and was staring at him with wide, dark eyes.

"It's okay. Just the candle."

"Fuck. I'm sorry. Your poor rug. It keeps taking a hammering when I come round."

The mood had shifted, and now instead of thinking of sweet torture, all Jeff had in his head was explaining to his mum just how the burnt patch had got there. He wasn't really a candle type. Could he blame it on a log having jumped out of the fire?

Then she'd want to know what he'd had a fire burning for in the middle of summer. Although she might have spotted the smoke out of her bedroom window already.

"Such a fucking disaster." Why did all Jeff's scenes have to end like this? Cut off before he'd had a chance to finish things his way, which would definitely have involved him coming all over Eddie's wax-splattered chest.

"God, what a mood killer," Eddie complained, slumping back onto the floor.

"Yeah. Maybe you should just get dressed and head off. I've had a practice with all the stuff now, anyway."

Eddie frowned, and something about his expression reminded Jeff of a particularly stubborn goat that one of the villagers owned. "I don't want to go yet."

"Yeah, but I don't think I can carry on any more of this."

"You didn't even use the ice yet."

"I forgot."

"You could cool my nipples with it. They're kind of sore."

"I could? Oh yeah. I suppose I could." Jeff wavered.

"Come on, we can get it back, I promise. Don't give up now. I really, really want to suck your dick. And your balls. Think you could cram them both into my mouth?"

Jeff's dick perked up at Eddie's words. He eyed Eddie's mouth, wondering what that would feel like. He'd never dared ask Sarah, as she'd made it clear she didn't do that kind of thing, but if Eddie was bloody well pleading for a tea-bagging...

"Stay there." Jeff unzipped his shorts. Would he be able to do this without taking them off? No, not likely. Fuck it, he'd just have to get naked and not think too hard about what was going on. He was going to get his balls sucked, after all. Yeah, that made any sacrifice worthwhile.

He shoved down his shorts and underwear, then looked down, figuring it out. He'd have to straddle Eddie's head. "Let go of the chair." Eddie obeyed, and Jeff shoved it away. Yeah, he wanted to be able to watch Eddie choking on a great big mouthful of bollocks. His bollocks. Fuck, yeah.

The bollocks in question were tingling with excitement.

Jeff stepped over his sub, standing with one foot each side of Eddie's head. He squatted, glad he'd stepped up his workouts lately. His balls were dangling just out of reach of Eddie's mouth. Eddie licked his lips and winked. Cocky bastard.

Jeff grabbed a handful of Eddie's hair and yanked his head up. "Suck them, bitch. That's it. Open your mouth wider. You can do it."

Eddie was making hungry noises that did peculiar things to Jeff's insides. And his mouth was wet and warm, and if Jeff had his way, his bollocks would live there for eternity. Even the threat of teeth added a certain excitement to the mix. "Oh yeah, that's it. Take them all. Want you choking on my nuts."

Eddie made a happy noise that sounded like he thought that was a great plan. What would he do if Jeff pinched his nose? Not for long, but just enough to make him a little bit breathless.

He couldn't, though. Not when Eddie had said no breath play. They'd have to discuss it first. At a point when Jeff didn't have his balls in Eddie's mouth. Mmm. He ground down against Eddie and watched him drooling with the effort. He was doing something clever with his tongue that felt like heaven. Oh yeah. Jeff lifted his dick up, about to start tossing off, but then Eddie opened his eyes, and they crinkled knowingly. Cheeky beggar. Jeff let go of his cock and let it whack down against Eddie's cheek instead.

"Unngh!" Eddie's eyes closed again.

Yeah, that was the stuff. Jeff used his cock like a club, battering Eddie's face. Claiming it. "Want you to smell like my cock. Want you to know you're my bitch."

Eddie made a choked-off sound and nodded, which tugged on Jeff's balls in a delicious way. Fuck it. He needed to come.

If he did it like this, though, he'd overshoot Eddie's face and paint the tablecloth. Damn it, he wanted Eddie covered in jizz.

"Hang on. Stop a minute. Yeah, that's a good boy."

Eddie whined as Jeff's balls plopped out of his mouth.

"Don't worry, you can have them back. Just need to move."

He got up, turned to face Eddie's feet and squatted again. Okay, so he was presenting a view of his arsehole to Eddie, but that was humiliating for Eddie, not for him. Yeah, that was right.

"Fucking love your balls," Eddie slurred before gobbling them back again.

Oh yeah, that was the good stuff. Right there. Jeff started fisting his cock, then remembered. He'd come first last time. And he was going to be considerate, wasn't he? He should let Eddie come first this time. No, he should *make* Eddie come first. There was an important difference.

But how did a straight bloke make another man come?

Eddie's hands were balled up into fists either side of his hips. "Touch yourself," Jeff ordered. "Go on. Do it. Make yourself come like a dirty little slut. Come all over yourself." Eddie reached for his cock, jerking it savagely. Fascinated, Jeff watched the head slipping out from under the foreskin. It was kind of primal. Kind of sexy.

Eddie's sucking redoubled, and he made a high, desperate sound. A jet of spunk shot out of his cock, then another. The scent of it hit Jeff's nostrils and made him giddy. Fuck it, he was going to come too. He grabbed his own cock harder and matched Eddie's rough strokes. There. The orgasm bubbled up from somewhere in the sucking heat of Eddie's mouth and shot out the end of his dick. Spunk sprayed from two directions, painting Eddie's chest with streaks of white over the flakes of wax and patches of reddened skin.

Oh yeah, that was fucking gorgeous.

When he was spent, Jeff reached down and ran his hand through the goopy mess. Eddie's mouth had gone slack, so it was easy to pull himself out and shift his legs so he was kneeling to one side of Eddie's head.

Eddie's eyes opened, black as sin. He spied Jeff's hand and grabbed hold of it with his own, pulling it to his mouth greedily.

"Yeah, that's it. Eat it. Eat it all." Eddie was probably eating bits of wax along with two lots of spunk, but he didn't seem to care. Did it really taste that good? The way Eddie was carrying on made Jeff salivate.

Jeff dipped his left forefinger into the mess.

Fuck it. In for a penny, in for a pound.

He licked his finger.

Actually, that wasn't so bad. Not as pungent and seaside-y as Sarah had tasted. It was more... Olives sprang to mind. Trust Eddie to taste like posh nosh.

Jeff dipped his finger in for another taste, then met Eddie's knowing gaze. He paused with his finger just in front of his lips.

"You know you probably shouldn't do that," Eddie said.

"Why not?"

"You don't know what I've got. One little cut in your mouth, and you're opening yourself up to infection."

"You sucked my finger first."

"Yeah, but I should really know better." Eddie gave a twisted kind of smile. "Fuck it. It's fairly low risk, and I know I'm negative, so you don't have anything to worry about there. I just... You should think about stuff like this. In future. Even with women."

"Huh." Since Eddie seemed to think it would be okay, Jeff raised his hand to his lips again.

"You really like it?" Eddie asked.

"Dunno." Jeff sucked his finger. No point pretending that wasn't what he'd had in mind. "'S'all right, I suppose."

"You must have more of an opinion than that. You must have tasted your spunk before."

"No. Why should I?"

"What, you never tasted it on a girl after she'd blown you?"

"No."

"Seriously? Bloody hell, you straight blokes have issues."

"It's not like that. It's just..." Jeff rolled onto his back. It was so much easier to do all this when he didn't have to look in those way too intelligent eyes. But he didn't want Eddie thinking he was being ignored and treated like a piece of meat. So he grabbed Eddie's hand and laced fingers, resting their joined hands on the centre of his chest. He'd always loved lying like that with Sarah.

"Just what?" Eddie prompted, and thank fuck he hadn't said anything about the hand-holding.

"It's just I never got the chance. Sarah wouldn't let me come in her mouth, so I wouldn't know."

"And what about other women?"

"What other women?"

"The other ones you've slept with."

"I've been with Sarah since we were sixteen."

Eddie exhaled noisily. "Are you telling me you were virgins when you hooked up?"

"Yep."

"And in all those years you never split up for a while, or found a bit on the side?"

"Never."

"And since you split up, what, six months ago, was it?"

"At Christmas."

"Right. So in all that time, you haven't slept with anyone else?"

It wasn't easy to shrug when you were lying on your back. "It wasn't for want of trying. I had a lot of first dates." Did it still count as one if she walked out before they got to the main course? "Well, only half a first date sometimes. I just don't seem to be very good with women."

"Fuck me. You must be bloody desperate for a shag." Eddie sounded in awe, like it was something incredible rather than just a few months of making friends with his right hand.

Jeff laughed, finally. "Yeah, so bloody desperate I'd do a bloke. Come on, it's not that bad. What's the longest you've gone without getting any?"

"It was that time I had the flu. Three weeks, I think it was. And had to stick to fairly vanilla stuff for a while after that till I got my strength back."

"Bloody hell. How many different blokes have you had, then?"

"Oh, one or two."

"Come on, I told you." Jeff squeezed Eddie's fingers.

"Okay, hold on, let me think." He could feel Eddie's fingers moving in his. Was he counting off his conquests on them?

"Well, I can't guarantee I haven't forgotten about a load of them, but I think it's probably about three hundred. Give or take."

"Fuck."

"Yeah, I did. All of them. If you count blowjobs as fucking, that is."

"Of course it is." Too late, Jeff spotted the mantrap he'd just stumbled into.

"Ah, so we have already fucked, then?"

"Shut up." Jeff should have let go of Eddie's hand then. Should have got up and started cleaning things away. Turfed the cheeky beggar out on his cute little arse. But it was nice lying there like that, and it wasn't like they were actually cuddling or kissing or anything.

He squeezed Eddie's fingers tighter and kept his mind carefully blank.

Chapter Twelve

"You're late," Eddie told Maddy as she sashayed into the coffee shop, but he was in too good a mood to really be bothered.

"Sorry, darling, but you know how it is." Maddy kissed both his cheeks before giving him an appraising stare. "So, you're looking like the cat that got the cream." She planted herself elegantly in the chair opposite Eddie. "Hope that coffee isn't for me. I'm after something herbal today."

"Looks like it's my second cup, then." Eddie pulled the latte over to him before calling the waitress. Once Maddy had ordered a lemon tea and a piece of cheesecake, she turned to him expectantly.

"You joining me?" she asked.

"Nah, I've already had breakfast."

"So have I, but it's half past ten already. I'm absolutely ravenous. So, how's it going with your trainee Dom?" she asked once the waitress had made her way back to the counter.

Eddie felt his grin stretch wider.

"I see." Maddy raised an elegantly painted-on eyebrow. "He's shaping up all right, then?"

"He's still rough around the edges, but I like 'em like that."

Maddy shook her head. "You always did like a bit of rough, didn't you? Remember that dreadful Aaron kid at college?"

"How could I forget?" Aaron had had a motorbike and wore a uniform of beat-up old leathers and a scowl. He'd been the star in many of Eddie's teenage fantasies, even if he had been unattainable. "Such a shame he was straight."

"And our Mr. White? Is he as straight as he makes out, then? Clearly not by the look on your face. Who would have thought it? Could have sworn he was as straight as they come."

"He's definitely more versatile than he thinks he is," Eddie said, choosing his words carefully.

"Come on, then, what have you been teaching him? You let him tie you up yet?"

"Maddy," Eddie hissed. "Keep it down. Not everyone wants to hear about my sex life." The café was quiet, but that just made their conversation even more audible to the few people in there—a white-haired couple stooped over their teacups and a hippyish-looking young woman with long plaits and a weather-beaten face.

"What? Anyone rude enough to eavesdrop deserves what they get. I'm not censoring myself for their benefit."

"Fine. Well then, can you at least drop the volume a little?"

Maddy rolled her eyes at him, and for an instant, they were back in college, sitting at the back of the lecture hall while Mr. Fox droned on about the Old Masters over the world's most boring PowerPoint presentation.

The tea and cheesecake arriving put a stop to their conversation for a moment, but Maddy clearly didn't want to be sidetracked and picked up again as soon as the waitress was back behind her counter. "So, how long do you think it'll be before he's got enough control to be let loose on a female sub?"

"Why should women need him to be more in control than a bloke would? I'm kind of insulted."

Maddy huffed. "Okay, let me rephrase. How long do you think it will be before you've knocked the rough edges off him enough for him to not frighten a less experienced and/or female sub?"

"And there you are again, assuming women are more delicate than men."

"We're not more delicate. We can take way more pain than you can. We give birth, for fuck's sake."

"Not this old argument. You know there's no way I can prove men would cope better with childbirth."

"Right. Because they wouldn't. They make enough of a fuss over man-flu. But that wasn't what I was getting at, anyway. It's more Jeff's rough edges generally that bother me. He just doesn't seem to care about treating subs with respect. He's got no manners or tact. I mean, I know I don't have much of a humiliation kink, but I still think he needs to learn that there's a time and a place for criticising women's bodies." Maddy clapped her hands to her cheeks. "No, wait. I didn't just say that. There is no time and place. Ever."

"What's he done now?"

"Last month at the social, he told Tilda her basque wasn't very flattering, and she'd be better off getting something she could cinch in at the waist like a corset."

"That doesn't sound so humiliating."

"Wait, I was paraphrasing. What he actually told Tilda was that she looked fat."

"Seriously, he actually used the f-word?" Eddie shook his head. "Okay, yeah, he probably does need to learn when to zip it."

"He insults you as well, then?"

"He does tend to take the piss out of me at times, but it doesn't bother me. My self-esteem is Teflon coated, baby."

Maddy narrowed her eyes at him. "Well, lucky you. Maybe that's because you haven't had a lifetime of the media telling you you're not thin or beautiful enough. Women have it much harder than men."

He refused to be dragged into an argument about feminism again, because he actually agreed with most of Maddy's views, but if she was in one of those moods, she still persisted in trying to force a disagreement, and he came out looking like a chauvinist. "So what you're saying is a man like Jeff would be better off steering clear of women and sticking to blokes, who don't tend to have their self-esteem issues tied up with their appearance."

"They don't tend to have self-esteem issues at all," Maddy grumbled.

"That's bullshit. Just because I don't, doesn't mean other blokes don't have their hang-ups. And I used to, didn't I? I just dealt with them. I refuse to have anyone take pity on me because I like being used and abused by working class men."

"Yeah, okay. I remember. You were as big a fuck-up as I was back at college." Maddy played with her cheesecake garnish with the fork, messing up the carefully presented strawberry slices and chocolate sauce. "Ignore me. I'm just being a bitch."

"Somebody's upset you. Is it Niall? What's that bastard done now?"

Maddy's mouth crumpled oddly, and for a horrible moment, Eddie thought she was about to cry. Maddy didn't do crying. Ever. Not even after that horribly messy breakup with her alcoholic boyfriend all those years ago. She'd just downed a bottle of tequila and ranted about the useless bastard until she passed out.

"Come on, pixie. You can tell me."

"It's not anything Niall's done. Well, it is. But you know, it wasn't his fault. And I really, really don't want to talk about it."

Eddie sat back and sipped his coffee. A big part of him didn't want to know, because if whatever it was had got Maddy that upset, then it was bound to be nasty and messy and the kind of emotional mess he really didn't want a part of. But then again, it was Maddy, and she didn't have many close friends. Him and Niall were about it, and if Niall was the problem...

"It's okay. You're probably best off not telling me, anyway. If it's straight people's relationship stuff, I'm the last person to offer advice."

Maddy took a sip of her tea and grimaced at it. "This stuff is bloody rank."

"You ordered it."

"Yeah, I did, didn't I?" Maddy heaved a huge sigh. "You're right. Oh, what the hell. I've probably got to tell someone, and I don't actually want any advice, so maybe you're the best person for this. But don't you breathe a word of this to anyone else."

Eddie leaned forward and took one of her hands.

"I'm pregnant."

He stroked her palm, wondering what you said to that. "Congratulations?"

Maddy snorted, then grabbed her napkin and looked dangerously teary again. "Yeah, thanks. I think."

This was so way out of Eddie's comfort zone, he'd need a map to find his way back there again, but at least he was okay with getting lost. "So, what's the problem exactly? Are you not sure if you want to keep it?"

Maddy hugged her arms around her middle and glared at him. "Of course I want to keep it. This is my baby."

"Yours and Niall's?"

"Yes, of course it's Niall's."

"Hey, don't blame me for wondering. I know you two have an open-relationship arrangement going on."

"Yeah, but I'm really careful. And besides, I've only been seeing other women for the last few months. It has to be Niall's. The dates are all right."

"Okay. And what does he think about it?"

The cheesecake was suddenly demanding all of Maddy's concentration.

"You haven't told him?"

"What if he wants me to get rid of it?" Maddy moaned. "That's our baby. I couldn't bear it if he didn't want it."

"What makes you think he wouldn't want it?"

"He's never talked about having kids."

"I think you'll find most blokes don't until someone else brings the subject up."

"Well, yeah, gay blokes don't, maybe."

"Hey, gay men can have kids too, you know."

"Not without a bit of help from a turkey baster. And a willing surrogate."

Eddie really didn't want that image in his head. "Look, whatever's going on, you need to talk to Niall. He'll probably surprise you. I mean, he's got that big old house and garden now. What's that if it isn't a family home? He's probably been planning for this but didn't want to bring it up in case you hated the idea." The more Eddie thought about it, the more he warmed to the idea. "All that work he's having done on the garden, that's not for his benefit, is it? He doesn't even like gardens."

"Why would anyone think I don't want kids?"

"Well, you never coo over babies, and you've always said you hate kids."

Maddy pouted. "That's other people's kids. Mine will be different."

"How, exactly?"

"They'll be mine, for a start."

"You know they'll still have dirty nappies and get sick and all that kind of thing."

Maddy waved her fingers dismissively. "It's fine. I can deal. I'm not squeamish. Anyway, how come you know so much about it?"

"Three younger stepsisters, perhaps?" Eddie had been twelve when the first of them came along, so his teenage years had featured a fair bit of babysitting. "It's hard to imagine you with a baby, but I bet she'd be cute."

"What makes you think it'll be a girl?"

"I don't know. I just never had to deal with any boy babies. A boy would be cool, though. With a mum like you, he'd never have to worry about it if he liked boys or dressing up in fairy costumes or what have you."

"Knowing my luck, I'll probably end up with a Neanderthal sports obsessive like Jeff."

"Mmm, equally appealing in its own way. I could train him up in the ways of the bear."

"Shut up. I'm not letting you anywhere near my little boy. You'll go putting all sorts of weird ideas in his head."

"That's better, you're smiling now." And more importantly, the threatened emotional meltdown had been avoided.

"Yeah, thanks, Edd. You're right. I'll have to talk to Niall. Tonight. Can't stand much more of being in a state like this." Maddy pulled a folding mirror out of her bag and set about righting her makeup, which, as far as Eddie could see, hadn't been affected in the slightest. She frowned critically before applying another coat of lipstick. She was busy doing something unnecessary with her eyebrows when she next spoke. "So, has your Neanderthal shagged you yet?"

Annoyingly, Eddie's cheeks started to heat. "Not exactly."

She looked up from her eyebrow surgery. "You're embarrassed! Oh, that's so cute. You must really like him. I've never seen you blush before."

"I'm not bloody well embarrassed." Eddie attacked the bowl of sugar cubes with his teaspoon. "It's just... I don't know if I'm hoping for too much from him. This is only ever going to be a series of training sessions, after all."

"You want a relationship with him."

It wasn't a question, so Eddie didn't bother answering. His cheeks flaming hotter was probably confirmation enough for Maddy, anyway.

"Oh, poppet, really? That's too bad. All those gay Doms you could have fallen for, and you have to pick a straight one."

"I haven't fallen for him. I'd just like to spend some more time exploring out mutual interests." Yep, that sounded about right.

And Maddy clearly wasn't having any of it. "You just keep telling yourself that, darling. Denial's not just a river in Egypt, you know."

Eddie flicked a sugar cube at her. "Oi, I sit here being all sympathetic and that, and then you tell me I'm in denial?"

Maddy put her shades back on again, neatly reassembling her celebrity-in-not-very-convincing-disguise look. "Yep, you're totally deluded. Now come on. Fill me in on the fun stuff. What else have you been up to since I last saw you?"

"Oh, a little bit of this and that. Work, mostly, if I'm honest."

"Come on. You must have bought yourself some new toys. And no, I don't mean dildos thank you very much."

"Funny you should mention that, because I found this guy in Bath who makes the most gorgeous glass dildos and buttplugs. Maybe you could get one for Niall to use. On you, not for him!" he added as Maddy flicked the sugar cube right back at him. It was good to see her laughing again.

Chapter Thirteen

Jeff was halfway down his brother's driveway when a passing van stopped him in his tracks. Eddie's car was the exact same colour. Why the hell hadn't Eddie phoned him like he said he would? It had been four and a half days. Four and a half days since Jeff had rearranged his front room to hide the burnt patch on the rug, and the new set-up kept reminding him of Eddie every time he went in there.

"Oi, keep going." Tony barged into him with a cardboard box loaded with what felt like rocks. "We've gotta get the van back to the hire place by six."

"Yeah, all right. Can't a bloke take a few minutes' rest?"

"We'll rest while we're having lunch. Come on, bro. You've been away with the bloody fairies all morning. What's the matter with you?"

"Nothing. I'm fine." The only reason he was stressing out about Eddie not getting in contact was he had an itch needed scratching, and Eddie certainly knew how to do that for him.

"Oh." Tony looked him up and down. "Girl trouble, is it? Yeah, you used to look like that when you were having a spat with Sarah. So come on, who is she, then?"

"Who's who?" Jeff climbed up into the back of the transit van so he could stack their latest boxes neatly on top of the others. And hopefully avoid this line of questioning.

"This mystery bird. The one you're getting all stressed out over."

"It's not a woman."

"Then what is it?"

Somehow, Jeff resisted the temptation to say it was a man. Tony would never get that. The man was as straight as...as straight as Jeff had been up till a couple of weeks ago. He had a wife and four kids, for Christ's sake.

"It's work," he eventually settled on. And it wasn't just to shut Tony up. Work genuinely was a puzzle right now.

"Yeah? Thought you was doing all right these days? More jobs than you could take on, you said."

"Yeah, that's just it. Dad reckons I should start hiring a team." Jeff wrestled a few other boxes into more stable positions—Tony was such a slapdash packer—before hopping down from the van's tailgate.

"Sounds good. You get to sit back and boss them around while you rake in the profits. Wish I was in a position to do that." Tony was part of a road-mending crew, but he really wasn't the kind of bloke you'd want as your boss. Not enough attention to detail, for a start. "So come on, what's the problem? Sounds like it's all going fine."

"I dunno. It's just sometimes I get to thinking like this is Dad's dream I'm living. Not mine."

"Yeah? Then what's yours?"

Jeff shrugged. "I like working outdoors. And with my hands. I just prefer doing stuff with plants than cement and shit. You know, proper gardening."

Tony gave him a lopsided grin. "You'll give the old man a heart attack if you tell him that. He already thinks you're a bit soft in the head putting in all that work on your own garden. Won't raise the value of your house, he says."

"Tell me about it," Jeff muttered.

But Tony slapped him on the arm. "Nah, don't worry about what that grumpy old bugger thinks. You want to do it, you do it. One thing I've figured out since having the kids, life's too bloody short to spend it doing stuff to please other people."

"You're all right, though. You're moving away from him."

"I know." Tony's grin grew wider, then faded. "Gonna miss the bastard, though. And Mum. You'd better look after them for me."

"You'll still visit every weekend, though?" Jeff didn't think he could bear the burden of being the only child still around.

"Yeah, don't worry. I'll be there to take the heat off you. And maybe I'll make a career change too. You know, get into retail or something. He'd go ballistic, wouldn't he? Probably smash all his bloody matchstick models."

They both grinned at the idea.

"Come on. Just a few more boxes to load, and we can get this show on the road. Denise just texted me to say they're going to be back by five, so we at least need to have the telly set up by then."

They loaded the rest of the van quickly and by twelve thirty were on the road to Trowbridge. However, they hadn't got any farther than Mells before Jeff's stomach gave a loud rumble.

"Next pub we pass, we're stopping for lunch," Tony announced.

"Yeah, sounds good," Jeff said without thinking. Of course, the next bloody pub would have to be Globetrotter. "Not here," he said as Tony pulled into the car park and into the exact same spot Jeff had last parked his truck.

"Why not? I've heard they do good food."

"Isn't it a bit poncy for the likes of us?"

"Jesus fuck, Jeff. We're not that bloody common. It's just a country pub, and our money's as good as anyone else's. Now get a move on. I'm fucking Hank Marvin."

Since Jeff couldn't give the real reason he didn't want to go inside, he followed Tony and hoped like hell it would be a different set of staff than the last couple of times he'd been down. If anyone told Tony that Jeff had been down here having a candlelit meal with a bloke, he didn't know how he'd live it down.

Fortunately, he didn't recognise any of the staff, and at the bar, they ordered their nosh. "And a bowl of olives," Jeff added after placing their order for pie and mash.

"Olives?" Tony wrinkled his nose. "Didn't think you ate that kind of rubbish."

"They're good here."

"Yeah? So when have you been before?"

Fuck. Jeff grabbed the wooden spoon with their order number on it and led the way to a table. Unfortunately, the only one he could see was the one he'd last shared with Eddie. Seemed memories had a way of ambushing him today.

"I've been here on a date," he eventually said. It wasn't exactly untrue.

"Yeah? So when are we going to meet this mystery woman, eh?"

"I said a date, not a relationship."

"Oh. Slapper, is she? Don't worry, Mum might not have liked Denise to begin with, but she got over it eventually. The kids helped."

"It's not like that." Fortunately, the olives arrived before Tony could wring anything else out of him, and Jeff took the opportunity to stab one of the oily Greek berries with the little double-pronged spear. Couldn't talk with your mouth full, could you?

Unfortunately, all that brought to mind was Eddie trying to speak with his mouth stuffed full of Jeff's dick. The organ in question got excited by that, and Jeff had to adjust his jeans. Fucking traitor. Was it possible for your dick to be gay, even if the rest of you wasn't?

Tony was still staring at him.

"What?" Jeff demanded.

"Don't think I've ever seen you eat an olive before. She posh, then, this bird you're not in a relationship with? You her bit of rough or something?"

"Something like that." Jeff chased another olive around in the earthenware bowl.

"Well, good on you, bro. Nah, don't look at me like that. I mean it. You were with that bitch Sarah for way too long. 'Bout time you had a bit of fun. Doesn't have to be anything serious, does it? Just mess around for a bit, and when you find yourself a bird like Denise, you'll be ready to settle down again."

"Sarah wasn't a bitch."

"Not to begin with, maybe. She didn't half get snotty with me that Christmas, though. You remember? You'd have thought I'd have done something awful." Tony launched into retelling one of his favourite anecdotes involving a prank the twenty-two-year-old Tony had played on Jeff's ex. And yeah, he had to admit there was a funny side to seeing Sarah covered head to toe in the custard Tony had rigged up to trap him, but still...

"She'd just spent two hours getting ready to go out. You ruined our entire evening. You think Denise would have seen the funny side if that'd been her?"

"Not at the time, but we'd be laughing about it now."

Maybe that was true. Denise had always been a lot more smiley and easy-going. Sarah had been...driven. And yeah, maybe a little humourless. She certainly hadn't been anything like Eddie, with his easy laughter and sense of fun.

Fuck it. He really had to stop thinking about that man. Jeff stabbed an olive with the fork, but all he could picture as the tines punctured the olive's skin was that pinwheel digging into Eddie's flesh. He had to try that again. When Eddie was tied up. He eyed the olive fork speculatively. Maybe something like that could have its uses too. It was sharp and pointy. So long as he sterilised it first...

He wrapped it in a napkin and shoved it in his pocket. He'd eat the rest of the olives with his fingers.

Tony gave him a weird look. "You know, most folk stick to nicking the glasses."

"I've got plenty of glasses already." Jeff eyed the container holding the wooden spoon with their order number. If the server didn't collect it when she dropped off their main course, he was having that too. What kind of a bruise would a wooden spoon leave on Eddie's pale, succulent arse?

Jeff licked his lips, tasting a salty bitterness that only reminded him of Eddie more.

Five hours later, and Jeff took his leave from an exhausted but happy family in their new home. The kids were over the moon about the large park at the end of the road, and even Jeff had to agree that there were some benefits to living in a larger town, at least where kids were concerned. The twenty-four-hour Tesco was another. Stomach rumbling again, he decided to call in there on his way home. He usually did the weekly shop on a Saturday, after all, and he didn't much fancy heading home to an almost empty fridge.

He was in the aisle full of grooming crap and all that bollocks, trying to decide which deodorant would smell the most macho, when his phone started ringing. He pulled it out of his pocket and stared at the screen. Fuck. Eddie. Should he answer in here? What if he got a hard-on in the supermarket?

Fuck it. He had to hear Eddie's voice.

He fumbled, nearly accidentally pressing Decline instead of Answer, but managed to save his cool by growling a "Yeah?"

"And hello to you too," Eddie drawled. "Got out of the wrong side of the bed today, did we? Bit too much of the old sauce last night?"

"Piss off." Jeff lowered his voice and turned to the shelf full of deodorants. "Been helping my brother move house. I'm bloody knackered."

"Ah, and now you're doing the weekly shop, which is very near the bottom of the list of things you like to do on a Saturday evening."

"How'd you know?" Was Eddie stalking him or something? Jeff looked up and down the aisle just in case, but there was no sign of that shock of straw-coloured hair.

"Relax, I'm not psychic or anything. Just heard the tannoy, and I'm good at guessing. I wanted to be a detective when I was a kid. Did I tell you that yet? I was obsessed for years. Used to buy all these solve-your-own-adventure books with my pocket money."

"Yeah? I used to buy crisps and fizzy pop with mine." Jeff pictured Eddie in a deerstalker, magnifying glass in hand. He'd look kind of cute like that. And then Jeff could be the big, bad cop who'd have to reprimand him for getting in the way of an official police investigation.

Shit. Now his truncheon was growing. Jeff stepped closer to the shelf and pretended to read the deodorant labels.

"What made you get into drawing stuff for a living, then?" he asked, as much to distract himself as to know the answer.

"I realised I wasn't quite up to challenging the institutionalised homophobia in the force, and I'd always been really good at drawing and designing on the computer, so it was the path of least resistance. And, you know, far more civilised hours. Unless I'm on a deadline like I am right now." Eddie sighed theatrically, so Jeff had to ask about it. "Oh, it's not going to be that bad, but the client phoned me up this afternoon with a different angle based on research from their latest survey, so now I've got to put together a whole new presentation for Monday."

"Can they do that? Seems kind of unfair."

"Yeah, they're just a potential client I'm pitching to. They can do whatever the hell they like. But it doesn't matter. I'll have fun doing the new ad mock-ups. It's what I wanted to do originally, but back then they didn't want to go down that road. Just means a late night tonight and working most of tomorrow." Eddie sighed again. "But if I get on with it, I should get it all done by early evening tomorrow. I'm going to need the thought of some kind of reward to motivate me, though."

"Reward, huh? What, like a drink?"

"Actually, I was thinking more of a bout of intense physical activity followed by a mind-blowing orgasm."

"Oh. That kind of reward." Jeff stared so hard at the can of Lynx his eyes started to cross, but it still didn't help him keep his dick under control. "Shit, could you not talk about that kind of thing? I'm in a public place."

"Mmm, you like the sound of that, do you? Yeah, you do." Eddie's voice went all honeyed and husky. Was this phone sex? Jeff hadn't had phone sex before, and the last place he wanted to try it out was in the body-care aisle of the Trowbridge Tesco.

That really wasn't a kink of his. Getting Eddie all hot and bothered in public would be a different matter, though.

Eddie was still talking, obviously not bothered by Jeff's silence. "I think what you'd like to do is come round here and put me in cuffs, then chain me to my bed. Yeah, you'd love that. And then you'd have me helpless and at your mercy. I wouldn't be able to stop you if you wanted to hurt me or fuck me or do anything to me."

"Shut up!" Jeff grabbed a gift box of assorted blokes' smelly stuff and held it in front of his crotch.

"I will shut up if you promise to come over here tomorrow."

"I don't know." Jeff wasn't about to give in that easily, even if everything inside him was screaming *yes!*

"Come on. I need this. And you do too. It'll be that third step we talked about."

"You make it sound like Alcoholics Anonymous or something."

"Except I'm not helping you avoid temptation. I'm totally enabling you to give in to your deepest, darkest desires. Come on, Jeff, what's going on in that head of yours? You'll be able to do it to me. I'll be yours to command."

Jeff groaned. "You don't know what you're asking for."

"No, but I'm going to have fun finding out. Oh, and we could do some more sensory play, couldn't we? You're in a supermarket. Pick up some root ginger. A nice big piece with a natural handle to it."

"Why?"

"You'll find out," Eddie purred, and Jeff had a sneaking suspicion he knew just where that ginger was destined.

"Pervert," he muttered.

"Takes one to know one."

"Text me your address," Jeff ordered before hanging up, hands shaking.

No, Eddie definitely didn't know what he was asking for. Even Jeff tried to avoid looking at his deepest, darkest desires. Who the fuck knew what was lurking in there? There was definitely stuff that scared him senseless. Mind you, the thought of kissing Eddie scared him senseless, so that didn't mean it would be anything too outrageous.

But what had he just agreed to?

Jeff detoured back round to the vegetables to pick up a piece of ginger, and by the time he'd reached the till, his dick had calmed down enough to no longer need camouflaging with the basket.

Chapter Fourteen

At four thirty, Eddie finally closed down his Mac and rubbed his eyes. He could have carried on working all evening, but after giving himself a near nervous breakdown a few years previously, he'd learnt to make sure he made time for himself. Being your own boss sometimes meant you were the one who had to order yourself to take a sanity break. He had to be strict with himself, but there was no one else to do it for him.

He glanced around the flat, idly wondering what Jeff would make of it. Compared to Jeff's place, it was cluttered and probably a bit over the top, what with the artwork on every wall and gadgets and whatnots all over the place. Be interesting to see how Jeff handled himself when he wasn't on his home turf. Edging him out of his comfort zone was an essential next step in his training.

None of that helped to explain why Eddie then set about the place like a one-man cleaning dervish, armed with a bin bag and a duster. Jeff wouldn't notice a bit of dirt. Hell, Eddie didn't notice a bit of dirt, but then again, he didn't want them rolling around on the floor and ending up with his bum stuck to an old plate of half-eaten food. There was comfortably lived-in and there was slobby, and Eddie's flat had tipped into the latter this last few months. He really should hire a new cleaner, but after the last one accidentally broke his plasma ball, he'd been wary of letting anyone else dust his stuff.

By five thirty, he'd got the flat looking reasonable again. His mother would no doubt find something to criticise, but it met Eddie's standards. The dirty dishes were all in the dishwasher and the stinkiest items out of the laundry basket were now whizzing around in the washing machine. He went through to the bedroom.

Should he change the sheets? But they'd only be getting filthy again in an hour or so, and couldn't face the idea of changing them again tomorrow. He brushed the worst of the biscuit crumbs out of the bed and straightened the covers instead. Then he rooted around in the drawer under his bed and pulled out everything they might be needing. One giant tub of Sex Wax, a heap of assorted condoms and a tangle of cuffs and rope. Would Jeff be bringing his kit too? Just in case he didn't, Eddie set out a row of toys on the top of the chest of drawers. Let Jeff choose if he wanted to use any of them. He paused over the giant black dildo—too scary?—but then left it out anyway. He liked it.

Then he got out the anal beads and buttplugs.

His arse clenched hungrily. What the hell. He might as well start the party now.

Eddie headed into the shower, buttplug in hand.

Forty minutes later, and the doorbell rang. Eddie sprang up from the sofa and ran to the view screen. Aww, there Jeff was, scratching his neck in that adorably tough-guy awkward way he had. From the angle of the camera it was hard to see just what Jeff was carrying, but there was something that looked promisingly gift-wrapped in his hands and a dark bag down by his feet.

Eddie pressed the intercom button. "Hey, tiger. I'm up on the top floor. See you in a minute."

Jeff squared his shoulders and looked for all the world like he was taking a few deep breaths to compose himself. Did he know he was being watched? Was he freaked out by the swankiness of Eddie's building? It was a converted riverfront warehouse, and the developers had spent a small fortune renovating the nineteenth-century building. Eddie spied on Jeff for a few moments longer, then went to his front door. He wanted to wait there, ready for when Jeff showed his face round the bend of the stairs.

He arranged himself in the doorway, leaning back against one side of the frame. He'd not dressed up, but he was in his favourite pair of soft old Levis and a skintight T-shirt that scooped low at the front. His feet were bare, and the buttplug was currently making an escape bid that his Lycra shorts really weren't helping stop.

"Fuck." Eddie wriggled and clenched his buttocks tight in an attempt to stop its downward trajectory. He should have gone with one of the light silicone ones, but he'd had to have his favourite glass one, hadn't he? It slipped a little farther.

"Bloody hell." Jeff's footsteps were sounding closer and closer, but Eddie couldn't exactly greet him with an escapee buttplug in his pants. What if it showed up as a lump when he turned round? Or worse yet, what if it fell out of his boxers and ended up dropping out of the bottom of his jeans? It would clunk on the floor, and Jeff would be bound to notice. The same thing had happened to him many years before at a club—luckily, that was just a cheap silicone plug, so he'd just kept walking and tried to pretend it never happened. Since that little episode, he'd taken to wearing a leather harness to keep the bloody things inside, but he hadn't wanted to put on something Jeff might find too freaky.

Because, of course, it was far less freaky to have a buttplug roll out of your jeans leg as you showed someone round your home.

Bugger.

He flipped his fly open and stuck his hand down the back of his jeans, feeling around for the base of the plug. "You little bastard." He grabbed it and went to push it back in again.

That was the moment Jeff rounded the corner. Jeff stopped on the step, his mouth open in an O of surprise.

"Hi," Eddie said, trying to play it cool. But it was no use. He'd been caught out, and the giggles were on their way. "Sorry, I just, erm, I'm having a bit of a moment."

"You don't say." Jeff resumed walking up the stairs, and the heat in his eyes was almost enough to overpower the urge to giggle. Almost, but not quite.

"Sorry," Eddie eventually managed to say through the giggles, at the same time as he got the plug pushed back in again. "Ooh, that's better." He wriggled his arse and winked. "Thought I'd surprise you by wearing a buttplug, but the stupid bloody thing didn't want to stay put."

"A buttplug, eh?"

Eddie scanned Jeff's expression for any signs of awkwardness, but all he saw there was curiosity and horniness. *Yeah, baby.* "You want to see it?" he offered.

"Later." Jeff slapped Eddie on the arse. "Now pull your trousers up and show me round, bitch."

Maybe there were benefits to acting like a complete klutz in front of the man you wanted to dominate your arse. If it made Jeff feel more in control, Eddie was all for it. He sorted his jeans out and led the way into his entrance hall. "Do you want to go straight to the bedroom?" He paused at that door, "Or would you like something to eat first? I think I might have skipped lunch." It was hard to remember to do mundane things like eat when he was working to a deadline.

"Are you hungry?" Jeff asked. The way he was standing there, feet planted wide and back straight, made Eddie want to drop to his knees and bury his face in his crotch. For once it looked like Jeff had made a bit of an effort with his appearance. He was wearing a black short-sleeved shirt, open at the neck to reveal the top of that gorgeous rug, and a pair of well-fitting indigo jeans. They might not give as much away as Jeff's shorts had, but he could still see a nicely outlined package down the left leg.

Eddie licked his lips. "I'm hungry, all right." He stepped forward and laid his arms on Jeff's shoulders. "Absolutely ravenous." His stomach decided to confirm that. "Oh bloody hell, I really am as well."

"Then we eat first," Jeff said. "Which way's the kitchen?"

"I was going to call for pizza." Eddie really didn't want to move from where they were, unless it was to get horizontal and splayed out.

"Need somewhere to put this, though." Jeff lifted something between them, and Eddie frowned at the blocky shape. Not gift-wrapped, after all, but it was in a nice paper carrier bag.

"For me? Thanks. Hey, not bad." It was a box set of Glastonbury Ales. "That beats a bottle of wine any day."

Jeff scratched his neck, giving Eddie a lovely view straight up his shirtsleeve. Hairy armpits. Was there anything sexier? But he had to get his mind out of the gutter, as Jeff was speaking. "I was going to get wine, but then I didn't know what you liked. And I figured you'd probably like this, since you had a pint of Golden Chalice at the Globetrotter that time."

"You noticed." Eddie couldn't stop grinning. "Don't know why Maddy thinks you don't have manners. I mean, you might come across as a bit of an opinionated bastard with no filter, but you know how to treat a man."

Jeff gave a resigned-sounding chuckle. "Yeah. Just don't know how to treat a woman, do I?"

"You should stick to blokes, then. We're much easier. In every way." Eddie thrust his hips forward, rubbing his crotch against Jeff's and pleased to feel an answering thickening down there. "I'd have put out even without the beers, but I'm happy you thought of me."

"Haven't been able to think of much else."

Eddie studied Jeff's face, trying to work out whether the gruffness of his words masked discomfort or horniness. Maybe a bit of both.

"I've been thinking about you too. In fact, I've been planning all sorts of things for today. So you know, much as I want to just drop to my knees and blow you, we probably should go and talk stuff through first. You've got to be careful when you're restraining someone." Eddie felt Jeff's cock plump up even further as he spoke, and he reached down to massage the solid length through Jeff's jeans.

"You could always blow me for a bit first," Jeff rasped.

"I suppose I could..." *Come on, make it an order.* While Eddie was perfectly capable of taking the initiative, it didn't get his motor humming the same way as if he was ordered to do something. Or better yet, made to do it by brute physical force. But maybe Jeff was being polite. He was a guest here, after all.

Fuck it. Eddie would just have to give him a hint. "Why don't you make me?" he whispered, his mouth a scant inch from Jeff's.

Jeff's breath tickled Eddie's lips, getting closer. Closer. Shit, was Jeff about to kiss him? Eddie held his breath, not wanting to spook him.

Teeth grazed his lower lip, then nipped.

Eddie moaned. Better than a kiss.

"Now get on your knees and blow me, bitch." Jeff backed up his words with a fist in Eddie's hair, and he gratefully lowered himself to the floor.

Eddie tore at Jeff's fly, desperate to get a taste again. Jeff's cock wasn't fully hard yet, but that was all the more fun—feeling it firm up inside his mouth. Eddie swallowed him whole. This was no time for teasing. Not with Jeff's hands on either side of his head, holding him still for a good face-fucking.

It was difficult to snatch a breath with the pace Jeff set, pushing fast and hard into Eddie's throat. Drool started to run down his chin, tears from his eyes, and he'd never been harder in his life. This was the good stuff. Made his head fizz and his heart race.

He was clinging on to Jeff's tree-trunk thighs for support, but the urge to touch himself was overwhelming. Couldn't ask for permission. Not with his mouth being used like this. Eddie groaned and gripped harder with his left hand, lowering his right to his aching cock. He settled for pressing and rubbing through the denim, too off balance to cope with something as complicated as a zip.

"Did I say you could touch yourself?" Jeff demanded.

Eddie forced his eyes open, looking up at Jeff's stern expression. Fuck it. He ground shamelessly against the heel of his hand, moaning his enjoyment around Jeff's cock.

"You dirty bitch. Just can't stop yourself, can you?" Admiration sneaked in under the veneer of toughness.

Eddie whimpered like a porn star, rutting hard against his hand.

"Stop that right now." Jeff pulled his cock clean out of Eddie's mouth, then a stinging pain exploded against his cheek. "Bad boy."

Eddie's vision swam as he stared up at Jeff.

Had he just been slapped in the face?

Chapter Fifteen

What had he just done?

Jeff glared at his hand, and at the pink mark on Eddie's face. Eddie's tear-streaked, puffy-lipped face. Oh God. Had he gone and got all out of control again? It had felt like the right thing to do at the time, but now Eddie was looking at him like that—all dazed—he was no longer sure of himself.

Jeff let go of Eddie's head and watched him fall back onto his heels. Should he apologise for taking things a step too far? But Eddie liked him acting the tough guy, didn't he? And Jeff was fairly sure tough guys didn't apologise when they slapped you in the face.

Jeff stood still, breathing heavily, waiting for Eddie to make his move. He'd follow his lead. Figure out how to play this.

Eddie got to his feet shakily, using Jeff's body like a climbing wall.

Sorry wanted to trip off Jeff's lips, but he held it back.

Eddie stopped when he was level with Jeff. Must have had his knees bent. Jeff appreciated that, because it was weird trying to assert yourself over someone taller. But it meant Eddie's eyes were right there, staring into his own. All golden coloured with that dark ring around the edges. The kind of eyes Jeff would have called beautiful if they'd been set in a girl's face. As it was, they were...fascinating.

And kind of scary, while he was waiting on judgement.

"Thank you," Eddie breathed. His eyelashes flickered down, and Jeff only had a split second to register what was happening before Eddie's lips crushed against his.

Fucking hell. Don't think. Don't think.

Eddie tasted of pure, naked sex, and Jeff kissed him back, chasing the flavour into his mouth. Eddie was every bit as enthusiastic, so Jeff grabbed a handful of his hair and dragged his head down, tight against his shoulder. There. Now who was in control? He nipped Eddie's plump lower lip before falling into his mouth again.

So fucking tasty.

He took his time conquering Eddie's mouth, exploring him thoroughly and coaxing out those sexy sounds he made in his throat. Like he couldn't help himself. Like Jeff was the best fucking kisser in the whole wide world. Who could kiss men every bit as well as he kissed women. Better, perhaps, judging by Eddie's reaction. The man was thrusting into Jeff's groin, and he had to use a hand to grip Eddie's arse and hold him there, or the friction would make everything end way too soon.

And he didn't ever want this to stop.

Eddie's jaw was smooth, like he'd only just shaved, except for a few spots that felt ever so slightly rough. But not in a bad way. What would it be like to feel scruff like that all over his jaw? Jeff's hard-on ached with want. It was so fucking tempting to slam Eddie back against the wall and rut against him till they both came. But they had other plans.

And Jeff could kiss him again later, couldn't he? He pulled back, still pinning Eddie's head to his shoulder.

Eddie gave him a dopey smile. "Mmm, thank you even more. Didn't think I was ever going to get one of those."

Jeff cleared his throat but couldn't think of a thing to say. *You won't get another* would be bullshit. That had been way too good not to repeat. But he didn't want to promise to do something so very un-straight again. So he stood there, holding Eddie tight to him and trying not to dwell on the fact he was holding a man tight to his naked dick and had every intention of ploughing his arse before the night was through.

He squeezed Eddie's arse instead of replying. Squeezed it harder than he needed to, perhaps, but Eddie gave a happy-sounding sigh and cuddled into him.

They stood there, swaying slightly, arms wrapped around each other, and Jeff told his mind to go fuck off. It'd been too long since he'd had a cuddle with someone he fancied the pants off. And he wasn't about to think about what that might mean either.

In the end, it was Eddie who broke the silence, with a warm, husky voice. "I suppose I should probably go and order that pizza." He didn't make a move, though.

Jeff's breathing was more or less under control now, and reluctantly he loosened his grip on Eddie. It was hard to do, like he was losing something precious, but he could have it back again later, couldn't he? Eddie wasn't going to act all weird and prickly like Sarah had done whenever Jeff tried to snuggle up to her over the last few years.

He'd been seeing Eddie for almost a month now, and no sign of prickly tendencies at all. If Eddie had been a girl, he'd have been bloody perfect. Jeff would have taken him home to meet the folks already. Shit, he'd probably have bloody well got a ring on her finger and all.

But Eddie was a man, so none of that was going to happen. And that was a fucking shame. It really was.

Eddie gave him a lopsided smile as he stepped back and ran his fingers through his hair. "So, what toppings are you after? No, let me guess. Meat, meat and more meat. Am I right?"

"Ham and pineapple's good."

"Really?" Eddie broke into a wide beam. "Hawaiian's my favourite. You like sweetcorn on that too?"

"Yeah, sweetcorn's good." Most toppings were good, really. "And garlic bread. And do they do those dough balls and the garlicky sauce you can dip them in?"

Eddie squinted at him. "Good thing I like garlic too, or you wouldn't be getting another kiss. And I reckon we'd both be upset about that."

To his horror, Jeff felt his cheeks start to heat. "Erm." He picked up the box of beer and his kit bag. "Which way's the kitchen?" He could use a beer or two right now.

"Down the hall, like I said earlier." Eddie grinned as he pointed his finger. "That open door you can see the fridge and stuff through. Want any help with your fly? Your hands are kind of full." And without waiting for Jeff's answer, Eddie took charge, tucking Jeff's cock back inside his jeans. Jeff groaned as Eddie gave him a squeeze before letting go to do up the zip, button and belt.

Eddie paused at the belt. "You know, I'd love to feel this doubled over on my arse. Been ages since I've had a good strapping."

"Doesn't that hurt?" Stupid fucking question. Jeff wanted to take the words back as soon as they were out of his mouth.

"Oh yes," Eddie said happily. "Stings like a bastard. And I bet you could put some real welly behind it. Just don't use the buckle end. Bruising's great, but I'm not keen on you drawing blood. Knew this guy once, he got an infected wound on his arse. Bloody disgusting it was. He couldn't sit down for weeks. Had to have antibiotics for blood poisoning. You should have seen the pus that came out of it. I've never seen anything so—"

"Could we not talk about this, please?"

Eddie peered at him. "God, you've gone green around the gills. You're squeamish? Really?"

"Not squeamish, just..." Jeff couldn't come up with a more macho-sounding word. "Yeah, all right. I'm bloody well squeamish. Just about infections and stuff like that, though."

"So you wouldn't get upset if I told you about the Top who forced his massive cock so far down my throat I actually threw up all over his leather jeans?"

Jeff's stomach heaved a protest. "Shut up."

"Just testing." Eddie winked at him and looked way too smug for someone who'd just been on his knees, sucking Jeff's cock. "Come on, this way." Eddie led him into the kitchen and dug through a drawer to find a bottle opener. Jeff glanced at the sleek bits of stainless steel equipment on the granite work surfaces and the big old enamelled sink, but he was too preoccupied with what Eddie had just told him to spend too much time comparing the swanky kitchen to his own bargain-basement version.

"Does that really happen?" Jeff asked as Eddie poured their beer into two tall pilsner glasses.

"Huh? Does what happen?" Eddie handed him a beer.

"You know. Uh, when you deep throat."

"Oh. Well, no, hardly ever these days. I had more of a hair trigger gag reflex when I was younger, but now I know how to relax my throat properly. Used to be I couldn't eat or drink for a few hours before a scene just in case." He leaned back against the work surface, all long, lean limbs and shining blond hair. "It was a bit like being in hospital. You know, before an operation. Nil by mouth in case you vomit while under anaesthetic."

"So you're okay having pizza now?"

"Don't worry, tiger. If any of us are going to spray bodily fluids over each other, it's going to be you doing it to me. While I'm tied up and can't do anything to stop you."

"Oh. Good." Jeff thought about it some more. "Call the pizza place now. I want to get going as soon as we can."

"You're a man after my own heart." Eddie clinked his glass with Jeff's and pulled out his phone.

Forty minutes later, they sat there on Eddie's sofa with a mostly empty pizza box on the coffee table in front of them. Jeff had now had the grand tour of Eddie's flat, which was smallish but packed full of stuff—most of which appeared to either need batteries or plugging in. The man's electricity bills must have been phenomenal. But he had to agree that the home planetarium looked pretty cool—or at least would have done if there hadn't been so much light leaking around the edges of Eddie's living room curtains. The only room he hadn't seen was the bedroom, and he was itching to get there. But first the food needed to be finished. Jeff picked up the last piece and stuffed it into his mouth.

Eddie stretched out like a cat and put his feet in Jeff's lap. "So, we need to talk about boundaries for bondage play."

"We do?"

"Yep. Absolutely. Think about it. I'm putting a huge amount of trust in you. I'll be helpless and at your mercy. You could gag me, and I wouldn't be able to do anything about it. And for all I know you could be some kind of serial-killing psychopath."

"I'm not."

"Yeah, I know that, but the point is, anyone could be. My gut tells me you're fine, but I'm still taking a huge amount on trust."

The very idea of Eddie putting himself in such a vulnerable position made Jeff's cock sit up and take notice.

"So I have boundaries. No gags for today. I need to be able to speak my safeword if necessary."

"I don't want to gag you anyway." Jeff liked the sounds Eddie made way too much.

"You sure? It's a real turn-on. Especially if someone does it with my sweaty underpants. Or better yet, yours. And you get to hear me making all these sexy muffled sounds, and you know I'm completely at your mercy."

"Fuck." Jeff closed his eyes as lust rampaged through his body.

"I will let you put your hand over my mouth, though. Not my nose too. You have to earn the trust to be able to do that."

"You'd really trust me?"

"Yeah, eventually. I hope."

Jeff pondered trust some more while gently stroking Eddie's bare feet. "So when I slapped your face earlier, that didn't upset you?"

Eddie's chuckle made him look up, annoyed. "Tiger, have you been worrying about that? Couldn't you tell I was happy afterwards?"

Jeff thought back to the kiss and scratched his neck.

"Nah, but you're right." Eddie stretched out his legs, and his T-shirt rode up, revealing a tantalising strip of skin. "It was a bit of a shock. A good shock to me, but you'd want to think carefully before doing that to someone you didn't know well. You're lucky I have a huge humiliation kink, but some people might object. Women, especially. Same goes for spitting."

"You'd like it if I spat on your face?" Jeff addressed Eddie's toes. Looking at him would reveal far too much about how much that turned Jeff on. And what kind of sick fucker got a kick out of that?

"I wouldn't want it all the time, but sometimes that can be just what I need to push me over. It makes me feel...dizzy. Like I can't believe I'm letting you do it to me. It's a real rush, even more than pain is sometimes. And what's even more amazing is knowing you're not doing it because you despise me, but because you really want to give me what I want."

"Pervert." Jeff smiled at Eddie's toes, feeling strangely reassured. "Okay, then. I might spit on you. I might not. And I might sometimes slap your face. But I'm definitely going to hurt you. And I'm going to fuck you."

"Ooh, I can't wait." Eddie's toes curled, and Jeff grabbed hold of them, feeling their strength. "So, what sort of bondage do you want to try? I have cuffs and a few bits and pieces you can use for joining them in various ways. A spreader bar too. Or if it's rope bondage you're after, I do have rope. Can take a while, though. Learning all the knots." Eddie flexed his toes, and Jeff finally dared to look up and meet the heat in his eyes. "I'm not sure I can wait that long for you to fuck me."

"You'll wait as long as it takes." Jeff didn't think he could wait that long either, but he wasn't about to admit it. And besides, cuffs sounded good. You had to start somewhere, didn't you? "Your bedroom. Now."

Eddie responded to the curt command by jumping up. "Want me to strip first, Sir?"

"I'll tell you when I want you to do that." But fuck, he did want to watch Eddie's naked arse on the way there. "Yeah. Strip now, bitch."

Jeff watched hungrily as Eddie bared his flesh. There was so much of it, all lean and pale, but with a golden undertone that seemed to promise he'd tan well if he ever got out in the sun. "You should sunbathe," Jeff said. "Naked."

"It's bad for you."

"So are all the fun things."

Eddie stepped out of his jeans, his cock already at half mast, Jeff was pleased to see. "I don't have anywhere to sunbathe naked. My neighbours would call the police if I tried to do it on my balcony. Plus I'd give everyone walking along the river path a free show."

"You can come and do it in my garden. Next weekend. The forecast's good."

"Yeah? Okay, then." Eddie slowly pushed down his briefs, drawing it out. Shouldn't have been sexy on a bloke, but Jeff was having to rethink some of his old assumptions. Like Eddie's cock and balls. The very thought of touching them made him hot and cold all over, but in a good way. In a way that made blood rush to his dick. He'd do it today. Not taste them or anything like that, mind—although now he'd already kissed Eddie, did it make any difference?

"Hey, you're thinking too hard. Just go with the flow." Eddie held out a hand as if to help Jeff up.

Jeff ignored the proffered hand and got to his feet. "I thought I was meant to be the one thinking and in control. Responsible and all that."

"Responsibility's one thing. Fretting's another."

"I wasn't fretting."

Eddie gave him one of those "I don't believe a word of it" looks Sarah had always done so well. Fuck that. "Get in the bedroom," Jeff snarled. "Facedown on the bed. Arms and legs spread."

"Yessir!" Eddie grinned like a loon and bounded out of the room. Jeff shook his head, unable to stop the smile that wanted out on his lips. The man was a nutcase. But he was Jeff's kind of nutcase.

Chapter Sixteen

Jeff walked through to the bedroom slowly, trying to brace himself for what he'd find. But no amount of mental preparation could lessen the impact of Eddie's naked body stretched out, all long limbs and golden skin. His arse pointed up in the air like it was inviting Jeff's cock to come and play.

Jeff groaned and shut his eyes, dizzy with the way the blood was all rushing out of his brain and into his dick. Right. He had to do better than this. Eddie needed him to keep his wits about him. And first there were cuffs and buckles and shit that would need his attention. Okay.

When Jeff opened his eyes, the vision was still as mind-bendingly hot as before, but this time, he forced his gaze to wander. Eddie's bedroom wasn't as cluttered as the rest of his flat, but that just made the tangle of black leather and rope all that more attention-grabbing. Jeff took a step over to the bed and lifted up one of the cuffs. Was it for Eddie's ankle or his wrist? Which would be bigger? He laid the four cuffs out in a row, and while there were definitely two longer and two shorter, he still couldn't think which would go where. Why couldn't they mark the stupid things with an A or a W?

He peered at Eddie's ankles and wrists, then grabbed hold of one of each to measure them with his thumb and forefinger.

"Mmph." Eddie's happy sound was muffled in the duvet, but then he turned his head to look at Jeff. "Want a hand with the cuffs?"

"Nah. I'm good." His rudimentary measuring had told him that Eddie's ankles were definitely a good inch wider than his wrists, which you wouldn't know to look at them. He had surprisingly slender ankles for a man. But not weak looking. Too much muscle and ropey tendon going on in his calf to ever mistake him for a weakling. Jeff bent Eddie's knees so his feet were sticking up in the air and waving around at a convenient height, then slowly buckled both cuffs.

The wrists were next. He did the one nearest to him, but rather than walk around the bed, he grabbed Eddie's other arm and pulled it behind his back, in the same way a police officer might restrain someone resisting arrest. Eddie moaned, and his hips bucked like he was humping the bed.

"You like that, bitch?"

"Yeah. Feels good."

Jeff buckled on the last strap and stood back to take a look. Somehow, the black leather made Eddie look stronger. Sexier. It was like he had a lion in a cage. Barely restrained, and it made it all the sweeter that Eddie was letting him do this. Jeff slapped Eddie's arse, just because he could.

"Spread your arms and legs. Wider. As wide as you can go. Good boy."

Eddie squirmed as he got himself spread-eagled, and it gave Jeff an excellent view of his backside. He hadn't wanted to see Eddie's cheeks spread wide before, and now he was wondering why. It was kind of appealing, especially with the base of that plug winking at him. It looked like one of the marbles Jeff had played with as a kid, all swirling reds and greens in the glass.

"Is this whole thing made of glass?" Jeff tapped the end, and Eddie whimpered.

"Yep. Cost a bloody fortune. Some bloke in Bath makes them to order."

"It's beautiful." He tapped it again, then pushed it in as far as he could. Eddie's reaction was gorgeous. That way he made those noises in his throat, like he couldn't help himself, and the way he writhed on the covers. "That feels good, does it?"

"Fuck me. Yes. Amazing."

"Can't really imagine how having something up your backside could feel good." Jeff grasped the plug and pulled on it, then plunged it back in again.

Eddie gasped and shuddered. “You should try it yourself.”

“Nah. It’s not for me.” But maybe he would. Eddie’s reactions had him intrigued. Maybe there were new erogenous zones Jeff could explore on his own body. He wouldn’t let anyone else see him do it, though. Purely self-exploration. In the interests of scientific research.

Yeah, right. He didn’t even believe himself anymore.

Jeff plunged the plug in and out a few more times, then remembered what he was really here for. The cuffs.

Along with the rope, there were a few other bits and pieces of leather kit. One was a cross with a trigger clip on each end. Okay, he could see how that would work. Maybe he should try it first.

He got up on his knees and grabbed Eddie’s hands, bringing them down behind his back. “First I’m going to hog-tie you. You’d like that, wouldn’t you, you dirty bitch?”

“Oh God, yes.”

The clips operated smoothly, and within a few moments, Jeff had Eddie trussed up with both his arms and legs linked together behind his back. It looked good, having him so helpless like that, but what exactly was he supposed to do now? He couldn’t really whack Eddie’s arse, because his shins were now in the way. He wouldn’t be able to fuck him like that either. Not enough room to get between his legs.

He stood, pondering the human puzzle, until Eddie craned his head around. “You could always fuck my mouth, you know. Seeing as how you’ve got me all helpless like this.”

“What do Doms normally do when they’ve got you like this?”

“Generally they fuck my mouth or torture my arse. Or they get me up on my knees and then they can torture my cock and balls too.”

“Ah.” That was a lot more variety than Jeff had been able to come up with. Clearly he did still have a lot to learn.

Figuring out how to get his cock into Eddie’s mouth would be a good start. He’d probably break the poor bloke’s back if he tried to lift his head up off the mattress too far. But if he moved him a little...

Jeff grabbed hold of Eddie under the arms and pulled him round so his head was positioned at the edge of the mattress. Eddie craned his neck up and winked. Cheeky bastard. Jeff was going to fuck his face so long and hard, Eddie wouldn't have the presence of mind to wink. And even if he did, he wouldn't have the energy to actually manage it. Yeah, that was a good ambition to have.

Jeff got his cock out in record time, then grabbed hold of Eddie's hair and fed him the whole length in one go. "That's it. Eat it, bitch." Eddie made hungry noises as he sucked and rippled his tongue, and Jeff ground in hard against his lips. Oh yeah. That was a good angle. He could go deep from here. Jeff flexed his hips, revelling in the heat and wetness of Eddie's mouth. It was tempting just to stay deep, giving shallow thrusts, but of course Eddie couldn't breathe like that. And while it was a buzz to hear him gasp for air whenever Jeff pulled out, he didn't want to suffocate him for too long.

It suddenly hit Jeff just how vulnerable Eddie was like this. That he was literally putting his life in Jeff's hands. How incredibly humbling that Eddie would do that for him. It slowed him down. Made him gentler as he gave long strokes in and out, cradling Eddie's jaw with one hand while he pulled his head back by the hair with the other. There. Nothing soft about that. It wasn't like he was just stroking Eddie's jaw. He was fucking his mouth too.

Jeff kept on fucking in and out, until he could feel Eddie's drool dripping down onto his balls. Balls that were drawing up tight. He had to save himself if he wanted a chance to fuck Eddie's other hole. The one currently plugged up with glass.

Jeff's cock throbbed, and he pulled himself out with a groan. Eddie was panting hard, his eyes closed and his lips all puffy and red. His mouth worked like he was trying to suck Jeff's cock back in again.

Shit. He really wanted to kiss Eddie right now.

Jeff dropped to his knees and gave in to temptation.

This time it felt more familiar. Like Jeff's tongue had finally found the place it most wanted to be, and had every intention of setting up home. Eddie's kiss wasn't as forceful as it had been earlier, but his slack-jawed submission was even more of a turn-on right now. Jeff kissed him thoroughly until they were both panting, then drew back. "I'm going to release you now, but I want you to stay flat on the bed. Like that."

"Not going to be a problem," Eddie slurred. "Not sure I can move right now."

"Shit, have I given you a dead leg or something?" Jeff crawled up behind Eddie to release the trigger clips, massaging Eddie's feet and hands after he'd done so. They felt a little cool, but nothing too unusual.

"Nah, just feeling floaty."

"Ah." So it was a good thing after all. Jeff let Eddie's legs crash down onto the bed, but released his arms more gently, lacing his fingers between Eddie's. He lowered himself to lie on Eddie's back. Eddie grunted but didn't complain, and when Jeff started kissing his neck, he made one of those gorgeous husky moaning sounds again. Jeff took a deep breath, smelling something warm and spicy with a hint of coconut from Eddie's hair. He didn't know if the spice was Eddie's shower gel or if it was just the scent of his skin, but it reminded him of warm earth after a rainfall.

Jeff's dick attempted to burrow between Eddie's arse-cheeks, and he reluctantly accepted that if he was going to do anything else along those lines, he'd better get suited up. And he'd better tie Eddie down too, because that was what this was all about, wasn't it?

Jeff examined the nearest bedpost. Eddie had a modern-looking, low, wooden-slatted headboard and footboard, but there weren't any handy chains already anchored to them like he'd hoped for. "How do you normally get tied to your bedposts?" Jeff asked.

"I don't. But I reckon you could do it with rope."

"You've never been tied to a bed before?"

"Yeah. Just not this one. Not had a man back here before."

Jeff digested that piece of information. It could be that Eddie had only recently moved in, of course, but it didn't look that way. This place certainly seemed well lived-in. "How long have you lived here?" he asked. It was kind of surreal, making casual chitchat while working on winding ropes around the headboard.

"Dunno." Eddie's words came out all muffled by the duvet. "Three years, maybe."

"Huh. You must like it here, then."

"And you don't?" Eddie's words were no longer muffled, but when he looked round expecting a touchy expression, all Jeff found was a glint in his eye and a challenging smile.

"I'd want a garden," was all he said.

"Yeah, well, I've got a river view, and you can't always have everything you want." Now Eddie sounded kind of morose, but Jeff was fucked if he was about to get dragged into a serious conversation right now. They could shoot the breeze about stuff next week, when Eddie came round to sunbathe. Amongst other things.

"You can have everything you want," he said, pushing Eddie down and encouraging him to spread his arms and legs wide, before grabbing one of his wrists to loop the rope through the D ring on the cuff. "So long as everything you want is my cock in your arse."

"Sounds good. Could you move the pillows, though? Gets kind of hot with my face buried in one of them."

Jeff pulled both pillows off the bed and chucked them on the floor. He'd never have thought of that by himself. Good thing he did have a sub who wasn't afraid to tell him what he needed. Even if he did get a bit too cheeky for his own good sometimes.

That thought led to a slap on Eddie's buttocks as Jeff moved down to deal with the ankle rope. Once he had Eddie all tied down and splayed out, he stepped back to admire his handiwork. Oh yeah. He was dying to screw that pert little bum.

But first... Jeff lifted up the black leather paddle Eddie had laid out for him. He'd never tried one like this. And there was the cane too. He picked it up and swished it through the air, surprised at the whizzing noise it made. Oh yeah. Time to get to work on that arse. He wanted it glowing by the time he sank his dick in there.

He started with the paddle, and Eddie pushed himself up into the strokes as much as he was able. The sounds he was making! "You're such a little painslut, aren't you? You love it. You're twisted, coz pain makes you all wet." Hold on. It was girls who got wet. But then again, maybe that worked. Eddie was probably dripping pre-come. Jeff certainly was.

He reached between Eddie's legs to check. Fuck, his dick was hot and damp and clammy. It felt debauched, holding that hot, damp, musky flesh. And kind of a turn-on too, as Eddie was whimpering like crazy and saying *please* a lot, although he didn't seem to be able to form any other words.

"Please what? What is it you want me to do, bitch?"

"Anything!"

Jeff gave a squeeze and a tug, which really wasn't so odd, as he'd tugged his own dick plenty of times. But this was Eddie's, and that turned him on even more than if he'd been fondling his own meat.

"I think..." Jeff said, getting into the rhythm of tossing Eddie off. "I think I'll cane you, then I'm going to fuck you. And you're not allowed to come until I say so."

"Fucking bastard! Gonna come right now if you keep doing that."

Jeff laughed and squeezed Eddie's dick, feeling his sub writhe underneath him as much as he could while tied down. "I think you'll find that's Sir Bastard to you."

"Please, Sir Bastard, will you bloody well stop that and cane my arse?"

"And then fuck you?"

"Yes! Yes please. Fuck me good and hard and rough."

"That's my dirty little bitch." Jeff stroked Eddie's arse with one hand as he gave a final tug to his dick with the other. Then he grabbed the cane.

It whizzed through the air like it was splitting it apart, and hit Eddie with a cracking sound. Eddie howled, and the white stripe quickly turned pink. Jeff did it again and again, surprised to see it was the far end of the cane that left the biggest marks. If he wanted to leave Eddie with stripes on both sides, he'd have to move around to the other side of the bed.

Jeff clambered over Eddie to get there, but on the way, the tip of his dick dragged over the hot skin of Eddie's arse. Oh fuck, that was good. He halted on his hands and knees over Eddie, dragging his dick up and down, left and right. Eddie was going fucking mental, making strange animal noises and jerking around like Jeff was fucking him hard already. Bloody hell, he was a real live wire. Jeff was going to get the ride of his life.

Hold on. Was this even going to work with Eddie's ankles tied? Would Jeff be able to get enough leverage to fuck him if he was pinned right down? He wouldn't be able to get him up on his knees, would he? And if he couldn't get him up on his knees, he wouldn't be able to look at all those glorious marks he'd left all over his arse.

And he really, really wanted to be able to see them while he fucked Eddie. But then again, if he did it like this, he'd be able to kiss and bite Eddie's neck, right where the skin smelled amazing. Mind you, even if he untied Eddie's legs, he'd still be able to lie on him like this. Yeah. Okay, then. He really should move and suit up.

But it felt so good right there.

Jeff forced himself up, undid the ankle ropes and spread Eddie's legs even farther apart. That ended up pushing Eddie halfway up onto his knees. Jeff had a great view of Eddie's erection, which looked bigger than he'd ever seen it before. Funny, but it was kind of nice having that visual to go by, so he knew Eddie was really turned on and not faking it. He'd had his doubts about Sarah's state of arousal at times.

Jeff slapped Eddie right between the arse cheeks, so he caught the plug too. Eddie made a broken sound, and his legs shook. "Stay like that, bitch." Jeff quickly stripped off his clothes. Eddie had left him a pile of condoms on the dresser, and he grabbed one at random. It smelled kind of minty when he opened it, but what the hell. Felt cool on his dick, and he probably needed that if he was about to bury it in Eddie's hot little arse.

Jeff had a moment of nerves when he was back, kneeling between Eddie's legs. He'd never actually taken Sarah up the wrong 'un—not for want of suggesting it, but she'd always refused. Was it going to demand some kind of special skills and attention? And hang on, you could write what Jeff knew about anal sex on the palm of one hand with a big fat marker pen, but the one word that fit there would be LUBE. "Erm, don't we need some lube or something?" Jeff asked.

"Huh? Oh, maybe. Yeah, I s'pose you'd better."

"You do it without sometimes?"

"Sometimes. With just spit. There's lube in the tub."

Jeff tore himself away to locate the tub. Sex Wax? Talk about unsubtle packaging. He dug his fingers into the goop and sniffed. Okay, not so bad. Now, did he just slather it on himself or would Eddie need some too? It seemed so lame for a Dom to ask.

In the end, he planted himself back between Eddie's outstretched legs and tugged on the plug a few times. It got wider up the shaft, stretching Eddie's arsehole around it as he moved the plug in and out. "I'm going to fuck you hard, and you're going to love it, aren't you?"

Eddie nodded frantically.

"Tell me what you want me to do."

"Fuckmefuckmefuckme."

"In detail. Step by step." There, that was getting around his little problem.

"I want you to pull the plug out and shove your big fat dick into me. Please. Sir."

Simple. Jeff slapped the side of Eddie's thigh. "Okay, then. You asked for it." He tugged harder on the plug, and the wide part popped out completely. Eddie made a guttural sound, and before he could think too much about what he was doing, Jeff slammed his dick home.

Oh.

Oh.

Oh!

So hot. So tight. Jeff pushed in as deep as he could go, feeling the resistance inside Eddie. But then it gave, and everything was rippling, pulsing heat. Like Eddie's insides were throwing a party in honour of his arrival. "So fucking good," Jeff growled, barely recognising his own voice. Eddie was spouting manic gibberish right into the mattress, but he seemed to be agreeing. He'd grabbed on to the ropes tying him to the bed frame, and all the muscles in his arms and back stood out. Eddie started to rise up onto his elbows, but Jeff pushed him down with a hand to his neck.

"Stay there, bitch. I'm going to fuck you good and hard."

"Yesyesyesyespleaseohfuckohfuckohfuck!"

Jeff slapped Eddie's glowing-red arse and the words descended into a grunty mess. "Noisy bugger aren't you? You always squeal like this when you're getting your arse reamed?"

"Nonono. Just you. Just with you. Please, Sir. Please."

"Please what?" Jeff paused with his dick deep inside Eddie and circled his hips. So fucking hot. Oh yes.

"Harder. Faster. *Please!*"

"And what if I want to go slow, bitch?" Jeff drew out as slowly as he could. All the way, so the tip of his dick was just kissing Eddie's rapidly closing hole. And then he surged back in again. The noise Eddie made in response was just beautiful. Kind of a gurgle mixed with a groan. Jeff did it again just to hear that noise. And again. And again, until sweat was dripping from him down onto Eddie's back.

Eddie was so carried away, it was kind of awe-inspiring. There's no way Jeff would ever dare lose it like that in front of anyone else, but Eddie didn't seem to have any inhibitions. He thrashed and sobbed and pleaded, and made noises that were so fucking sexy, they should have been illegal.

Now he thought about it, Eddie was a hell of a lot braver than Jeff was.

It was an unsettling thought, so Jeff did his best to fuck it out of his mind. He picked up his pace, driving into Eddie so hard he knocked him flat on the bed. Jeff lay on top of his prone sub and gave in to the temptation to bite that spot where his neck met his shoulder.

Eddie howled and writhed. "Please. Gotta come. Please, Sir!" His body tensed under Jeff's, like he was fighting to hold back the orgasm with every muscle he owned. From the slice of Eddie's face Jeff could see, it looked like he had his eyes squeezed shut and was grimacing.

Next time they'd have to do this face-to-face, so Jeff could watch every last expression. And so he could kiss him. Would Eddie's kisses now be as frantic as his body language?

He drew out Eddie's discomfort a little longer, making shallow, jabbing thrusts, which seemed to punch all the air out of Eddie's lungs, if his grunts were anything to go by. But before long, Jeff's own orgasm built up in his balls.

"Do it," he panted. "Come now. Like this."

He pushed in as deep as he could and stayed there, circling his hips slowly.

Eddie gave a pained gasp, arched his back, and his entire body stiffened. He clamped down on Jeff's cock like he was never going to let him go, and then his insides spasmed like crazy. The delicious pressure pulled Jeff's orgasm out of his balls, and he sank his teeth back into Eddie's neck.

When Eddie's shuddering had milked every last bit of spunk from Jeff's balls, he collapsed all his weight onto Eddie and lay there, waiting to catch his breath. Eddie heaved underneath him, obviously suffering from the same problem.

Jeff pressed an openmouthed kiss to the back of his neck, wishing he were taller so he could reach Eddie's mouth.

"Too heavy," Eddie mumbled into the pillow. "Roll off."

"Sorry." Jeff grasped the condom before pulling out, then chucked it onto the floor. It was a crying shame to have to leave that hot little arse, but he'd get to do this again. As soon as he could, hopefully.

"Cuffs?" Eddie reminded him, his voice hoarse. No doubt that was from all the noise he'd been making. Shit, Jeff hoped Eddie's neighbours were hard of hearing.

He couldn't work out how to untie the knots he'd made quickly, and so he settled for just unbuckling the cuffs. Eddie sighed and his arms flopped down, like he didn't have the energy to move them anywhere more comfortable.

Jeff lay down to one side of Eddie and put an arm around him, and Eddie responded by rolling over so they were facing each other. Eddie looked well and truly fucked, and he gave a sleepy smile before burrowing his head into the crook of Jeff's neck.

"Mmm, that was amazing. Knew you'd be a great top."

Jeff grunted in response. It was just dawning on him that he'd just screwed a man, and that he didn't feel weird about it. Well, maybe a little bit weird, but more puzzled than disgusted. He didn't know how to share any of that with the man in his arms, though.

"Meant to come all over your arse," he eventually said, because that seemed like a safe topic of conversation.

"Mm, and I meant to ask you to bring that ginger and stick it up my arse first, but there's always next time."

"Next time?" Ginger up the arse?

"Next time." Eddie yawned and snuggled in closer. Jeff gave in to the urge to stroke his back, and Eddie made a happy sound like a cat.

"Tomorrow?" Jeff suggested.

"Huh?"

"I could come round tomorrow. Fuck you after work. With ginger, if that's really what you want."

"Mmm, you're keen. That means either you're really desperate and making up for lost time, or I'm the most fantastic shag ever."

Jeff snorted. "Stop fishing for compliments." But when Eddie didn't say anything else for a while, he added "You were great." It didn't go anywhere towards explaining how incredible the whole experience had been, but it seemed to satisfy Eddie, who made one of his happy cat noises again and started combing his fingers through Jeff's chest hair.

"Wish I could do tomorrow, but I've got a busy week ahead. Might be best to save it for the weekend. When I come round to yours for naked sunbathing."

"Yeah. All right." Jeff pretended an acceptance he didn't really feel. A week felt like an awfully long time to have to wait to see Eddie again.

They lay there for some time, Jeff wanting to kiss Eddie again but not really knowing how to ask. Maybe Eddie only kissed as foreplay. Was kissing the kind of thing gay blokes did just as an end in itself? He could have just grabbed Eddie's head and forced himself on him again, but the energy had changed. Now it felt more like they were equals than Dom and sub, and he didn't want to screw with that balance.

He'd just have to wait. He'd stuck things out with Sarah for thirteen years, so he must be patient enough to manage without Eddie for a few days.

Chapter Seventeen

"So, how's your Dom training going?" Maddy asked, planting her feet on Eddie's coffee table. "Got him fully converted to cock yet?"

"Not exactly, but I think we're getting there." Eddie lounged back in the armchair and remembered the feel of Jeff's hand wrapped around him, calluses rubbing just right. It had only been a few days ago, but already he was craving Jeff's touch. And not just on his cock.

"Ooh, you're doing one of those smiles. Come on, what are you remembering? Did he give you a blowjob?"

If only! "Excuse me, but I don't ask you for the gory details of your sex life."

"You don't have to, because you know I'll quite happily give them to you anyway." Maddy pouted. "Not that there're any to give right now. I'm getting bloody sick of vanilla sex. How do people put up with it all the time?"

"Vanilla? You? Why?"

Maddy folded her hands over her still very flat stomach. "Niall doesn't want to risk doing anything to harm the baby. And apparently that includes hurting me. I mean, I can understand why suspension, fisting and breath play are out of the picture for a while, but he's taking things way too far."

"Maybe he's worried you'll get too, I don't know, excited?"

"I could do with a bit of excitement. Honestly, he won't let me wear my corsets or even have a glass of wine with dinner. Is a light spanking over the bench too much to ask for? He's treating me like I'm made out of china or something."

"At least he cares."

"Oh yeah." Maddy got a smile that bordered on soppy. "He's being ridiculously overattentive. And he's treating me to a spa break in the Cayman Islands next month. Apparently the best way to spend my pregnancy is flat on my back having my nails manicured. Even wants me to give up work."

"And will you?"

Maddy snorted. "Not bloody likely. I'd go doolally if I couldn't work. And besides, you can't take time out in the fashion industry. Got to keep up with every last trend, or you're hopelessly out of date."

"Sounds a bit like graphic design." Eddie frowned at the latest set of designs he'd sketched out for a client, pinned up over his workstation. Were the faux-retro stylings too passé now? But it was what they'd said they were after, so he'd gone for a vintage take on their current logo. "Knowing when a trend has passed is a tough call sometimes."

"Darling, if you're even asking yourself that question, it's over."

"For the fashionistas, maybe, but for the rest of us mortals, trends stick around for a bit longer."

"As evidenced by the fact you're still dressing exactly as you did at college. You do know the rave scene is well and truly over, don't you?" It would have sounded bitchy from anyone else, but since Maddy was like this with everyone, it didn't really mean anything.

"I like this look. It's me."

"You look like the least gay gay man ever. Honestly, you could at least do me the favour of being obsessed with clothes so I could take you shopping. Worst GBF ever."

Eddie grinned and planted his naked feet next to hers. "What if I tell you all about my relationship issues. Will that earn me gay points?"

"It might do. They'd better be juicy ones, though. With plenty of emotional drama. Extra points if you get all weepy."

"I don't know if I'd go that far, but they're kind of juicy." Although using that word just reminded him of Jeff's copious love juices and what it felt like to be covered in them. That probably wasn't the kind of juicy Maddy was after. "I don't know. What does it mean when a man fucks you and then asks to see you the next day? Is that just a sex thing, or does it mean more?"

Maddy leaned forward. "So he has fucked you at last. About bloody time."

"Hey, I'm not surprised it's taken a while. He does still think he's straight. Or at least, I think he does. I don't know. That's what I'm trying to figure out."

"You could try asking him. That's what I do when I want to find out what someone thinks."

"Yes, thank you, Ms. Stating-the-Bloody-Obvious. It's not that simple, though, is it? Not with Jeff. He gets this terrified look whenever I mention anything too gay in conversation. I really don't want to push him and scare him off. Coming out is a really big step."

"Not for you it wasn't."

"Hey, I had my share of angsting over my sexuality."

"Yeah, but not about being gay. You said it was easy for you. Family support, being in some unconventional private school where no one batted an eyelid. You certainly didn't seem to have any issues with liking cock when we were at uni, anyway."

"No, true." And there had been plenty of available cock to like. Happy memories...for the most part. "But I did have issues with liking pain and humiliation. Took me a while to be okay with that one. And think about it, it must be worse for the sadists. I mean, if it's frowned upon for people to enjoy pain, think how much worse it looks if you enjoy dishing it out."

Maddy harrumphed. "Bullshit. We live in a society surrounded by media glorifying violence towards women. Did you know in the States, they rate films showing women experiencing sexual pleasure as adults-only, whereas scenes of violence towards them only merit an R?"

"What's an R when it's at home?"

"Means teenagers can go with their parents, I think."

"Really?" For once, Maddy had stumped him. "Okay, that's pretty terrible. And not just the whole scenario of going to the cinema with your folks. I'll join you waving a placard to protest against that one. But it isn't violence towards women in this case, is it? It's towards men. One man in particular. Me."

"Yeah, and you love it."

Eddie couldn't help grinning. "Okay, guilty as charged. But I still think it must be tricky for some blokes. You know, they must start questioning whether they're a psychopath or something."

"Do you think Jeff thinks that deeply? He doesn't seem the sort."

"Hey! Just because he's working class doesn't mean there's nothing going on between his ears. He's an intelligent man. Not educated, perhaps, but he's not thick."

Maddy gave him a way too knowing smile. "You really do love him, don't you?"

"Love is just a short-term hormone-driven infatuation, evolved to reinforce the pair bond so that children have the best chance of survival."

"Right. You just keep telling yourself that. And how does science explain the fact homosexuality hasn't gone the way of the dodo, then?"

"You really want to argue about this again?" They'd hashed this one out many a time over the years, with Eddie taking the staunchly empirical position and Maddy giving the new-age spiritual mumbo jumbo. And even if secretly he agreed with some of her arguments, he'd never let her know.

Maddy yawned. "Nah, you're right. I'm not really in the mood for that one." She brightened visibly. "But I did have an idea while we were chatting. If you want to help the feminist cause, would you mind posing for a little photo?"

"What kind of photo?" Eddie had learnt the hard way to be wary when Maddy got that look on her face.

"Nothing too risqué. You remember that photo of that bloke holding up a sign saying 'This is what a feminist looks like'. You know, I tagged you in it on Facebook."

"You tag me and poke me every day. How am I meant to remember every single last lolcat?"

Maddy rolled her eyes at him. "This wasn't a lolcat. It was a beardy bloke in a Regency dress."

"Oh. That one." Yep, how could he have forgotten?

"Right. So me and the girls were thinking we should add our pictures to the meme. I mean, fair play to everyone getting involved, but an awful lot of them fit the whole lentil-munching, butch-lesbian stereotypes the world already has of feminists. And I'm not entirely sure beardy dress man was helping matters. What they need is a bit of glam."

Eddie caught the gleam in Maddy's eyes. "Oh no, I'm not having a makeover. No way."

"Darling, would I? Far be it from me to bestow my expertise on someone for free. No, I just thought maybe you could pose for one in some of your bondage gear. Not in a submissive pose, though. In a way that makes you look tough. Maybe even a little dominant."

"I'm not sure a leather harness and arseless chaps will make me look all that dominant."

"The gear doesn't matter. It's the look in your eyes that will. You'll just need to look happy and confident. You can do that with your eyes shut."

"But then how will they see the look in my eyes?"

Maddy threw a cushion at him. "You know what I mean."

"Okay. And this will go online, will it?"

"That's right. Might even go viral, you never know. So what do you say?"

Eddie sighed. "Yeah. I'll do it. So long as you don't tag the picture with my real name. Wouldn't want clients to see it."

Maddy waggled her fingers dismissively. "Don't worry, as if I would."

"You tagged those drunken pictures of me as a student."

"Well, if you're that embarrassed, you should get yourself a professional profile as well as a personal one."

"Yeah, I know. It's just a hassle I could do without. Having to remember what I'm logged in as." He caught a mischievous look in Maddy's eyes he knew spelt trouble. "What? What have you done now?"

"Nothing, darling. I was just wondering, you think Jeff would want to take part?"

"Don't you dare ask him."

"Why not?"

"Because..." Because Eddie really didn't want to find out just how unreconstructed a man Jeff was. What if he thought women should "know their place" like they did in the old days? He was pretty old-fashioned in other ways. And if Jeff turned out to be a total chauvinist arsehole, Eddie was pretty sure all those mushy feelings inside him would congeal to a lump of lead.

"Just, erm, let me ask him. I'll be able to put it in a way he'll understand."

"Darling, I do know how to talk to men."

"You know how to seduce them. That's different."

"Hardly." Maddy pouted but soon cheered up when Eddie brought through a selection of bondage gear for her to choose from. "Oh, these are fabulous! And I just had a marvellous idea. We could style you wearing black tie over the top, you know, with the bow tie and shirt all sexy and undone. You've got a dinner jacket somewhere, haven't you?"

"This isn't a fashion shoot, you know," Eddie grumbled, but he went to do her bidding.

In less than half an hour, Eddie watched as she sent the picture of him from her iPad through the ether, to be shared with who knew who? Eddie adjusted his harness and idly played with his nipple through the metal ring. He hoped this wouldn't come back to bite him on the bum. Maddy's schemes had a way of doing that.

Chapter Eighteen

Friday seemed to take forever to come round. While Jeff knew that objectively it had taken exactly the same time as it did every week, the four days of slogging away building a raised pond for some overpaid carp-fancier had really dragged.

Friday was now even more appealing than ever. And not just because he'd clock off for the weekend and the fact it brought him one day closer to seeing Eddie, but because it was now his regular day in Niall's garden, doing proper gardening. He picked his tools up out of the back of the truck with enthusiasm. Today he'd work on tackling the overgrown pond that had really been bothering him. The overhanging plum tree needed branches cutting right back so they didn't shade the water, and there was a bunch of vegetation that had all but obscured the water. But it would be nice and cool down there, and he'd be doing something useful involving plants rather than bricks and mortar.

And of course, there was always the knowledge he'd be seeing Eddie tomorrow. As he made his way down the side of Niall's house, he contemplated all the things he wanted to do to Eddie. He'd tie him down—faceup this time—and play with him. Maybe he could ask Eddie to bring that wicked little pinwheel again. And he'd run it over Eddie's body, all the time watching his face and drinking up those desperate, turned-on sounds he made when he was being tortured.

Fuck. If Jeff wasn't careful, he'd end up having to work with a boner in his shorts. That really wasn't going to help with all the bending down he'd have to be doing.

Bending down... He could untie Eddie's legs, bend him in half and fuck him like that, Eddie's legs up over Jeff's shoulders. He could lean down for a kiss then too.

Bloody hell. He had to stop imagining kissing Eddie. Trouble was, he couldn't think about much else.

Fortunately, distraction presented itself in the form of Niall, out sunning himself on his back patio. He was wearing a pair of micro shorts that didn't leave much to the imagination, and Jeff found himself surreptitiously checking out Niall's body. Was he really gay if it was only Eddie who turned him on? Niall certainly didn't do much for him. A bit too paunchy, and the chest hair really wasn't Jeff's thing. God only knew what Eddie saw in Jeff's monkey body.

Niall tilted his head in Jeff's direction and yawned. "You know, it's kind of creepy when someone just stares at you while you're sunbathing."

Fuck. Had Niall been able to tell he'd been checking him out? Even if he hadn't particularly been into what he was looking at, it still counted as checking out, didn't it?

Jesus Christ. He really was gay.

The realisation he'd been holding at bay all week slammed him between the eyes.

His fingers went limp.

His tools clattered to the ground.

"Hey, are you all right, mate? You look like you need to take the weight off your feet for a minute."

Jeff staggered over and collapsed into the other sun lounger.

"You're not sick or something, are you? I know you self-employed types don't usually get sick pay, but I'd be happy to pay you something if you're really unwell. I don't want you working here if you've got something infectious."

"Nah, it's nothing like that. I just didn't sleep all that well last night. And I skipped breakfast." It was only a partial untruth. He'd only had a plain piece of toast that morning, and he'd spent the night drifting in and out of fevered erotic dreams of Eddie and him and—oh God, there'd been other men too, hadn't there? In some kind of sauna. And the gym, and on the football field. All those hard, masculine bodies around him, under him, on top of him…

"I think I might be gay," he blurted out, then immediately really did feel sick. Nauseous to the pit of his stomach. What if Niall was disgusted by him? Jeff stared down at his clasped hands, unable to meet Niall's gaze.

He'd been expecting Niall to sound disapproving or, at best, carefully neutral, when he began speaking again. What he wasn't prepared for, however, was a chuckle.

"Oh yes? Is this young Eddie who's got you feeling that way? Well, not so young Eddie, really. He's older than you, isn't he?"

"He is? He doesn't look it."

Niall shrugged. "I think he's Maddy's age, and she's thirty-three."

"Seriously? She's looking good for it."

"It's really not that old, you know. Being an old fogey like me gives you a different perspective."

"You're not that old," Jeff said, despite his judgement about the greying chest hair and paunch.

"Well, I'm certainly starting to feel it. You realise that by the time this baby is born, I'll be fifty-two? That means I'll be seventy when he or she goes off to university. Seventy, I ask you! It hardly seems possible."

"Baby?" Jeff floundered. What did any of this have to do with him being gay, and why on earth wasn't Niall more shocked by his revelation? A man could feel miffed, having his soul-baring shoved aside like that.

But Niall was yammering on again, and it wasn't anything to do with Jeff. "Yes, a baby. Maddy's pregnant. That's why I'm not at work today. Going to be taking her to her first scan later on. It's so exciting!"

"I didn't know."

"Sorry, I just assumed you would, what with you being thick as thieves with Eddie these days. Maddy tells me he's taken quite a shine to you. So, it's all going well? I knew you two would get along. You're the kind of man Eddie needs in his life. Steady and stubborn. One he can't wind around his little finger like he has with every other boyfriend he's ever had."

"Other boyfriends?" Jeff didn't want to know. But then again, he couldn't bear not to know either. "I didn't think Eddie had ever been serious with anyone before."

"Well, no, he hasn't been serious with them, but they've always seemed smitten with him. That's how he manages to manipulate them. But you, I figured you'd be a tougher one for him to charm. Especially with the whole not-being-gay thing."

"But I just told you I was."

"Really? Because the way you look at women, I'd never have guessed."

"How do I look at women?"

"Like you want to cover them in whipped cream and eat them up."

"I do?" Jeff thought about it. "I'm not into sploshing. As far as I know." Getting all sticky with foodstuffs didn't really appeal to him, although if Eddie suggested it, he'd probably want to give it a try.

But only if it was with custard. Yum.

"Okay, then, you look at women like you want to strap them down, smack their cunts and then eat them out. Is that a better image for you?"

"Yeah. I suppose." Jeff had wanted to do those exact things, hadn't he? And so maybe he still did. But right now, he couldn't imagine doing kinky stuff with anyone but Eddie.

"Jeff, you don't just suddenly turn gay overnight. You're probably just a bit bi, that's all. Well, join the club. I mean, if any bloke's going to turn an otherwise straight bloke's head, it's Eddie. I certainly enjoyed fucking him."

If Jeff hadn't already been sitting down, he'd have collapsed at that point. As it was, he just opened and closed his mouth a few times, trying to think of some way of responding to that. "You didn't," was what eventually came out. *Please tell me you didn't!*

"Yeah, it was how I met Maddy. Me and Eddie used to have this thing. Well, it wasn't anything serious on my part—I was just experimenting. Seeing if I preferred a male to a female sub."

"You met Maddy while you were shagging Eddie." It was a horrifying thought, for reasons Jeff wasn't about to analyse.

"Not literally while. Well, sort of. We were only weekend playmates for a few months. I took him to this club, and Maddy was there. They've been best mates since forever. And I ended up leaving the club with her rather than him. He was pretty pissed off with me at the time, although he phoned to apologise the next day. He's that kind of bloke, you know? Doesn't hold a grudge."

Eddie might not, but Jeff was fast discovering that he did. Although who exactly he held it against he couldn't rightly tell.

"Why didn't you tell me any of this?"

"None of your business, really."

"I think it is. You know, if Eddie's some kind of tart, out to seduce straight men."

Niall snorted. "Oh come on, it was hardly like that. I approached him on Fetlife and set up a meeting. I wanted to try things out with a man. And anyway, I identify as bi, not straight. Although I'd say I was only about twenty percent bi."

"There are percentages?" You could write down the sum total of what Jeff knew about bisexuality on the back of an envelope. He had a lot to learn. But maybe this was a good thing. After all, if he was bi, he might only be a little bit gay after all. "How do you know what percentage you are? Is there a test?"

Now Niall really was laughing. Jeff bristled. "A test? I expect you could find a Kinsey test online somewhere, but I just came up with what felt right for me. Eight times out of ten, I'd rather be with a woman, but sometimes I'm attracted to men."

"Men like Eddie."

"Exactly." Niall raised his glass like a toast, but Jeff couldn't see anything there to be happy about. Was Eddie really that desirable to other men? Was Jeff going to have to beat them off with a stick? Or would he just have to face up to the fact Eddie would never be interested in a bloke like him? Beyond the sex, that was. It wasn't like Jeff could offer the kind of lifestyle Niall could, with his huge house, well-equipped dungeon and fancy cars. The best Jeff could offer was a terraced miner's cottage, a sad little suitcase of toys, and a beat-up, smelly old truck full of mud.

No, Eddie would be better off with a man like Niall, and he'd have to know that himself. Jeff had better not get too attached. And really, if he was only a certain percentage bisexual, then it would be dumb to get all invested in a man, wouldn't it? Especially one who didn't do serious relationships. Jeff should keep that in mind. He should keep going to the socials and keep his eye out for a woman. Once Eddie had finished his training, Jeff would have the confidence to approach them and get it right, wouldn't he?

Yes, once Eddie had finished his training.

Just two more sessions, and Jeff could get back to a normal life. He took a deep breath and tried to force his head straight.

"Niall?" Maddy's call cut through the air between them. "Where are y— Oh, there you are." Maddy strolled out onto the patio in her amazingly high heels and leant down to give Niall a kiss. And not just a polite peck in front of company either. The two of them looked like they were trying to eat each other's faces off, and Niall's hand had worked its way up the back of her skirt by the time Jeff realized he'd have to announce his presence.

He cleared his throat loudly, and Maddy turned her head. "Hey, Jeff. How are you?"

Jesus Christ, how did she manage to make those three simple words sound dirty? Like she knew exactly what he'd been up to with Eddie at the weekend. Then again, maybe she did. Maybe Eddie was the kiss-and-tell type.

Shame he'd never thought to tell Jeff about Niall. Bloody hell, that still hurt.

And he still hadn't answered Maddy. "Yeah. Fine." Okay, Maddy was still looking at him like she expected more, and Niall was still fondling her legs like they were alone in the bedroom. Not that she seemed remotely fazed. Would Eddie like being handled like that in front of other people? And would Jeff enjoy doing it?

But he had to make conversation. He couldn't just sit here, transfixed by the sight of the two of them canoodling. "Oh yeah. Congratulations. How's the baby?"

It was the right thing to say as Maddy settled down on Niall's lap and seemed perfectly happy to chatter on about scans and morning sickness. Jeff let it all wash over him.

I want some of that.

He wanted that closeness, that casual intimacy that poured off the two of them in their little touches and shared glances. Like they were speaking to each other through a whole secret language no one else could ever hope to share.

Yes, finding himself a woman would be the best thing to do, because he could never hope to have that with Eddie. Two men never found that level of closeness, did they? Well, not in Jeff's experience, anyway.

Although with every day that passed, he was starting to realise just how little experience he had. And he wanted more. Lots more.

Chapter Nineteen

On Saturday morning, Eddie pulled up around the corner from Jeff's house, not wanting to brave the parking on his road. It was the first time he'd been here during the day. In fact, it was the first time he'd been here without following Jeff back from the pub.

Bloody hell. It was only the third time he'd been here in total. Felt like they'd known each other for a lot longer than they had. Maybe it wasn't the amount of time you spent with someone that counted, but rather the intensity of the time you spent with them.

That'd go some way towards explaining the weird feeling he had in the pit of his stomach. Nerves and excitement all rolled into one squirming ball. It was just the anticipation of getting a good seeing-to. It had to be. Not that he'd ever felt it quite like this before, but it was probably just the natural end result of having spent a week burying himself in his work so he could legitimately take the whole weekend off.

Yep, the whole bloody weekend. Eddie had stowed a micro keg of a strong local ale inside the suitcase of kink, and he fully intended to drink too much of it to be able to drive home. Jeff would have to ask him to stay the night. He couldn't avoid it. It was devious, but Eddie didn't mind stooping to such a low tactic. Not if it meant he got to wake up next to Jeff and have some sleepy morning sex, kink optional.

Eddie's arsehole clenched in anticipation as he walked down to Jeff's house. Fuck yes. He was going to be a dirty stop-out and do the walk of shame back down this road in the morning. One of Jeff's neighbours—a white-haired man in an incongruous knitted hat—sat out on his tiny front lawn, staring at the view. He must have been baking under the midday sun with all those layers on, but he just gave Eddie a nod of acknowledgement and a toothless smile, like he hadn't a care in the world.

Jeff's cottage looked even more welcoming in the daytime, with the roses spilling their sweet scent down over him as he walked up to the door. And Jeff must have been waiting for him on the other side, because no sooner had Eddie raised his hand to knock than Jeff was opening the door.

Jeff gave a shy smile, and Eddie let out the grin that he'd been holding in.

Jeff stepped back. Eddie followed him in, and the door slammed shut as Jeff pushed him back against it. He dropped the suitcase. "Fuck, there was beer in there."

"Don't care." Jeff's eyes glowed with lust, and Eddie let his knees bend to bring him down to the same height. Jeff took full advantage of that, just like he'd hoped, and ransacked his mouth with a spine-tingling, dick-firming kiss.

Oh yeah, someone had been missing him. Eddie kissed Jeff back as fiercely as he'd been dreaming of, pressing his whole body against Jeff's solid bulk. It was a wonder their clothes didn't catch fire with the heat building between them. No, scratch that. It was a wonder Eddie's dick hadn't burst out of his jeans and rubbed up against its favourite playmate, which was currently trying to drill a hole into Eddie's thigh.

Bloody hell, Jeff's dick got harder than any bloke's he'd ever known. Eddie scrambled for Jeff's fly, desperate to finally get a good feel of it. He'd had it in his mouth and his arse now, but he still hadn't had a chance to explore it properly with his hands. And it had never touched his own dick. Would that be too gay for Jeff? Only one way to find out.

Eddie attacked Jeff's fly and then his own, freeing their cocks at almost the same time. He kissed Jeff ferociously all the while, not giving him time to object as he grabbed hold of Jeff's cock and brought it to his own.

Oh! So hard and sweaty slick. Eddie wrapped a hand around them both, and rather than stop kissing him, Jeff made a hungry noise and reached down to grab Eddie's buttocks, squeezing them hard.

Yeah, this was a time for fast and dirty. They could get the toys out later. Eddie tested Jeff's grip by leaning his weight on him, then gave in to what he'd been wanting to do and wrapped both his legs around Jeff's middle. Now he was suspended from Jeff's body, hanging on to his sturdy frame and letting it take his weight, with only the door against his back giving any other support.

Felt so fucking amazing, being able to do that. Eddie bucked his hips and pumped his hand, determined to bring them both off before Jeff's grip gave way.

Their cocks slid together in his hand, the ridge on Jeff's giving just the right amount of friction as Eddie thrust his hips.

Jeff broke the kiss, panting. "Fuck! Oh shit, that's good." He buried his head against Eddie's shoulders, and his whole body convulsed. His dick pulsed in Eddie's hand as wet heat burst against his stomach.

Eddie fucked into his hand, lubricated by Jeff's come. "So good," he agreed, before the pleasure barrelled through him and shot out the end of his dick.

"Ungh." It wasn't the most articulate summing up of the situation, but it was all he could currently manage as his legs slipped down over Jeff's bum. He clung on to Jeff's neck and let them fall.

"Fuck me," Jeff wheezed.

The urge to do just that nearly bubbled up—Eddie didn't mind topping every now and again, especially if the other bloke was still in charge in some way. And who knew? Jeff might love having a cock rammed up his arse. Eddie certainly did. But instead he just chuckled. "Hi. How's things?"

"All better now." Jeff bared his teeth to nip at Eddie's neck, giving him a delightful shiver. "How about you?"

"I'm grand, thanks." Eddie peered over Jeff's shoulder. "Hey, you're rearranged your living room. I like it." The absurdity of chatting with their soggy dicks pressed together up against the front door hadn't escaped Eddie, but if Jeff wanted polite chitchat, he could have it.

"Do you like runner beans?" Jeff asked.

It took a moment for Eddie's brain to wrap itself around that non sequitur. "To eat? Yep. So long as they're not overdone. My stepmum had a habit of murdering them."

"Good. You can help me pick them." Jeff gave Eddie's arse a quick squeeze and then stepped back. "Better get yourself looking respectable. Some of the bits of the garden are private, but the neighbours can all see the back door."

It was pointless feeling let down about that little command. Eddie knew Jeff wasn't ready to come out. He couldn't even come out to Eddie and admit he was, at the very least, bisexual. But that didn't stop the irritation rising as Eddie tucked himself back into his jeans and wiped his hand clean on his T-shirt. "Shit. I should have brought a change of clothes."

"You look like you've brought a whole weekend's worth of stuff." Jeff glanced at the suitcase, but Eddie couldn't for the life of him tell if he disapproved of that.

"Nah. Just beer and toys. It's step four of my Intro to BDSM class later. I hope you've done your homework."

"I didn't know I had any."

Fuck. Eddie never had sent that text in the end, had he? He'd been going to suggest Jeff went and looked up genital torture online—specifically cock and ball torture—but then he'd bottled out, worried it might give Jeff the fear.

And now here he was, about to spring it all on a man who was totally unprepared.

Eddie thought fast. "Figure of speech. But I think I will set some this week. I've got plans for next weekend."

"Our final session." Jeff's face was unreadable again, his voice flat. "You said five in total, didn't you?"

"I did." *Ask me for more. Ask me for more.*

But Jeff just pulled a face and turned away. "Come on. Let's go pick beans.

Jeff strode out of his back door, not looking back to check if Eddie was following. That had been so fucking confusing. That whatever-it-was they'd just done at his front door. Resentment seethed inside Jeff, but he hadn't a clue why. Maybe it was just at the way Eddie made him feel. All messed up. It had been easier yesterday. Much simpler to imagine a humdrum straight life without Eddie in it.

Strangely enough, it had been easier to imagine himself alone. His mind refused to put a girl in the picture. Perhaps the whole thing with Sarah had just rocked his confidence a bit. Yeah, that was it. He'd get back in the swing of things eventually. Get back on the horse that threw him.

The thought of riding Eddie hard—whacking him with the crop all the while—made him groan. He paused under the rose arch, resting in the shade to help cool him down. Overheated and horny, that was all he was. These gay fantasies would pass eventually, and he'd remember how to fantasise about shagging women.

Maybe he should watch some straight porn. That might help. Yeah, he'd do that later after Eddie had gone home. That one on his hard drive with the woman with the huge tits and gorgeous white skin, being fucked by all those men with huge, veiny cocks...

"Hey, this is beautiful!" Eddie's voice made Jeff start, guiltily. Did it count as being unfaithful in the mind if you thought about other men's cocks? Sarah certainly hadn't been happy when she caught him watching porn.

But you couldn't be unfaithful to someone you weren't in a relationship with, could you? So thinking about other blokes' cocks was fine. Right. Good thing he had that sorted.

"Earth to Jeff? You all right there, mate?"

"Yeah." Jeff's voice cracked as he realised what a weirdo he must seem, spacing out like that. "Um, yeah, fine. Just checking the roses for black spot." He pulled a handy leaf out, turning it over to examine it.

Eddie reached out to touch the leaf, and his arm brushed against Jeff's. "What are we looking for? No, let me guess. Is the name a hint?"

"Yep. They're black spots on the leaves, and they spread like crazy once they get started. It's a fungal disease, and they should be okay in this dry weather, but you can never be too careful."

"You really do know your plants, don't you? Is this all your handiwork?"

"Yep. Sarah liked sunbathing, but she didn't really want to put any work in on the garden. You should see the rest of it."

Jeff led the way from the upper patio section, down a couple of steps and into the vegetable patch. He walked the pathway between the raised beds, pausing every few steps to examine the squash plants trailing over the edge, and pinching out the tips of the shoots that had already set fruit.

"Wow! You really grew all this? My stepmum's garden never looked this good. She used to plant everything in straight rows. You've got it all jammed in together."

"Some things are still in rows," Jeff said absently as he picked the greenfly off a pea shoot.

"Yeah, but not in the same way. Not with these raised-up beds. Do you mind if I take some pictures? She's getting kind of arthritic now, and I bet she'd find something like this much easier to manage than having to stoop down to the ground all the time."

"Yep. Knock yourself out."

Eddie paced between the beds with his phone in his hands, kneeling down to get shots along the pathways between the low stone walls Jeff had built to edge the beds. It was good to see his garden appreciated. Sarah had always been on at him to install a sauna and hot tub down here instead, complaining that he'd spent way too much time and money on growing something they could simply buy from the supermarket. She'd never understood that gardening brought him peace and contentment. The same kind of peace and contentment she found at the gym or the spa, no doubt.

Eddie seemed to get it, though, even if he didn't share Jeff's green fingers. They were much better suited than Jeff and Sarah had ever been. For a moment, Jeff allowed himself to imagine a life with Eddie living here, perhaps taking the spare bedroom as his office. Of them sitting out on the patio with their coffees to catch the morning sun. Perhaps Eddie could even do some of his work out here while Jeff gardened. There were shady spots where you could still see a laptop screen.

Jeff gave his imagination a kick up the backside for being ridiculous. That wasn't going to happen. Couldn't happen. For a start, Eddie had no interest in settling down with anyone. Secondly, there was no way Jeff was going to move in with a man. Thirdly, what would his parents say? And fourthly... Well, he didn't need a fourth. He'd already constructed a solid argument. Solid as the walls he'd built. He tapped one of them with his boot, and a layer of stone flaked off. Oops. He leaned down to push it back into place. That was often the way when you used recycled old stone, though. But it looked so much better than new brick.

Eddie's hand landed on Jeff's shoulder, startling him. "So, Jeffy-Jeffy, just how far down does your garden grow?"

Jeff stood and walked over to the next set of steps down. "You see that line of trees down there?"

Eddie shaded his eyes and squinted, his shoulder rubbing against Jeff's in a distracting way. "Yep. I see them."

"That's the end of the garden."

Eddie gave a low whistle and clapped his arm around Jeff's shoulders in a way that could probably have passed for blokeish companionship, if it weren't for the way Jeff's body reacted to the touch. But Eddie didn't seem to notice his discomfort. "Bloody hell, this really is a garden and a half. Must take you forever to look after it all."

"Not really. The bottom part is all pretty wild. And it's only narrow." Jeff peered at the rooftops on his parent's road, counting the chimneys to locate their house. From this spot, you could just see a patch of their patio, which meant, of course, that anyone there could see him up here. Should they be looking. There was no one there, but Jeff stepped down and away from Eddie just in case. “This part’s the fruit garden,” he said to explain why he’d moved. “I don’t quite manage to keep myself in fruit and veg all year round, but I have more than enough in the summer months.” The scent of ripe berries and the low humming of insects were always calming, and Jeff moved between the net-covered fruit cages, glad for a reason to keep going, down into the most private part of the garden.

But Eddie wasn’t following him. Instead, he was peering into one of the shady cages and rubbing a leaf between his fingers before smelling them. “Blackcurrants, right? My stepmum grows loads of these. Ooh, and is that raspberries? I adore raspberries.”

Jeff opened the door to the cage. “Come on, then,” he said.

Eddie had to stoop to get inside. “Mind your feet,” Jeff told him. “Stick to the straw paths. There’re strawberry plants all over the place.”

“I thought I could smell strawberries too. You must be able to make the most amazing summer pudding.” Eddie’s eyes glowed in the greenish light, and he looked like an overgrown school boy, all filled with excitement.

“Yeah, summer pudding’s okay, but I prefer Eton Mess.”

“Eton Mess!” Eddie’s eyes darkened, and he licked his lips. “Even better. My stepmum never made that. Said she couldn’t stand meringue. But what’s not to like about meringue?”

“Exactly.” Jeff couldn’t stop staring at Eddie’s lower lip, still glistening with his saliva. He’d make Eddie Eton Mess for pudding if it meant he got to see that expression on his face again. He had plenty of eggs, and he was sure there was some cream in the fridge. Hopefully it was still in date.

“What?” Eddie asked, grinning knowingly and taking a step closer. “You’re spacing out on me again.”

“Uh, raspberries. Over there.” Jeff pointed so he didn’t have to put together more coherent directions.

“I see them.” Eddie bumped into him as he went past, and although it was a confined space, surely he was closer than he needed to be? Jeff's heart rate sped up, and he had to stop himself from grabbing Eddie and throwing him onto the ground, squashed strawberries or not. What was wrong with him? He'd come about ten minutes ago. He shouldn't be raring to go again quite so soon. Not with this level of desperation, anyway.

To distract himself, Jeff plucked a fat, juicy raspberry and ate it, but the tangy flavour bursting across his tongue was almost too much stimulation. As was Eddie, moaning with delight. "Oh my God. These have to be the best raspberries I've ever tasted. You're going to have to stop me, or you won't have any left."

"That's okay. I've got more than I can eat, anyway."

"What do you do with the excess? Somehow I can't see you making jam."

Jeff couldn't tear his gaze away from the pink juice staining Eddie's lips. Utterly sinful.

But Eddie had asked him a question. "Erm, I give most of it to my mum. Sometimes my brother too, but he's moved away to Trowbridge, so that's not going to happen so often."

"You're a real family man, aren't you?" Eddie sounded pleased about that, which was weird as Sarah had always said he needed to cut the apron strings.

"I dunno. I just do what I can. And they help me out too."

"It's nice. I wish I could see more of mine, but they went and moved to Devon a few years back. Takes me a couple of hours to drive there now. Not really handy for Sunday lunch. It's a bloody shame. I really miss having a roast at the weekend."

The urge to invite Eddie round for Sunday lunch at his parents had to be tamped down and a large rock put on top of it. Okay, so he could introduce Eddie as a friend, and that would be fine—his mum was always ready to cater for an extra body or two—but his folks would be bound to wonder how someone like him had ended up being friends with the likes of Eddie, and knowing Jeff's dad, he'd probably sniff out Eddie's queerness a mile off. According to Bert White, all posh blokes were a bit gay anyway.

"You're drifting off on me again," Eddie said. "What's a man got to do to keep you in the here and now?" He'd moved closer as he spoke, brushing against the bushes bordering the path, and all that separated them was a few inches of super-heated air.

Chapter Twenty

The scent of sex mingled with the sharp tang of blackcurrant leaves, leaving Jeff's head swimming. All he wanted to do was lean forwards and kiss—

Eddie did it for him, crushing his lips onto Jeff's. He tasted of ripe fruit, but when Jeff tried to lick into his mouth, Eddie pulled back, keeping the kiss light. Strange. Jeff had never kissed this way before, but after a minute more of gentle lip sucking and teasing, he had to admit it was good. It gave him time to appreciate the plump firmness of Eddie's lips, and the hint of shaving gel lingering under the scent of raspberries.

He could get used to that shaving gel scent.

And more to the point, this kind of kissing was good because it gave Jeff time to slowly map out Eddie's back with his hands, exploring his lean torso, before drifting down to cup his arse. He should probably order Eddie onto his knees to suck him off right now—Jeff's cock was certainly ready to go along with that plan—but it didn't feel like the right moment. This wasn't about dominance and submission. This was about...

Jeff hadn't a clue what this was about.

"What's going on?" he asked, right up against Eddie's lips so they brushed against his as he spoke.

"You're showing me your garden, and I seem to remember you said something about picking beans for lunch."

"Oh." That wasn't what he'd meant at all, but he supposed it was as good an answer as any. Jeff cleared his throat and wiped a hand over his head. "Yeah, it's getting kind of late. We should have dinner soon."

Eddie glanced at his watch. "It's only half one."

"Exactly. I've usually had my dinner by now."

Eddie frowned. "You mean lunch."

"I mean dinner. It's only lunch when it's a sandwich, and I'm cooking something proper."

"Ah." A look of understanding dawned on Eddie's face. "So what do you call the evening meal, then? Supper?"

"Don't be an idiot. It's tea."

"Tea? What, you're going to make a pot of tea and serve crumpets?"

Jeff wondered if this was a subtle upper-class way of ripping the piss out of him, but Eddie seemed genuinely interested.

"Um, no. I'll probably be making egg, chips and beans for tea."

Eddie's eyebrows shot up, but he smiled. "Sounds delicious. Can I stay?"

"I don't see why not. And if you're lucky, I might make some Eton Mess for pudding."

"Jeff White, you'd better watch it, or I'll fall hopelessly in love with you." Eddie grinned mischievously and turned on his heel, leaving Jeff struggling for words.

He definitely didn't want that to happen. Did he?

Dinner seemed to go down well, even though Eddie kept insisting on calling it lunch. But he said how much he liked the quick pasta dish Jeff had whipped up, and the way he cleared his bowl and went back for a second helping reassured Jeff he was telling the truth. And while they ate, they chatted about football—turned out Eddie had a reasonable knowledge of the premier league goings on that season, even if he didn't actually support a specific team—which was just weird, if you asked Jeff. But Eddie didn't ask him, so Jeff didn't bring it up.

But then they were finished, and Jeff didn't want to talk football anymore, but he didn't know quite how to bring up what was on his mind. This business of there only being two more sessions and exactly what they involved. It should have been simple enough to ask, but for some reason, he didn't dare.

Finding out would just make the end of their sessions together even more concrete, and he couldn't bear facing that.

Because Jeff was really enjoying just hanging out with Eddie. He didn't exactly feel relaxed—not with the end hanging over him—but for minutes at a time, he'd forget about that and feel more comfortable than he remembered being in a long time. And, okay, Jeff could always talk footie with his mates down the pub, but they didn't know all the other stuff about him that Eddie knew. He felt like he could be properly himself, and Eddie wouldn't judge him for it. Wouldn't think he was a creepy weirdo for all the sadism shit, or a pansy for all the gardening shit.

"So." Eddie leaned back in his chair and stretched, his T-shirt riding up to show a few inches of white skin. "I think last week you said something about naked sunbathing."

"Yep. You're right. I'd forgotten." And that was a much better idea than heading upstairs, because it meant he'd get to spend a few more hours in Eddie's company.

"How could you possibly forget that? I've not been able to think about much else."

"You're really that excited to get the sun on your skin?"

"No, I'm really that excited to get a good leisurely look at you, naked."

"Oh no. I'm not taking everything off."

"You bloody well are if you want me to."

Jeff stared at him for a few minutes, doing his best to look forbidding, but Eddie didn't back down. It would be pointless to argue. Besides, Eddie had said he liked Jeff's hairy body, hadn't he? And Jeff wasn't going to judge him for that. Much.

"Fine," he eventually agreed. "But you'll have to rub sun cream on my bum. I don't want to burn."

"My pleasure." Eddie eagerly rubbed his hands together.

"Okay, let's go." Jeff grabbed a couple of bottles of cold lager out of the fridge and led his way out into the garden.

The heat had intensified while they'd eaten inside, and it was like walking out into an oven. Jeff led the way down the path and through the different terraces, before getting to the wild section. This was where he'd stopped terracing levels, and so the land sloped down the hill, evening out as it neared the bottom of the valley. There were trees here, and long grass, and to the untrained observer, it probably looked like Jeff didn't do any gardening here at all. But it all still needed managing. Jeff kept the brambles from taking over, and he mowed a path through the grass, and he even cut it all back in the autumn so the tough grasses wouldn't take over from the wildflowers. It took a lot of work to give the impression of effortless natural beauty.

Eddie pulled ahead of Jeff, almost running through the meadow, which was crazy in this heat. Jeff watched him strip off his shirt, and he had to admire his lean, muscular body. Did Eddie have to work at that too, or did he really lead a charmed life?

"You go to the gym?" Jeff asked.

"Yeah, a few times a week. Mostly for the pool, though. Training is so boring."

"Even with all the fit blokes there?" Not that Jeff would be checking them out, of course. Why did he feel like he was blushing?

Eddie shot him a sly smile. "You clearly haven't been to my local gym. Very few fit blokes there. Lots of yummy mummies working off the baby fat, though."

"Ah. Sounds like the place Sarah used to work." Jeff led the way to the large mown circle by the pond. There was enough room here to lay down the blanket, and he was reasonably certain it wasn't overlooked by anyone. Sarah had used to sunbathe naked down here, anyway, and he didn't think she'd have done it anywhere she could be seen.

Jeff threw off his clothes and stood there, trying to ignore the fact his dick was straining up towards Eddie. An Eddie who was still half-clothed and staring at Jeff with a hungry look on his face. "Take 'em off," Jeff ordered. "Now."

"Yessir!"

Eddie was so pale in the bright sunshine, his skin glowing white. "You're going to need sunscreen."

"I thought the point was to get me tanned."

"Yep, but I don't want you to burn."

"You do know I'm a masochist?" But Eddie didn't keep up with the smart-arsed remarks and submitted to Jeff, offering himself up to be covered in sun lotion. Jeff took his time applying it, making sure every last patch of skin was covered up.

"I don't think I'm going to be getting any sun there," Eddie remarked as Jeff slid a finger right down his arse crack.

"You never know. I might order you to spread your cheeks for me." The idea of having a good inspection of Eddie's arse was an appealing one. But maybe not out here. Jeff slid his finger down to prod him in the balls instead, enjoying the surprised noise Eddie made. But then he patted him on the freshly lotioned arse and asked Eddie to return the favour.

When they lay down on the blanket together, Jeff had expected he'd want sex, but in the heat, there didn't seem to be any rush. Instead, he took hold of Eddie's hand and pulled it up to his chest. Not quite cuddling, but it still gave him the intimacy he craved.

They lay there, talking drowsily about nothing in particular, until Eddie suddenly sat up. "I have to ask you something," he said. "I promised Maddy."

Bloody Maddy. Jeff had been enjoying lying there like that. "What is it?" Eddie was now off rifling through his clothes. Jeff was liking this less and less.

"Take a look at this." Eddie held up his phone, and Jeff had to squint to make out the picture in the bright light.

Was that what it looked like? Jeff held his hand up to shade the screen. Bloody hell. It was a torso shot of Eddie smiling cheekily at the camera, wearing some kind of bondage harness under his open shirt. Jeff could see the straps of it over his shoulders and down at his waist, but his nipples were blocked from view by some sign he was carrying.

"You like it?" Eddie asked.

"Why can't I see your nipples?" Jeff complained. Eddie had lovely nipples. He snuck a look at them right now. In the hot sunshine Jeff's own nipples were as flat as pancakes, but Eddie's still stuck out proudly, as if they were begging for a good squeeze or suck. Imagine what they'd look like if Eddie was chilly!

"Never mind about my nipples. What do you think about the message? Would you be willing to take part? Maddy thinks you'd be perfect for it."

Perfect for what? Jeff squinted at the writing on the sign and scissored his fingers on the screen to zoom in. Huh. "You're a feminist?"

"Don't say it like that."

"Like what?"

"Like it's some dirty word."

"I didn't. I just don't understand how you could be a feminist. You're a bloke."

Eddie huffed at him, and Jeff had the uneasy feeling he'd stepped into a mantrap. "Men can be feminists too. Anyone who believes in equality for both genders is a feminist. It doesn't matter what you have between your legs."

"Oh." Jeff pondered that for a minute. "I'm totally behind women having the same rights and pay and all that. Seems only fair."

"Right. Then you're a feminist. It's a simple as that."

Was it? Jeff would just have to take Eddie's word for it, he supposed.

"So? Will you do it?"

"What's this for? Who's going to see it?"

"It'll go on Tumblr. Anyone could see it. Is that okay?"

"I'm not wearing any kinky gear." He'd never live that down if one of his mates saw it. He'd get enough of a ribbing about the whole feminist thing as it was.

Eddie flapped his hands. "You wouldn't need to. Maddy wants someone who looks like your average bloke to take part."

"Okay, then. We can do it later."

"Seriously?" Eddie was looking at him like he couldn't believe what he was hearing. "You don't want to make any more conditions?"

"Maybe one." Would Eddie agree? It was a lot to ask, but faint heart never won fair maid—erm, lad. "First I'd like to take some photos of you. In bed. Today."

Eddie's lips curled. "Only if you send me copies too."

"Deal."

They shook on it.

"Let's go," Jeff said, getting to his feet. He pulled his shorts back on, but he couldn't be bothered by the rest. If his neighbours wondered why he was walking half-naked through his garden with another bloke, and a very obvious hard-on, they'd just have to draw their own conclusions. He could live with that.

Chapter Twenty-one

Eddie followed Jeff back up to the house, oddly nervous now they were about to get into the zone. Maybe that was because this was more of a teaching session than others had been. After all, Jeff probably wasn't going to know what half the stuff in Eddie's suitcase actually was. And yep, he might be totally freaked out by some of it.

Eddie just had to hope the lust he'd seen blazing in Jeff's eyes would be enough to carry him over any "I'm not gay" wibbles.

"Where do you want to do this?" Eddie asked. Jeff was standing at the base of the staircase, but he was staring over at the empty grate.

Jeff cleared his throat. "Upstairs. I want to tie you to my bed."

"Sounds good to me. I'll just need to show you how some of this kit works first." He lifted up the suitcase.

Jeff's eyes widened, but he nodded, and his erection certainly didn't seem to be flagging. Eddie followed him up the stairs, eager for a first glimpse of Jeff's upper level.

It was plain and simple up here, much like the downstairs, but the daylight revealed evidence of empty picture pins sticking out of the walls, and darker spots on the paper below them where frames must have once hung. Eddie wanted to ask more about this Sarah woman, and what she'd taken with her when she left—a large chunk of Jeff's heart, he was guessing—but he didn't want to kill the mood.

And all thoughts of Jeff's ex fled from his head when he entered the bedroom. "Oh my God, that bed is perfect!" It was an old brass bedstead, painted cream, with a plain white duvet on it. It looked so innocent and countrified, and it was going to be so thoroughly debauched in just a short while.

Eddie salivated at the prospect of being the first man to be tortured on it. There was something special about christening a bed.

He looked up from his appreciation to find Jeff giving him a puzzled look. "It's nothing special. We got it in IKEA. I mean, not *we*. Me and my ex."

"Shh! Don't tell me. Let me imagine it's some heirloom passed down from your grandmother or something. It'll make it all that much more titillating for us to do what we're about to do. Or rather, for you to do to me what you're about to do to me, and for me to take it like a good boy."

Jeff shook his head. "You're nuts, you are."

"Actually, that's a good idea. We can start with my nuts." Eddie placed his case on the bed and unzipped it. The toys were a heap inside—he should really get some kind of case with handy storage pockets in it, but then again, it wasn't like he'd have to bring them over here ever again. Not with their last session taking place elsewhere.

No, no point dwelling on that. Eddie leaned in and started taking things out, placing them in a row on the bed. He felt movement beside him and heard Jeff's throat working like he was bracing himself to say something.

Eddie would spare him the embarrassment. "These are all intended for genital torture, but that doesn't mean they all necessarily hurt. This one, for instance, is bloody amazing for a while." He held up the magic wand and wondered if Jeff had a plug socket anywhere near enough to the bed for them to use it. "But, like any kind of pleasure, you can have too much of a good thing, and it can be used past the peak of enjoyment, to where your sub is begging you to stop because they just can't take it anymore."

Jeff took the magic wand from Eddie's hand and frowned at it. "This is one of those massage thingies, isn't it? Sarah had one."

Bloody Sarah again. Seemed like they couldn't get away from her today. "Didn't Sarah tell you they're commonly used as vibrators?" Maybe she'd kept it her little secret.

"Women put these inside them?" Jeff's eyes went wide, as well they might. This particular magic wand was a good three inches wide at the end.

"They're not intended for internal use. Too tricky to keep clean, and probably way too powerful. You want a vibrator inside you, you'd be better off going for one of these."

Eddie picked up his favourite vibrating dildo. It was thick, black and looked pretty mean. Jeff blanched. "I thought vibrators had those bunny ears on them. You know, like you see in Ann Summers shops." He scratched at his neck like crazy, as if to ward off the blush Eddie could see creeping up it.

"Since when have you been in an Ann Summers shop?"

"Erm, a couple of years ago. Sarah thought some new underwear might liven things up for us."

"And did it?"

"Kind of." Scratch-scratch-scratch. "I mean, it was sexy, but what I really wanted was to get some of the toys, but she said no. She wasn't going to let me tie her up or hurt her. Which I totally respected."

"Of course you did." Poor Jeff, being stuck in a vanilla relationship for so many years. Eddie's heart went out to him, and although he wanted to find out more, he didn't want to make the poor bloke feel any more awkward than he already was. "Well, those vibrators you saw there are intended for women. If you want one for your arse, you need a wide base so it doesn't get accidentally sucked in by your muscles."

Jeff was nodding now. "Yeah, I read about that. Does it really happen?"

"Never to me, but this bloke I know, he's had to go to hospital four times to get things pulled out of his arse. You'd think he'd have learnt his lesson, but he just gets off on sticking everyday household objects up there, and they don't usually come with the right kind of base."

"He sounds like an idiot."

"Yep. Solo BDSM is fun, but it can be risky. Like all those people who die of autoerotic asphyxiation. Doing it with a partner is much more exciting, and usually safer."

"Not everyone's lucky enough to find a partner who likes kinky sex." Jeff sounded really morose now.

"That's what the Internet's for. Hooking up with other kinky types. Although it's probably easier for gay men. I don't think there are nearly as many straight women out there looking for hookups."

"You're telling me."

"Don't worry. We'll find you someone." It hurt to get the words out, but since Jeff was never going to settle down with a man, Eddie should help him find someone to make him happy. "Our last session. We're going to a club. We'll be covering public humiliation and exhibitionism. You can look for someone there."

"We're going out together. To a gay club?" Jeff looked terrified.

"Not a gay one. A kink club. There might be a few gay couples, but it's likely to be mostly straight. Gay men tend to find the straight fetish clubs a bit tame. And there are far too many scantily clad women in them, but I figured that would be a good thing in your case."

Jeff pulled a face Eddie couldn't interpret, but at least it wasn't a leer at the prospect of naked female flesh. "And you want me to publicly humiliate you?"

God, did Eddie want that! But he knew not to push Jeff too far past his comfort zone. "No, this is more of a field trip. We can just observe and talk about what we see. I won't be there as your sub. Just your..." He searched for the right word. "Mentor?"

"Oh." Jeff's expression went blank. "Okay. I've never been to one of those clubs before. Should be exciting."

"Perhaps." Privately, Eddie thought it would all be rather boring—especially as he wasn't going to be there as Jeff's sub—but he wasn't about to burst Jeff's bubble.

"Whereabouts were you thinking?" Jeff asked.

Eddie had done his online homework and lined a few possibilities up. "Well, we don't have as wide a choice out here as people do in the southeast, but there are a few places that do the occasional fetish night. The next one coming up is down in Bournemouth this coming weekend, but that's not going to be so good in terms of meeting someone local. And to be honest, we could probably get into London in the same time it will take us to drive down there."

"That's okay. Bournemouth sounds good." The speed at which Jeff rushed to say that made Eddie pause, but maybe it was simply embarrassment on Jeff's part.

"We'd have to stay in a hotel," Eddie said. "But there's plenty to choose from. How about I book us a room somewhere? My treat." If he left it to Jeff to book a hotel, they'd probably end up in a Travelodge.

"No. I'll do it."

"But..." Eddie floundered, trying to think of a way of putting it that wouldn't offend Jeff.

"Don't you trust me to look out for us?"

Us. He'd said *us*. Eddie couldn't stop himself grinning stupidly. "Yeah, you're right. I trust you." And if it was a Travelodge with paper-thin walls, so what? He'd just have to find a way of getting a thrill out of slumming it for a night. And he could always wear a gag to keep the noise down.

Jeff met Eddie's gaze for a moment, then looked down to the bed. His eyes widened. "What the hell is this thing?" he said, picking up the stainless steel ball-crusher press. "Bloody hell, it's heavy." He played with the handle, twirling it around so that the base moved up on its internal screw thread. He turned it over, fiddling with the fastenings that opened the cylindrical body of the press and running his fingers around the small opening at the top. A kind of horrified fascination dawned on his face. "Oh my God, is this what I think it is?"

"I don't know. What do you think it is?" Eddie fought the urge to cup his hands protectively over his crotch. He loved the press—for fuck's sake, he'd bought it himself, hadn't he?—but the thought of its immanent use always made him squirm. It was intense. And painful. And dangerous. And oh-so-fucking-good in the right hands.

"Erm, you put your dick in it?" Jeff had blanched under his tan.

"Not your dick. Your balls. If you wanted something to put your dick in—sorry, to put my dick in," he corrected as Jeff really did slam a hand down over his crotch, "then you'd be looking at a cock cage. But I don't have any of those."

"Why not?"

"I don't like them. I want to be able to get hard when I'm turned on. A cock cage hurts when you get an erection. Some of them don't even let you get a semi-on. They're fucking horrible. And don't you even think about buying one, you bastard."

"I won't. I like you having an erection. I mean, I, erm, I like to know you're enjoying what I'm doing." Jeff scratched his neck like a dog with fleas. "But you actually like this thing? Really?" He stared at the ball crusher like it was a medieval instrument of torture, which perhaps it had been. There was a certain resemblance to a thumb screw.

Eddie closed his hands over Jeff's. "*Like* is a tricky concept sometimes. I don't exactly enjoy it when it's being tightened. It bloody well hurts, but there's a kind of pleasure in that too. And it's fucking sexy to be at someone's mercy like that, because if it was tightened too far, it could do some serious damage. Takes a huge amount of trust for me to get this one out with someone else."

Jeff's eyes widened. "Do you want me... I mean, would you let me use it on you?"

"I'd love you to. Just go slowly. Not more than a half turn at a time. And once I've reached the point when I'm pleading with you to stop, no more than one more half turn. And don't leave it on for longer than about thirty minutes, max."

"You need me to set a timer?"

"Nah. It should be okay for the time it takes you to either shag me silly or beat the crap out of my arse." Eddie showed Jeff how to operate the quick-release catch. What with the way Jeff's breath had sped up, he thought he was about to get thrown onto the bed and trussed up right away, but Jeff held on and seemed to concentrate for the rest of Eddie's little toy talk. He seemed interested in the cock rings—especially the ones that went round both balls and cock—and out of the various nipple clamps Eddie had packed, he was definitely drawn to the huge, fierce-looking ones. "They're engineered so they get tighter as you pull on them," Eddie explained after clipping one on the end of Jeff's finger. He yanked on the cord to demonstrate.

"Ow! For fuck's sake." Jeff released it and stuck his finger in his mouth.

"Lightweight. You should try one on your nipple. Or clamped over your foreskin. Or on the loose skin behind your balls."

Jeff was definitely looking green around the gills. "I think I'll stick to your nipples."

"Probably a good idea. For now." Although Eddie wanted to beg Jeff to use them everywhere, if this was to be their last session in bed like this. But no, they'd have their hotel next weekend too. Eddie could pack all the toys he still wanted Jeff to use, couldn't he? For one last festival of kink. A farewell fuck.

"Did you bring the cuffs?" Jeff asked, and Eddie fished them out of the case. "Put them on. Wrists and ankles."

Jeff began gathering up the toys. Oh. Weren't they going to use any of them? Eddie did his best to smother his disappointment. After all, it wasn't like Jeff was gay. Although he did do a bloody good impression of being bi-as-you-like.

But then he noticed Jeff lining up some of the toys on the top of his chest of drawers.

Eddie smothered a smile and bent down to buckle up his ankle cuffs.

Chapter Twenty-two

Tying Eddie to the bed went much faster than it had the previous week. Jeff glanced at the clock. Okay, maybe not that much faster, but definitely smoother. He wasn't as jumpy as last time, and he handled the rope confidently, making deft knots like he'd learnt to when he was a kid. If only his Scout leader could see him now, putting his highwayman's hitch to good use. Jeff tugged carefully on the end before lifting the rope to where spread-eagled Eddie could see it. "This is a quick-release pull. Should you need it for any reason."

Eddie raised his eyebrows. "That's nice of you, but I've never met a man who's given me so much I needed to escape."

"I'm not thinking of that. It's just in case I, you know, if anything should happen to me. Wouldn't want my mum finding you tied to my bed while I'm dead on the floor." He thought about that some more. "And if I did collapse for any reason, I'd want you to be able to dial 999."

Eddie's brow crinkled. "Are you feeling all right? Is there something I should know about? A health condition?"

"I'm fine." Jeff flexed his muscles, tempted to drop down and do some press-ups, just to show Eddie how fine he was. "I've just been reading up on scene safety. You know. Responsible Dom stuff." He didn't mention he'd been paying special attention to breath play. The website had strongly recommended that a good Dom would let the sub bring that up, should it be something they wanted to try. And besides, admitting you wanted to choke someone had to be creepy for them, didn't it? Jeff would certainly run a mile or ten if someone said that to him.

Especially if he was tied up at the time.

Although, in that case, he probably wouldn't be able to run anywhere. Hence the quick-release tie.

"You've been doing your homework. Even though I didn't set you any. I like that." Eddie was studying him in a way that made Jeff want to go and hide in the wardrobe, but he brazened it out instead and knelt down to fetch his homemade spreader bar from under the bed. Eddie's eyes darkened in response.

"I've been reading about these. Ways to use them. And I thought it might be more interesting than having you in four-point restraints. Gives me more access." Access to the bits of Eddie Jeff really hadn't wanted to go near to begin with. Funny how a few short weeks had desensitised him. He had a good ogle at Eddie's cock and balls. His dick was straining up, all ripe and inviting, and his balls dangled beneath, plump and juicy looking. Jeff's own cock and balls got all worked up over it, making him think they must be in league with his eyes and somehow his brain had been left out of the loop.

That would certainly explain why he felt like such a clueless moron around Eddie, but at least he was getting better at acting like he knew what was going on. He had to maintain the impression of always being in charge. Even when he knew the man he was with could probably lead him around by the balls, should he decide to.

Even when he was bloody desperate to taste him. But Doms didn't do all that, did they? And straight ones certainly didn't suck cock. Jeff was pretty sure about that, even if it was all he could cling to in a stormy sea of desire. He anchored himself more firmly by concentrating on the spreader bar. He'd screwed an eye-hook into each end of the length of broom handle, and then attached trigger clips using split rings. It was pretty bloody satisfying to attach it to Eddie's ankle cuffs and confirm it worked every bit as well as the fancy, store-bought one Eddie had shown him the previous week.

Eddie flexed his legs and grinned. "What are you going to do to me now you've got me at your mercy?"

"I haven't finished with tying you up yet." Jeff rooted around under the bed for the collar he'd bought, then realised his mistake. "Shit. I should have put this on you first."

Eddie gasped when he saw what Jeff was holding. "Is that a collar?"

"Yeah. You got a problem with that?"

"I haven't. But some people in the scene give them a real significance. You should definitely check how someone feels about collars before springing one on them."

"Shit. Sorry." This whole BDSM thing was a bloody minefield at times.

"Nah, don't worry. I'm fine with it. Worn a collar plenty of times."

"Oh yeah?"

"Been led around on a lead too."

"You like that, do you?"

"It's better in public. I mean, not in public, public, but in a club. Yeah, it's fucking sexy when everyone can see you're owned like that."

Jeff couldn't imagine anything more embarrassing. "Wouldn't let anyone do that to me."

"Yeah, but that's because you're not a depraved submissive with a humiliation kink." Eddie stuck his tongue out and winked, which made him look kind of cute.

Oh God. Now Jeff was finding men "cute".

No, not *men*. One very specific man. Whew. Jeff distracted himself by buckling the collar round Eddie's neck, yanking more roughly than he strictly needed to. Eddie's Adam's apple bobbed. "Not too tight," he warned.

"I'll decide when it's tight enough." Jeff made his voice all growly, but he did leave a finger under the collar when tightening the buckle, just to make sure it wasn't too snug. "There. You like that, bitch?"

"Yes, Sir."

"Hmm. Well hopefully you won't like this quite so much." Jeff yanked on the spreader bar, forcing Eddie's knees up. He'd put in a third eye-hook and another trigger clip, exactly halfway along the bar, but no matter how much he bent Eddie in half, he couldn't make it quite reach the D ring on the collar. Damn it, he was going to need that extra length of chain after all. "Stay like that, bitch," he ordered and smothered a smile as Eddie cursed and visibly struggled to keep his legs up.

The chain was in the crate under the bed, and Jeff grabbed it, along with the big bottle of lube he'd bought. It looked like gay stuff, what with the picture of Greek guys up to no good on the label. Better yet, it had a squirty dispenser top just like bottles of liquid soap did, so it would be easier to use than that bloody tub of Eddie's.

"I see you've been planning ahead."

"Yep." Jeff attached the chain clip to Eddie's collar and forced the spreader bar as close as he could. Eddie grunted, his knees almost touching the pillow either side of him, and his arse pointed high in the air. Jeff clipped the bar to the chain and then stood back to admire his handiwork. Fuck it. He wanted a picture. Something to remember this by. "Smile," he ordered when he'd pulled out his phone. "No, wait, scream."

Eddie stared at the phone, and for one horrible moment, Jeff thought he was going to refuse, but then he threw his head back, slitted his eyes and pulled one of the most convincing orgasm faces Jeff had ever seen. Fuck that was sexy. He took several photos, kneeling above Eddie to get as much of his face in the shot as possible. Then he took a few from the foot of the bed, giving him a great view of Eddie's hole. Bloody hell, it needed filling. Jeff's cock twitched at the thought of burying himself deep in there. He turned to the toys. He should use one of those first. Get something in there while he tortured Eddie's cock and balls.

The beads were the first thing he landed on. The set Eddie had brought round were stainless steel again—he seemed to have a thing for metal and glass rather than silicone—and they were way, way larger than the ones Jeff had seen in sex shops. Also, far more rigid. For some reason, when he'd first heard about anal beads, he'd imagined them attached together by a cord, like a mutant necklace. Instead, they resembled a stylised Christmas tree, stacked up in ever decreasing height on a foot-long steel pole. The lowest bead was fatter than Jeff's cock, although only just, he was pleased to note. Not like that black dildo, which had gone back in the case. Toys like that could make a man feel inadequate. Jeff palmed his dick through his shorts, wishing he'd thought to get a bit of a blowjob in before tying Eddie up like that. The angle would be impossible now. Not without releasing the clip on the collar, and he didn't want to do that just yet. Fuck it. Jeff could wait. It would make it all the better when he finally did get to stick his dick inside Eddie.

He squirted a good load of lube on his fingers and took a quick swipe over Eddie's hole. Then he took a slower one, exploring the feel of that twitching ring of muscle. Last time he hadn't done this. He'd just played with the plug, and ever since he'd been wondering what it would actually feel like to finger Eddie. Screw it. Only one way to find out. He stuck the tip of one finger in, and Eddie immediately clamped down.

Jeff's dick pulsed like it was the part of him being squeezed. Stupid thing. Jeff told it to wait its turn, as he circled that fingertip around. He fluttered it then—the same way he used to when fingering Sarah—and it seemed to have the same effect in arseholes as it did in a pussy. By which he meant Eddie arched off the bed, gibbering something unintelligible. Oh yeah, that was fun. Jeff played with his fingers some more, driving Eddie wild, until he judged it time to introduce the beads.

The first two beads slid in easily. The third required a bit more pressure, and the fourth had to be pumped in a few times until Eddie's ring stretched to take it. It was mesmerising, watching Eddie's hole stretch. Jeff pulled the fourth bead back out again just so he could watch it go in a second time. The soundtrack Eddie was providing was pretty bloody sexy too. All choked-off whimpers and raspy "Oh Gods". And the fact he couldn't do a thing to stop Jeff was a real turn-on.

No, wait. It was the fact he'd trusted Jeff enough to let himself be tied up like that that was the real turn-on. Thank fuck for dirty little painsluts.

Thinking of pain…

Jeff slapped Eddie's bum hard, watching the way his hole twitched. He did it again and this time forced the fifth and final bead up against it. Yep, there was a definite response. He got up nice and close and slapped with one hand while the other kept up the pressure on the bead. Eddie cried out as Jeff pressed harder, and then the bead popped inside.

"You like that, slut?"

Eddie squirmed. "God, fuck, ow, fuck. Good. So good."

Jeff played with the beads for a few more minutes, popping the last bead in and out. It seemed to get easier all the time. Made him wonder how many of his fingers he'd have been able to get in there, had he kept going. "You ever been fisted?" he asked.

"Why? You want to try?" Eddie panted.

"Just curious. Maybe." If Eddie responded like he had with the beads, it would be a huge amount of fun for Jeff. He squished his fist up as narrow as it would go. Still an awful lot wider than that last bead. Wider even than the monster dildo. "Think my hands might be too big, though."

"You'll be fine. Lots of lube. Gloves. Have a go if you want. Just take it slow."

"Maybe I will. But not yet." Jeff leaned over and grabbed a couple more toys from the chest of drawers. "Got some other things I want to try first." He held up the nipple clamps and examined the loops at the handle end of them. Eddie had said they got tighter if pulled on, and so Jeff had imagined being the one to yank on them, but what if he got Eddie to do that for him, so Jeff's hands were free to torture him elsewhere? He turned to examine the distance between Eddie's chest and the spreader bar. Yep, that should work.

First he needed to unclip Eddie's ankles. He did one, then slipped the loop of the clamp onto the end before clipping Eddie's ankle back again.

"Huh? What are you doing?" Eddie's eyes weren't really focused.

"What do you think?"

Eddie blinked a few times, and his pupils widened. "Oh no."

"Oh yes."

"No, no, no. That's not fair."

"Who said anything about me playing fair? Where's the fun in that?"

"You total fucking bastard."

"That's Sir Bastard to you." Jeff slid the other clamp onto the other end of the spreader bar before reattaching Eddie's ankle.

"Oh please, no." Eddie's last "no" trailed off breathily, and it didn't sound anything much like a no at all. It sounded more like a moan of pleasure. And since he hadn't safeworded, Jeff was guessing this was one of those times when a no could safely be ignored.

The clamps dangled from the bar, the jaws of them just an inch or so above Eddie's chest. Right. Now Jeff had to work out how to get them on Eddie's nipples. Fuck. Maybe he should have done it the other way around. Nipples first, bar second. He'd remember that for next time. Eventually he managed to get one hand around behind Eddie's leg to grab hold of his nipple and squeeze it up towards the clamp, while the other hand pressed the clamp so the jaws opened. It took him a couple of tries to get the meat of Eddie's nipple between the jaws, but when he did, Eddie yelped.

"Fuck. Ow. You fucking bastard. Sir Bastard. Whatever."

"Shut up and take it, bitch. I thought you said you liked pain."

"I do. Fuck. Arrrgh!" That was the other clamp going on. Eddie's complaining might have bothered Jeff if it weren't for the fact the man's dick was hard as blackthorn and digging into Jeff's arm as he leaned over.

"How's that?" Jeff asked, tilting the spreader bar down to one side so it pulled on the clamp on the opposite side of Eddie's chest.

"Nnngh! You're a cruel bastard, sir." But Eddie sounded approving rather than upset, breathing flirtatiousness into the words. "I fucking hate you sometimes."

"So you keep saying."

"Did I tell you I love it when you're mean to me?"

"You don't need to. I can tell you do." Jeff took hold of Eddie's cock and gave it a few hard tugs.

"Oh yeah. So good. Owww!" Eddie had squirmed with pleasure, and Jeff watched as the spreader bar tilted and tugged on his nipple clamps.

"This will give you pleasure and pain. All mixed up together so you don't know where one ends and the other begins." He pumped on the anal beads with one hand, while the other massaged Eddie's cock. Jeff was stimulating Eddie's nipples, cock and arse, but what about his bollocks? Jeff let go of the beads to give them a firm squeeze.

Eddie wheezed a yelp in response, arching his back so his left nipple stretched out. He whimpered and settled back down again. This gorgeous flush had covered his chest and spread up his neck, and he was dripping with sweat. And the best bit was, Jeff was still totally in control. Not just of Eddie, but of himself. He held his hand to his chest. Yep. His heartbeat was faster than usual, but not too fast. He was feeling relaxed rather than frantic. Yes, he wanted to get inside Eddie very much indeed, but he could wait a while. Especially if that meant he got to torture him some more.

He wanted Eddie worked into a state by the time he fucked him. He wanted him so desperate to come, he could do it at a word. And so he told Eddie that while squeezing his balls.

"Fuck, yeah, please. Do it."

Jeff glanced back at the toys on the chest. The ball-crusher press was a scary-looking thing, but it would mean he'd be able to properly concentrate on Eddie's arse and cock, and not have to worry about his balls dangling around, all lonely and neglected.

Getting it on was a little tricky, especially with the way Eddie arched and protested, but eventually Jeff had the cold steel cylinder clamped shut, trapping Eddie's balls inside. He tugged down on it a little, watching the strip of skin at the top stretch.

"Remember," Eddie rasped. "Just a quarter turn at a time."

"You said a half turn."

"Changed my mind. Sir."

Jeff smiled as he met Eddie's challenging gaze. "I'll tell you what I'm going to do. I'm going to turn this thing really slowly. So slowly a dirty pain slut like you is going to be begging for more. But I'm going to keep on going until you're begging me to stop. And then I'm going to get to work on your arse. I'm going to see how many fingers I can get up there, and if you're a good boy and open up for me, I'm going to give you my whole fist. How does that sound?"

"Fuck me!" Eddie moaned, breathlessly.

"I'll fuck you after. I'll open up your arse with my fist, and then I'll fuck right into it, so deep you can feel me banging into your throat. How's that?"

"Yes. God, yes." Eddie was gabbling and nodding his head, and Jeff felt a surge of pride. Not just in himself for finally getting the hang of this domming and dirty talk, but in Eddie for being so bloody brave. He had to be in a huge amount of pain from those clamps already, yet there he was, begging for Jeff to crush his balls and fist him. What a trouper.

Jeff wound the press with an almost glacial slowness. But he didn't want to hurry. Not when this was making Eddie's toes curl and his head thrash. Even his cock was joining in on the fun, dripping onto his belly. The sparse hair there was slick with sweat, and if Jeff could have reached in without risking knocking the spreader bar and causing even more pain, he would have licked him there. As it was, Jeff had to settle for licking his lips.

Although there was one place he could still lick... As he twisted the press, Jeff stared at Eddie's hole. It was looking pink and puffy now that Jeff had played with the beads for a while. He could yank them all out and lick it. He hadn't realised blokes did that to each other, but in his searches for gay BDSM video clips, he'd found one where the Dom was licking his own spunk out of a well-fucked sub. It had made him hot and cold all over, and he'd barely been able to watch it. He'd never risk screwing Eddie without a condom, but in principle, the licking probably wasn't so bad. Eddie was clean. He could see that. And the way that sub had reacted in the video was just obscene.

It couldn't be so very different to giving head to a woman. Less juicy, but then again, there was all that lube oozing out. Jeff swiped his finger through it and licked the tip.

Okay, maybe not. That tasted horribly sweet and made his tongue feel numb. Revolting. He'd have to do it before getting any lube in there. Next time.

The last time.

But he didn't want to dwell on that. He wanted to work on Eddie. The man whose voice was now so hoarse Jeff could barely understand him, but he seemed to be begging him to stop. Jeff let go of the press carefully, and took hold of Eddie's cock with one hand—still hard, thankfully—reaching in carefully to cup his jaw with the other. "You okay?"

"Yeah, fuck, yeah. Think so. Phew!" Eddie's eyes finally focused on Jeff's, and he smiled weakly. "Knew you'd be good at this. Knew it from the start."

It was kind of humbling, to know that finally someone believed in him. Jeff's eyes stung. Must have been the sweat dripping into them. "Next you're going to know you can take my fist." He held it up in front of Eddie

Eddie groaned, but his pupils dilated. "Make sure you don't get it into a fist until you're way inside. Fingers first, not knuckles."

"I know. I've been doing my research."

"And plenty of lube. And a glove. Shit. We don't have any gloves."

"Don't worry. I've got gloves."

"Not washing-up ones. You need the thin ones. Like doctors have."

"Yeah. I've got them."

"Knew you were a pervert."

"Absolutely." Jeff didn't mention they were for cleaning the toilet, as it just didn't sound all that sexy. "I'll be back in just a moment. You okay being left like that?"

"Yeah. Don't be long, though."

Jeff raced down the stairs and dug around in the under-sink cupboard. There they were. He pulled a single glove on as he ran up the stairs, not wanting to waste a moment. Or to give Eddie time to change his mind.

Eddie was still lying there. He looked so fucking sexy, his balls in a steel can and his nipples stretched out by the clamps, arms and legs spread wide by the cuffs and bar and rope. And that collar round his neck! Jeff picked up his phone and snapped a few more pictures. Wank fodder for the week ahead. Better than anything you could find online.

"You'll have to send those to me," Eddie rasped.

"You'd get off on that, would you? Seeing yourself like this? All spread open, used and abused."

"Too right."

"Dirty bitch." Jeff slapped Eddie's arse and yanked on the beads.

"Fuck, fuck, fuck!" Eddie yelled as the beads tore out of him. "Fuck, that's good. Again!"

"You don't get to choose. You just get to lie there and take what I give to you. And next I'm giving you a surprise."

For a moment Jeff thought Eddie was going to protest, but then he gave him a slow smile.

Yeah. What a trouper.

"Surprises are good. I like surprises." Eddie thought he did, anyway. "It had better be a good one, though."

"It should be."

Eddie heard a drawer open and shut, but because of being tied up, he couldn't crane his head to get a look at whatever Jeff was fetching. The mattress dipped as Jeff climbed back on, and then Eddie felt whatever it was at his hole. It was moist and cool. Some kind of buttplug? Jeff pushed it inside a little way, then eased it out and circled it round.

"Mmm, that's nice. What is it?" Eddie was starting to be lulled by the sensation when the burn started to hit him. "Oh my God. Is that ginger?" Of course it was bloody ginger. Nothing else felt quite like it. He started to clench up, but Jeff was already pushing the ginger root back into him.

Jeff chuckled. "You told me to buy some. Seemed a shame to let it go to waste."

Eddie tried to calm his breathing. The ginger heat was amazing, but only for a while. "You've got to be really careful not to lose it inside me. Seriously. It fucking kills if it's left in for too long."

Jeff plunged the root deeper inside him. "Don't worry. I've been reading up on figging. I know what to do. You just trust me. Give in and enjoy yourself."

Eddie took a few more deep breaths and started to relax into the sensation again. He knew he'd be whimpering with pain in a few minutes, but for now it was good. So fucking good. If he could just let go and trust Jeff. And stay still, because every time he wriggled his nipple clamps squeezed tighter. Yeah, Jeff was turning out to be a wonderfully creative sadist. Curse him.

The ginger was becoming unbearable when Jeff finally pulled it out. Of course, that didn't stop the burn. That would keep building for a while yet, but he was grateful for another squirt of lube to cool him down.

"Ahh, thank you, Sir."

"Good boy. You've been such a good boy. You ready for more?"

"No more ginger."

"No. Now you get my fingers. I'm going to fist you, and you're going to take it all." Jeff prodded some fingers inside. They slid in easily, reactivating the ginger burn, but in a fucking gorgeous way.

Eddie moaned with pleasure.

"You like that, bitch?"

"Yessir." Eddie's voice came out thick. "How many's that?" He could never tell by feel alone.

"Just two. Here's the third." That was a bit more of a challenge for Eddie to relax into, but Jeff persisted and eventually it slid in too.

Now Eddie's attention was entirely focused on the stretching burn in his arse. He'd never have chosen to have a figging right before a fisting, but it was actually working quite well, taking away some of the sharper, stinging pain and replacing it with a hotter, fiery pain. He could deal with that better. At least, he kept telling himself that as Jeff worked his hand.

"I've got four fingers in you now. Can you feel that? All four. I'm going in right up to my knuckles. Just my thumb to fit in now. You think you can take my thumb?"

No! But Eddie nodded anyway. "Please. Yessir, please. Now." It felt so fucking good, being stretched that wide. Pain and pleasure blew away his awareness of everything else.

"Jesus fuck. That's so sexy," Jeff was saying. "I've got my thumb in there too. Almost there. You've just got to relax a little bit more for me. You can do that, can't you? You can be a good boy and let me in."

Eddie whimpered every time Jeff plunged his hand in. He couldn't take it. Those knuckles were just too fat. But he wanted to. God, how he wanted to. "Yes," he found himself saying. "Yes. Do it. Come on." He repeated the mantra over and over, and with a bright burst of pain, Jeff's fist pushed all the way inside him.

"Oh my God. I did it. You did it."

Eddie panted desperately, so full he could barely breathe, let alone speak. He wanted Jeff to take his hand out, and he wanted him to plunge in deeper. But Jeff kept perfectly still, and eventually Eddie managed to get himself back under some kind of control.

He managed to open his eyes and peered past the chains and spreader bar at Jeff, who was staring down at Eddie's arse. Jeff appeared to be as in awe of the whole thing as Eddie was. "I can feel your heartbeat," Jeff said. "Or maybe it's your pulse, I don't know. I've never felt anything like it."

"Feels great," Eddie managed to force out.

"Can I move now?"

"Yeah. Move. Please." Eddie almost regretted giving Jeff permission when he started pulling his fist back out again—the stretch!—but then Jeff plunged back in, and this time the sting of his knuckles was more bearable. And he kept doing it, until Eddie was sobbing with the mingled pleasure and pain, wanting it to go on forever and to stop right now. His nipples burned as he writhed, his balls throbbed in the press, and it was all too much.

"Enough! Stop," he pleaded. His safeword was on the tip of his tongue, but then Jeff withdrew completely.

Eddie moaned, regretting it already as the exquisite fullness gave way to an empty void, but he had to something about his balls. "Please. The press. Take it off."

"God, sorry. Of course." Jeff did something, and blood rushed back into Eddie's balls, the pain of it making him cry out. He was going to come if he wasn't careful.

"Please. Fuck me. Please. I want to come. You inside me."

Jeff went to undo one of Eddie's ankle clips, and he protested. "No, like this."

"Are you sure you'll be comfortable?"

"No, but it's so fucking sexy. Please." Comfort was overrated. During sex, at any rate. "Do me hard and fast."

"You don't get to give the orders." Jeff was gazing at him through the tangle of legs, clamps, chain and spreader bar. The intensity of his gaze made Eddie feel even more naked and debauched. "But lucky for you, I'm fucking desperate to give you a good pounding."

Eddie had to wait for an age while Jeff went to get suited up, although it had probably only been a few seconds. And then Jeff was back, pushing into him with brute force. "This how you want it, bitch?"

"Yes, yes, like that." Eddie's balls throbbed, his nipples burned, and his arse was tender from the combination of ginger and Jeff's fist, but all those aches and pains only turned him on more. He concentrated on them, and on the glorious thrusting of Jeff's cock. He was holding on to Eddie's legs and slamming in hard. So hard Eddie was pushed up the bed so his head slammed against the headboard.

"Oh God!" Jeff said. "Gonna come. You first." His face contorted in what looked an awful lot like pain. "Come on, bitch. Shoot all over yourself. Do it. Now."

Eddie didn't even need to touch himself. That command, along with Jeff nailing his prostate, set off a chain reaction inside him. His balls hurt so good as he shot, drenching himself in come.

"Yeah, that's it," Jeff said. "Good boy. So fucking good. Feeling you come."

Eddie forced his eyes open to watch Jeff as his face went slack, and he groaned, hips jerking.

"So fucking good," Jeff mumbled, leaning heavily against Eddie's legs.

Eddie hissed. There was good pain and there was bad pain, and now he'd come, the bad pain was making itself known above the rush of endorphins.

"God, sorry." Jeff had forced himself up onto his knees and was fumbling with the spreader bar.

One of Eddie's nipples screamed in protest. "Clamps first!" he demanded.

"Yep. Right. Uh, how do these things work?"

After a few moments of mind-bending pain and sobbed instructions, Jeff finally released both of Eddie's nipples, followed in quick succession by the collar, bar, arm and leg cuffs. Eddie couldn't move. He just let his limbs fall to the mattress, powerless to stop them. "Ungh," seemed to be the only thing he could manage to say right now, and he wasn't even sure it was a proper word.

He tried again. "Ugg." No, those were boots. "Hug." That was it. What he wanted.

And Jeff seemed to understand him this time, because the next thing Eddie knew was a pair of powerful arms wrapping round him, and being pulled over to pillow his head on a beautifully furry chest.

"That was amazing," Jeff said softly, and Eddie could hear his voice rumbling inside his chest. "Thank you."

"Meant to be my line," he mumbled before giving in to the inevitable and sleeping.

Chapter Twenty-three

Jeff woke to the sound of birdsong and a soft breeze stirring the curtains. That wasn't particularly unusual. What was unusual was the warm body pressed up against his back.

And more to the point, the hard cock pressed up against his arse.

Jeff lay there, not moving, trying to work out whether or not he liked it. There was something dangerous and exciting about the feel of Eddie's erection resting there. Like he was only a few inches away from breaching Jeff's most holy of holies. And that was also terrifying, because wouldn't it hurt like buggery? Well, of course it would. It bloody well *was* buggery.

But buggery didn't seem to hurt Eddie. And, to be honest, given the size of what came out of Jeff's arse some mornings, Eddie's cock should be able to slip in easily enough.

The thought made him squirm. He didn't know whether to push back against Eddie or to roll away. But he'd been reading up on anal sex—thank fuck for the Internet—and it seemed even straight blokes sometimes liked a bit of action up the back passage. He'd spent an uneasy half hour watching home videos of blokes being "pegged" by their girlfriends, and hadn't known whether he was more turned on by the submissive men or the girls with strap-ons. That was one confusing, hot and sweaty wank session. No, sorry, *research* session.

Jeff wriggled some more, unable to help himself as his own dick stiffened right up to match Eddie's. Eddie just snuffled against his neck, his breathing still slow and deep.

If Eddie started humping Jeff's bum in his sleep, he wouldn't move. Well, he would if there was any danger of penetration going on, but he'd just lie there and take a frot against his arse crack. It wouldn't mean he was gay or anything. Just a little bit bi. And he wouldn't be being submissive if Eddie was asleep. Jeff was fairly sure it was impossible to dominate if you didn't have any of your conscious brain involved.

And so that was why he didn't mind being the little spoon. It was kind of nice having Eddie's heavy leg draped over his, and the gusts of warm breath against the back of his neck. He'd certainly never felt like this with Sarah. He'd always been the big spoon. Back when spooning was still in the picture. It hadn't been welcomed for the last couple of years.

He probably should have realised something was very wrong back then, but he'd just slowly become used to the idea that the sex and intimacy were tailing off the longer they spent together, and he hadn't realised quite how much he'd lost until he tried to cuddle up to her one night and she ended up getting so grumpy with him, she buggered off to the spare room so she could get a "decent night's sleep".

And she'd stayed sleeping in there for the last six months of their relationship.

Somehow, Jeff didn't think Eddie would do something like that. Eddie was an altogether more tactile kind of person. And if there was a problem, Eddie would tell him about it. He wouldn't expect Jeff to somehow be able to figure out what it was from spiky body language and cryptic messages left on the fridge.

Although those might genuinely have been shopping lists.

Eddie nuzzled a bit closer and murmured something sleepy sounding.

Jeff's hips twitched without his say-so, pushing his arse back against Eddie's cock. Oh my God, it was nestling right in the crack now. Hot and damp and heavy. Shudders quaked up and down Jeff's spine. Felt like he was falling. Spinning out of control into some new state of being. And he just wanted to throw his arms out and enjoy the ride.

Although that was just a figure of speech. If he threw his arms out now, he'd probably wake up Eddie and end up pitching the duvet onto the floor. Sexy snuggling wouldn't be nearly as much fun in the cool morning air.

A sound scraped across Jeff's consciousness. A sound that shouldn't have been there. A key in the front door.

Oh fuck! There were only two people who had access to his spare key—his folks—and he didn't want either of them seeing Eddie here. He sat bolt upright. The clock read 9:30. Shit, had they really slept in that late?

"Mmm, come back to bed," Eddie mumbled sleepily.

"Shhh!" Jeff clapped his hand over Eddie's mouth. Eddie's eyes widened, then he blinked the sleep out of them.

Footsteps sounded on the bottom of the stairs.

"Shit. Oh shit." Jeff was paralysed. He had to do something. Now.

"Jeff sweetheart? You still in bed?"

"Hang on, Mum. I'm coming down."

He leapt out of bed and pulled on his dressing gown.

Eddie was propped up on his elbows now, giving Jeff a look that wasn't exactly a challenge but definitely questioning.

"Just, erm, be quiet for a bit, yeah? I'll get rid of her."

Eddie rolled his eyes and slumped back onto the pillows. Jeff made a quick scan of the room. Nope. Even if he hid Eddie in the wardrobe or under the bed, there was still way too much kinky stuff on show for his mum's eyes. There were cuffs tied to the bedstead, for fuck's sake. "Back soon," he promised and nipped out the door.

His mum was halfway up the stairs. "I heard voices. You got a girl up there, Jeff White? Well, come on, let me meet her."

"I said I'd come down, Mum. For Christ's sake, give a man a bit of privacy. What are you doing here anyway? It's not cleaning day."

"Well, that's a charming welcome." Mags huffed and walked up the rest of the stairs. Jeff blocked the bedroom door with his body. "I was going to make you both a cup of tea, but I reckon you can get your own now. Anyway, you're a dark horse. You never told me you was seeing a girl this weekend."

"Mum, keep it down."

"What? You ashamed of your old mum now? Or is it her? Had a case of the beer goggles last night, did you?" She gave a dirty laugh. "Your little brother certainly brought a few tramps home in his time."

He bloody well would be ashamed of her if she kept this up. "No. She's sleeping. Come on, downstairs."

Mags gave the bedroom door a longing look and spoke in a stage whisper. "Well, if this is going to be serious, I want you to bring her round for lunch later. Been dying to see you settled down with a nice girl. Not like that Sarah turned out to be. Snotty cow. Come on, you bring her over so me and your dad can make sure she's good enough for you."

"She's got to go home before then."

"Why? Oh Jeff, she isn't married, is she?"

"What? No! Just, oh come on. Downstairs. It's none of your business. I'm a grown man, for fuck's sake. And we need to have words about you just letting yourself in here without warning me."

"I sent you a text half an hour ago. It's not my fault you're knackered after a night of passion." At last Mags set off down the stairs, saying something about needing to borrow a pair of secateurs. The reason for her visit, apparently. Jeff gave the bedroom door one last guilty glance and set off after her.

Chapter Twenty-four

Eddie slumped back onto the bed and tried not to give in to disappointment, but it proved impossible. He should have known Jeff wasn't ready to own up to loving a man. Well, okay, shagging a man at any rate. Love didn't come into it, what with all that romantic nonsense being nothing but a short-term hormonal imbalance.

Although that didn't explain why his heart had screamed in protest when Jeff fobbed his mum off, calling Eddie a "she".

No, he had to admit it, he wanted more out of Jeff than that. He wanted a chance to have a proper relationship and see where it led. To see if he could, in fact, fall in love, given the opportunity.

But it was abundantly clear what Jeff was really after, and while Eddie might be a great match for him in many ways, he was short a pair of breasts, and had that whole inconvenient cock-and-balls thing going on between his legs. Maybe if he'd been one of those blokes who got a kick out of cross-dressing, then they could have worked something out. He could have pretended to be "Edwina" until Jeff's family got to know him, and once he'd charmed his way into their hearts, he could have revealed his true identity.

Although to be honest, that probably wouldn't have worked. Even the best drag artists weren't one hundred percent convincing when you got up close. The Adam's apple was always a giveaway, as was the size of their hands. No, it would never have worked. Eddie let that daydream fly away on a cloud of perfume.

And if Eddie couldn't make himself female, and Jeff wouldn't come out, there was absolutely no way they could be together, beyond the odd snatched night here and there.

Eddie wasn't about to be someone's dirty little secret. Yes, the sex was amazing, but he wanted a man who was proud to be with him. Not someone who lied and hid him behind closed doors. He was getting too old for that shit.

Eddie scowled at the door in question and slowly, carefully, eased himself out of bed. The springs made a noise, but hopefully it wouldn't be audible downstairs. His shorts were lying by the bed, and he'd packed a spare T-shirt in his case.

By the time he was dressed, he could still hear muffled voices downstairs. Impossible to tell what they were saying, but he'd probably end up being heard if he tried to open the door and listen in. And then Jeff's mum would charge up here, and Jeff would be busted, and he'd never forgive Eddie for forcing him out of the closet in such a spectacular fashion.

For a brief moment, Eddie entertained the idea of just walking down there and kissing Jeff in front of his mum. He could say good-bye and stroll on out, leaving Jeff to deal with the fallout. The idea had a lot going for it. Revenge at being referred to as a "she" for a start. And it might help Jeff get over the whole "I'm straight" lie he'd been telling himself and everyone else who would listen.

Eddie paused with his hand on the door handle. He could stride on down there and destroy Jeff's carefully constructed world, but it wouldn't be fair. Who knew what kind of shit Jeff would have to deal with as a result? His dad sounded like a total bigot. And besides, outing people against their will was wrong, plain and simple. Yes, probably universal acceptance and end to homophobia would come around sooner if gay sports stars and celebrities didn't lie through their teeth, but they had to find the courage to come out by themselves. It didn't mean much, otherwise. Tom Daley's YouTube confession must have been a hell of a lot more inspiring to young gay men than poor old George Michael's scandalous arrest had been for Eddie's generation.

Although it had had the bonus of making public toilets seem incredibly glamorous and exciting for a short while.

The voices downstairs grew louder—they must have been walking through the living room. Eddie pressed his ear to the door.

"—don't know why you don't just wake her up and bring her down, love. I'm not that scary, am I?" Jeff's mum was saying.

"Maybe I want her to keep the bed warm. You think about that?"

"Okay, okay. Spare me the details. I'm just saying, though, I want you to pass on the invitation for lunch. Anyone you're interested in is welcome at our table, you know that. There's always room for one or two more, and I can always chuck in a few more veg to stretch the meat out further."

"Thanks, Mum. I'll mention it, but don't get your hopes up."

There was a sound of kissing, and Jeff grunted like he was being hugged tight around the middle. Eddie's chest panged. He'd had hugs like that off his stepmum many a time, but never from his real mum, who just air-kissed and held his shoulders with her carefully manicured talons. Jeff didn't know how lucky he was, having someone like that to look out for him. He'd bet anything she was all grey-haired and mumsy, in a cosy cardigan and sensible skirt. Eddie crept over to the window and peeped through a crack in the curtains. Moments later, a small, blonde woman in leopard-print leggings and an alarming sequinned T-shirt appeared on the path, tottering along on a pair of gold high-heeled sandals.

Okaay. Good thing he hadn't bet anything on that, after all.

At the end of the garden path, she turned back to face the house, looking right up at Eddie. Shit. He closed the curtain a crack so that only his eye was peeking out.

Jeff's mum smirked and waggled her fingers up at him.

She couldn't have seen him. Not really. Just the movement.

Eddie kept stock-still, not even breathing until she'd turned back and started off down the road.

Phew. He was still calming his beating heart when Jeff clumped back up the stairs again.

"Oh, you're up."

Eddie turned to find Jeff pouting.

"I thought you'd still be in bed."

"I'm all wide awake now."

"Yeah, but being wide awake in bed can be fun too."

Eddie's dick stirred in interest, but the rest of him really wasn't in the mood anymore. "I should get going. Got lots to be getting on with."

"But it's Sunday."

"There's no such thing as a day off when you're self-employed."

"I don't work at the weekends."

"No. You have Sunday lunch with your loving family. Who would be ever so happy for you to invite me along. Oh, except not me, after all. They want you to invite your mythical girlfriend. Is that what you've been telling them all along? That I'm some bird you're seeing? And nothing serious either. Certainly not important enough to invite to a family meal."

Jeff frowned. "Come off it. I thought about inviting you as a friend, but they'd be bound to find it weird. I mean, aside from the sex, what have the two of us got in common anyway? They'd never understand why we were friends. And my dad, he'd know as soon as he clapped eyes on you, you was gay."

"And that would be a bad thing?"

"Of course it bloody well would. He's never had a good thing to say about gay blokes. Ever. He'd be muttering insults under his breath the whole meal. And that's the best-case scenario."

"You think I haven't had to deal with raving homophobes before? I know how to stand up to a bit of bullying. I've been out since I was sixteen, so I've had my fair share of it."

"Yeah, but you've never met my dad, and it would all get messy. Trust me. He'd end up arguing with Mum and me. You wouldn't want to be there."

Eddie fought down the urge to tell Jeff it was all a bit "messy" already. "Fine. Look, I'm just going to head off home. You can deal with your arsehole of a dad by yourself."

"He's not an arsehole." Jeff didn't sound too sure of himself.

"He certainly sounds like one." But what did he really know about the man, after all? Maybe Eddie was the one being the name-calling bully now. Shit. "Sorry, I'm being judgmental. I'm sure he has his good qualities too. He raised you, for a start."

Jeff gave a grim smile. "Yeah, but I think I turned out all right despite that."

"Maybe. I'll say one thing, though. I think you'd be a lot less mixed up in the head about your own sexuality if you hadn't had to deal with a homophobic bully as your male role model. Just something to think about."

Eddie could see he was about to outstay his welcome by the pained and resentful expression on Jeff's face. "I'll be off. Don't forget to book that hotel for next weekend. I'll send you the details of the club so you can find somewhere near. And hey..." He picked up his suitcase on the way to the door. "I had a great time last night. Just thought you should know."

Jeff really looked at him then. "You did?"

"I did." Eddie wiggled his arse a little. "Still feeling it too. Double bonus." He winked and headed on out of the door. He wasn't going to push his luck going for a kiss. Jeff was already floundering. He didn't want to push him hard and meet resistance. Because resistance in blokes like Jeff often came backed up with fist power.

Eddie wasn't about to risk ending it all like that. He wanted to part as good friends, not enemies.

Although, in actual fact, he didn't want to part at all.

Chapter Twenty-five

That week, the weather turned muggy, with hazy clouds trapping the heat of the day so that even at night, Jeff could find no escape. It was horrible weather for toiling outside, and even worse when you were in a bad mood.

Much as he wanted to blame his mood purely on the humidity, Jeff knew that was only half the reason he hadn't been sleeping properly. The things Eddie had said as he left kept swirling around in his mind. Jeff kept trying to compose a text to clear the air, but it was impossible to pin down his own feelings. He thought about simply sending Eddie the photos he'd taken of him all trussed up, but he wasn't sure how that would go down after the way they'd parted. And besides, he was paranoid about keeping them on his phone in case someone got hold of it and had a look, so he'd already downloaded them to a password-protected file on his computer and wiped them off the phone. In the end, he just booked a hotel and texted Eddie the details, asking if he wanted to meet there or drive down together.

Parking looks bad. Let's go in my car, Eddie responded.

Okay… Jeff stared at his phone. *Are we okay?*

We're fine. See you on Saturday. Can you be ready for five?

They arranged the timings, and Jeff didn't ask any more personal questions. *Just friends.* That was what Eddie had said, wasn't it? He'd said they could go as equals. Nobody would need to know their relationship.

But what about if Jeff wanted people to know? Not anyone local, of course, but in Bournemouth, in a kink club, he could test it out. See what it was like being gay for a night. They'd be an accepting crowd, used to seeing all kinds of stuff. You wouldn't get close-minded arseholes like Jeff's dad there. Hopefully.

With a plan in his head, Jeff got surfing online.

By the time Eddie pulled up outside on Friday afternoon, Jeff had almost worked himself up into chickening out of the whole thing. But since Eddie was driving, he'd decided on opening a cool can of liquid courage, and that had gone down rather too easily. He was halfway through his second can of Stella when Eddie honked the horn outside.

Eddie had the top down, so Jeff just tossed his suitcase over into the backseat before settling down, can between his knees. Eddie raised his eyebrows at it. "You're starting early."

"I'm allowed to. I've been slaving away in the heat all week."

"I'm not judging. Think I'll be joining you as soon as we get there. God, I hope the hotel has air-conditioning."

"It does." Jeff had checked. It also had a king-size bed and a hot tub, but he thought he'd save the surprise for later. He was looking forward to seeing Eddie's face when they walked through the door of their room.

Jeff had expected the drive down to be awkward, what with all the unsaid crap in his head, but Eddie kept up the lighthearted chatter about his week and childhood outings to the places they were driving through, and they had fun spotting peculiar place names. Sandy Balls was a favourite.

"Sounds painful," Eddie said. "And not in a good way."

Jeff chuckled. "Should be all right if it's Weymouth sand. That stuff's really soft." He'd loved holidaying there as a child, staying with his gran. In some ways, he'd liked it even better than their annual jaunt down to the Costa del Sol.

"I suppose so. Did you know their sand's so fine, it's only just big enough to be classified as sand. Any finer and it would be silt. That's why it's so beautiful for making sandcastles."

"You've been there?" Jeff couldn't hide his surprise. Weymouth was hardly the kind of posh resort he'd have expected Eddie to holiday in.

"Oh yeah. Used to go at least twice every summer. Had to visit my aunt."

"Me too. Well, not my aunt. My gran." It was good to discover they had that much in common, at least, and so they spent the next twenty miles swapping memories of the beach resort while the car whizzed through sleepy little villages crammed full of thatched cottages, like something you'd see on a jigsaw puzzle or Dorset souvenir tea towel.

Part of Jeff wished they were going to Weymouth instead of Bournemouth, so they could spend a lazy weekend exploring old haunts together. But a larger and more aggressive part of him was thrumming with nervous anticipation of the night ahead, and he wasn't about to suggest changing their plans. But as they drew closer to the seaside town, Eddie switched on his sat nav, and their conversation grew sparser while the roads grew busier.

Jeff had forgotten how built up Bournemouth was. It surely must have been big enough to be classed as a city these days, and the urban bustle and hectic traffic was a far cry from dozy little Hook St. Norton. But Eddie seemed to feel at home on the roads, navigating the traffic with only the occasional mild curse. It was a good thing they'd taken his car, as Jeff would have been spitting insults left, right and centre by now. The roads had far too many lanes, and the number of signs gave him a headache. Or maybe that was just him being dazzled by the headlights of the other cars as the sun slowly set.

But finally Eddie turned down a side street, and then into a car park, announcing, "Here we go. Oh, looks much nicer than I'd imagined."

"What's that supposed to mean?"

"Nothing. Just that I'd been picturing a traditional seaside B&B for some reason. This is a proper hotel. But really, I hope you didn't spend too much on it. I'd have been fine anywhere. I don't mind roughing it."

"Maybe I do, though."

Eddie lay his hand down on Jeff's thigh. "You're full of surprises, aren't you? Every time I start thinking you're just a typical straight bloke, you go and show me another side of you. You have hidden depths, you know."

This conversation had gone way out of Jeff's comfort zone now. Bloody good thing he'd never bought Eddie flowers, after all. "I just like a decent night's sleep, that's all. And I wanted somewhere with thick walls." He grabbed hold of Eddie's thigh and squeezed, sliding his fingers up the inseam of Eddie's jeans.

"Hmmm, carry on like that, and I'll make sure you don't get any sleep tonight. You'll turn me on so much I'll be insatiable." Eddie leaned over to speak right into Jeff's ear, his voice low and seductive. God, it was tempting to just get Eddie's cock out and make him come here in the car.

But Jeff could control himself until later. "I'll make you come so hard you'll pass out."

"What if I've scored some Viagra? I could keep going all night then. We could both keep going all night. Imagine that. Staying hard for hours on end. You could give me such an epic shafting, I'd be begging for you to stop."

Jeff's cock jumped up and screamed *yes, please*, even as his mind lectured him on what a terrible idea that would be. "I don't do drugs," Jeff eventually stammered, even as Eddie's hand massaged his erection through his jeans.

"Me either. And I've never actually tried the little blue pills before, but I reckon it could be fun someday, don't you?"

"I think I'll save them till I actually need them. Which means hopefully never."

"Mmm, you certainly don't seem to have a problem getting it up." Eddie squeezed the tip of Jeff's cock, and it was almost too much to bear. Jeff grabbed his wrist and pinned his hand down to the edge of his seat before kissing him briefly yet thoroughly.

When he pulled back, Eddie looked kind of dazed. His lips also looked deliciously tempting, all glistening with spit. Jeff wanted to see them painted in his jizz.

"Out of the car. Now."

"What are you going to do to me? Surely not here, in a car park? Anyone could see." Eddie didn't actually sound like he objected to the idea, all wide eyes and breathy voice.

"You'll get your chance for a bit of exhibitionism later," Jeff promised. "For now, I just want to get us checked in and into our room."

"And then what?"

"And then I'm going to push you down onto your knees and fuck your throat until I come."

Eddie made a turned-on sound in his throat that just revved Jeff's engine even harder. Jeff opened his door. "Out of the car. Now."

"Yes, Sir."

They made it to reception somehow, and Jeff was glad of the bag he could hold in front of his crotch. It didn't seem like the kind of place that would appreciate men wandering through the lobby with obvious tents in their pants. It was definitely a good few cuts above a fleapit that charged by the hour. They had a giant vase of fresh flowers on the counter, and not the kind of flowers he grew in his garden or that you could buy on a garage forecourt. Nope, these were all sculptural and tropical looking, and the only ones Jeff actually recognised were the giant artichoke flowers. Seemed a bit of a bloody waste of good artichokes, but posh people were weird like that.

He reassessed his opinion when they got to the room, though. He'd been worried it would all be over the top and he'd get paranoid about breaking some overpriced knick knack, but the room was actually pretty simple. And entirely white, from the plush fluffy carpet to the iron bedstead to the giant ornate mirror frame.

"Wow." Eddie had stopped just inside the door, his eyes as round as pennies. "This room is something else. It seems a shame to have our luggage out and spoiling the colour scheme."

Jeff didn't really give a fuck about the colour scheme. Not when Eddie was standing there looking good enough to eat. He felt an absurd urge to drop to his own knees on the fluffy carpet, but he wasn't about to do that.

Although what if tonight was his last chance?

But what if he loved it, and then he couldn't give it up? It was going to be hard enough doing without Eddie as it was. He didn't want to spend the rest of his life pining after the bloke's cock. Better if he didn't know what he was missing. And besides, Jeff wouldn't have a clue what he was doing down there, whereas Eddie was a fucking expert.

Jeff stepped right up to Eddie and put his hands on his shoulders, then pressed down.

"Mmm, are you not even going to let me get unpacked?" Eddie asked, but he didn't seem bothered by the rush. Not with the way he got to work on Jeff's fly, and then his cock, swallowing it down whole.

Jeff tried to make it last, but it was so fucking good in Eddie's mouth, and he'd been wanting this all week. And the desperate, gasping noises Eddie made every time Jeff drew back far enough for him to gulp a breath were so fucking erotic. In the end, he let go and painted spunk all over Eddie's mouth and cheeks, just like he'd promised. Looked great, dripping down his chin. Jeff swiped his finger through it and fed it to Eddie, who was still clinging on to Jeff's bum with both hands.

Jeff gazed down, taking in the glazed stare and the erection still filling out the front of Eddie's jeans. "Good boy. That's it. Now, are you going to behave for me tonight? There'll be a reward in it for you."

Eddie nodded.

"I can't hear you."

"Yes, Sir." Eddie cleared his throat, but his voice still sounded raspy and raw. "I'll be good."

“That’s what I like to hear. You’re not going to come until I say you can. Which isn’t going to be until much, much later. I want you bursting with the need to come the whole time we’re at the club.”

The pout Eddie gave him was way sexier than it should have been. “Please, Sir. I’ll be good to go again later. I promise. It’s not going to be a problem.”

“But I want you to be squirming with the need to come all evening.” Jeff glanced at his watch. Half seven already, but they still had a couple of hours until the place opened. “Come on. We can eat downstairs, then come back up to get ready.”

Eddie looked like he was about to refuse, and his hand drifted down to rub his cock through his jeans, but Jeff just raised an eyebrow, and Eddie stopped. “Fuck! You’re a right bastard, you know that? I’ve trained you too well, I have. When am I going to learn?” Eddie continued grumbling in that vein as he got to his feet and put his case on the bed, but Jeff could see he was smiling too.

Although they chose to eat in the hotel’s bar rather than the restaurant, the food was still a bit fussy sounding for Jeff’s liking, but fortunately Eddie pointed him in the direction of fish and chips—even if it described itself as a fillet of sea bass coated in beer batter, with hand-cut pommes frites—and it turned out to be delicious.

And what was even more delicious was watching Eddie fidget and adjust himself during the meal, and the way he glared whenever Jeff brushed their legs together. “Don’t blame me if I pop the moment a stray breeze brushes my cock,” Eddie muttered. “I don’t know how I’m going to calm down enough to take a piss. I’ll be splashing all over the ceiling at this rate.” He glared over the top of his glass as he took another swig of orange juice.

“Maybe you shouldn’t be drinking anything, then.” Jeff took a long draught of his beer and smacked his lips noisily. “Mmm, delicious.”

“I really hate you sometimes.” But then Eddie smiled, and Jeff smiled back, and he stopped caring that they were out in public. He took hold of Eddie's hand across the table and stroked it rhythmically.

"You can do it. I know you can. You'll do it for me. It'll be worth it."

"What? Pissing on the ceiling?"

"You know what I mean."

Eddie's mouth twisted into a smile. "All right. All right. Just don't make me wait too long."

"I'll make you wait as long as I want to. I'm the one in charge here."

Eddie blinked hard, but when he finally met Jeff's gaze again, his eyes had softened.

"Yes, Sir."

Chapter Twenty-six

When they returned to their room, Eddie excused himself to use the bathroom, and he had half a mind to quickly whack one off. It would be an awful lot faster than waiting to calm himself down. But then he remembered the heat in Jeff's gaze as he gave his orders, and that little catch in his voice that had betrayed just how turned on he was by Eddie's suffering.

"Bastard," Eddie muttered as he stared down at the toilet bowl. He couldn't let Jeff down. Not now the man was finding his confidence. The fumbling, awkwardness of their first couple of encounters had given way to this self-possessed, relaxed calm, and it was incredibly sexy. But thinking about that really wasn't helping matters.

In the end, Eddie started contemplating his latest commission, and just how he was going to provide the client with something both traditional and cutting edge, and eventually his dick was soft enough to aim at the porcelain.

"Ahhh!" At least the full bladder wasn't going to be bothering him again for a while. And if Eddie only sipped a drink at the club, he should be okay for a good few hours.

Bloody hell, Jeff had better not make him wait a few hours.

At the thought of that, Eddie's dick stiffened again, and he groaned, leaving his fly open as he went back into the main room. "Look at what you've done to me," he complained, before catching sight of a vision in black leather.

"Oh my God."

Jeff stood in the pool of light by the bed, wearing a pair of thick leather jeans, biker boots and not much else. Eddie had caught him in the act of pulling a black, short-sleeved shirt on.

"No, wait a minute." Eddie almost stumbled over his own feet in his hurry to cross the room. He was vaguely aware of more black stuff strewn over the bed, but he ignored it in his lust to get to Jeff. He leaned down and nuzzled into Jeff's chest hair, which earned him a surprised grunt. "Wish you didn't have to cover all this up," Eddie said before licking one of Jeff's nipples.

"Maybe I'll open my shirt later." Jeff grimaced as he pulled the shirt on fully. "Actually, I think I'm going to have to. I'm sweltering in these bloody things. Fetish gear wasn't exactly designed for hot weather."

"Oh, I don't know. Some people love getting all sweaty and slippery."

"Yeah? Well, I don't. Wish I'd gone and got me a kilt too."

"Huh?"

Jeff's grin was positively feral. "Turn around, boy."

Eddie did as instructed. There was a long black leather skirt on the bed. "You want me to wear that? Seriously?"

"Have you got a problem with kilts?"

"Not on Scottish blokes, no. But..." *I've never been into cross-dressing,* he wanted to say, but he didn't want to get into an argument about it on their last evening together. He picked the kilt up. The leather felt soft and it looked quite well made. Fully lined, and there weren't any over the top details to make it look too girly. But still, it was a skirt. "I've got some of my own leather jeans to wear," he said, pointing in the direction of his suitcase.

Jeff stepped up behind him and spoke into his ear. "You said you were going to be a good boy tonight, didn't you? You said you were going to do what I say to keep me happy."

"Yes, but..."

"No buts. Just you, in the kilt and your boots. I want you naked underneath."

Eddie took a deep breath and felt kind of dizzy. It was like that, giving in to someone else's will even while a part of you protested. But it was better that way. Something about it not being exactly what he would have chosen made his head swim. That bliss of giving himself up to be Jeff's fantasy. And so he dropped his jeans and stepped out of them before slowly stepping into the kilt.

Jeff slapped his arse as he bent down to pull it up, and that made Eddie hurry. Moments later, he zipped the fly shut and wiggled his bum. Actually, that was quite freeing, although his hard-on could now swing around disconcertingly, rubbing against the slick lining fabric. "You know I'm probably going to come just from this rubbing against me, don't you?"

"Oh, I forgot. Sit down." Jeff patted the edge of the bed. "Kilt pulled up. Legs wide. That's it. Wider." He shoved Eddie's knees wider with his hands and reached over to pick something else up behind Eddie.

Eddie groaned. "It had better not be a fucking cock cage. I hate those."

"You should probably shut up about them then, or you'll put ideas into my head."

Cool leather wrapped around the base of Eddie's cock and balls, and he sighed with relief. Just a cock ring. He could handle that. Welcomed it, in fact. And the snap on leather bands were an awful lot easier to get in and out of than some of the more elaborate metal contraptions. He'd have to introduce Jeff to those next time. Although there wouldn't be a next time. Shit.

"Are we good to go now?" Eddie asked, when he was finally upright again. Jeff was staring at him in a disconcerting way. "What's up? You don't like the kilt? I can still change."

"Shut up. I fucking love the kilt."

"Then what is it?" Eddie felt naked under that gaze. He shivered.

"Nothing." Jeff hesitated, then took Eddie's chin in his hand. Eddie was about to make a smart remark, but something in the intensity of Jeff's gaze stopped him.

Jeff ran a thumb over Eddie's lower lip. "You know how good you look right now?"

"I do?"

"Fucking gorgeous." Jeff hooked a hand around Eddie's neck and tugged him down to meet his lips. His tongue licked over Eddie's lips before thrusting inside and claiming him.

Had Jeff just called him gorgeous? If Eddie's mouth hadn't been otherwise occupied, he'd probably have teased him about it, but then again, maybe he wouldn't. Because there was something sad about it all, what with it being their last night together.

So when the kiss finally broke, he said nothing. Just rested his forehead against Jeff's and caught his breath.

"We should go," Jeff rasped. "Get a T-shirt on, or everyone's going to stare at you. Hope we don't have to park too far from the club."

Romantic moment over. Eddie gave him a wry smile. "Don't worry. If anyone asks, I'll just put on a Scottish accent. *Nothing to see here, Jimmie.*"

"That's a bloody awful accent." Jeff hefted up a packed rucksack and handed Eddie his T-shirt. "Come on. You're driving. Just the car," he clarified when Eddie smirked.

It was only a short drive to the club, and there was a large car park just over the road so they wouldn't have to walk far, which seemed to make Jeff happy. Eddie snuck glances at him whenever he could during the drive. Was he nervous? If so, he was doing a good job of keeping it hidden. Fuck. He looked hot like that. Such a pity they were only going to be observers at the club. Exhibitionism was always such a turn-on.

The big bloke at the door gave them the once-over, but after Jeff answered a few cursory questions and handed over their money, he obviously decided they were kinky enough to head inside. "Play nicely, boys," he called after them. "And remember, no photos."

The anonymous-looking door opened into a dark vestibule, with doors ahead of them to the area where the doorman had said they'd find the playrooms, and steps leading up to the bar. Eddie felt Jeff's hands on his shoulders. "On your knees."

"Here? Are you sure?" Eddie dropped to the floor anyway, never minding that he was in the vestibule of a straight club. His dick had softened on the drive down, but now it pumped back up to full mast, totally obvious under the kilt. The thought of anyone being able to see him there, kneeling and hard, only made more blood rush to his groin.

He'd been expecting to find himself with a mouth full of dick, but instead, Jeff was scrabbling around inside the bag. "Ah, here it is."

As the leather band of the collar closed around Eddie's neck, he swayed. Oh God, now everyone would know how he liked things. No pretending he was another Top on the prowl. And then Jeff clipped something onto the collar's D ring.

"Are you serious?" Eddie stared at the lead. It was only a short one, and when Jeff tugged on the end of it, he had to stand up.

"You need to stop questioning everything I do, slut. I'm the one in charge here, and what I say goes."

"Yessir." Eddie held his arms out gratefully to take the cuffs when they appeared, and he leant down to buckle the ankle ones himself when Jeff ordered him to. Fortunately Jeff didn't mention attaching them together. It was virtually impossible to walk gracefully when shackled. "So we are actually playing tonight, then?"

"Looks that way, doesn't it?" Jeff looked kind of smug, and Eddie couldn't find a trace of fear.

"You know people will think we're a couple."

Jeff tugged on the lead and gave him a pointed look. "And?"

And nothing. If Jeff wanted to have a little taste of being out, Eddie wasn't about to persuade him otherwise. He did want to give some warning, though. "It's probably going to be very tame in there. I don't think much public sex happens in straight clubs."

"They said on the website they have a sex licence."

"Yeah, but that doesn't mean anyone's going to take advantage of that. You might see a bit of flogging and spanking, but that'll probably be about it."

Jeff shrugged. "We'll just have to see what happens. Don't you go worrying about it. Your job is to do as I tell you. Nothing more, nothing less. And right now, you're going to follow me up those stairs, and we're getting a beer. Come on, bitch. Get a move on." Jeff winked, tugged on the lead and started up the stairs.

And just like that, all Eddie's resistance crumbled. Damn it, this man was so perfect at topping him.

And besides, he bloody well had to follow when he was on such a short lead. Eddie winced as the collar bit into his neck, then took off after his man.

Chapter Twenty-seven

Walking into that room with Eddie on a lead behind him was probably the most frightening thing Jeff had ever done in his life. But mind over matter and all that. He forced his hands to stay steady and strode over to the bar.

"Pint of Becks, please," he said when the barman looked his way.

"Right up." The bloke set it down in front of him, and Jeff took a deep draught for courage. "Anything for your pet there?" the barman asked. He was a skinny young thing with long red hair in a ponytail and a face full of metal bits and bobs. Sub or Dom? Jeff thought he caught a whiff of sub, despite the cocky attitude.

Jeff looked back at Eddie, who was standing behind him, smiling as he took in the scene around them. "I'd love a pint of coke, if that's all right with you, Sir."

Jeff pretended to ponder it. "I suppose so. Since you've been a good boy."

Once he'd paid for the drinks, he realised he'd just acted gay in front of the barman, and the bloke hadn't even raised an eyebrow. Not that he was probably able to with all those metal rings weighing it down, but still... A band of tension inside him released, and he took a deep breath. Time to look around properly.

There were plenty of women in the usual leather and PVC, corsets and stockings. One even had her tits out and was also being led around on a lead. He watched her wobble on her ridiculously high heels. Eddie could probably walk better in a pair of those. And his legs would look better in those hold-ups, the fishnet all stretched over his lean muscle.

He spotted another couple of blokes wearing kilts too. It was hard to tell who was submissive and who was dominant up here, as everyone seemed to be treating it like an overgrown version of his local fetish club, just socialising rather than doing anything too obviously sexual.

"You're right. It does seem pretty tame."

Eddie leaned against him. "If this were a gay BDSM club, all you'd be able to smell would be testosterone, sweat and spunk. You'd see subs in slings with blokes lining up to fuck them, and if you paid a bit extra, the barman would've dipped his dick into your pint."

"Why would anyone want that?"

"It's fun to watch? You could have made me drink it if you didn't like the idea of dick-swirled beer."

"Yeah, I suppose that could be humiliating." Jeff could always dip his own dick in Eddie's coke. "Must be sticky, though. You know, beer and coke and stuff on your nob."

"I'd happily lick it all off for you."

"I bet you would." Jeff's dick hardened at the thought, and he reached down to adjust it. Fuck it. If there was one place in the world he didn't need to be ashamed of having a hard-on in public, it was at a sex club. Even if there wasn't any actual sex going on.

"Is this really it? No floggings or anything?"

"We could go and take a look downstairs," Eddie suggested. "That's where the bloke on the door said the private rooms and stuff were."

"He did?"

"Weren't you paying attention?"

How could Jeff admit to the fact he'd been so bloody anxious his blood had been roaring in his ears? He'd not taken in anything the man had said, he'd been so caught up in the idea of getting that collar on Eddie's neck and somehow plucking up the courage to lead him inside.

And now they were in here, he wondered what he'd ever been nervous about. No one seemed remotely scandalised by him leading a half-naked kilted bloke around on a lead. In a strange kind of way, it was slightly disappointing. He glanced down at Eddie's erection, still tenting the front of his kilt.

"If this is nowhere near as fun as the usual clubs you go to, what are you so excited about?"

"Must be the company." Eddie smiled, and something inside Jeff ached. God damn it, it was so bloody unfair that Eddie wasn't a woman. He'd be totally perfect if he was.

Jeff needed to get his mind off Eddie's cock and back onto pussy. Maybe if he saw some girl bits being tortured downstairs... "Come on, let's go." He yanked on the lead and headed off to the stairs.

The room downstairs definitely had a different sort of vibe. That was largely down to all the subs strapped to various crosses and benches, being spanked, paddled or flogged. There were plenty of spectators too, and Jeff could see several curtained-off doorways with signs on them saying time inside was limited to fifteen minutes. He could take Eddie into one of those rooms and fuck him every which way, then drag him out again all dazed and smelling of Jeff's cock.

Bloody hell, he was hard enough to drill through concrete. That had to be down to being in a room full of female subs being hit though, hadn't it? Yeah. Of course. Never mind that he hadn't really looked at any of them yet. And of course, they weren't all female...

"God, they really should put a bit more effort into their floggings. Call that painful? I think not." Eddie sniffed at the nearest bench to them, and Jeff followed his gaze. A large woman was being flogged by another one. Oh my God. Live lesbian sex!

Jeff's brain almost short-circuited.

He watched for a minute, disappointment slowly welling up. This had to be the least sexy flogging he'd ever witnessed. The Domme was flicking the tails really gently, like she either didn't want to hurt the sub or just couldn't be bothered to put any more effort into it. And for her part, the sub looked like she'd fallen asleep. She wasn't even naked. The flogging was going on over a pair of black lacy granny knickers.

Jeff shook his head. "If she's going to keep her knickers on, she could have at least worn a thong."

"A lot of female subs are really self-conscious about going naked in public. Maddy told me all about it."

"And I'm guessing male ones don't have the same problem?"

"I'm sure one or two must, but not that I've noticed."

Bloody hell, why did the gay kinksters get to have all the fun? "So you're saying you wouldn't have a problem if I were to turn you over a bench and lift your kilt so everyone could see your naked arse?"

"I'd be absolutely delighted." Eddie rubbed up against Jeff's side, purring. "In fact, I'd spread my legs wide so they could see this cock ring too. Let them all know just how much you own me. And you could fuck me too. In the mouth or the arse. Or both. That'd give them all something to write home about."

Jeff glanced around. There really didn't seem to be any sexual contact going on at all between the subs and Doms. It wasn't how he'd fantasised a sex club would be. Taking Eddie the way he'd suggested was tempting, but Jeff wasn't quite ready to break the unspoken rules about how much sex went on in public here. "Let's look around some more first. Then I'm going to take you into one of those curtained booths and fuck you like the dirty little bitch you are."

"Mmm, yes please, Sir." Eddie licked Jeff's ear.

"Oi, less of that!"

Eddie grinned like the cat that had scoffed down the whole bloody pint of cream.

Jeff led them over to a group of people standing around a St Andrew's Cross. It was the biggest crowd, so clearly something special was going on here. He glared at the shoulders of a tall bloke in a long leather coat. Why couldn't Jeff be four inches taller? Okay, so he'd still be shorter than Eddie, but at least he'd have a better chance of seeing stuff in crowds.

Just then, the couple in front of them left, and Jeff got to see what was going on. A woman was strapped to the cross. She was pretty. Long dark hair. Relatively normal looking despite her collar, corset and fishnets. Better yet, her tits were hanging out the top. He recognised her then for the woman he'd seen being led around on the lead earlier. And right now she was getting spanked between the legs and looking like she was enjoying every moment of it. Properly enjoying it too, if the wetness on her Dom's fingers was anything to go by.

"So, what do you reckon?" Eddie asked. "Is this more what you were after?"

"Yeah, she's cute," Jeff said. It was a shame about the tattoos, but at least they were just on her arms. And he had no objections to piercings through nipples. Especially when it was a pair as juicy and prominent as those. He adjusted his dick, which was currently attempting to drill through his fly. "I'd do her."

Eddie snorted. "Yeah, okay. I'd do him, for what it's worth."

Jeff hadn't even looked at the Dom, other than to register the wetness on the bloke's fingers, but he tore his eyes away from Miss Wobbly-heels to see what Eddie was going on about.

Just a bloke. Leather trousers and a black shirt, like just about every other Dom here. At least this one didn't have a ponytail. He had sensible cropped hair like Jeff's, and he was fairly well built. Not all that tall, though, he was pleased to see. "Dunno what you see in him. There's better-looking blokes here."

"Like who?"

Fuck. Jeff glanced around, trying to make it look like he wasn't checking out the blokes even when he quite blatantly was. "I dunno. That one over there. The bloke in the funny harness thing." It looked nice, the way those metal circles went round his nipples. Like the one Eddie had been wearing in that photo he'd showed him. Damn, Jeff should have asked him to wear it tonight.

"What, the one in the fishnets and hot pants?" Eddie asked.

"Yeah, that's the one."

Eddie squinted at Jeff.

"What?"

Eddie shook his head. "Trust you to pick out the most girly-looking man in the room."

"He doesn't look girly. Get a load of those muscles in his legs. Bet he's flexible as well as strong. And you'd never get a harness like that over a pair of tits. He's got a nice pair of nips too. I could have fun with those." Great. Now he was discussing the merits of another man's body in terms of sex. What the fuck was going on with him these days?

"He's got a really pretty face, though."

Eddie sounded so put out about it, Jeff struggled to understand what was going on beneath the surface. Jealous? Nah, couldn't be. Eddie was too confident to feel jealous about other men. "I wasn't looking at his face," Jeff admitted. He turned back to fishnets-harness man. "Nah. He's not pretty. Just looks like a bloke to me. Blokes aren't pretty."

"But she is?" Eddie gestured in the direction of Miss Wobbly-heels, who was currently licking her Dom's fingers clean. Fuck. Had they just missed her coming?

"Yeah." Jeff rubbed at his cock, absentmindedly. "She's pretty. Sexy too. Nice tits. You think they're going to go at it some more?"

"I doubt it. We should move on."

"Nah, it looks like he's going to hit her with the crop next. We'll stay." Jeff wound the lead tight around his hand and pushed on Eddie's shoulder to get him down on his knees. There. Now he could use the top of Eddie's head as an arm rest, and he got the comfort of touching him like that. It was even nicer when Eddie leaned in and plastered himself against Jeff's leg.

Chapter Twenty-eight

Eddie knelt on the floor, fuming. He had no right to feel this way, he knew. Jeff was straight. Or at least, Jeff thought he was straight. Mostly. And he had every right to look at women. Especially when they were exhibitionist painsluts who clearly got a thrill out of being leched at by a group of strangers.

But it didn't mean Eddie had to like it.

So when he pressed himself up against Jeff's side, it was pure possessiveness. Fuck it. Jeff was his for this last night, and Eddie wanted everyone to know it.

He ignored the spectacle going on in front of them and concentrated instead on working his hands carefully up to Jeff's fly. So far so good. Jeff didn't seem to have noticed. Now if he could slip a hand inside maybe they'd be the ones everyone was watching. Public gay blowjobs had to beat public pussy spankings in terms of spectator value, surely?

Eddie was just struggling with the button at the top of Jeff's leather jeans when a hand clamped down on his.

"What do you think you're up to?" Jeff growled.

Uh-oh. Jeff grabbed a fistful of Eddie's hair and dragged him to his feet. His scalp was on fire, but being treated like that just got Eddie even more turned on. Maybe there was something wrong with him, but a virile, pissed-off man was the epitome of sexiness. If it weren't for the cock ring holding him back, Eddie would have come there and then.

"Well?" Jeff demanded.

"I thought you might enjoy the show more with your cock in my mouth."

"You don't get to make the decisions. You see this lead? This collar?"

"Of course I can't see the fucking collar. I haven't got eyes under my chin."

"You know exactly what I mean, smart-arse." Jeff glared forbiddingly, and Eddie glared right back at him. He wasn't going to do humble right now. He wanted an angry Top to match the way he was feeling inside.

But all Eddie's posturing didn't seem to make the slightest bit of difference to Jeff. He continued in the same stern tone. "This collar?" He tugged the lead hard so Eddie stumbled against him, and now Jeff was talking right into his ear. "This collar means you're mine, and I'm in charge of everything you do. You don't even get to go and take a leak without asking my permission first."

"You wouldn't deny me, though, would you?"

"I don't know. It depends how well you've been behaving yourself." Now Jeff smiled, the smug bastard. He knew just how to play Eddie, it would seem. "But first I think you're going to need punishing for what you just did."

Punishment! Eddie shivered with delicious anticipation. What would Jeff do to him here in public? All these people would get to see what a wanton slut he was. It was humiliating, but in the very best kind of way.

And so when Jeff led him over to one of the curtained booths Eddie had to bite back a moan of annoyance. "Can't we do it public, Sir?"

"Not what I've got in mind," Jeff said, letting the curtain drop back behind them. The space inside was dimly lit, the walls, ceiling and floor black, all except for the mirrored wall. And the only bit of furniture was a low spanking bench. "Down you go." Jeff grabbed the back of Eddie's neck and steered him until he was leaning over the bench. It was pretty wobbly and didn't appear to be fixed to the floor, making Eddie suspect the equipment had just been brought in for the night. Still, there was something seedy about being spanked over a dilapidated bench. It was the sadomasochistic equivalent of sex in an alleyway, or something.

But he stopped thinking when Jeff pulled his kilt up and yanked down on his balls. “Ow!”

“Legs apart. Wider.” Jeff’s voice had a hard, commanding edge to it that turned Eddie into a puddle of lust. It was tough to move when your limbs had liquefied, so Jeff had to help him by kicking his ankles out.

“Are you going to stay like that, or am I going to need to strap you down?”

Normally Eddie would want to be tied down, but not to a bench this wobbly. “I’m good.”

“You haven’t been very good so far.” Pain exploded across Eddie’s buttocks. “You’ve been a dirty slut, and you need to remember who’s boss.”

“Yessir.” Another blow landed, and another. Eddie arched into them, floating on the pain. Jeff’s hand was the best. Even as he picked up the pace and the stinging reached the point of unbearable. “Arrrgh!” Eddie couldn’t help wriggling, trying to turn away from the onslaught.

“Stay still, bitch.” Jeff’s hand pinned him down to the bench, and now he concentrated on slapping between Eddie’s buttocks, right over his tender hole and occasionally catching his balls. It was simultaneously too much and not enough. Eddie sobbed and bucked against Jeff’s hand, loving the way he was held so securely in place.

Sometime later, Jeff stopped, and by now Eddie was floating, his arse on fire but in a way that felt oh-so-very good. He tried to thank Jeff, but his mouth refused to work properly. His entire body had gone limp, all except for his dick, that was.

Jeff lifted his chin, and Eddie smiled. He could manage that much, at least.

The wolfish smile Jeff responded with warned Eddie his ordeal wasn’t over yet.

Goody.

Jeff unzipped his fly and got out his cock. It looked even more impressive than usual in the dim light, dark and throbbing with veins. Eddie salivated and opened his mouth.

"Good boy." Jeff held Eddie's chin while he fed him that mighty cock. He went deep, forcing into Eddie's throat so he could take every last inch.

Eddie stared up into Jeff's eyes, unable to breathe. Jeff was looking down with something like awe in his expression. "Yeah, that's it. That's my slut. You can take me all, can't you? Feels so fucking good in your mouth. Your throat." Jeff's hands roamed over Eddie's face and neck in a rough caress.

A tightness welled up in Eddie's chest, but it wasn't the need to breathe. It was more than that. Something painful and incredible and beautiful.

And that was when it hit Eddie. He loved this man. Really fucking loved him.

This was the real deal, he was sure of it.

His eyes watered, and whether that was because he was full of love or full of cock, he couldn't tell. When Jeff started to thrust, Eddie held on to that feeling and let Jeff's cock pump him full of more love, more sensation. His body was a balloon filled to bursting point. He needed Jeff's firm hold in his hair to stay tethered.

And he needed that pain at the back of his throat too. The battering and the hungry gasps for air every time Jeff pulled back far enough.

Just when Eddie's jaw was aching to the point of unbearable, Jeff pulled out and stroked his hair. "Well done. You're going to get a reward for that."

Jeff moved out of sight behind him.

Eddie wished he could turn his head to see what Jeff was doing back there, but that wasn't about to happen, so he just relaxed there, drifting on the sensations.

Cold wetness splattered on his hole, making him gasp, but before he'd had the chance to think anything more than "lube!" Jeff's dick was pressing into him. It was a rough, brutal entry, and Eddie's bruised hole ached, but it was everything he craved.

"Fuck, yeah," he managed to pant. Felt like Jeff's cock was pushing all the air out of his lungs. And there was no time to get his breath back, because Jeff started up with a punishing pace. He fucked Eddie's arse like they were competing for an Olympic gold medal, and every time those hips slammed into Eddie, his abused skin flared with heat. So fucking good. *Yes.*

Eddie tried to help out, to thrust back, but Jeff was holding his hips so firmly he couldn't move. He could only rock with the bench and clench inside, riding out the storm of Jeff's lust.

"So good," Jeff was saying, sounding almost as breathless as Eddie felt. "Yeah, they can all hear you out there, wailing and grunting. They know you're getting a good fucking, and when you walk out, they're all going to see your blowjob lips, and they'll know just how I've used you. You're going to smell of my cock. Of my come. They're going to see it. All over you. And they'll know you're a dirty bitch. My dirty bitch."

Eddie moaned his agreement and reached out for the wall. The bench was rocking so wildly now he needed to brace himself.

His fingers slipped on the mirror, and he opened his eyes. He'd forgotten about the mirror. Oh God, he could see Jeff behind him, ploughing into him. Jeff was staring down at the point their bodies joined. Staring with a look of intense lust, like he'd never seen anything as amazing as his cock pounding in and out of Eddie's arse. Eddie lifted up on tiptoes to try to see too. Oh God, his skin was red. So dark red. He whimpered with the sheer dirty pleasure of being used and abused. He wished Jeff would lead him out naked, so everyone could see the state of his arse and know just what had happened to him. To know that Jeff owned his body. For a short while, at any rate.

The bench creaked ominously below Eddie, but he didn't care. He planted his hands on the mirror and thrust back as hard as he could, meeting Jeff's need with his own. And yes, he needed to come, but more than that, he needed Jeff to come in him. On him. Whichever. He wasn't fussy, and he'd take it as it came.

He just needed to be the one Jeff was focused on when he did it.

Eddie squeezed his muscles inside, and Jeff grunted. "Bloody hell, do that again."

Eddie worked his arse, aiming to give Jeff the fuck of his life. He'd spoil Jeff for anyone else. Make him an Eddie addict. Make him fall for him. Crave him.

Love him.

"Jesus fuck!" Jeff bellowed and pumped his hips harder.

The bench creaked. It shuddered.

Eddie flung his hands out as wood splintered beneath him.

He crashed into the floor with a tooth-rattling crunch.

Jeff landed on top of him.

"Oh my fucking God."

Jeff's cock twitched inside Eddie as he came.

Eddie couldn't move with Jeff pinning him down. Couldn't work out if he was injured or not. Couldn't even come with the fucking band around his cock and balls. He wanted to cry.

But then Jeff lifted him up, onto his lap. "Hey, are you all right? You hurt anywhere?"

Eddie flexed his arms and legs gingerly, relieved to find there was nothing worse than a scrape on his knee. "Just my jaw and arse, you fat-cocked bastard. You broke the bench."

Jeff chuckled. "I can see that. You want to come all over it?"

"No." Although maybe he did. Just to make this whole experience even more sordid than it already was. "Please, no."

"Tough. You're going to." Jeff fiddled with the cock ring, and all at once blood rushed to Eddie's cock with a dizzying surge. He leaned back against Jeff's hairy chest, helpless to protest as Jeff took hold of his cock and pumped it, squeezing hard and putting a mean foreskin twist at the top of each stroke.

He couldn't have held back the tidal wave of spunk even if he'd wanted to. It jetted out, painting white lines across the padded bench and splintered legs. Pleasure surged through his body, igniting every last nerve ending. Jeff milked him and milked him until he was spent and every last muscle fibre ached.

"Hey, are you finished in there?" a voice called from outside. "You're only meant to be in for fifteen minutes, you know. You've been hogging it for twenty-five now."

Eddie groaned. All he wanted was to sink back into Jeff's arms, but the woman outside wouldn't shut up, and she was getting shriller and shriller.

"We'd better get up," Jeff said.

"Mmm, I s'pose." Eddie looked down at the bench. "How are we going to explain that?"

"Leave it to me." Jeff shouldered his rucksack without buttoning up his shirt again. If Eddie hadn't just come, he'd have done so at the sight of those hairy pecs bulging.

Jesus, he was so far gone he'd follow Jeff anywhere. Do anything.

The bloke didn't even need the lead.

But Jeff jerked it anyway, pulling Eddie to him for a quick, mind-searing kiss.

"What was that for?" Eddie asked.

"Just to say thanks. You've been a great teacher." Jeff smiled shyly before leading them out to face the music.

Chapter Twenty-nine

In the end, Jeff had the club owner apologising for not having checked the safety of the equipment, which Jeff considered a bloody good result, seeing as how initially the jumped up little tosspot had been threatening to charge them to replace the bench. He'd claimed it was worth over three hundred pounds.

"Then you've been ripped off, mate," Jeff told him. "I could build something better than that for less than twenty quid and a day's labour." And perhaps he would. There was definite potential to a piece of furniture like that. He'd enjoyed the way he'd had such easy access to both Eddie's arse and mouth, and with some sturdy eyehooks at the bottom, he'd be able to cuff him in place.

But how the hell would he explain it to his mum when she came round to clean?

Bugger. That put paid to that idea. And besides, Eddie wouldn't be coming round anymore, would he? This was it. Training complete.

At the door of the club Jeff unbuckled the collar from around Eddie's neck. He had a horrible sensation of finality. But it was best this way. Jeff wasn't gay, and Eddie wasn't the settling-down type anyway. And at least Jeff now had confidence in himself as a Dom. He hadn't even let a collapsing spanking bench faze him.

He was dynamite.

Shame he felt more like a budget firework that had been left out in the rain. But maybe that was just the come-down from an amazing orgasm.

They didn't speak much in the car. Eddie was uncharacteristically quiet, and Jeff realised just how much of their normal chatter was down to Eddie's efforts. Eddie always seemed to know what to say to sort out Jeff's head. Except for right now, when Jeff really needed him.

"Are you okay?" he asked as Eddie pulled into the hotel car park.

"Apart from all the aches and pains? Yeah, I'm golden." Eddie smiled, but under the wan streetlight, it just looked sad, like a painted-on smile.

Jeff grunted, not knowing what else to say, and they headed on inside.

The bar was still open.

"Fancy a drink?" he asked, wanting to get back their usual easy conversation.

"Nah, I'm good." Eddie yawned. "Think I should be getting to bed. Got to drive back early tomorrow. Seeing my dad and Belinda for lunch. And all my sisters will be there too."

"Oh." Jeff had imagined there'd be time for a trip down to the beach together. "What time do we need to leave?"

"Earlyish. I was thinking eight to make sure we miss the worst of the traffic."

"Right. Eight." Jeff tried to hide his disappointment. Definitely no time for the beach. They'd be cutting it fine if they wanted morning sex, and since they hadn't managed to have any the week before, he was desperate to try for some this week.

But what he'd really wanted, more than anything else, was to walk hand in hand with Eddie down the beach, early in the day before it got crowded.

"I'll head up, then," Eddie said. When Jeff made to follow him, he stopped him with a hand to his chest. "Nah. You have a drink. Seriously. I just want to crash out now. I'm not up for company."

When Eddie left to go up those stairs, he must have taken part of Jeff with him. It was the only explanation for the way he felt so hollow inside.

But he stayed for a couple of pints, followed by a large vodka, and when he finally stumbled into their room, Eddie was fast asleep.

Jeff kept to his side of the bed and tried his best to feel happy about the prospect of going out and looking for a kinky girlfriend.

The shrieking of gulls woke Jeff up with a start. It was nothing like the mellow twittering of the birds around his house. He lay there, heart pounding, facing the window. Light filtered in around the edges of the blackout curtains, but it still had that early morning washed-out quality. Jeff checked his phone just to be sure. 6:15. They had time.

He rolled over to wake Eddie up, but Eddie was already awake, his eyes glittering in the half-light.

“Hey,” Eddie whispered. “Last morning.”

If there was more, Jeff didn’t want to hear it. He cut Eddie off with his mouth, roughly taking possession of him and rolling on top. Eddie tasted like sin, and he made a broken, yearning sound in his throat that turned Jeff on even as it broke his heart. They tangled, both grasping and rutting hungrily, until Jeff finally pinned Eddie’s wrists to the mattress above his head. “Stay there. I want to fuck you.”

Eddie’s body went limp with surrender, his eyes heavy lidded. Jeff ransacked his backpack, trying to remember where he’d put the condoms and lube. Eventually he found one of the foil wrappers and suited up. Lube? Where the fuck was it? Something heavy sounding rolled out of the bag, but he wasn’t about to turn a light on and go rooting around on the floor. He needed inside Eddie. Now.

Jeff pushed Eddie’s legs up to his shoulders and stared down. Eddie was looking up at him with a strange expression.

"Fuck me. Now," Eddie demanded.

Okay. That was one order Jeff didn't mind taking. He looked down at Eddie's hole. There was only one lubricant that sprang to mind. Jeff called up as much spit as he could and let it fall onto Eddie, working it into his arse with his fingers. "This okay?" he checked, once he'd lined himself up ready to push inside.

"Yeah. Do it. Come on. Now."

Jeff spat once more for good measure, aiming for the point where their bodies joined. He surged forward, meeting resistance but jabbing through it with short, sharp thrusts. Eddie hissed and winced, but he urged Jeff on all the time. "Come on. I want to feel you. Burns so fucking good."

Jeff pushed on into the clenching heat of Eddie's body until he couldn't go any farther. He groaned, light-headed with need. Eddie looked so fucking good below him, his hair stuck to his forehead with sweat, his brow furrowed and his mouth open and panting. Jeff leaned in closer, forcing Eddie's legs farther back still until he could reach his mouth.

They kissed in desperation, messier and messier as Jeff began to move. Shallow stabs at first, aiming for that place inside Eddie that made him whimper and leak pre-come. Yeah, that was it. Jeff could feel the dampness on his belly. The urge to go deep and hard was lurking at the back of his mind, but for now he wanted to work Eddie into a state.

Only problem was, he was working himself into one too.

If he wasn't fucking careful, he was going to blurt out something stupid. Something about wanting to keep seeing Eddie. And Eddie had made it perfectly clear how he felt about that.

Best to just keep kissing him so neither of them could talk. And Eddie tasted so fucking good.

Jeff kissed along his jaw and down to his neck.

"Harder. More. Please!" Eddie demanded, his hips bucking beneath Jeff.

Jeff nipped at the skin of his neck before pulling out.

Eddie whined.

"Quiet, boy. You'll get what you're after. Come on. Over here." Jeff tugged Eddie to the edge of the mattress and stood by the side of the bed. Now he could thrust away as hard as he liked, using his whole body to push. He drooled on Eddie's hole again. More light was spilling in around the curtains now, and he could see the bubbles in the spittle as it dripped down. It probably shouldn't have been erotic, that sight, but it turned him on something chronic. He wanted to spend the rest of his life inside Eddie, like some freaky Siamese twins, joined at the groin.

Their bodies crashed together, building momentum, and no matter how long he wanted to draw it out, Jeff was powerless to resist. When the sharp tang of Eddie's spunk hit his nostrils, the tide of his own orgasm swept over him, scouring out every last drop of pleasure.

They lay there panting, beached and broken. Jeff raised his head. "Thank you."

"What for?"

"Everything."

"My pleasure. You'll be a great Top now. Some lucky woman isn't going to know what's hit her."

"My cane, hopefully," Jeff joked, but his heart wasn't in it.

Eddie smiled sadly, then twitched his arse. "I need a shower. Then breakfast."

Jeff didn't want to move anywhere.

"I'm going to need you to let me go," Eddie said firmly.

Yeah, that was about the size of it, wasn't it? Jeff pushed himself up on wobbly legs and set about gathering his things from far-flung corners of the room.

Breakfast was over quickly, and Eddie picked up a paper to read while he ate, so Jeff did the same. Of course, Eddie had some poncy leftie paper with way too serious headlines, and Jeff had *The Mail on Sunday*.

"Jesus. I didn't think I knew anyone who read *The Daily Mail*," Eddie eventually commented. "You do know it's full of made-up bullshit and scare-mongering, don't you?"

Jeff grunted and filled his mouth with toast so he didn't have to reply. He turned to the sports section. It wasn't like he'd bought the bloody thing himself, was it? But it was the paper his dad always read, and so he'd grown up with it.

Besides, there was always something that caught his interest. This time it was an article about the offside rule, and he read that until it was time to leave.

The drive back was mostly silent. Eddie didn't seem to be in a chatty mood, and Jeff certainly wasn't. Part of him was frustrated he was missing out on his last chance to have a natter with Eddie, but then again, it didn't absolutely have to be the last, did it? They might live very different lives, but surely they could meet up now and again? It wasn't like that would have to interfere with any other relationship Jeff started, was it? Not in the beginning stages, anyway, and by the time it got more serious with his new girlfriend, he wouldn't be needing Eddie's company anymore.

The more he thought about it, the more he warmed to the idea, and so when Eddie pulled up outside Jeff's house, he knew he had to speak.

"I was thinking," he began.

"Sounds dangerous," Eddie quipped.

"Shut up. I was thinking about us. This *thing*. I know you've finished my training, but I was wondering if we could carry on seeing each other, you know, every now and then. Just to keep up my skills. At least until I've found a steady girlfriend, anyway."

Eddie had his sunglasses on, and it was impossible to see his eyes, but his lips had set in a hard line.

Jeff blundered on, aware this wasn't going well but hoping if he kept going, he'd be able to explain himself better. "I know you aren't after anything like a relationship, but that's fine, because I'm not gay anyway. So it would be okay, you see? Just like two mates meeting up every few weeks to muck around.

You know, have a few beers. Me tie you up and screw your brains out. That kind of thing."

"You're saying you want to be friends with benefits?" Eddie's hands were still gripping the steering wheel tightly.

"Uh, yeah, if that's what you want to call it. Yeah, actually, that's exactly what I'm after." Friends with benefits still got to sleep over and kiss and cuddle in the morning, didn't they? Something they hadn't had time for this morning.

"So let me get this straight. Now your training's over, you want to be able to carry on using me as a practice body, just until your perfect female sub comes along?"

Jeff scratched his neck. There was something not quite right about the way that sounded, but then again, it was exactly what Jeff was suggesting, wasn't it? "Yeah, that's about it. But, you know, I don't mind doing some of the gay stuff too."

"Oh, you're going to give me a blowjob now, are you?" Eddie didn't sound too thrilled about the idea, and Jeff was starting to feel riled by his tone.

"I never said nothing about that. Just, you know, the cock rings and stuff that goes on your bollocks. I don't mind torturing you with those."

"Right. Well, as much as it's been a pleasure being tortured by you, I don't really fancy being some substitute for your perfect woman, and I certainly don't want to spend any more time with a top who's revolted by the idea of going down on me. I know I'm a pretty easy-going sort of bloke, but I do have some self-respect."

"I never said you didn't."

"You offered to make me your bit on the side."

Jeff scratched his neck. "I thought that's what you wanted."

Eddie stared at him. "Jesus Christ, Jeff. Are you really that thick?"

Chapter Thirty

Bloody hell, had Eddie really just called Jeff thick? Had he insulted that swaggering gorilla of a man? The one who could probably knock Eddie out with one punch? No, if anyone was thick, it was clearly Eddie, but he was so angry he ploughed on regardless. "You mean to say you actually believed all that crap I fed you about not wanting a relationship? What the fuck? You really think I'm that shallow, I was only in it for the sex?"

"Erm, I don't really know what you want me to say."

"For fuck's sake, Jeff, I don't want you to say anything. Words are cheap. I want actions. I want you to love me and to show it by owning up to that in front of the whole wide world."

Jeff had gone pale under his tan. "I didn't know…"

"Well, of course you didn't know. I wasn't about to broadcast all that and send you running for the hills. Needy is never an attractive thing, and besides, it's never going to happen, is it? So I thought I'd better keep it all to myself. And judging by the way you're looking at me right now, I wish I'd bloody well kept things that way." Except that wasn't strictly true. Part of Eddie was relieved to own the truth, even if the rest of him was wailing that now he'd ruined everything by rushing and he should have just taken the fuck-buddies offer.

Jeff scratched his neck like he had fleas. "Erm, that's okay. It's kind of good to know how you feel." He didn't sound at all convinced by his words. "But you're right. Even if I did have, uh, feelings for you, I'm not about to tell the whole world I'm gay."

"You have feelings for me?"

"Maybe." Scratch-scratch-scratch.

"What kind of feelings are we talking about here? Sexual feelings? Emotional feelings? Romantic feelings?"

"Erm, I'm not really sure? Feelings that mostly make me sick and afraid." Jeff suddenly brightened. "But you could come inside, and we'll talk about it, and maybe you could help me sort them out. You're better at all that shit, what with you being gay."

"Right. Of course, because loving men automatically makes me all sensitive and so on, unlike you red-blooded heterosexuals who just enjoy an occasional roll in the hay with other blokes. And even then, I was the one doing all the putting out. I might as well have been a woman for all the attention you paid my cock."

Jeff flushed. "That's not true."

"Isn't it? Come on, admit it. If I was a woman, you'd have no problem going down on me. And you'd probably have fallen head over heels in love with me too. But because I've got that pesky Y-chromosome, you won't even kiss me in public."

"What about last night? Everyone knew we were together."

"Yeah, but you still didn't kiss me. You just yanked me around on a lead like a piece of meat."

"You said that's what you wanted!" Jeff's voice was getting louder now.

"I did! But I also wanted you to kiss me and hold me and fuck my face in front of everybody. I wanted you to make a public spectacle of me, so everyone would know just how much I turn you on. But instead, you dragged us off into some dark little room. Probably you were thinking of her while you doing me too."

"Her? Who the fuck do you mean?"

"Her. The slapper in the corset who you couldn't take your eyes off."

Jeff looked blank, but that was probably all an act. Eddie elaborated. "The one with her tits out who was getting spanked between the legs."

Jeff's forehead uncreased. "Oh. Her. Yeah, I remember. She was hot."

"Well, thanks a fucking bunch."

"Wait. I didn't mean it like that. You're hot too."

"Really."

"Of course. I wouldn't be so into doing you if I didn't fancy you."

Coming from Jeff, that was probably a major confession, but Eddie wasn't going to be mollified by a few crumbs chucked his way. "So you fancy me enough to keep shagging me, but not enough to want to make it a proper relationship. Well, at least I know where I stand. And I know exactly where you can shove that fuck-buddies offer. Let me give you a clue. It's a hole you'd never let me near. Not in a million years. Because that would be way too fucking gay for you."

Jeff's forehead creased, and he looked around furtively. "Could you keep it down, please? Come on, let's talk inside."

"Right. Because we wouldn't want the neighbours to see you having an argument with the bloke you were screwing just a few hours ago. They might put two and two together, mightn't they? And then your cover would be blown wide open. Nowhere to hide. Well, excuse me if I don't feel a huge amount of sympathy for you right now, Sir Bastard."

"Do you have to be such a bitch?" Jeff asked.

"Get out." That hurt, having what had become a pet name of sorts thrown back at him as an insult. "Get out of my car, right now. And take your stuff with you. I don't want to have to see you ever again." Eddie was vaguely aware he was being overly dramatic, but he was so fucking angry he didn't care. And wounded too. Jeff had reached inside him and torn out all his pathetic little dreams of them shacking up together. Now they were just fading scraps of paper, blowing away on the wind.

Jeff didn't say anything else while he got out of the car and took his bag from the boot. Eddie thought for a moment that might be it, but Jeff came back to the door and opened it. "I didn't want things to end like this."

"I know. You wanted your handy little tart on the side to text whenever you needed a booty call. Well, that isn't going to happen. Get used to it, Jeff."

Jeff shook his head. "That isn't it. I wanted us to be friends."

But that would be too painful, when Eddie wanted so much more. "I think it's best I just keep my distance. Wouldn't want to compromise your otherwise perfectly heterosexual lifestyle, would I?"

Jeff's face shuttered, and he slammed the car door before stalking up the path to his front door.

Eddie wasn't about to hang around waiting for him. He peeled off with a squeal of rubber, and drove way too fast all the way home.

Life without Jeff should have been fine. Eddie knew this for a fact. He'd only been seeing Jeff one evening a week for the last month or so, along with the occasional text and phone call. Not much to miss, really. And Eddie had always been perfectly happy with his own company, hooking up online when he felt the need for some kink and domination.

Yep. Intellectually, he knew that nothing had changed, and it should be easy to slip back into his old ways.

It was a shame his heart had missed the memo.

It was ten days before Maddy called him up, angrily demanding to know why he hadn't been responding to her texts and Facebook pokes.

"I'm kind of busy with work right now," he told her, staring at the screen of his computer.

"Oh come on, you can't be that busy. You've never been too busy for a quick chat before. Come on, Eddie. I need you."

"Why? Can't Niall look after you? He's the man you're tying yourself to for the rest of your life, you know. Even if you split up, he'll still be the baby-daddy."

"Yes, thank you. I'm well aware of that. But he's also really busy at work right now, and I'm feeling lonely. Anyway, I'm coming over with food and booze in half an hour. Thought I'd better warn you, although you're being such a miserable sod, I'm wishing I hadn't bothered."

"Maddy, I really need to work."

"Bullshit. You need to take a break and have a proper meal. And a few glasses of red. Seeing as how I'm not meant to be drinking anymore, I can't very well go and open the whole bottle for myself, can I? But if you're drinking it, I could just have a little splash to keep you company."

In the end, Maddy bulldozered over all his objections, and he found himself choosing his favourites from her hastily recited list of specials at the local Thai takeaway.

He hung up with a sigh. Maddy was right, of course. He really wasn't all that busy, as he'd turned down his last job offer—it really hadn't appealed, and it wasn't like he was desperate for the cash—and had been working on something that had never even been commissioned. He'd sketched out and scanned a retro-looking illustration of a burly gardener digging in a lush garden, before adding colour on the computer. And now he was trying to choose the right font to add "Jeff White, Gardener extraordinaire" to the top.

Of course, Jeff would never want to use it. He'd probably say it was far too gay for a straight bloke like him. But Eddie couldn't help himself. He had to do something to feel closer to Jeff. Except for picking up the phone and calling him. That was way too scary.

Eddie cast his gaze around the place. He should probably tidy up a bit before Maddy arrived. But then he had an idea for a font that just might work and set about trying it out.

When the doorbell rang, Eddie was still fiddling with the font kerning. He buzzed Maddy in, then set about feverishly tidying the worst of the crap off the sofa and coffee table.

Clearly he didn't do a good enough job, from the way Maddy's nose wrinkled. "Oh my God, it smells like a sock graveyard in here. Have you even opened the windows this week?" She muttered under her breath as she thrust her achingly hip insulated picnic bag in his direction, then set about airing his flat.

"Oi! If I'd wanted the windows open, I'd have done it."

"It stinks in here. And fresh air is good for you. It'll help cheer you up, for a start."

"Maybe I don't want to cheer up. Did it ever occur to you I might want to wallow in my own misery for a while?"

Maddy turned from his window. "That's such bollocks. You've never wallowed before in your life. You're the bouncing-back type. Come on. Open the wine, and that'll cure what ails you. It's a good one. I nicked it from Niall's cellar."

Knowing Niall, that probably meant they were breaking into a bottle that cost more than Eddie usually made in a month, but what the hell. He poured them both a glass, but Maddy stopped him before he was halfway through hers. "That's plenty, thanks."

"You really are serious about all this earth-mother, healthy-living stuff, then."

Maddy wrinkled her nose. "Yes, I suppose. But mostly it's because I'm getting acid reflux pretty much constantly. And the bloody morning sickness! That's a total misnomer, you know. It happens all day long. There's no morning about it."

"You're not going to throw up here, are you?" Eddie looked around in alarm. He wasn't that house proud, but puke on his sofa cushions really wasn't going to improve the place.

"Don't worry. I haven't actually been sick yet. It's just the constant nausea that gets me. And the oversensitive nose. I can't actually go near the bin anymore. Or clean the lavatory."

"You've never cleaned a toilet in your life."

But Maddy was ploughing on regardless. "And as for the oversensitive, swollen breasts. Don't get me started on those."

"No. Please don't start on those."

Maddy gave him a sly look. "Better find something to distract me, then, or I'll start talking you through milk ducts and birth canals and all that malarkey the midwife keeps telling me about. But a true tale of an unrequited gay love affair could be the kind of thing that stops me mentioning just exactly what's happening to the inside of body right now."

Eddie was done for, he knew. No point fighting it anymore. "Fine. You want to hear about me and Jeff? Then you're getting every sordid little detail, whether you want it or not."

Maddy sat up straighter with a gleam in her eye.

"Are you sure you're not a sadist after all? You seem to enjoy me suffering."

"Don't be ridiculous. I just think it will do you good to talk."

"Even if I really don't want to?"

"Especially then."

So Eddie told her everything about their trip to Bournemouth, including the collapsing bench and the bitter ending. She moved over closer to him as he spoke, and somehow he ended up with his head on her lap, speaking almost directly into her stomach.

"I hope the baby can't understand any of this," he said. "Don't want to corrupt the poor little mite before he's even taken his first breath."

"Don't worry, pickle. He'll be fine."

"You talking to me or the baby?"

"You, obviously. The baby's a girl."

"You know that for sure?"

"As sure as the sonographer could be. I'm going to buy unisex clothes to be on the safe side, though."

Eddie was still confused. "But you said 'he'll be fine' to me. Who's he?"

"Jeff, obviously. Come on, Eddie. I'm meant to be the one with baby-brain here. Use your head. Clearly, Jeff just needs a bit more time to get used to the fact he's in love with a man. Give him a chance to wrap his head around it. It's a big step for a straight bloke."

Love? "What makes you think he's in love with me?"

"I don't know. Maybe it's the way he's been treating you so well. He's never done that with any of the girls he's had dates with, so far as I've heard. But with you? He's smitten. Giving you pet names. Cuddling up all night. Even being out in public for you."

"In a kink club."

"And in the hotel too, you said."

Eddie thought about them holding hands over the table. "Yes, I suppose he was. But still—"

"But nothing. Did he, or did he not, want to carry on seeing you?"

"He did. But only as a fuck-buddy."

"Did he actually use that word?"

"Well, no, but I could tell that's what he was—"

"No buts, I said. Trust me, Jeff White is not the kind of man to mince his words. If he'd meant fuck-buddy, that's what he would have said. Now think about it, what did he really say?"

Eddie thought hard, then shook his head. "I don't know. I was pretty furious with him at the time. I'm not sure my testimony would stand up under scrutiny."

"Then talk to him. Give him another chance. And really listen this time, because it sounds to me like he's just scared of having feelings for another man. He's going to need some time and patience, but from the way you talk about him, it sounds like he's perfect for you."

"He's an arrogant, pigheaded bastard."

"Like I said. Perfect for you."

"Thanks a bunch. Fine friend you are." Eddie started to get up, but Maddy held him down.

"You need someone you can't easily manipulate. Someone down-to-earth. Can you have a laugh with him? Chat easily?"

"Yeah, we used to be able to."

"And the sex is fantastic?"

"Off the scale," Eddie said morosely.

"And you think you love him."

"I do love him. Even if he doesn't deserve it."

"Deserving it has nothing to do with it. If you wait around for someone who truly deserves your love, you'll be waiting forever. We've all got our flaws. You can be a good Dom and still have issues."

"I thought you used to say Niall was perfect."

Maddy snorted. "Hardly. But he's perfect for me. And he's very patient with me too. That helps. Although I think the pregnancy hormones are proving to be a bit of a challenge for him. But he's doing well, bless him. I can't complain. Not much, anyway."

They sat like that for a while, with Maddy twirling her fingers in his hair, while Eddie mused on the whole situation. "I'm not saying I won't give him another chance," he eventually said, "but he'll have to earn it. There's stuff he needs to do. I don't want him hiding in the closet, too afraid to even touch my dick in case it makes him visibly gay or something."

"Just give him a bit more time," Maddy said. "He'll come around. And if he doesn't, I'm setting Niall on him."

"Oh." It was nice to know his friends were looking out for him, but still. "I can fight my own battles, you know."

"Of course you can," Maddy soothed, but he was sure he heard doubt in her voice.

Damn it. Eddie would prove he had backbone. He wasn't about to give in to Jeff just because he could do The Voice and The Look. That would be pathetic.

He wasn't going to give in to Jeff's toppy ways. And if this was going to work out, Jeff would have to apologise and make things good without attempting to dominate Eddie. He was going to have to grovel.

Chapter Thirty-one

The Fox and Hen was absolutely heaving—standing-room only—as it usually was when there was a premiership match on the big screen. Chelsea were playing Arsenal, and so Tony had driven over from Trowbridge and insisted they watch the game together, just like old times. Nothing out of the ordinary, really. Nothing except Jeff, who just couldn't get his heart behind cheering the boys in blue on.

But he did his best, watching the screen and joining in with the outraged insults and jubilant cheers when everyone else did. He even made the mistake of joining in with the Arsenal supporters at one point, but a dirty look from his brother set him straight. No one seemed to have noticed he wasn't his usual self. No one except Tony, anyway, who'd told him he was being a miserable git and had gone to get another round in. Jeff was still only halfway through his first. Maybe he did need to drink more. He took another swig of his lager, but it might as well have been fizzy water. Nothing seemed to have any flavour these last few days. He'd been chewing his meals mechanically, no real enjoyment in the act.

Tony jostled his way between a group of cheering Arsenal supporters—they'd just scored—and made his way back to Jeff's pillar. He put two full pints down on the shelf next to Jeff's half-empty one. "God, you still nursing that one? You sure you're not coming down with something, mate? You're looking kind of green around the gills."

"Nah, I don't think so." Not unless gayness counted as an illness, and Jeff was fairly certain Eddie would have something to say about that. "I'm just knackered." That much was true. He'd spent the morning lugging a truckful of sacks of sand and cement around, and that was on top of a restless night.

"You work too bloody hard," Tony said. "Don't want to end up like Dad, do you? You should get yourself something a bit easier. My new job's well cushty. I could see if they've got any vacancies coming up. Put in a word for you." Tony was now a security operative, although as far as Jeff could see that was just a poncier way of saying night watchman.

"I don't want to work nights." And more to the point, he didn't want to spend his working life wandering around a deserted industrial estate in the dark. "Dunno how you put up with it. And having to wear that stupid uniform."

"Hey, Denise loves the uniform. Says it makes her hot. She went and bought a pair of fur-lined handcuffs to go with it too, so we can play, if you know what I mean." Tony's eyebrows waggled up and down suggestively.

A memory of Eddie cuffed to Jeff's bed, legs spread wide, taunted Jeff from behind his eyelids. He tried to ignore it. "You're into all that kinky stuff, then?"

Tony screwed up his nose. "It's all right. I dunno. I'm happy with whatever so long as I get to come, but Denise has got a bee in her bonnet about spicing things up. Next thing I know, she's going to get me a doctor's coat or something. Or maybe I should suggest a nurse's outfit for her. You know, a really short one, maybe in PVC." Tony's eyes lit up.

"Nice one." Jeff raised his glass and forced himself to have another gulp.

Tony was clearly warming to the idea. "I could get it for her for her birthday. Where do you think I'd buy something like that? On eBay?"

"You could try Honour Fetish Wear," Jeff suggested, then took another swig of beer to shut himself up.

Tony tipped his head back and gave him a sly look. "Oh yeah? You've been shopping there before, have you?"

Yes, just last week, because he hadn't wanted to let Eddie down on their club night. He'd been determined to make a good impression, even if he never got to wear his leather jeans again. But he didn't share any of that with Tony. Instead he just shook his head. "I've just heard about it. You know. From Niall."

Tony just kept looking at him, and it made Jeff want to scratch his neck, but he couldn't. Not when he was holding his pint in one hand and leaning against the pillar with the other. Jeff rushed to fill the awkward silence with words. "You can get other stuff online too. You know, for the nurse's outfit. Medical examination kit. Pinwheels and so on."

"What the fuck's a pinwheel?"

"Pretty much what it sounds like. A little metal wheel with sharp points on it. You run it over someone's skin. All the especially sensitive parts."

"Never had no doctor do that to me before."

"It's meant for testing your reactions."

"Yeah?" Tony narrowed his eyes. "You seem to know an awful lot about this for someone who's never been on this pervy website."

"Niall showed it to me. You know what a dirty bastard he is."

Tony sipped his lager with a thoughtful expression. "He's one of them Doms, isn't he?"

"I think so."

"You should watch it, mate. Next thing you know, he'll have you tied up and strapped down over a table while he does unspeakable things to your backside. You know, like that scene in Pulp Fiction. You remember? When they've got those rubber balls in their mouths? Bloody disgusting, that was. Dunno how any self-respecting man can get off on being used like that."

"That was a rape scene," Jeff pointed out. "I don't think they were meant to be getting off on it."

"Yeah, but some blokes do, don't they? Bloody weirdos. Imagine wanting to do that. Being tied up and abused, or, you know, getting down on your knees and sucking cock. That's a woman's job. Revolting."

Jeff was filled with the urge to punch Tony's big fat mouth. He'd gone along with that kind of homophobic ranting in the past, just because that was what they'd been brought up with.

But now it wasn't some faceless, stereotypical gay man Tony was insulting. It was Eddie.

And if he was perfectly honest, it was Jeff too.

And come to think of it, he was fairly sure Tony had just insulted women too. He recalled Eddie's photo holding up that feminism sign, and why he'd done it. It had struck a chord at the time. Jeff had even agreed to do one himself, he seemed to remember, although since that hadn't happened yet, it seemed unlikely it ever would.

"You think it's a woman's job to suck cock?"

Tony smirked and raised his glass. "I'll drink to that."

But when Jeff didn't respond in kind, Tony's smirk faded. Jeff placed his glass down carefully, determined not to give in to temptation and throw the dregs of his beer at Tony's smug face. "You think that's all women are good for, do you?"

"Well, that and cleaning and bringing up kids and shit. I mean, yeah, some of them are pretty shit hot at work too, but there's some stuff birds are just naturally better at than men. Like sucking cock." The smirk was back again.

"Yeah? You ever had a bloke suck you off? You know, for comparison's sake?"

Tony grimaced. "Don't be disgusting."

"It's not disgusting. Best blowjob I've ever had in my life was off a man, so don't you go telling me all women are naturally better at it."

Tony's slack-jawed expression would've been amusing if Jeff had been in a better mood. But then something shifted in Tony's eyes, and he laughed loudly. The sound grated on Jeff's eardrums.

"Nice one, mate." Tony slapped him on the back. "You really had me going there. As if you'd ever let a bloke suck you off! You're straighter than a fucking ruler, you are. Thirteen years with the same bird. Speaking of which, you need to let me set you up with this mate of Denise's. She's well up for it, she is."

"I'm okay, thanks."

"What? You must be gagging for it by now. Or have you had luck with that dating agency at last?"

"Something like that."

"Oh yeah? What's she like? Come on, mate. Spill the beans."

"I really don't want to talk about it right now."

Tony pulled a face. "All right, all right. Keep your hair on. I was only making conversation. Jesus, you're touchy today, bro. You sure you're not coming down with something?"

Yes. An overwhelming urge to punch you, then head over to Eddie's place and shag him senseless.

"Maybe I am." Jeff glanced up at the big screen and couldn't even bring himself to care that Chelsea had now equalised. "I think I'd better head home and lie down for a bit."

"You'll miss dinner." The plan had been to head back to Tony's new place in a taxi and spend the night there, but since Jeff had only had a pint of weak lager, he should be okay to drive still.

"You know what, I'm feeling kind of funny. Wouldn't want to pass a bug on to you or the kids. Probably best I just clear off now, out of everyone's way."

"Yeah, you do that. I'll text you to let you know who wins."

"Nah, don't bother. I'll catch the highlights later."

"Suit yourself." Tony pouted a little, but he slapped Jeff on the shoulder as he left, and told him to drive safe.

Outside, Jeff sat in the cab of his truck with the engine running, trying to calm his breathing. He'd been so bloody close to punching Tony's lights out, and while it certainly wouldn't be the first time in his life he'd beaten up his brother, he was a hell of a lot bigger now than the last time they'd fought. As far as he could remember, it had been over who got to have the next ride in their go-cart.

Scuffles between kids was one thing. With adults, it was quite another, and half the reason Jeff had shaved his head and pumped his muscles up so large was to look intimidating enough to be able to avoid fights altogether.

And what would his mum have said if she'd found out he'd hit Tony? She'd want to know why, and she was a lot sharper than Tony. She'd just be able to take one look at Jeff's face and know what was really going on. And then his dad would find out Jeff was carrying on with a man. And then all hell would break loose.

No, best he kept his family out of this altogether.

But he did want to prove Tony wrong about it being degrading and disgusting for men to give blowjobs. And there was really only one way to do that.

Jeff eased off the handbrake, shifted into first gear and headed out of the car park. The main road ran south to Jeff's house, and north towards Bradford on Avon.

Jeff turned north.

Fifteen minutes later, he was standing outside the main door of Eddie's building. Should he have texted? What if Eddie wasn't even in?

Fuck it. Only one way to find out.

Jeff pressed the buzzer.

What felt like hours later—but which his watch assured him hadn't been more than a few seconds—Eddie's voice crackled through the speaker.

"I think you'd better come on up." The door clicked as the lock released.

Jeff decided to take that as a sign he'd been forgiven.

All the way up the stairs, he tried to think of what he was going to say to Eddie. He'd already planned out what he was going to do to him, but words had been left out of his fantasies. Maybe he wouldn't need to say anything. Maybe Eddie would welcome him with open arms and kisses.

One look at Eddie's face made him realise he wasn't going to get off that lightly.

Jeff halted on the last step, suddenly unsure of himself. He should have taken the time to stop at the garage and buy flowers or wine or something. Did gay men like that kind of thing? Or was it just for women? No, he had to stop thinking that way. It wasn't fair to anyone if he kept comparing Eddie to a woman.

And of course, that brought back their argument on Sunday morning. "I'm sorry," tumbled out of his lips before he'd had a chance to bottle out.

Eddie's glare softened a little, but he still looked wary.

"Can I come inside?" He didn't want to have to do all this out on the stairwell. What if the neighbours heard?

Eddie paused, and for one horrible moment, Jeff thought he'd been let up here just to be given the brush-off in person, but then Eddie gave a peculiar, tight-lipped smile and stepped back, holding the door open.

"Thanks."

Eddie's smile twisted again, and even a knucklehead like Jeff couldn't miss the sadness in his eyes. All of a sudden, the anger that had driven Jeff here evaporated. Why did he even give a fuck what an idiot like his little brother thought anyway? Even if he lost Tony's respect, they'd still always be brothers. That tie couldn't be broken.

But whatever it was that held him and Eddie together was new and fragile, and if Jeff didn't do some rapid repair work, it just might snap.

And he didn't think he could bear that.

"This is going to take more than a blowjob to fix, isn't it?" Jeff said.

Eddie's eyes went hostile again. "If you think I'm going to get down on my knees and suck your cock, you've got another thing coming, *mate*. I might be a total slut for your whole toppy vibe, but I've got some self-respect."

Jeff ground his knuckles into his eyes and sighed. "Fuck, that wasn't what I meant. This isn't how this was supposed to go in my head."

"Uh-huh. I suppose by now we'd be naked and humping like crazy?"

"Yes. I mean no! Not like that. I was going to... I mean, I wanted to..." Could he say it? "Eddie. I think I'm gay."

"Really. Because just last week you were adamant you were no such thing. You'll have to forgive me if I treat your sudden conversion with a great big dollop of scepticism." Eddie's tone was acid, but Jeff could still see the bruised hurt in his eyes.

"Look, I know you get bitchy when you're hurt, but please, could we just sit down somewhere so I can explain myself properly?"

Eddie stared at him for a long moment. Then his shoulders slumped, and all the fight went out of him. "Okay. Jesus Christ, I really must have it bad if I don't object to you calling me bitchy. Do you want a drink? I see you haven't brought any yourself. Tip for the newbie gay guy: men appreciate kiss-and-make-up presents every bit as much as women do. I'd have been happy with anything. You know, a bottle of something nice, chocolates, fancy undies. Even a bunch of flowers picked from your own garden would have been a nice gesture."

"I wanted to get here as fast as possible. While I still had the nerve," Jeff mumbled, his cheeks heating.

"Well, at least you're being honest rather than giving me some bullshit about the shops being closed or your car breaking down. I suppose that's something." Eddie turned and walked down the hall to the kitchen, and Jeff followed gratefully.

"So tell me," Eddie said, his head in the fridge. "What happened to make you change your mind about the whole sexual-orientation thing?"

"I don't know, exactly."

"You'll have to do better than that."

Jeff watched Eddie fill the kettle and ready the mugs while he pondered his answer. Would it seem naff to admit to it being down to an argument with his brother over the football? Maybe he should say something about a divine revelation or something. But then Eddie seemed to want honesty.

"I've been miserable for days," he said eventually, after Eddie had handed him a mug of tea. "Ever since Sunday morning."

"Sounds like a classic guilty conscience."

"It's not." Jeff paused at Eddie's sneer. "Yeah, okay, it's that too. I shouldn't have said any of that crap, and I've apologised already, but that's not all it is, okay? I've been looking around. At other blokes, and I'm noticing stuff about them that's sexy."

"But you still fancy women, don't you?"

"Yeah, I do."

"So you're bi. Not gay."

"Does it matter?"

Eddie shrugged and took a gulp of his tea.

"Look, I might fancy women still, but I don't want to be in a relationship with one of them anymore. I want to have a boyfriend, not a girlfriend."

"So why does that make you miserable? You can have all the cock you want. Gorge yourself. The gay world is your oyster."

"I don't want lots of cock. Just yours."

"Really? Because you haven't acted all that interested in it so far. Other than a couple of very brief reach-arounds, I don't think you've ever touched it. You certainly haven't tasted it."

"But I want to. It's all I've been thinking about."

"Really." Eddie didn't look like he believed a word of it. "Well, it's not the most romantic come-on I've ever had, but lucky for you, I'm not the romantic type. But you are going to have to prove all this to me." Eddie went for his fly and very deliberately unbuttoned it. He tugged out his limp dick and stood there with his arms crossed.

Jeff nodded and dropped to his knees.

This wasn't how it was meant to go at all. His first blowjob wasn't meant to be given on his knees on the kitchen floor. And of course, in his fantasies he'd pictured Eddie gagging for it, already hard and dripping with pre-come.

But if this was the hand he'd been dealt, he'd just have to do his best. And he figured the way to start out would probably be with a kiss. He'd have preferred to work his way down

Eddie's body, starting at his lips, but here went nothing. He didn't have to feel submissive, though. He gripped hold of Eddie's hips and pushed him back against the fridge, letting him feel the strength in his arms. Eddie gave a surprised "oof", but Jeff was pleased to see his cock stir as it began filling with blood.

He pursed up and leaned in to kiss Eddie's dick. It felt so smooth and vulnerable beneath his lips. Protectiveness welled up inside him. He was going to cherish this cock. It was his to look after now. Even if Eddie didn't know that just yet.

And hopefully it would be his to spank and abuse too, but only with Eddie's express permission. For now, it was all about convincing Eddie he could do the whole dick-loving part. They'd deal with the cock torture another day.

Eddie sniffed. "Well? Is that it? Because I've got to tell you, I've had better. Blowjobs generally involve getting a cock inside your mouth. Not just kissing it."

"Shut up." Jeff inhaled deeply. Eddie smelled of citrus shower gel and musk. "I'm working my way up to it." This time, he licked a stripe up Eddie's cock. It was definitely plumper now and starting to lift up a little. He took one hand off Eddie's hip to take hold of it, carefully peeling the foreskin back. The smell here was stronger, and he just touched the tip of his tongue to Eddie's piss slit, wanting to sample the flavour before going the whole hog.

"Jesus," Eddie breathed as his cock hardened in Jeff's hand. Jeff's own was busy fattening up too, clearly excited by the smell and taste of another dick. Yup. Definitely gay. Or bi. Whatever. The important thing was, Jeff loved cock.

Eddie's cock in particular.

But Eddie probably wouldn't believe him until he took it inside his mouth. Jeff looked up at him, trying to judge how he was doing. Eddie's eyes were wide open and staring, but Jeff couldn't figure out his expression.

"Go on, then," Eddie said.

Right. Only one thing for it. Jeff opened his mouth and filled it with flesh.

After a few moments of struggling with keeping his teeth out of the way, Jeff began to relax and explore with his tongue. Eddie had almost reached full mast now, and he was making those super-delicious turned-on noises Jeff always enjoyed. Oh yeah, he was obviously doing something right.

Confidence poured through him, warming him inside. He could do this. He could get the hang of being a gay man and having gay sex. Proper gay sex, where he took as well as gave. His arsehole clenched at the thought, but if that was what Eddie wanted to try, he'd happily give it a go. He'd give anything a go if he got to spend more time like this, with Eddie in his mouth and in his life.

"Okay, that's enough. Christ, that's enough, stop it!" Eddie pushed Jeff's head back until he popped out of his mouth. "Oh Jesus bloody fuck, why did I let you do that?"

"Because you wanted me to." That was a no-brainer. "No man turns down a blowjob. Ever. Even I didn't, back when I thought I was straight."

Eddie didn't reply, and his arm was still shielding his eyes.

Oh fuck. Doubts bubbled up from somewhere in the region of Jeff's gut. Had he really been that bad at it?

"I'll get better with time," he promised. "And practice. Lots of practice."

"That's not it. You were fine for a first-timer."

"Well then, I don't get it." Jeff sat back on his heels, perplexed. This was starting to remind him of one of those times Sarah would get all moody and he'd have to figure it out or she'd end up sleeping in the spare room. "Come on. Tell me what's up? I can't read minds."

Eddie finally took his hand away from his eyes and looked down at Jeff. His eyelashes were all wet and sticking together in clumps, and then Jeff realised why he'd been hiding them.

He'd been crying.

Chapter Thirty-two

Eddie buttoned up his fly and swallowed back his tears as best he could, determined not to give in to them. It was bad enough letting Jeff see this.

It was humiliating, and not in a good way.

Eddie had been splayed out and sexually tortured in front of an audience many a time, but he'd never, ever felt as naked and as exposed as he did right now. And that look of earnest bewilderment on Jeff's face was only twisting the knife into his heart.

"I don't get it," Jeff was still saying. "Talk to me Eddie. Tell me what it is so I can put it right."

Eddie swallowed a few more times, not really trusting his voice yet, but he had to give Jeff something. The poor bloke was getting to his feet now and hugging himself like he didn't trust his arms not to do something crazy.

"Eddie? Please?"

"This isn't going to work," Eddie said.

"What isn't? Me giving you a blowjob? I don't see why not. I could tie you up first if that made it any better for you."

Eddie snorted, snot bubbling out of his nose. Oh, that was attractive. Way to pull the newly bi bloke. "I'm sure being tied up would make it more fun, but it's still not what I'm after. I can't do this, Jeff. I can't be your dirty little secret. I haven't gone through my whole adult life as an out gay man, only to go running back into the closet and pretending to be just your friend. Or your mystery girlfriend who hides up in your room when your mum comes round."

Understanding dawned on Jeff's face. "Oh, you're still upset about that?"

"No, not exactly. I get why you want to pass as straight if your family are really that bad. It's much easier for bi guys to get away with that. But there's no future for us, is there? If you won't come out and I won't hide, I don't see how it can work."

"Wait a minute." Jeff grabbed Eddie's shoulders now, dislodging a fridge magnet, which clattered to the floor. "Who says I'm not coming out?"

"You do. Ever since I've known you, you haven't missed a chance to remind me of how straight you are. Why should things be any different now you've had a taste of my cock?"

Jeff shook his head impatiently. "You're an idiot. Everything's different. And not just coz I tasted your cock either."

"No? Why then?" Eddie held his breath waiting for the answer.

"Because I figured something out. I love you."

Eddie stared, dumbstruck. He wasn't being given a line, he was sure. Jeff looked deadly earnest and intense. Eddie's heart trembled, and for some reason, he felt like he was about to vomit.

"You love me? How do you know?"

Jeff huffed. "Maybe because I can't stop thinking about you? And not just the sexy bits. I miss chatting with you and stuff like that. And your smile. I miss that. Yeah, there it is. I want more of that smile in my life."

Eddie's heart swelled dangerously, but there was one last thing he had to get clear before he kissed the living daylights out of Jeff. "And you'd be willing to come out? It doesn't have to be straight away, but I'd want you to work your way up to it."

Jeff ran his hands down Eddie's arms and took hold of his hands. "I can't pretend the idea doesn't scare me shitless, but..." Jeff's gaze skittered about the room. Then it landed somewhere, and his eyes widened. Eddie found the source of his fascination pinned on the noticeboard: the printout of his ad for Jeff's gardening business.

Shit.

"What is that?" Jeff strode over to the board and now all Eddie could see was the back of his head. Hard to get a read on what Jeff was thinking.

"Just something I was working on. More to keep myself amused than anything else. I mean, I don't expect you to use it or anything."

"You did this for me?" Now Jeff had turned back to him, and if it weren't so patently ridiculous, Eddie would have said there were tears glittering in his eyes. Men like Jeff didn't cry, though.

But maybe this one did. Jeff walked back to him, and up close, the awestruck emotion in his face was obvious. "I can't believe you did that for me. And you never even said anything about it."

"We haven't exactly been talking this last week."

"Nobody's ever made me anything like that before. I'm truly honoured."

Eddie wanted to protest it was only a design, same as he'd do for any of his clients, but that wasn't exactly true, was it? He'd put his heart and soul into that drawing, and he'd worked late into the night even though he knew he'd never be paid for his efforts. And so he simply smiled and said thank you.

It was the right thing to say. Jeff smiled back, then pulled a resolute expression. "I'm still scared, but after you doing something like that for me... Yeah, I want you to come for lunch with me at my folks' tomorrow. My brother and his wife and kids will be there too, so you can meet the whole family."

"They already know?"

"Not yet, but they'll figure it out pretty quickly when I introduce you as my boyfriend." Jeff's determination wavered, and he gave Eddie a shy look. "You are my boyfriend, now, aren't you?"

Eddie pressed a gentle kiss to Jeff's lips. Jeff exhaled shakily, and for the first time, Eddie realised just how keyed up Jeff had been inside, even if he hadn't given much away on the outside.

"Of course I'll be your boyfriend. But if you're after a twenty-four/seven lifestyle thing, you're out of luck. I'm no one's slave, and I'm only submissive in the bedroom."

"Just the bedroom?" Jeff smiled wickedly. "Are you sure?" He grabbed hold of Eddie's wrists and pinned them back against the fridge. "Coz there are all these other rooms I'd like to dominate you in too." He finished by nipping Eddie's lower lip. Not hard, but enough of a bite to make him shiver and his cock perk right back up again. Jeff ground his groin against Eddie's, and he could feel just how happy Jeff was too.

Fuck it. "You can dominate me wherever you like," Eddie agreed, "Just so long as you keep doing that."

"Yeah? That's a shame, because what I really want right now is for you to stay there with your hands on your head, and for me to get back down on my knees and finish blowing you."

Eddie whimpered and ground shamelessly back against Jeff.

"No, wait..." Jeff mused, his grin wolfish. "That's not it. I think I want you on your back on the breakfast bar, naked, holding on to your ankles and presenting yourself to me, so that I can sit in comfort at the end while I eat you out."

Eddie couldn't get up there fast enough.

Now that he was sitting on the high stool with Eddie spread out before him like a feast, Jeff's nerves got the better of him. There it all was. Eddie's cock, balls and arsehole, ready for his attention.

There was no going back and pretending he was straight after this.

But what if he didn't like it? Sucking the tip of Eddie's cock was one thing, but his balls? His arse?

"It's okay. You don't have to if you don't want to. It must be kind of weird for you. Scary, even."

Jeff looked up to find Eddie giving him a disappointed kind of smile.

Fuck it. He wanted to prove himself worthy of this man. This man who bravely took every bit of pain and humiliation Jeff doled out. "I'm not bloody well scared," he growled. "Just admiring the view." He stuck his tongue out and very deliberately swiped it over Eddie's ball sac and up to his cock shaft.

There. That wasn't so bad. And it stole a surprised-sounding huff from Eddie.

He did it again, this time trailing the tip of his tongue down, from Eddie's balls to the strip of skin behind. There was a little ridge leading all the way down to his hole, and Jeff followed it there. The saltiness of Eddie's skin gave way to something musky—almost metallic. It reminded Jeff of the scent of freshly turned earth. Not so bad after all. In fact, it was one of his favourite smells. He played with his tongue, pulling Eddie's cheeks wide and licking every which way, exploring the unfamiliar textures and flavours.

Eddie's reaction was turning him on too. He couldn't seem to keep still, constantly making these gorgeous, desperate sounds as he writhed about. He was going to fall off the breakfast bar and do himself an injury if he didn't calm down. "Keep still," Jeff ordered, using his hands to pin Eddie's hips down.

He worked his way up to Eddie's bollocks again, and this time he experimented with sucking one into his mouth. It was odd. Slightly prickly textured. But not unpleasant. Not in the slightest. He sucked in the other as well, pleased Eddie's balls weren't as big and hairy as his own.

"Godohgodohgod," Eddie whined. Jeff could feel him straining and pressed him down even more firmly.

"Keep still, or I'll have to tie you down."

"Please do that again," Eddie pleaded. "So good."

What was good? Holding him down? He was still doing that. Oh, the tea-bagging. Or was it actually considered tea-bagging from this angle? Jeff didn't know. He'd ask Eddie when he was back to normal again. Although keeping him in a state like this for hours on end was incredibly tempting.

As Jeff sucked on Eddie's balls, he contemplated all the things they could now do together. He had so many plans.

He could hogtie Eddie and fuck his throat while he held his nose shut.

He could tie him spread-eagled and kiss him all over.

He could watch the sunrise with him from Jeff's garden, then go inside for coffee and toast before heading back to bed.

It was all good.

Happy thoughts filled Jeff's head as he turned his attention to Eddie's cock. There were so many things they could do together. So many first times for them still to come.

And the one he was going to concentrate on enjoying right now was getting Eddie to come in his mouth.

Jeff opened wide and sucked Eddie as deep as he could. Oh, not so far. He was only halfway down when the urge to gag hit him. How the fuck did Eddie take him all the way into his throat? Jeff wasn't going to be able to do that in a hurry. But if he couldn't go deep, then he'd just have to concentrate on the bit he could fit in his mouth.

Jeff moved one of his hands to circle the base of Eddie's cock, pumping up and down with it while he worked on sucking and licking the crown. Eddie was moaning like crazy now, and the olive-y flavour in Jeff's mouth grew stronger. Yeah, he was getting there. Him, doing this to Eddie. Felt so fucking powerful.

And at the exact same time, so fucking humble.

"Can I come? Please, Sir?" Eddie pleaded.

Oh, what a good sub he was. Jeff hadn't even thought of this as a situation requiring permission. He pulled off for just long enough to growl "Do it," before getting back to the job in hand. In mouth. Whatever. The important thing was, Jeff had his lover's cock in his mouth, and he was determined to show him a good time.

"God! Now, Sir. Coming now."

Jeff might have been warned, but the first jet of spunk was still a surprise, making him splutter and draw back. He watched the next two coming out while getting his breath back, then sucked Eddie in greedily. He wanted this. He'd earned it. And it tasted good. Like Eddie. And like sex. His two favourite things in the whole world.

When the spunk stopped splurting and Eddie's body had gone limp, Jeff got up, kicking the stool over in his rush to get his jeans undone. He walked round to where Eddie's head rested. Fuck. He hadn't thought this through. He'd wanted to come all over Eddie's face, but the height of the breakfast bar put paid to that idea. He frowned.

"You okay?" Eddie asked. He was frowning too. "Shit. You didn't like it."

"Don't be an idiot. It was fucking fantastic. As you should be able to see by this bad boy." Jeff grabbed his erection and almost came on the spot. "My nuts are fucking bursting. I was just trying to figure out how I was going to come all over your face."

A slow smile dawned on the face in question. "Help me down."

And that was how, less than a minute later, Jeff had a kneeling Eddie in front of him, smiling dreamily as Jeff painted his lips with come.

Jeff's orgasm rippled its way up to his heart too, and when he'd finally finished pumping his love all over Eddie, he pulled him to his feet. And kissed him. Both of their flavours mingled on his tongue.

"I fucking love you," he said, squeezing Eddie tight.

"Love you too, you bastard."

Chapter Thirty-three

"So you're going to do all the talking?" Eddie asked, for what must have been the twentieth time, as they walked down the hill to Jeff's folks' the next day. Jeff had contemplated bringing the truck for a quick getaway if necessary, but it was always a nightmare parking it down there on the narrow roads, and it was a lovely day.

Also, his hands had been shaking too much to trust himself driving.

"I told you, I've got it sorted. I'll be fine." He was kind of terrified, but he just wanted to get it all over and done with as soon as possible.

"I just want you to know I'm there for moral support if you need me."

"I know that." Jeff smiled at his boyfriend. *Boyfriend.* The thought made him all gooey inside, like someone had scooped out his innards and replaced them with warm caramel sauce. He wanted to take Eddie's hand as they walked, but knowing the Hook St. Norton grapevine, someone would see them, ring up his folks and steal his thunder.

Although maybe that would be the best way to do it, and save himself the ordeal of coming out.

Nah, that was the coward's way out. Eddie would respect him far more if he told his family face-to-face.

He just had to keep thinking about that and how amazing things had been last night. And this morning, when he'd spanked Eddie scarlet before fucking him every which way. And the way Eddie had looked afterwards, all blissed out and happy. The warm caramel sauce bubbled, and Jeff was in danger of popping a stiffy if he carried on in with that train of thought.

But then they turned the corner, and he could see his dad outside the house, smoking, and his dick shrivelled. Bert watched them approach, smoking his ciggie with a kind of defiant rage. That must mean Tony and co were here already, as Mags wouldn't let Bert smoke in the house when the kids were there.

"This your mate, then, is it? The one you texted about?" Bert said, tipping his head back so he could look down his nose at Eddie, who towered a good six inches above him. Jeff rolled his eyes at the macho posturing. And it was only going to get worse when Bert found out the truth.

"Yep, this is Eddie. Eddie, this is my dad, Bert. Come on. Mum'll be in the kitchen, I expect."

Bert held out a hand, and Jeff watched as he squeezed Eddie's hand hard. That had to hurt. "You got a last name, son? I don't recognise you from round these parts."

"Powell. And I grew up in Bradford on Avon."

"Ah. Bradford on Avon, eh? Bit posh there, isn't it." Bert was clearly doing his best to wind Eddie up.

But Eddie just smiled. "I suppose it is."

"Not sure what you're doing hanging around with a reprobate like my Jeff, then."

"Dad! Since when have I been a reprobate?"

"Since that time you stole a car and crashed it."

"You mean the time I borrowed your car without asking and backed it into a wall? Come on, Dad. That was ten years ago. One little dent is hardly writing the thing off. And it wasn't like I'd been drinking or anything. And I'd passed my driving test and everything." Jeff turned to Eddie, who was giving him a look he recognised as amusement. "Come on, let's find Mum."

They headed inside, and Jeff pulled Eddie to one side in the hall before heading through to the noise of the kitchen. "Sorry about that. Did he hurt you? He's always trying to prove he's the top dog when he shakes hands."

"I'm fine." Eddie flexed his fingers and winked. "Good thing I'm a masochist, that's all I can say. And you know how I love a dominant man."

"If you're getting turned on my dad's handshake, that's just wrong."

Eddie gave him a challenging look. "You think you can do better?"

"Arm wrestling. Later. My place. Winner gets a blowjob. And a rimming."

"Mmm, I like your thinking."

Jeff licked his lips, sorry they had to go through with the whole coming-out-to-the-family ordeal first, but that was just the way it was. He squared his shoulders and headed into the kitchen.

"Hi, Mum. I've got someone for you to meet."

Mags was bent over the oven, and all they could see was her ample bottom in leopard-print Lycra. Jeff groaned inwardly, wondering what Eddie made of his folks. Eddie's own family sounded so very different. Respectable, for a start.

"Hold on a minute," Mags called. "Just testing the bird. Okay, another half hour should do it." She slammed the door shut and turned to give him a hug. "Hello, darling. You're looking good." She narrowed her eyes. "You look like a man who got lucky last night."

Jeff scratched his neck, which was getting very hot.

"Oh sweetie, I am happy for you, you know that. Now why couldn't you have brought her with you? Not that I mind having your friend instead. Eddie, wasn't it?" Mags turned to Eddie and hugged him tight. "Ooh, you're all skin and bone. Good thing I've got plenty of grub to fatten you up, isn't it?"

"Mum, he's hardly starving."

"This is all lean muscle, Mrs. White," Eddie said, his face serious but his eyes twinkling. "I can assure you I eat plenty. I just don't seem to be able to pack much weight on. Unlike your son."

"Ooh, listen to you. Dead posh, you are, aren't you? And it's Mags, sweetheart. No need to stand on ceremony here. Now why don't you two get yourselves drinks and head on out to the garden. Your brother's here, with all the family."

Jeff went and fetched a couple of lagers from the fridge, handing an open bottle to Eddie. "Come on, then," he said when Eddie lingered over a pile of vegetables.

"Can I help you with anything, Mags?" Eddie offered. "I could peel these carrots if you like."

"Well I never. A man offering me help in the kitchen! Jeff, you can bring him back anytime. But no, love, it's all under control. I do this every week. You want to come back and help me on Christmas Day, though, love, and I'll gladly take you on."

"It's a date," Eddie said, kissing her hand.

Mags giggled and blushed. "Be off with you, Casanova, or my Bert'll be getting jealous."

Jeff just shook his head at Eddie and let him out to the garden.

"All right, bro. You feeling better today?" Tony called from over in the improvised goal.

"Yeah?" Jeff puzzled for a moment, then recalled his hasty exit from the pub the night before. So much had happened since, was it really less than twenty-four hours ago? His whole life had changed since then. "Oh, yeah, I'm fine. Just needed to sleep on it. This is Eddie, by the way. Eddie, this is Tony, and that's his wife Denise." He pointed out Denise, who was flicking through a magazine, her feet up on a sun lounger. "And these four balls of energy are Jayden, Tyler, Jackson and Chardonnay. Don't laugh," he muttered to Eddie. "It was better than some of the other names they came up with."

"It's a pleasure to meet you all," Eddie said. "Do you need a couple of extra players on the field? Because it's been a few years, but I was a pretty mean midfielder when I was at college. And I think we could put together a game of three-a-side if me and Jeff join in."

In the end, they played football with Tony and the kids for a good half hour until Mags called them in, and Eddie proved to be pretty bloody amazing with the ball. Jeff could see him gaining points with the kids and with Tony, and he was feeling pretty positive about the whole situation when they headed inside. This would go fine. It had to. They'd all liked Eddie. Even his dad had shown a kind of grudging admiration when Eddie didn't wince at his monster handshake.

The table was set up in the front room, as there just wasn't space for them all in the kitchen, and Jeff looked around at everyone. Eddie was listening to Jayden's recital of footie statistics with an expression of interest—definitely a masochist—and even his dad was smiling at something Tony was saying. It would be a shame to break up the happy party with his announcement. Maybe he should leave it till after the main course. When everyone was feeling too full of food to object to anything much.

Unfortunately, Mags got in there first. "So, Eddie," he heard her asking, and the sly tone to her voice set off alarm bells. "You know anything about this new girl of Jeff's? He's being awfully secretive about her. He hasn't even given me a name. I'm going to start thinking she's married or something if he doesn't introduce me to her soon."

"Or completely fictional," Tony chipped in.

"Have you got a girlfriend yourself?" Mags asked Eddie. "Oh, are they friends or something? She some posh bird he doesn't want to bring round coz he's ashamed of us or something?"

Eddie was looking at him expectantly. "Jeff? I think you'd better handle this one."

Right, yes, because Jeff had said he'd do all the talking, hadn't he? Now why had he said that, exactly? Jeff stared down at his half-eaten dinner, but the roasties weren't giving him any inspiration, other than reminding him that they were just about the same size and shape as Eddie's balls. Balls which he'd had in his mouth for the first time yesterday. And he'd enjoyed it, oh so very much.

"Eddie doesn't have a girlfriend," Jeff found himself saying. It was a roundabout way to get to the point, but he needed to build up to it. "He has a boyfriend." There, he'd outed Eddie. Now he just needed to out himself. "Me." He cleared his throat and looked up from his roast dinner. "I'm Eddie's boyfriend. So now you know."

Chapter Thirty-four

Every pair of eyes at the table was staring right at Jeff. All except for Chardonnay, who was looking at Eddie. "Does that mean you're my uncle?" she asked. "Cool. Mum, Dad, I've got another uncle. Shakeisha's going to be well jealous. She's got two mums," she announced proudly, "but she ain't got no gay uncles."

"Hasn't got any," Denise muttered absently, "not *ain't got no.*"

Jeff looked from one to another of them. The boys had all lost interest by now and were eating. Tony was staring at him with his arms folded, like Jeff was a Sudoku puzzle that needed solving. Denise was wide-eyed, but she gave him a small smile. His dad was... Well, his dad was getting up and walking out of the room. His mum was biting her lip and worrying her charm bracelet, and Eddie was looking at him with those big golden eyes all suspiciously bright, but he was smiling proudly, and that was the best sight in the whole bloody world.

Better than Jeff's garden in full bloom at dusk.

Better than the most spectacular sunset.

Better than his mum's treacle sponge, which he could smell cooking in the oven.

Jeff took hold of Eddie's hand on the table and squeezed it in full view of everyone. It was scary but exhilarating. "Mum, I know Dad's not going to like it, but I hope you can get used to Eddie. He's good for me. He makes me happy. And I...I love him."

Mags was dabbing at her eyes with a tissue now and making a right mess of her mascara. Oh dear. This really wasn't going too well. Now Tony was staring at Eddie. He looked like he wanted to start trouble, but he'd be up against the two of them if he tried anything with Eddie.

"I think we should probably go," Jeff said to Eddie, who grimaced and nodded. "Mum, I'm sorry for spoiling dinner. We'll be off now and let you finish in peace."

"Oh, don't be ridiculous." Mags got up from her chair and trotted round the table. "You're my firstborn. You'll always be welcome here." She wrapped her arms around Jeff and suffocated him in a perfumey hug. "Honestly, I think we're all a bit shocked, that's all. I never in a million years would have thought you'd turn gay, Jeff White. You always had such an eye for the girls."

"I still do. I'm bi, not gay," he protested. "Uh, not that it matters either way," he added hastily, catching Eddie's raised eyebrow. "I'm off the market now I'm with Eddie, so no trying to set me up with anyone, you hear?"

"As if I would." Mags let go of Jeff and turned to Eddie. "Come here, you. You're not getting off that easily, my boy." Jeff just caught Eddie's look of alarm before his face was squashed against Mags's boobs. "Never thought I'd see the day when I had a son-in-law. But that's good. Always did get on better with men than women. 'Cept you, of course, Denise. But then again, you and me could be peas in a pod, couldn't we?"

Denise grinned back at her. "Yeah, that's right. And we're dead chuffed for you, aren't we, Tone? It's nice to see your brother happy again, isn't it?"

Jeff's brother mumbled something he couldn't quite catch, but at least it didn't sound like an insult.

Mags huffed. "You'll have to do a bit better than that, my lad. You and your dad both. Don't you worry about Bert," she said to Jeff and Eddie. "It'll take him a while to come round, but he'll get there, I promise. I have my ways of getting him to do what I want. It's amazing what a few weeks' withdrawal of conjugal rights will do, ain't it, Denise?"

Denise smirked back at her, and Tony and Jeff both said "Oi!" at the same time.

"I don't want to hear about your sex life, Mum," Jeff protested.

"And we don't want to hear about yours either," Tony added.

"Like we'd sit here and give you all the juicy details," Eddie said. "I absolutely don't kiss and tell. And Jeff doesn't either."

"Ugh, kissing. That's gross." That was Jayden. His other two younger brothers were flicking peas at each other across the table.

"Okay, enough of that, boys. Anyone ready for pudding? I don't think I can manage any more of this. I see you've eaten all of yours, though, Eddie."

"It was delicious. Thank you, Mags. It's been ages since I've had a roast dinner, so that really hit the spot.

Mags flashed Eddie a big grin, and Jeff relaxed some more. So long as Eddie devoured her treacle sponge with the same enthusiasm, he'd be welcomed into the family.

When they were all settled down with treacle pudding and custard (or ice cream in some cases, or both in Jeff's), Jeff noticed his mum heading out of the room with a bowl of pudding. Was his dad hiding upstairs, or outside smoking himself into an early grave? The treacle sponge turned to flavourless paste in his mouth. He'd have to face the music and talk to the old man. Today, really. Leaving it any longer could do more harm than good.

But he should let him finish his pudding first. He was always grumpier with an empty stomach.

They stuck to harmless talk about what was on the telly while they polished off pudding, and afterwards, Eddie offered to help wash up. Jeff hovered for a while, more in the way than a help, but Eddie and Mags seemed to be having a whale of time laughing about some celebrity he'd never heard of on Strictly Come Dancing, so he decided he'd better seek out his dad. He'd try out the front first. But Tony grabbed him by the arm first.

"A little talk, bro? Let's go for a walk. Out the back way."

It'd be practice for talking to his dad, he supposed. The junior version.

"So you're really a bummer?" was the first thing Tony asked.

"Looks that way, doesn't it?"

"I don't get it. If you still like birds, why'd you want to go and get involved with a bloke?"

"Because I love him?"

"Yeah, but women are sexy."

"Eddie's sexy. Really fucking sexy. And filthy too. You would not believe some of the things he does." It was fun watching Tony's expression turn to horror.

"Oh my God, I don't want to know. That's disgusting."

"No more disgusting than if it was a woman doing it to you. You'd love it then."

"So it's just the sex, is it?" Tony pulled out his packet of Marlboros and lit one up.

"For fuck's sake, weren't you listening to a word of what I said in there? I love him. End of story. He's not just some sex object. I mean, it might have started out a bit like that..." But had it really? They'd started out by talking. From what he'd heard from Eddie, they'd talked a lot more before they first had sex than Eddie had with some of his previous hookups. "It's not just sex. He's a good bloke, and we have a laugh, you know? He gets me in a way that Sarah never did. And I get him. I don't have to spend my time wondering what's going on in his head. He just tells me if he's got a problem, and then we fix it."

Tony was staring down at a pebble like it was fascinating. "So this is why you got so weird at the pub yesterday. You weren't really sick after all, were you?"

"I was sick of hearing that shit coming out of your mouth."

Tony pursed up his lips and blew out a long stream of smoke. "Sorry," he eventually muttered. "I didn't know."

"Yeah, well even if you didn't, you should try thinking about who you might be offending before you open your mouth. Could be any number of gay blokes around that you don't know about. You can't always tell from the way people look. Eddie, for instance. Bet you never figured that one out before I told everyone."

"All right, all right. I said I was sorry, didn't I?"

"Words are cheap. I just want to know you're not going to be saying homophobic shit to your boys when you get home. This crap has to stop somewhere, you know? I've had enough of it from Dad over the years. I don't want to be hearing it from my nephews too. I deserve better than that. Eddie deserves better than that. We need to break the pattern. Not let the old bastard poison everything."

Tony flicked his eyes up to meet Jeff's. "Yeah, okay. I'll do my best. But Jeff, mate, what are you going to say to everyone down the pub? You gonna bring Eddie down there to watch the footie? You think he'd fit in? What if someone tries to gay bash you?"

"I can look after myself. And so can Eddie. He's tougher than he looks. And we can count on you too, can't we?"

"Yeah. I s'pose." Tony didn't sound all that enthusiastic, but at least he wasn't trying to persuade Jeff to give Eddie up. Or that he wasn't really gay.

"You're really serious about him, aren't you?" Tony said. "I never heard you talk like this about Sarah."

"I think Sarah and me got together too young. We weren't really all that suited, but we stuck together for some reason."

"Your house, I reckon," Tony muttered. "Good thing you never married her or you'd have had to sell it and give her half."

"No, it wasn't that. I think we were both too comfortable to want to shake things up. And probably a bit scared of going it alone. But I'm glad she left me now. Really glad. Because if she hadn't, I'd never have found Eddie, and I'd still be miserable but not admitting it to myself. So I've got to thank her, really. I might do that, actually." The more he thought about it, the more he warmed to the idea. "I could call her, and we could all meet up. Better she hears it from me than on the grapevine."

"Rather you than me," Tony said. He sighed deeply as he ground out his cigarette. "Listen, you want me to talk to Dad for you, I'll have a go. He's not all that bad, you know. He was laughing at Julian Clary the other day."

"At him or at his jokes?"

"Does it matter?"

"Yeah, it kind of does." Jeff kicked a stand of nettles back that had encroached on the path. "Don't worry about it. I should be the one to go and talk to him. It's my life. My responsibility." And something had lifted inside him since he'd told everyone. Like he'd been tethered down and now he was free to take off in whichever direction he wanted. It was kind of scary, but also exciting. He'd just have to focus on that feeling, rather than the dread of facing his old man.

They turned to walk back towards the house, and their dad was waiting for them on the pathway. He looked smaller than usual, and out here it really struck Jeff just how much of a toll the accident had taken on him. The large, powerful machine of a man from their childhood was now wasting away. Stooped and paunchy where he had been broad and muscular. It was easy to see now what he'd be like as an elderly man. He was almost there already, despite not having hit retirement age.

Seeing him that way deflated some of Jeff's righteous anger, and he approached him with reconciliation in mind.

"I don't want to talk to you," were the first words that came out of Bert White's mouth, but this time Jeff listened to the hurt and fear underneath them.

"I know you don't. But I think you should, seeing as how I've spent the whole of my life listening to you."

"Me? You never listened to a bloody word I said."

"Of course I did. Why do you think I went into building when what I really wanted to do was the horticultural course at Lacock? But that wouldn't have been man enough for you, would it? Well, I'm sick of living up to your standards. I've got different ones, and as far as I'm concerned, loving another man doesn't make me any less of one."

"But it's wrong."

"Who says?"

"God, for one."

"Don't give me that. You don't believe in God. You've never even been to church."

"Yes, well... There's other people that think it's wrong too."

"Like who? Some of your old workmates? Some blokes down the pub? You know what, Dad, I really don't care about what a bunch of homophobic bigots think. I can look after myself. And I can look after Eddie too. Not that he probably needs it. He's tougher than I am."

"He doesn't look particularly tough." Bert sneered a little, but it didn't seem like his heart was in it. "What d'you have to go and take up with a posh bloke like that for? And all this rubbish about you messing around with flowers and so on. What's wrong with the life I brought you up to? It hasn't done me any harm."

There was no point in bringing up the injury or the fact the man was chain-smoking himself to an early grave. If he couldn't see those problems himself, then the stubborn old git was hardly going to accept it from Jeff. "I'm not you, Dad. I have to make my own choices, and they're not always going to look like yours."

"You're telling me. Are you seriously saying you'd rather have some man like that rather than a bird like my Mags? You're going to give up all that soft skin and a nice pair of tits? What exactly can you do with a man, anyway?"

"You really want me to fill you in on our sex life? Because it's pretty wild."

"Don't be disgusting."

Jeff shook his head, starting to lose patience. "I'm not being disgusting, Dad. You're the one who's disgusting. And if you can't accept me and Eddie, then I don't want anything to do with you. I've had enough of trying to keep you happy. I'm living my own life now."

Burt sniffed loudly and looked like he was about to start a tirade but turned away instead. Fine. If he didn't want to listen, Jeff wasn't going to waste his breath.

As he walked away back to the house, Jeff felt something lifting inside him. His steps were bouncy, like gravity had finally gone and given up on holding him down.

It felt like he could fly.

And when he saw Eddie smiling at him through the window before turning to flick bubbles at Jeff's mum, he knew everything would work out somehow.

The worst was over, and what didn't kill you only made you stronger.

This was going to make him and Eddie stronger together. He was sure of it.

As they walked back up the hill towards Jeff's house, Eddie was surprised to feel Jeff's hand land on his waist. "Someone might see," he warned, but Jeff just grunted and gripped him tighter.

Eddie's insides curled up into a body-sized smile. "I'm really proud of you, you know."

"It's no big deal. Hardly anyone around at this time of day, anyway. They'll all be inside, too stuffed full of roast to move."

"Not for holding me in public. For coming out to your family. That took a whole heap of guts. And then some. I mean, I remember how scary it was for me, and my family were a hell of a lot more liberal than yours."

"Yeah." Jeff frowned, and Eddie felt bad for even mentioning it. Who needed to be reminded of being rejected by a parent? But Jeff's expression soon turned to curious. "They took it okay, did they?"

"Absolutely fine. Belinda said she'd always known anyway, and Dad just gave me this excruciating lecture about safe sex."

"You know what, I should probably be grateful the old man's never going to do that." Jeff smiled at last, and Eddie's heart bounced around with joy.

"You're amazing, you know that?"

Jeff's smile broadened. He picked up his pace, yanking Eddie along with him.

"Whoa! What's the hurry?"

"I've got to take this amazing man home and kiss him stupid."

Eddie fizzed inside, like he was about to burst with happiness. "Just kissing?" he teased.

"First kissing, and then we'll see where it leads. I've still got this pointy little olive fork I've been meaning to use on you. And I've been wondering what kind of mark a wooden spoon would leave on your arse."

"Ooh, I've never been spanked with a wooden spoon before. Or tortured with an olive fork."

"Good. Nice to know I can still show you something new."

They were at the end of Jeff's road, and Eddie had to get it out now before they got inside and he couldn't speak any more.

"You know what the most amazing new thing you've shown me is?"

"It's not my dick, is it?"

"Shut up." Eddie would have punched Jeff's arm, but with the way they were huddled together, he had to settle for slapping his thigh. "You're dick's gorgeous, but it's not that."

"What could be more amazing than my dick?"

Eddie slapped Jeff again for good measure.

"The most amazing new thing you've shown this old tart, is how to fall in love."

"Oh." They stopped outside Jeff's front door. Jeff turned Eddie round to face him, his eyes searching Eddie's. "You seriously mean you've never loved a bloke before?"

"Never. Not until now."

"Then I'm proud to be your first."

"And last."

"And last," Jeff agreed. "Now get your arse inside so I can turn it purple."

"Yessir!"

Epilogue

One year later

Being on the beach with Eddie was dangerous, Jeff decided. August had decided to put on one last, late burst of heat, and so they'd descended on their old haunt of Weymouth beach, along with Maddy, Niall and the sproglet, and just about every other bugger in the whole of Somerset and Dorset, it would appear. And despite there being so many people around, Eddie insisted on wearing one of the skimpiest bathing costumes known to mankind. It was obscene. You could see almost everything. All those acres of golden skin, for a start.

Jeff really had to stop looking.

Eddie rolled over in the sand and put a hand on Jeff's leg. "You know you should take your shirt off. This is probably the last chance we'll get this year. September's only a couple of days away, and then it's a fast downhill slide to winter."

"I think you'll find we've got autumn to get through first," Jeff said, doing his best not to look around him as he shrugged off his T-shirt. "Don't blame me if everyone runs screaming when they see the gorilla on the loose."

"Mmm, my gorilla." Eddie ran his fingers through Jeff's chest hair.

"Fuck! Don't do that." Jeff glanced over at Maddy and Niall, but they were too absorbed in cooing over the baby to notice Eddie touching him up.

"You worried people will know we're gay?"

Jeff huffed. "If they haven't already figured it out by the way we've been holding hands for the past few hours, then they must be idiots. What I'm worried about is me popping a boner on the beach. There are children around, for fuck's sake." He was going to have to take a dip in the sea to cool off at this rate.

"We need to find ourselves a gay beach," Eddie said. "They're the best. Everyone knows the score, and hard-ons are only to be expected. Welcomed, in fact."

"There aren't any gay beaches around here."

"Oh really? And who made you the expert in all things gay, Mr. White? I'll have you know there's one at Studland Bay, and another near Sidmouth."

"Well, what the hell are we doing here, then?"

"You love it here. Come on, admit it. You're having a whale of a time. It's like being a boy again."

Jeff looked around at the kids playing in the surf and the boats out on the water. The sandcastles and ice cream and sheer hubbub of family life. "Yeah, okay. But I think we're going to have to head back to the hotel before long. I can't even look at you in those shorts. How can you wear them? What happens if you start getting hard? There's no hiding it in them."

"I think you'll find I have enough self-control not to get hard."

"Oh really?" The sadist in Jeff wanted to come out to play. "And what if I started detailing all the things I'm going to do to you when we get back to the hotel? Like hog-tying you and fucking your throat so hard you can barely snatch a br—" Uh-oh. Jeff's little fantasy was making someone hard, all right. It was just a shame it was him instead of Eddie.

"I'm all ears. Carry on, Sir."

Oh God. Just hearing that one word from Eddie's lips was enough to pump more blood into Jeff's cock. He grabbed his T-shirt and pulled it back on. It was long enough to cover his groin, thankfully. "Let's go."

Eddie raised an eyebrow. "Seems a shame to waste the sunshine."

"We're not going to waste it. I think you'll find it comes in the hotel window too."

"You think so? At this time of day?"

"Only one way to find out."

Jeff stood and held out a hand to help Eddie up. Not that Eddie needed it, but Jeff liked everyone knowing they were together. Strange, that. He'd thought he'd have been terrified to do something so simple in public, but once he'd got through the ordeal of telling his friends and family, a bunch of strangers held no fear for him. He was too conscious of just how close he'd been to missing out on all this to want to hide his love for Eddie.

And okay, so not everyone had taken his news well. His mates down the pub had given him a right good ribbing about it, but when he'd started taking Eddie down for the regular match night, most of them seemed to get on all right with him. And the ones who didn't? As far as Jeff was concerned, they weren't worth bothering with. Anyone who didn't adore Eddie was an idiot.

And yeah, that included his dad, but who knew? Maybe he would come round one day. He could have all the time he needed, because he was family. And besides, Jeff wasn't sure how much longer he'd hold up under Mags's denial of sexual contact.

That woman definitely knew how to manipulate men.

Jeff just had to hope Eddie wasn't taking notes.

"Are you two getting ice creams?" Maddy asked from under the shade of the giant umbrella.

"Actually, we were headed back to the hotel." Eddie smirked as he goosed Jeff's arse. Cheeky begger.

"God, didn't you two get enough of each other last night?" Niall complained. "There was me, expecting a bit of adult conversation after dinner, and you two scarpered the moment you'd polished off your dessert."

Jeff tamped down the urge to scratch his neck. "I was tired after the drive."

Maddy snorted. "Eddie drove, didn't he? Honestly, there's me with a four-month-old baby, and even I can manage to stay up later than you two. No thanks to you, mister." She made a face at Oliver and then blew a raspberry on his tummy. He gurgled back at her.

In some ways, Jeff thought, it didn't matter if his dad never came round. These people were his family in a way his blood relatives never had been.

Although that didn't mean he was doing an ice-cream run for them when Niall had a perfectly good pair of legs.

"See you for dinner later," he said, before throwing his arm around Eddie's shoulder and steering them both back towards the Esplanade.

"Can we get an ice cream on the way back?" Eddie asked. "I've got a bit of a sore throat. Somebody bruised it this morning."

"Yeah, I think you'd better, because somebody's about to bruise it again very soon."

"Goody."

Eddie took Jeff's hand, and they walked back to the hotel.

Half an hour later, Eddie lay on his stomach on the hotel bed, completely immobilised. Jeff had bound his arms and legs in a mean hog-tie, and there was absolutely no play in the rope. Eddie had strained against his bindings to check, and now he could just relax, knowing there was absolutely no way he could move anything other than the safety bell in his hand. Well, that and his head.

And even that was clamped fast in Jeff's hands while the man in question fucked Eddie's mouth. Eddie was lying on the bed with Jeff standing in front of him. Eddie looked up and winked. Jeff saw it and grinned. This had become a new favourite position for them to play in.

Jeff's fingers pinched around Eddie's nostrils as he pushed deep into Eddie's throat. There was no way of getting any air into his lungs. No way of moving, even.

Eddie had never felt safer in his life.

Total, utter trust.

Jeff had earned it.

Eddie's lungs burned, and he started heaving for breath. Just as it got uncomfortable, Jeff pulled back. Eddie took a huge gasp around his cock, before Jeff pushed back in again. Jeff did it a couple more times until Eddie's head was swimming. His eyes watering and his whole body deliciously alive.

And Jeff stared down at him, that look on his face again, like Eddie was doing something utterly amazing and awe-inspiring. That look Eddie had come to recognise as love.

"So good," Jeff said. "Want to do this all day. But then I wouldn't get to come all over your face."

"You're such a bastard," he croaked, when Jeff eventually pulled out.

"Shut up, bitch." Jeff smiled fondly and stroked his cheek before painting it in come.

About the Author

English through and through, Josephine Myles is addicted to tea and busy cultivating a reputation for eccentricity. She writes gay erotica and romance, but finds the erotica keeps cuddling up to the romance, and the romance keeps corrupting the erotica. She blames her rebellious muse but he never listens to her anyway, no matter how much she threatens him with a big stick. She's beginning to suspect he enjoys it.

Jo publishes regularly with Samhain, but has also been known to edit anthologies and self-publish on occasion, although she prefers to leave the "boring bits" of the book creation process to someone else.

Visit JosephineMyles.com for more about her published stories, saucy free reads and regular blog posts.

When Mr. Glad Rags meets Mr. Riches, the result is flaming fun.

Stuff

© 2014 Josephine Myles

The Bristol Collection, Book 2

Tobias "Mas" Maslin doesn't need much. A place of his own, weekends of clubbing, a rich boyfriend for love and support. Too bad his latest sugar daddy candidate turns out to be married with kids. Mas wants to be special, not someone's dirty little secret.

When he loses his job *and* his flat on the same day, his worlds starts unraveling...until he stumbles across a vintage clothing shop. Now to convince the reclusive, eccentric owner he's in dire need of a salesman.

Perry Cavendish-Fiennes set up Cabbages and Kinks solely to annoy his controlling father. Truth be told, he'd rather spend every spare moment on his true passion, art. When Mas comes flaming into his life talking nineteen to the dozen, he finds himself offering him a job and a place to live.

He should have listened to his instincts. The shop is already financially on the brink, and Mas's flirting makes him feel things he's never felt for a man. Yet Mas seems convinced they can make a go of it—in the shop, and together.

Warning: Contains an eccentric, bumbling Englishman, a gobby drama queen, fantastic retro clothing, scary fairies, exes springing out of the woodwork, and a well-aimed glass of bubbly. Written in brilliantly British English.

CPSIA information can be obtained at www.ICGtesting.com
Printed in the USA
LVOW07s2003071015

457328LV00005B/436/P